MARRIED TO THE ALIEN DOCTOR

Renascence Alliance Series Book 2

ALMA NILSSON

Printed in the United States of America

First Printing: June 2019

ISBN-10: 1073315185
ISBN-13: 978-1073315185

Sometimes we feel we straddle two cultures; at other times, that we fall between two stools.

Salman Rushdie, *Imaginary Homelands, Essays and Criticism 1981-1991*

Abbreviations

Universal Credits: UC
Instant Communicator: IC
Video Message: VM

Traded to the Alliance Empire

Dru stood up quickly when her captain entered the brig. She and her 25 female crewmates, from the human starship *Dakota*, were being held in a tiny cell on an Alliance Alpha Warship. Humans were at war with the Alliance Empire. Not directly of course, humans weren't quite that stupid. They had joined their allies, the Jahay, to push the Alliance back from colonizing their desolate corner of the galaxy or so they were told. The war had been going on for about one year and it had not been going well for the Jahay and their allies. The Alliance was far too strong and their military prowess too great. Surprisingly, instead of being destroyed in their last encounter with an Alliance fleet, all the humans had been taken prisoner after their ship had been disabled. And their captain had not returned in over a day, until now.

There were rumors that the Admiral of this fleet had married her. It was the most unlikely thing any human could imagine. It was true that Alliance people and humans were genetically similar, however, the Alliance had never taken any real interest in humans and humans liked it that way. The Alliance Empire and humanity could not have evolved any differently. The Alliance ruled the galaxy, their population was in the trillions and they had thousands of colonies throughout the galaxy. Conversely, humans had barely made it out of their solar system and only had Earth and some small settlements on Mars and Europa. Additionally, humans had purposely capped their population at 12 billion so that Earth's ecosystem would be as balanced as possible. The Alliance was a military and technological powerhouse, no one civilization could defeat them alone. Humans, despite their renowned ingenuity, were the least technologically advanced species in the galaxy and any other civilization could take them within hours without much trouble. However, no other civilization had ever tried.

Not only were humans known for their originality, but they had beauty. Other species in the galaxy adored the exotic pink and brown hues of human skin and the variation of human colored eyes and hair. Although it was rare to meet humans outside their solar system. If you did, they were usually members of the tiny human fleet. A fleet that was known for a bit of piracy and stealth, never for its military competence. When meeting human fleet starships, most other species would be worried that in passing they might lose some of their cargo. But humans were charming and if they were contacted about the missing cargo, humans would smile and end up sending the complainer away with some Earth goods. It was annoying but the galaxy just couldn't be upset with humans for long, they were too adorable with their awkward universal translators, substandard ships and beautiful faces.

Despite humanity's small population, many people in the galaxy still knew what humans looked like, the Galaxy Court often had images of humans in their advertisements, despite that humans were too lowly to even have a seat on the Galaxy Court. The Galaxy Court takes actions on issues in the galaxy concerning its members, over 50,000 species. These actions include, peace and security, sustainable development, galactic species rights, disarmament, governance and more. The Galaxy Court also provides a platform for its members to express their views. However, only 1,000 seats are available for the General Assembly, most of which are taken by the richest and most powerful members, never humans. More adventurous travellers, would even made the trek to visit Earth, and even if other species never actually met a human in their lives, they knew about human products. What the galaxy loved most about humans, besides their good looks and charming attitudes, was their obsession with beauty in all forms; clothing, food, music, architecture and art. Humans had shrugged off a lot of machine-made products and most of what they used in their daily lives, such as clothing, china, textiles, housing, were all handmade. Whereas in the rest of the galaxy these things were all ubiquitously machine made without any thought to beauty or uniqueness. The Off-worlders that visited Earth, usually liked humans, but in a condescending kind of way. As beautiful things were admired but worth very little in terms of universal credits, UC, the common galactic currency. Even so, humans still had a superior attitude towards other species because they were so adored, despite their low position in the galactic ranking order, both financially and technologically. Humans were the little darlings of the galaxy and they knew it.

The Alliance had little beauty. Their skin was a dull grey, they had either grey or green eyes and all had black hair. Their fashions, as their society, was mainly focused on order, simplicity, efficiency and function. Off-worlders who were lucky enough to be invited to any of the Alliance home planets, as there were three with one large capital planet, called in the simple Alliance style 'Capital Planet', were awed by the highly structured technological modernness of the society and its inhabitants. It was rumored that nothing was more perfectly run and set out in the galaxy than the Alliance Capital City and its law-abiding religious citizens. The Alliance was respected and feared by most, but they were also viewed to be fair overlords. Alliance people believed their pantheon of gods had tasked them with the role of being the chosen people to guide all others away from chaos in the galaxy.

The Alliance Empire had always kept one eye on humans, and this was what the Alliance felt kept humanity sovereign for so long. Opposingly, humans believed that their creative ingenuity and charisma had kept them free from being colonized or destroyed by a stronger civilization in the galaxy. Perhaps it was a mixture of both, but one thing was certain, the Alliance was struggling now with a demographics issue and felt humans owed them for all their protection in the centuries prior. Unfortunately, the Alliance was not going to humble themselves and directly ask humans for help, they were going to trade for it. Or at least make it appear like a trade, and thereby legal, so that the Galaxy Court would not interfere in their solution to integrate human women into the top tiers of their society.

Dru knew very little of galactic politics. She was young and she had been raised in a conservative pocket of Earth that rejected technology and embraced traditional human culture. All she knew about the Alliance were some vague generalizations and one of them was that they never took prisoners. Given the tiny brig and the even smaller cell she was in, she guessed this was probably not just a rumor. And she was just as confused as the rest of the crew as to why they were there, still alive. That is why she stood curiously and respectfully to attention as her captain walked into the brig. The Alliance Admiral stood next to their captain; they were flanked by his heavily armed guards all carrying modern weapons and traditional Alliance short swords. Dru took in her captain's appearance and thought she didn't look tortured. She looked tired, but she was wearing a clean human fleet uniform and her short brown hair was not the matted, dried blood mess it had been yesterday. Dru closed her eyes and focused on the Captain, entering her mind. And then said out loud, "Oh you've got to be kidding me."

None of the other women in the cell noticed Dru's small outburst. They were too busy trying to listen to what Captain Rainer was saying. The male crew, being held in the other cell, were told that they could return to Earth if they promised not to participate in this war any longer. The women were all hoping the same would be applied to them.

Dru knew that it wouldn't be though. She had looked into Captain Kara Rainer's thoughts and saw intimate images of the Admiral and her. Not only that, Captain's mind was running on a loop, *If I can survive a couple months of marriage to survive this war at all, they can too. I can't rescue dead people.*

Dru agreed with the Captain's sentiments. She had come too far in life to die over something so ridiculous, if her options were to be executed or to become an Alliance man's wife, she would take the latter. There was always a possibility for escape if she was alive. Dru had grown up in a cordoned off area of Earth known as the Exterior. It was where people who rejected modern technology and or insisted on believing in religion were sent. Usually these two traits went hand-in-hand. To keep the residents of the

Exterior 'safe' the whole area was sealed with a forcefield and guards. No one left. No one but Dru, that is. She had escaped at 16 years old. However, she only realized when she was out, that she was supposed to be 18 years old to be considered an adult. Instead of returning, she just began telling people she was 18 years old. She joined the fleet to become a doctor because she couldn't afford to live otherwise, and they would provide for her if she provided for them. Although she had never had a formal education, she had apprenticed with her mother, who was the Exterior's priest, medicine woman, counselor and witch all rolled into one and what Dru lacked in understanding about technology, she more than made up with basic skills and understanding of what she called 'fundamental humanity', all the basics behind the technology. Her entrance exam had been a verbal examination by a panel of doctors, psychologists and fleet instructors as well as an old-style IQ test. Both were easy for her. The fleet felt lucky to have her and dismissed that she had no place of birth, no parents, no surname, no money, only the clothes on her back with a small bag of personal effects and was clearly lying about her age.

As far as the human fleet was concerned, she was young, and she would be one of them now with no more questions asked. She was just too valuable to the fleet to be returned to the Exterior, which by the law, was what they were supposed to do. She was given the middle name of Anne and the last name of James. And Dru liked it. Her new names represented her new life. She even had considered going by the name 'Anne' rather than Dru but decided against it as most people called her 'Dru' anyway and commonly misspelled it as 'Drew', which she never corrected. She kept her real full name a secret, it was a link to the Exterior and she didn't want to be sent back as a criminal or worse, face her mother's wrath. As the years passed in the academy many people just referred to her as 'James' which she liked the best.

At the fleet academy Dru learned how to be a modern human woman. She copied her roommates in many things, unbeknownst to them that she was doing almost everything with technology for the first time. When people asked her where she was from, she named a town just on the other side of the Exterior where many of the guards' families lived, so that the lie wouldn't be too great. She said she wasn't close with her family and that was it, no one asked anymore questions. She was accepted as she was a good student and was decently social. She accepted invitations for coffees, shopping, and parties, however, she always kept herself at a distance. She was afraid to show her true self fearing that her classmates would find out the truth and she would be returned to the Exterior. She never had a boyfriend, as she assumed there would be time for that later and she spent most of her time studying and catching up on everything she had missed over the last couple hundreds of years, as she gauged the Exterior to be about 200 years or more behind the greater part of humanity she was now living in. She, of course, did keep some of her old Exterior ways in private, even though part of the deal with the fleet lying for her was that she had to swear to give up all her 'religious and backwards ways'. But the truth was she still prayed, still would have the odd hang up about luck and still used her mind to read others' thoughts, could manipulate people with her mind and sometimes she could even see the future. It was that last trait that had given her strength to leave the Exterior. However, in all her premonitions about life in the fleet, she never once felt that she would be taken prisoner. She was blindsided now, but it didn't feel wrong either and she couldn't help but think,

Maybe I kept this from myself or I would have never left the Exterior if I saw myself intimate with an alien. And then remembering a terrible experience she knew she subconsciously hid from herself before, she thought, *Maybe I should fear what happens now?*

Captain Kara Rainer stood in front of the holding cell where her female crew were waiting to hear their fate. She looked at them all evenly, "All female crew of the *Dakota* will be sent to the Alliance Capital Planet to be married to Alliance men. They have a demographics problem. We must sacrifice ourselves to preserve humanity. I have been assured that if we cooperate, less human women will be taken." Kara had been assured of no such thing, but she couldn't tell these women that they were just being taken as wives, a social practice that was only observed by the most backwards of civilizations in the galaxy. "Alliance men will treat you with respect and there are laws to protect you. Ask for new translators so you can read and stay in contact with each other. Be strong and be proud to be human. They need us more than we need them right now, don't forget that. I will find you all." Kara felt guilty and silently vowed that she would escape and free them from this Alliance slavery, even if it took the rest of her life. These women were her responsibility and human women were owned by no one.

As Captain Rainer was speaking Dru had a flash, a premonition, of her captain in a different uniform on a different ship. She couldn't concentrate on the image as all the other women around her were protesting loudly and flaying around as guards tried to corral them into a move-able bubble like forcefield. If one of them moved too fast or too slow in the bubble they would all receive a painful shock. Dru was hit in the face by one of the guards and told to stop resisting and get into line. She hadn't been resisting but she had been inadvertently shoved out of line with all the chaos of women around her shouting and trying to run.

Eight armed guards stood around them dispersed evenly around the forcefield. Dru looked at the Admiral and read his thoughts easily. She wanted to find out why they were doing this, if their intention was more sinister than a demographics problem. It was clear that Admiral Tir didn't trust humans, he felt they had already proven more difficult than he assumed, and they represented his reputation somehow. Dru probed further, but she was violently shocked as she stopped to try and grasp his thoughts but as she stopped the bubble forcefield moved forward. She fell to the floor with all the other women in pain. The pain was so intense throughout her whole body she didn't get the chance to read the Admiral's thoughts any further. But she had picked up enough to know that this was more than just the demographics issue, that the Admiral was planning something revolutionary and human women were just one small piece in his plan.

Kara looked at her crew and let them protest. She hated that she was doing this to them, and she vowed she would retrieve every last one of them from the Alliance.

Tir looked at Kara, "Calm your crew, Wife." He purposely used her new title to humble her in front of her crew because he knew humans thought it was a disgrace to be married.

Kara pretended she didn't hear him. She knew he would do nothing to hurt her or them. The Alliance desperately needed human women as they were too religious to employ their superior medical technology to manipulate nature. When she saw the last woman go through the door she said under her breath, "Don't give up on me."

. . .

Aboard the supply ship, Dru and the other women were put into a large empty room with only a silver toilet and no window. They were let out of the bubble forcefield once they were all in the room, but they didn't disperse from one another because Alliance ships were kept at a frosty 15C, so the women remained close together for body heat just as they had done onboard Admiral Tir's ship, but Dru had noticed this room seemed slightly warmer, and she wondered if that was just the numbness from the cold talking or if these men had taken some pity on them. An Alliance officer spoke to them before locking them in, "Welcome to the supply ship the *Igu*. It'll take a week to reach the Capital Planet. We will feed you vegetables once a day with clean water. And we have increased the temperature in this room to 19C for your comfort. Please be calm and good. I don't want to have to punish any women aboard my ship. You can be assured humans; a much better life awaits you in the Alliance."

Then the officer left, the automatic doors closing behind him, and a red light appeared above the door, no doubt to show it was securely locked. All the women looked at one another, some with tears streaming down their dirty faces and others in complete shock. Jane, the oldest of them and the *Dakota*'s Chief Engineer, began to speak. Her very short brown hair was sticking up at odd angles and there were dark circles under her blue eyes, but they were clear, and she spoke confidently, "We aren't defeated yet. Let's stay close for body heat as we did before. And, when they do come with food, let's look for any chance we might have to take over the ship and escape. I don't want to be any zombie's sex slave." 'Zombie,' was the derogatory word humans used to describe Alliance people because of their grey skin.

Some of the women nodded at Jane's words, but Dru reckoned most of them were too stunned to think about escape or mutiny right now. They all huddled together quietly in what now was their familiar scents of unwashed bodies and wounds. Some began to cry, but mostly no one made a sound. Except Dru, who spoke quietly, "I'll ask them for a med kit to clean our wounds. At the very least, we can use clean water."

"James," Rebecca, 'the beauty queen', as they all called her for her perfect golden face, big golden-brown eyes and straight brown hair, called out to Dru. "One of the guards smashed my toes when they were moving us. Can you have a look?"

Dru shifted in the group to move closer to Rebecca. She was surprised that despite Rebecca's sweat and blood she even smelled somewhat pleasant. *Some people have all the luck*, Dru thought as she asked Rebecca to remove her boot and sock. It didn't take long for her to assess the situation, "These two smaller toes are broken. Keep your foot elevated and try not to use it. It'll probably heal well enough to walk on by the time we reach the Capital Planet. However, by then I suspect we will be seen by medics anyway." Dru left off saying, 'To determine if we are fit to breed children.' She looked into Rebecca's brown eyes and then added, "Don't worry, it hurts worse than it is. I promise."

"Are you sure?"

Dru nodded, "Yes, I'm sure. Try to rest." One thing Dru couldn't get used to outside the Exterior was how fragile her modern counterparts were. Growing up she had had broken bones, overcome illnesses, seen countless babies born and countless people die. These women had never been really ill. If they broke a bone it was healed almost immediately and now birth and death were almost painless, as long as there were no surprises.

Dru moved back over to sit next to Jane. There was an unspoken hierarchy among them and Dru was second to Jane despite her young age. Dru supposed this was because she was the doctor, which especially now, they needed. She closed her eyes and closed her mind to block all of their thoughts out. She tried to focus on the crew of the supply ship. To see if they knew anything like what she had sensed from the Admiral. After a few minutes she sighed, *This crew knows nothing except we are to be married and they are under strict orders not to converse with us more than necessary*. Dru thought to herself, *Obviously, the higher ups are worried about us using our womanly charms to take over the ship*. She made a note to mention this to Jane when she woke up. Perhaps they could use this to their advantage. Of course, Dru would try to manipulate the minds of the crew to gain control of the ship if possible.

The days went by quickly on the supply ship. As promised, they were fed once a day, the food was terrible, which was no surprise as Alliance food was just as much the running joke in the galaxy as was human technology. They had no med kit for the women to use, as human translators were for the spoken word only and their med kit was an ancient one that had to be manually operated with only Alliance hieroglyphics on it. The crew of the supply ship had brought it to Dru but none of the officers were allowed to get close enough to the women to use it. Dru couldn't figure anything out on the old Alliance med kit, so she handed it back and did the best she could with extra water and clean cloths. When her crewmates complained she explained that if she put in the wrong combination into the ancient med kit, she could do more harm than good. She sensed they didn't believe her, they believed they were in so much pain that she should take the chance to heal them. She held back saying, 'You have no idea what real pain is, and I don't want to accidently inflict it on you now.'

Unfortunately, the officers on the supply ship took extreme precautions when bringing them food and water. There were always three or four officers together and always with weapons pointed at them. Despite the women's best efforts to open personal dialogues, it was always in vain. By the last days, they had given up even trying and even among themselves they were beyond the point of hypothesizing about what awaited them. They just huddled close together for warmth in silence. Thankfully, 19C was more comfortable than 15C but without blankets or any soft comfort it didn't feel luxurious.

Finally, they reached orbit around the Alliance Capital Planet. The most prestigious of all the planets in the galaxy. The supply ship docked at Alliance Capital Space Port One. They were lined up and guided off the ship into the port where they were met by a group of six Alliance women of various ages. The women were all dressed in the signature Alliance dresses, solid, dark colored, loose fitting garments with floor length hems, mandarin collars and quarter length sleeves. They adorned themselves with copious amounts of intricately designed jewelry both on their person and in their long, braided black hair. Their jewelry was much more colorful and detailed than any of the men's they had seen onboard the ships. They wore no makeup, which was strange for humans as almost all humans now, men and women alike wore makeup, especially on planet or in space ports. One of the Alliance women spoke firmly with the officers from the supply ship and immediately their bubble forcefield was released, but the officers remained around them, frowning, weapons drawn.

Anu, the Chief Medical Officer on Alliance Capital Space Port One stepped forward to address the human women. She was angry that they had been treated so poorly on their voyage here. She looked over the 26 women and was disappointed. Most of them were smaller in stature than the average Alliance woman and they all were of varying body shapes, health and age. What was even more disturbing was that all the women seemed to be wounded in one way or another. Not one of them had a clean uniform without some blood on it.

In the Alliance Empire, women were treasured, there were so few of them and without women, there would be no more Alliance. Humans were the only other species in the galaxy that were genetically compatible. The only differences between the two species were skin colors, small variations in eyesight and slightly different body temperatures.

Anu berated the guards from the *Igu*, "Why haven't these women's injuries been attended to? Why haven't' you given them clean clothing?"

The guards just looked at the Chief Medical Officer and said nothing. They had their orders not to get close to the human women and if she wanted answers, she could speak to Admiral Tir.

Anu shook her head in disbelief, "You should be ashamed of yourselves, treating women in this way. I'll have a strong word with the Admiral about all of this." *If they were going to steal human women, they should at least be civilized about it*, Anu thought angrily.

Anu looked at the sad group of women and said with some compassion, "Human women from the starship *Dakota*, welcome to the Alliance, your new home. From now on, you'll be given proper meals, warm clothing, education and a decent place to live. I apologize for the treatment you've received up until now. Men are lost without women to guide them. Now if you will all follow me, we will get you started on your medical checks, a final precaution before you are taken to your new home on the Capital Planet." Anu and the other doctors turned and began walking, telepathically talking amongst themselves about the ragtag humans. The humans and the guards followed.

Dru knew they carried a stench of unwashed women with them as they walked behind the doctors and it didn't surprise her that the people passing by in the space port stopped to stare at them. Humans were not a common sight in the galaxy. Dru was surprised by their thoughts though as they passed the curious onlookers.

What are all those human women doing here?

So, it is true.

They will depopulate adorable little Earth. Will no one say 'no' to the Alliance Empire?

This is good for us. Finally, some relief from the gods.

Gods, it is true. They are beautiful and no one can doubt, the Lost People have returned.

. . .

After walking for about 15 minutes through the busy port, they entered a medical screening area. There were five med stations set up with silver medic robots and large medical beds surrounded by virtual walls of transparent computer screens. The human women were lined up and examined five by five. Dru was the last called to be examined, while most of the women tiredly watched on without emotion.

"Drusilla Anne James," her name was called by the Chief Medical Officer and she was assigned a bed with a doctor and a robot.

Dru could hear gasps from most of the *Dakota* crew when they heard her full name. 'Drusilla' was an ancient name and not many knew the name she went by was only a nickname. Dru didn't know what to do, so she pretended that all was normal as she walked up to her assigned medical bed, hoping her crewmates would think the Alliance had made a mistake that she didn't care to rectify. She quickly removed all of her clothing as she had watched all the other women's examinations and knew this was what was required, so she didn't wait to be told. She just wanted to get this over as quickly as possible so that they could all get to wherever they were going to next.

Dru was asked to lie down on the medical bed and was scanned with three different lights over her body, she felt nothing though. Multiple readouts were shown on the virtual 3D screens to her left. She could not help but look at them, and marvel at the superior Alliance technology, while the robot fussed about her person, taking blood, salvia, ear wax, looking into her eyes, groping her breasts, probing her vagina and all kinds of invasive tasks while the doctor began asking her questions.

"How old are you?"

Dru looked up at the Alliance woman standing next to

the medical bed, her long black hair was braided into four heavy braids and adorned with intricate silver jewelry. She had smooth grey skin and big grey eyes. *Zombie,* Dru thought. "Twenty-two years old." This was a lie she was actually only 20 years old, but a lie she was so used to telling she almost believed it herself. And she had no reason to think the Alliance would question it either.

The doctor looked her in the eye and asked again, "How old are you?"

"Twenty-two years old," Dru said confidently.

The doctor noted,

Possible discrepancy in age. She says she is 22 years old however, the computer suggests a couple years younger. Yet, I don't believe she is lying.

"Profession?" The doctor was trying to reach out to Dru telepathically too. She could see on the read out she had an exceptionally high level of telepathy, *And do you hear me like this too?* she transmitted the words without speaking, but she felt Dru mentally blocking her, so she made note of that too and continued with the examination orally.

"Junior Doctor."

"Does your hair color make you special in some way? Out of all the human women here, you are the only one with this red color."

"It's rare. A recessive gene, only a small percentage of humans have red hair, but among people with red hair, I'm more common with my green eyes. I'm only different from humans with other hair colors in that I'm more sensitive to ultraviolet rays and extreme temperatures, I've a higher threshold for pain and prefer to use my left hand over my right."

"I see. We have recessive genes that express themselves differently. Are you married?"

"We don't marry on Earth. We stopped doing that centuries ago," *And none of us ever want to marry one of you*, she thought.

The doctor looked into Drusilla's green eyes with surprise at hearing her project her thoughts so clearly and then asked through telepathy, *We don't have to speak out loud. We can do this naturally if you like?* But again, she could feel the young woman block her, "Have you any children?"

"No."

"How many full siblings do you have?"

"Three. Two sisters and one brother."

"Any half siblings that you know of?"

"No, we don't marry but we are not feral," but this was a lie. She didn't know for certain who her father was and some of her siblings might even be half siblings, but her life had not been normal for modern human society, so she didn't want to draw attention to this. Especially since her crewmates were now all listening to her examination.

The doctor looked into her patient's eyes and easily knew that she was lying about her siblings. That she was not positive they were all her full siblings. She noted it and then continued with the examination, "When did you get your first period?"

"Twelve years old. Are you really going to use us for breeding?"

The doctor was not surprised by her question as the other women had all asked her this same thing after that particular question about the onset of menstruation. She reckoned that humans must be very backward indeed if they used women as breeders like livestock. But it only made her feel more relief that these women had been saved from their barbaric lives on Earth and brought to the Alliance, no question, under dubious circumstances. No one really believed that Admiral Tir traded for them. The doctor ignored her question though, "How often does your period come? And how do you deal with it?"

"Every 28 Earth days, one of our calendar months, pain killers and a menstrual cup."

"You all seem to be affected by your lunar calendar. That may change here. We'll have to wait and see. There is only one human woman living on the Capital Planet now so there is no way to know for sure. Alliance women's cycles are governed by our two neighboring planets and last three times as long. As for the excess blood, we have a better solution which I'll give you before you leave. Your method seems to be more primitive than the other women, is there a reason for that? Are you religious in some way? All the other women were taking birth control so that they did not bleed." Without asking the doctor began probing her mind. She sensed this human was different from the rest, not only for her red hair and being telepathic but something else as well. Drusilla's thoughts and memories were well guarded, but the doctor waited at the edge of her mind so that she was able to catch the odd word or image to explain these differences and it was enough to note,

Her childhood might not have been on Earth. I picked up images of very rugged interiors and filth both on the people and surroundings, like a colony gone wrong. However, her record shows nothing of this.

Dru had always used the menstrual cup her mother had given her. Even though she was a doctor she never thought

19

about changing it as it had always worked. The blood was useful for prayers or spells, her mother was a kind of medicine woman or witch, depending on who you asked and Dru sometimes still used her blood for spells or offerings to spirits. "My mother is old-fashioned, and it's always worked for me, but I am more than happy to try something modern as I obviously didn't have time to take it with me when we were taken prisoner."

"You're not our prisoners. You came of your own free will," the doctor said and Dru began to protest until she heard the doctor say to her telepathically, *I'm sorry Admiral Tir took you this way. I hope that you will find we are offering you a good life here. Please remain calm and don't call yourselves 'prisoners' or you might receive punishment.*

Dru had never had someone speak to her telepathically. She could read others' thoughts but not this. This was sophisticated. She tried to talk back with her mind, but it was like a toddler trying to speak for the first time.

The doctor looked at her and said telepathically, *And we will teach you how to use this skill properly. We have saved you from the barbarians of Earth. What a talent you are, and you were almost wasted.* The doctor then spoke out loud to her, "I'm glad you are willing to try something more modern. Some of the other women were more reluctant. The more you all resist the longer integration will take. It's better if you all just accept this as your new life. Are you also taking some kind of birth control?"

"No," Dru answered and then was echoed by the shocked gasps from her crewmates. She knew now that they would guess she was from the Exterior. Everyone else took birth control. Births were planned on Earth. You had to get permission to reproduce. Only people in the Exterior were allowed to reproduce as they wished, as without technology, a lot of people of all ages died, so population regulated itself naturally. They would know now that she was born outside the system and was assigned no physical regime that was monitored by the human government set. When the fleet registered her, they forgot to do that and then by the time someone noticed, her superior on the *Dakota,* John, he just ticked the box saying casually, 'They must have made a mistake.' She knew that he knew she was from the Exterior. It was one of their unspoken bonds.

"I'm glad to see that some humans have some sense not to poison their bodies. Women in the Alliance never take birth control. It's preposterous that you would control a woman's fertility as it's fleeting like a flower for only a few days every cycle and only for a couple decades of her life. It goes against nature and the gods to alter women's bodies."

"Do the Alliance gods care so much about women's bodies and sexuality then?" Dru's experience with gods and worship was from her mother. She definitely believed in unseen forces, but not necessarily deities. And definitely not deities that cared too much about what the mortals in the world did daily.

"It's blasphemy to even question it. The gods control all of our fates."

Dru definitely believed that she had a future set out before her, but whether or not a god had planned it, or it was just how things were going to play out, she hadn't decided yet.

When the doctor realized Drusilla was not going to reply, she continued with the examination, "You're also the only one young enough to fully utilize our anti-aging techniques. You'll have the opportunity to live as long as we do. You should feel lucky."

"Three-hundred years on the Capital Planet. All my

friends will be dead and gone. How will that be a better life than the one I was living, the life I chose for myself?"

The doctor looked at her somewhat sympathetically, "You'll make Alliance friends and it's double the life-span of humans and probably more than that as you were most likely going to die in the war. Why other species choose to have women on starships I don't know?" The doctor said the latter more to herself than to Drusilla. "And as far as choosing your life, none of us choose. The gods choose our paths. You've no control. You'll see," the doctor said dismissively and resumed her exam. "On Earth, are children conceived naturally or artificially?"

"Mostly naturally."

"Just a few more questions. What about you and your siblings? Naturally or artificially?"

"Naturally."

"All born naturally?"

"Yes. How are babies born in the Alliance?" Dru didn't want to go into any more detail, babies in the Exterior were born completely naturally, not 'modern human naturally'. She suddenly felt sorry for her crewmates if they were going to have to birth hybrid zombie babies the old-fashioned way, to experience pregnancy and all with no practice at all in managing pain. They didn't even get their periods; they were completely unprepared for that kind of strain and pain on their bodies.

"You'll find that all out in good time, but for the moment let me put your mind at ease that we've reverted back to doing things naturally as well with very little intervention. We've found that that is the best for both mother and child. Babies born from artificial wombs lacked emotional attachments that couldn't be cured."

"Obviously," Dru said thinking, *What kind of technological maniacs are you? Thinking that fetuses nurtured outside a living woman wouldn't have emotional issues? Even humans knew that there were some things that could not be substituted.* "How many years did it take the Alliance to come to that conclusion?" She wanted to know if any of the men she would be coming into contact with would be emotionally defective because of being nurtured in an artificial womb.

The doctor picked up her thoughts, "It's been centuries since we have had children that were bred in artificial wombs. It was a mistake that we corrected quickly." The doctor then got back to the exam, "Have you ever had sex with a man?"

"Yes," Dru answered sharply while she began swatting away at the robot as he was trying to put something rather large in both her anus and vagina.

"Let the assistant continue and try to relax," the doctor said calmly as the robot began sprouting more hands to restrain Dru on the bed and complete its task.

"How often?"

"Five times," Dru didn't want to admit that she had only had sex on one occasion when she gave her body to five male guards so that she could escape the Exterior. It had been both a degrading and terrifying experience. She had been a virgin. She thought she knew what to expect but those men had been brutal to her. The last thing she wanted was to let anyone here know what she had done. She knew the computers monitoring her would show a lie, so she answered this question as honestly as she could, five guards had sex with her once, one right after the other and some at the same time. She didn't want to think about it more than an instant to answer the question.

"A week?"

"Ever," Dru hoped this would be the end of the questioning.

"Five times with one man or different men?"

23

"Different men."

"How old were you?"

"Six…Eighteen."

"Sixteen?"

Dru nodded.

"And the time after that?"

"All when I was sixteen," Dru could see the other women from the *Dakota* looking at her in shock and looked away. She didn't want to answer these questions in front of them. They would think she was wanton just giving herself to five men as she couldn't explain it was to escape. It was illegal to escape the Exterior. There was supposed to be a legal way to apply to leave, but she had never seen or heard of it until she was already on the outside, and she doubted it truly existed. Dru looked up at the doctor and pleaded mentally, Please *don't ask me anymore about this*. She repeated this mantra over and over in her mind, hoping the doctor would hear her.

The doctor did hear her and gave her a slight nod and noted,

First sexual encounter, raped, possibly more than once by five men. She is blocking me. The memory is too strongly connected to so many others to erase or decrease its visibility without strong personality alteration. No sexual relationships following. Recommend monitored sexual therapy and psychoanalysis.

The doctor said quietly, "Sex is a natural part of life. A healthy adult should be averaging at least one sexual encounter a week or every two weeks minimally. Your lack of experience after your first encounter makes me wonder if you are somehow physically defect. We'll need to perform more exams to make sure you are completely healthy in this regard."

Dru suddenly felt sensations in her anus, clitoris and vagina and jumped. She looked up at the doctor for an explanation.

The doctor was looking at her brain scans.

"What are you doing?" Dru demanded trying to squirm away from the robot, but she knew what the robot was doing, thrusting the equivalent of a penis in and out of her vagina in a very pleasing motion. She was sure her cheeks were hot with embarrassment. She looked over and everyone was watching her. She was too upset to read any of their thoughts, and she didn't want to hear them anyway.

"We're checking that you are sexually healthy, that the reward centers in your brain are activated with arousal and orgasm. Your lack of experience makes me wonder if your libido is healthy or if you have a mental block that hampers your sex drive. Just relax Drusilla."

Dru tried desperately again to remove the devices from her body. She felt that was the least she could do to show her crewmates that she was not just lying down to enjoy this in front of them all. The robot just spouted more arms to hold her down. It was humiliating, she didn't want to orgasm in front of everyone while a robot pleasured her. She stole a glance again over at the rest of her crew mates, hoping that they would turn away for her sake, but they were all watching her, and in that moment, she hated them for it. She tried to free herself again, but the robot was holding her down so tightly she could not move even a millimeter. It wasn't long before she could feel her body reacting to the robot's movements, in and out of her vagina, the deft feather like touch on her clitoris and the slight spread in her anus. Her vagina was becoming so wet with her own fluids she could hear the swishing sound of the robot's appendage moving in and out of her. Minutes passed and she felt the building sensation in her body, even though she was doing everything she could to resist it, but she couldn't stop it. Her body began tensing and finally the release of an orgasm went rushing through her like a hot trembling wave, but the robot didn't stop, it kept going.

She heard the doctor somewhere say, "We are checking multiple orgasms now."

Dru closed her eyes; her body was riding out these forced orgasms right there in this clean and clinical space port medical center with an audience. She almost blacked out from the sensations and in that moment, she didn't care that everyone saw or heard her moans of pleasure. She couldn't help herself. She couldn't control her body's responses. When she came back from the bliss of the orgasms, the robot released her and removed the devices and then cleaned her with a cleaning solution. She could see on the medical screens what she assumed was a record of her heart rate, temperature, breathing, brain activity and convulsions. She felt deeply embarrassed and violated. She knew tears began streaming down the sides of her face, when she came to terms with what had just happened, but she didn't care about that either. *How dare they do this*, she thought angrily.

"You never had an orgasm like that with any of your lovers?"

She ignored the doctor and the doctor asked three more times. Finally, the robot gave her a small electric shock. "No," she replied quietly as she tried to wipe away the tears.

"Never?"

"No."

"By yourself?"

"No," Dru had never masturbated. At home she shared a bed with her sisters. During the days, she was never alone, except in the outhouse, and there was nothing sexy about a hole that smelled of excrement. After her sexual encounter with the guards. She never wanted to be reminded of what had happened to her. She never wanted to relive it, but her mind wouldn't let it rest. Whenever she was turned on sexually, her mind would return to that night. When a man got too close it would remind her of one of the men who used her.

"Never?"

"No."

The doctor shook her head, "Let me assure you, despite your lack of experience, there is nothing wrong with your sexual responses or anatomy. You are perfectly healthy. I would recommend though that you practice sex. It is unhealthy for you to continue this way. Sex is an integral part of Alliance culture; you must learn to enjoy it. I'm perplexed why you feel so violated now. Your responses to the exam were natural and healthy. You're among women now and our sexuality is natural. As I said, there is nothing to be ashamed of. Please stop crying." After a minute, the doctor decided to move on with the exam even though Dru had not stopped crying, "Any serious illnesses in your life?"

"No," another lie.

The doctor noted,

Lies about past illnesses. Telepathic probing reveals she is concerned what her crewmates think, not about the illnesses. She is the only one of the humans I have examined to have suffered broken bones and childhood illnesses. She has clearly not been raised in the same community as they have. If she were Alliance, I would suspect a child born out of wedlock, but since humans don't marry, I can't speculate on her differences.

"Have you always been this weight? Is this considered acceptable physical health by human standards?" The doctor asked sizing her up. Alliance people deemed health as one of the most important factors in life. They all strived to keep as perfect and athletic bodies as they could for their entire lives. Drusilla was just below average height for an Alliance woman standing at 170 cm, but her breasts and hips were considerably larger, and the doctor didn't know if this was because she was overweight or if this was natural.

"I'm healthy," Dru said somewhat defensively. She was not fat, but she did have curves. She had breasts that were not made for running, but she practiced yoga, had a flat stomach and had a very nice figure in mid-drift shirts and fitted A-line skirts, her preferred outfit when she wasn't wearing her uniform. Alliance citizens had the reputation for being all muscle and it was rumored they tortured over-weight people. *I hope it's just propaganda and that they really don't torture people who are deemed overweight,* she thought trying to discern the doctor's slim figure through her boxy Alliance dress. Then she looked around the room at the other doctors and she reckoned under their loose dresses they were streamlined, muscled athletic women without protruding hips or breasts. Her mind began to race then, *Were they going to cut fat off of me, right now?* She didn't doubt anything they might do to her after making her publically orgasm.

"I didn't mean to insult you. Alliance women don't have extra weight in these areas," referring to Drusilla's breasts and hips. "Your scans show that you have an acceptable amount of body fat, 26%, however you must not exceed 30% or that will be deemed obese. Do you understand?"

"In my life? Even if I am pregnant?"

"Pregnancy of course does not count, but yes, for the rest of your life. We take our health very seriously. To become overweight is to shame the gods."

Dru said sarcastically, "Of course, it does," she was done being overly nice after the orgasm incident.

The doctor overlooked her rude remark, "Most Alliance women only have about 15-22% body fat, with a limitation of about 25% before punishment ensues. It's a privilege I'm granting you by moving your limit all the way up to 30%, you should be grateful. Now, how long had you served in the human fleet?"

"I joined when I was 18 years old, but I had only been onboard a starship for eight months."

"Not very long. I assume you had just finished your studies?"

"Yes."

"It's good you are young; it'll make your adjustment here easier. You can probably still become a doctor if you would like to pursue that. Physically, you meet all the requirements," Dru had no idea what the doctor meant by that but didn't have time to question it because she was already focused on the next thing the doctor told her. "We just need to do one more cosmetic procedure and then we are finished. We're going to pierce your nipples now."

"I noticed that some of the other women didn't have this done. I don't want this done."

"Women older than 30 years old are given an option by the Contracts. You'll not be given an option. You are young and you will definitely marry. Men expect this as part of the Contracts."

"I don't know what the Contracts are, and I don't care, this is mutilation of my body and I won't allow it," Dru sat up and put her hands over her large breasts defensively. The robot then held her hands behind her back and two other doctors came over to speak to Dru.

"This is mandatory," the Chief Medical Officer Anu told her as if that would sooth her. "You must marry and to marry you must conform to our physical standards. To marry without pierced nipples is to go against the gods. Your husband will not want you. You'll bring shame on all human women."

"None of the human women standing over there would feel any shame if I didn't do this. I won't let you do this to me," Dru said aggressively and tried to wiggle out of the robot's grip which she knew all too well was futile.

"I'm putting this in your record if you don't stop resisting you young barbarian," Anu threatened.

"Am I supposed to be intimidated by that threat you old zombie bat?" Dru heard some of her crewmates laugh at her insult. "You've taken me prisoner, humiliated me and I'm refusing to have my body mutilated by you and you think I would care what you put in my official Alliance record?" She gave the woman a good kick in the chest then and Anu almost lost her balance, "Put that in my record too." Dru heard her crewmates laugh with her at that and it gave her more courage to fight the robot and the doctors. She felt good even as she was being pinned back and held down. Dru knew her body would be covered in bruises from where the robot held her, but she thought this act of resistance was worth it.

Three Alliance doctors and the medical robot held Dru down and she screamed as they pierced her nipples without any anesthetics on purpose. "You didn't need to make this so difficult or painful. You've no choice in these matters. You're an Alliance citizen now. The outcomes will all be the same. You only have the choice to make the road to becoming one of us easy or difficult. In the end, you will observe our traditions and become a member of society. Accept and obey," said the Chief Medical Officer Anu trying to make this young human see reason. She had seen more humans than most Alliance people in her career and she was unsure as to whether or not they could ever be civilized. She would make a note in Drusilla's file that she needed to be kept on the strictest tether. She was the most valuable among this lot, their best hope for the future and they needed to give it their best shot at taming her. *It was a shame that the most promising on paper was the most barbaric among them,* Anu thought as she looked down at the red-haired woman.

Dru's tears were streaming down her face again, she looked at her mutilated breasts, her spirit momentarily gone, "I'll never be one of you. You have abducted me, disgraced me and now expect me to be grateful?" Her voice rose then, and she found her strength again, "I'll hate you all until the day I die. You're ugly zombies and I hope your civilization dies! The whole galaxy would rejoice!"

Anu, slapped Drusilla across the face as if she were a disobedient child and pinched her newly pierced nipples so hard Dru fell back dizzy and nauseous from the sharp pain, "You will be grateful. Admiral Tir saved you from certain death and now you are being given the chance to be a wife and a mother in the Alliance Empire. There is no greater gift in the entire galaxy. Now you will say, 'I am grateful.'"

Dru looked at Anu defiantly. Tears were streaming down her face, but she didn't look away.

Anu slapped her face again.

Dru thought, *Do you think I've never been hit before? I'm not like these other precious humans. I was fine until you humiliated me you stupid zombies and right now, I don't feel like giving you the satisfaction of breaking me completely.*

"If you don't say the words, I'll take every bit of clothing from all of you human women and parade you through the station like the barbaric animals you are. Then I'll have you all publically whipped for disobedience. This is the Alliance. All you women form one House. House Human. If one of you steps out-of-line, you all are punished. Now what is your choice Drusilla? Should I arrange for the public whipping in the port or will you obey?"

Dru looked at the other women from the *Dakota*. Jane mouthed the words, 'Just say it.'

Dru looked back at Anu and said begrudgingly, "I am grateful."

Anu was annoyed with this human's pride and was not prepared to stop there. She demanded Drusilla repeat another phrase, "Say, 'I will honor the Contracts of the Alliance.'"

"I will honor the Contracts of the Alliance," Dru said, even though she still had no idea what that was. She didn't care anymore; she saw the rest of her crew looking at her. They were exhausted and they had no more fight. She needed to just jump through these hoops for her crewmates now despite the hatred in her heart and her desire to make this doctor's life just as difficult as she was making hers.

"I will be a wife and a mother in the Alliance. It is the greatest gift in the galaxy."

Dru repeated the words and then Anu gave her dirty fleet uniform back to her roughly. She could feel the tears still streaming down her face as she put on her uniform. They had won with this medical examination and she felt filthy from it.

Anu went to a nearby computer and Dru could hear the words, "Obstinate human. Failure to comply. Failure to understand her situation. Strict routines. Punishments."

Then Anu addressed all the human women in a stricter voice than she had when she had first greeted them, "Now that your medical examinations are complete you are all clear to begin your new lives on the planet. As you have witnessed, any disobedience or lack of gratitude will be met with punishments. If one of you steps out of line, the rest of you will know it. I'm not sure why some of you think that we have abducted you or mean you any ill will. You have been brought here to help us and in turn help yourselves. It says right here," she held up her instant communicator, IC, where a document was open in Alliance hieroglyphics, a written language the human translators could not translate, "Your captain commissioned you all to become wives to Alliance men to help us in exchange for her male crew's lives and return of her ship to Earth. You cannot read the document, I know, but you can read her signature. Come closer and have a look. That is your captain's signature and she supervised your disembarkment from the *Refa* to the supply ship *Igu*. You are here willingly. We are the Alliance Empire. We don't abduct women." She paused, looking in all of their colorful eyes and said, "Accept this gift with the gods grace and I wish you all good fortune in your new lives."

"Release us then if we are not prisoners," Dru said quietly to her examination doctor as she was still standing next to her.

"We cannot do that. We need you," the doctor said gently. "The best thing for you to do now is to embrace your new life here as a second life. I've no doubt Admiral Tir would've destroyed your ship if the gods had not guided his hand in saving you." The doctor handed her a

33

small circular case with an even smaller circular silver disc in it, no bigger than the size of a fingernail. "This is for your menstrual bleeding when it comes. Colloquially, we call it 'the disc'. It's very easy to use, when your bleeding begins, press the button and insert it just a centimeter into your vagina. It is a tiny device that manages the blood, some will be released when you urinate if there is excess, don't be alarmed by this. It also eases the pains of menstrual cramping and will keep track of your cycle in the main medical data base. Your bathroom mirror will keep you updated on your cycle." The doctor could see on Drusilla's face that she was alarmed by this. "Rest assured everyone's health is tracked in the Alliance. All the toilets and mirrors keep track of everyone's health so that we can keep everyone as healthy as possible. This is nothing we are singling human women out for. I've also given you some general vaccines against some alien diseases that reach us here from our men coming home and not being properly screened." Dru must have made a face again because the doctor continued, "I know, in this day and age, you would think it wouldn't happen. But we are especially worried about you humans as you have been so isolated in your corner of the galaxy and we don't want to test your immune systems or our medical prowess in trying to keep you alive if we can prevent it now. Do you have any questions?"

"Can I take these out ever?" she said motioning to her nipple piercings over her fleet uniform where they were still throbbing.

"No, you are an Alliance woman now. Your future husband will buy you other jewelry for them. Men expect this. It's part of the Contracts."

"What are the Contracts?" Dru was exasperated.

"The Contracts are a long list of compromises between

men and women to keep our society fair and equal. Many agreements have been added to it over the centuries, nipple piercings are one of them. Do you have any other questions?"

"What if I don't want to marry?"

"Every Alliance woman must do her part now. If the Alliance falls, the galaxy will be in chaos and that includes Earth. Humans wouldn't stand a chance without the Alliance. Do you really think that everyone else stayed away from you because you were so adorable? No, they did it because the Alliance always protected Earth and your small colonies. You are the Lost People. Now you have an obligation to marry and have children, to have daughters specifically, for the Alliance. This is your destiny now. It's a blessing from the gods that you have been chosen. Don't tempt fate by speaking such blasphemy about not wanting to marry. Go embrace your new life, your new home and be grateful. You don't want the gods to take this gift away from you or punish you for your lack of gratitude."

Dru didn't say anything more to the doctor as she had nothing left to say to such blatant racism. Concluding that her examination was over, as the doctor said no more, she put the disc in her pocket and walked over to join the rest of her crewmates.

Jane took Dru's arm and whispered, "You did well James. I'm sure that was the worst of it for today."

Dru nodded trying to stop the tears that were again running down her cheeks. She was so angry and humili-ated, and ultimately, frustrated as she knew in this moment and for the foreseeable future there was nothing, she could do to change her situation. After a few minutes of self-pity, she tried to get her emotions under control, looking around at her crewmates and berating herself, *We are all in this together and you are the only one crying like a child.*

35

Her attention was drawn now to another group of Alliance women that stood before them. Dru tried to focus on what they were saying; her nipples were throbbing with pain every time she moved her bra would put more pressure on her nipples and it would hurt. She was wiping her tears away. She half listened to the older Alliance woman who began to address them. The woman had greying hair that she wore in one long braid down her back. She was wearing a traditional light blue Alliance dress on, with a lot of silver necklaces that denoted her rank. Dru reckoned she must be relatively important as she wore a lot of jewelry.

"Welcome human women from the *Dakota*. We are so pleased that you have come to live among us on the Alliance Capital Planet. My name is Madame Bai and you can think of me as your Alliance cultural guide. My assistants," she pointed to the five younger women behind her, dressed very similarly to herself but in different colors of black, blue and grey, "will also be helping you in this great transition. You're no longer prisoners and therefore, you have no need to think about escape. Alliance citizenship is a gift that has been bestowed upon all of you. Now, if you will follow us, we will take you to your new home that has been especially prepared for you with warm clothes, warm beds and vegetarian food in the Capital City."

The human women obediently followed Madame Bai and her assistants to a transport that would take them down to the planet. No one was going to protest against a warm bed and food. They were all so cold and exhausted.

Dru vacantly looked out of the transport window at the dark blue and black-green planet below as they quickly descended towards its atmosphere. The planet was slightly darker than Earth's as the Alliance's sun was not as bright or warm. She silently marveled at the size of the planet, it was at least six times the size of Earth, and she couldn't help but remind herself, ironically, *This was one of the planets I was so keen to visit when I first joined the fleet.* The Alliance Capital Planet was legendary and its security tight. Off-worlders were only allowed to visit by invitation only. Dru had seen pictures, videos and of course heard a lot about it and its people, but there was such an abundance of information about them and their civilization it seemed it was a way for the Alliance to keep their secrets in plain sight.

Soon they landed in the largest megapolis Dru had ever seen, one of the Alliance women said to them passively that over three billion people lived in the Capital City alone. The Alliance Capital City had an almost mythical status as one of the most technologically advanced cities in the galaxy. Dru had only met one person, an old professor at the fleet academy who had ever visited it. He had told the class that it was a technologically advanced city but at the same time, devoid of any sense of life. Dru looked out and thought it was fitting that people who looked like zombies lived in a city without anything worth living for. Humans both in and outside of the Exterior spent a lot of time cultivating art in one way or another and focusing on social interactions with each other. They saw it as the only purpose for living. Obviously, the Alliance had other ideas about their purpose for living.

When they exited the transport, Madame Bai and her assistants led them towards a large yellow rectangular stone building. Two guards stood to attention outside at a little gate house at the end of a small stone drive. The guards greeted them and then momentarily released a transparent light blue forcefield to allow them entry. Dru thought to herself when she saw the large forcefield surrounding their 'new home,' *Okay, not prisoners, then why the forcefield? For protection?* She could not help but be reminded of her own escape from the Exterior and looked at the large Alliance guards as she passed them. The guards bowed and Dru wondered if she would ever have to seduce them to escape. Suddenly, images from her sexual encounter with the human guards flooded her thoughts and she almost vomited. She bent over and one of the guards seeing her distress came to ask if she needed assistance. Dru acted on instinct alone and just hit the guard square in the face as he had put his face at her level.

The guard only smiled at her and said, "I see that you are fine, little fiery one." And then went back to his position outside the guard house.

Jane came to Dru's side, "James, are you okay?"

Dru had regained her composure, "I'm fine. It's just the pain from the piercings," she lied and rubbed her knuckles. It was all the emotional distress of being brought there as a prisoner, humiliated and momentarily reliving one of the worst hours of her life all in one day. And a day that was still not over.

"Not much longer now," Jane said reassuringly, and they walked into the large building. Madame Bai was waiting for them by the door with a look of sympathy.

Dru looked up as they walked through the entryway and thought this was the tallest building she had ever been inside. There were no windows on the bottom floor except one line of windows that extended all the way up to the roof and then curved around the top of the building. Once inside, Dru realized that the line of windows going up to the higher floors was the glass elevator they took to the living quarters. Dru could not help but admire the sprawling metropolis around them as the elevator quickly climbed up the side of the building. The city was buzzing with countless transports flying between the tall skyscrapers that ended somewhere in the clouds. The scene seemed so alien but at the same time familiar, *How many times have I seen this in pictures or videos about the Alliance?* Dru asked herself as she found the two iconic nearby Alliance planets in the sky making the scene complete. It was midday and the sun had reached its highest point but only managed to be as bright as it would be on an Earth evening. Dru couldn't help but think, *And this is your new alien home, forever.* But she had to reflect that it didn't look devoid of life as her professor had said. It did have a certain charm as all the buildings, for being so modern were built out of what looked like natural stone. And even though most of them were only various sizes of rectangles, the windows on every building had their own unique patterns, not unlike some of the patterns she had seen on the women's jewelry. A lot of geometrical shapes all falling together, and she thought it was almost pleasing to look at, but she couldn't admit to it being nice, not yet. She was still shaken from all that had brought her there, the abduction, the holding cells and finally the invasive medical exam.

Their new home was the most modern building Dru had ever been in. The floors and walls were a combination of black and yellow stone punctuated by small computer panels and floor to ceiling windows, showcasing the city and the tops of the numerous buildings disappearing into the clouds. The lights were low and Dru remembered, *Alliance people have excellent night vision comparable to the big cats on Earth,* she wondered if that now also translated into poorer vision in bright light. She smiled suddenly thinking about having a husband and being able to hide from him by just turning a lot of lights on.

The women were led into a room filled with tables and chairs arranged as if it were some kind of circular conference room. Once they were all in the room, Madame Bai addressed them. "Welcome to your new home," she spoke

39

excitedly and almost warmly even though her audience was reluctant to show any kind of emotion except exhaustion and despair. "As I said before we left the space port, we will be teaching you all you will need to know for your new life in the Alliance. Today, we will just introduce you to the building's basic technology, allow you to clean yourselves and get dressed in some fresh clothing. Tomorrow, we will begin formal classes which will all take place in this room which we will call the 'classroom'. It's our hope, the Alliance Empire's hope, that in time you will find peace and comfort here. Now let me give you a quick tour. We will begin with the dining room and kitchen," Madame Bai began walking out of the classroom and everyone followed as her assistants brought up the rear.

They walked through the expansive dining room that was all black stone with two long black wooden tables that would easily sit 100 people at each. Large and unintelligible Alliance banners in different shades of blue were hung on the walls. Madame Bai pointed to the banners, "These say 'Human' on them. Typically, Alliance dining rooms have their House banners hung but since you have none, we created these for you. You all belong to House Human, which I will explain in detail later." Madame Bai was proud of all the work she had done for these women in their new home and she hoped that they might try to appreciate some of it, but she kept telling herself, *Don't expect much at first. They are ignorant barbarians and they are scared.* After she had shown them the dining room, she led them through to a silver modern kitchen where three Alliance women were cleaning and talking, all dressed in green. They stopped talking when Madame Bai began speaking and eyed their new human guests suspiciously. "These," Madam Bai said, "Are your slaves, they will do most of the cooking and cleaning for you. They aren't to be consulted on any other matters and you'll be grateful for whatever food they serve you. I understand that you are all vegetarian, but it's possible for you to eat meat according to our doctors. I would encourage you to begin to try to eat meat, your future husbands and their families will expect it and frankly, it's healthier. Mealtimes in the Alliance are strictly regulated by the sacred times of the day. We eat three times a day, never more. The times are as follows: 7:00, 13:00, and 19:00. If you miss a meal, you must wait for the next one. We have cameras and trackers throughout this building, and you'll be punished if you go against the gods and eat outside of mealtime. If you can all adhere to these rules, at the end of the month you'll be rewarded with human food as there is a human who owns a shop here in the Capital City. When we go out on one of our city tours, I'll make a point to go to his shop. It's not in the best area, but as you are human you probably won't mind. Now let me show you the gymnasium."

Madame Bai led them down the hall to a small gymnasium. Inside there were only swords hanging on the walls and more House banners. This room was different though, as there were no windows in it. The room was lit only by artificial candlelight and it had dark yellow lines painted across the rough stone floor. All the women came into the room and Madame Bai began explaining, "In the Alliance we all practice with swords. This is to both maintain good health as well as to protect ourselves," when she looked around at the amused faces, she clarified her point sharply, "We don't have a justice system like many other civilizations do. Our judges and juries do not settle personal disputes. Our personal disputes are resolved through duels to the death. You must all be prepared. As humans you will be exempt from being challenged only for the first 100 days. I implore you all to learn how to use your swords and practice every day. An instructor will begin training you all tomorrow."

"I haven't seen any women carrying swords," Jane commented. She couldn't help but notice that every man she saw had been carrying one. It reminded her of some movies she had seen about medieval times on Earth.

"And you won't. Women aren't as headstrong as men. We plan our duels and they always have a seven-day waiting period. Men may challenge each other in the moment as long as there are sufficient witnesses. I know you must be shocked by this, but men refuse to give up their right for an instant duel. It is in the Contracts." When Madame Bai was content there were no more questions about the gymnasium, she led them across the hall and explained, "Your shrine is here." The women peeked in through the entryway, the room was half the size of the dining room, with no windows and the walls were lined with different black statues of the deities, mostly women with shoulder length hair. The room smelled heavily of incense and there were some burning white candles in front of one of the statues. "I have taken the liberty of already thanking the goddess of home that you have arrived safely. Tomorrow, when we begin classes and you begin to learn about our religion, your religion now, we will spend some time there. Now let's move on to your bedrooms."

The women were then shown one room as an example upstairs, as all the rooms were identical. The room itself was large with more yellow stone walls and a wooden black floor. Dru was beginning to realize that these dull colors were the favored colors in the Alliance. Each room had a very large bed with a mustard colored fur of some kind of animal on it, Dru was used to the use of animal furs from her upbringing but the rest of her crewmates were disgusted by this. As humans valued their animals almost equal to their own right to life, so to use an animal's fur was almost like using human skin.

The rest of the bedroom had no other furniture except for a black wooden wardrobe and a yellow desk with a computer panel. All the bedrooms had floor to ceiling windows on one complete wall that overlooked the metropolis that would now be their home.

"From this panel here next to your bed," Madame Bai brought up the unintelligible Alliance hieroglyphic menu, "You can access the shades, the room temperature, entertainment, and internal communication. The temperature can be turned up to as high as 23C however all of the communal areas will continue to be kept at 19C as you become accustomed to our normal room temperature."

"Why 19C? Onboard the *Refa* it was only 15 degrees."

Madame Bai looked at Drusilla and wondered if humans were even more backward than what the research showed. "Men and women operate best at different temperatures. Men prefer cooler temperatures and science has shown 15C to be the optimal temperature for men so everywhere in the Alliance Empire that is for men only, starships, barracks, Alliance headquarters, etc. the temperature is set at 15 degrees. However, everywhere else in the Empire, the standard temperature is 19 degrees. Women's optimal temperature for work and comfort is 19C. However, as you are human that is still too cold for you all so we have added these features to your private rooms and no doubt when you marry, you can ask for the same in your homes."

"And our husbands?" Jane asked.

Madame Bai smiled, "Well, they won't be home to wear too much clothing, will they?" She thought she was making a joke, but none of the human women smiled so she cleared her voice and then went on with the tour. "You will all be given Alliance translators tomorrow, so that you can read Alliance." Madame Bai began showing them the bathroom next. It was a beautiful large room made of black and silver stone, lit as if natural light was coming in. "The toilets will adjust to each one of you after you press this button," she pointed to a small blue button on top of the sleek black toilet, "after you use it for the first time it'll remember you and adjust to your individual comforts. Your health will be tracked by local doctors through your waste and appearance in the mirror to make sure you are healthy. As for the showers, they have been set to go to higher temperatures as well so that you do not have to suffer through cold showers. We want you to feel at home here. The shower will provide shampoo, soap and moisturizer appropriate for your individual skin and hair. These shower treatments also provide a lasting and pleasing scent to blend with your own natural scents throughout the day."

"What is 'a lasting and pleasing scent'?" Rebecca asked. Humans bathed regularly but did nothing to mask their natural scents.

Madame Bai looked at the humans and didn't want to insult them, but it had to be said, "In the Alliance we combine our natural scents with more pleasing scents. As we all live so closely together it makes everyone more comfortable."

"What's wrong with the way people naturally smell?" Rebecca didn't want any Alliance scent mixed with her own. "I'm not opposed to soap, but we all smell the way we are supposed to. If you want us to marry someone isn't it better that they really smell us to know if they like us? Don't you know about pheromones?"

"It's interesting you should say that as you were almost all on birth control and that changes your smell as well.

Since Drusilla is the only one who wasn't on birth control," everyone looked at Dru then, at the sound of her real name again with some shock as if they had forgotten it, and then with the reminder as there was something not quite right about her not having been on birth control, but those looks were lost on Madame Bai as she continued, "I'll allow her to forgo the pleasing scents if she wants, but the rest of you will use what is offered to you as you showed little regard for your pheromones before by taking birth control. Let the gods be thanked you were brought here to us to save you." Madame Bai nodded at Drusilla, "Do what you like in this regard, Drusilla."

Dru did not want any Alliance scent on her. It sounded disgusting. To wear something artificial. However, she didn't want to make any enemies either, so she replied, "I'll do what everyone else has to do." She could feel that this made a lot of people feel better and they went back to their mindless apathetic listening mode. And she hoped they forgot about her real name and her lack of birth control usage.

"As you wish, now, the mirror," Madame Bai pointed to the large round mirror over the sink with two panels on either side, "is able to provide you with information about your health, based on your toilet samples and appearance, to local news, weather or even hair style suggestions." Then she opened a drawer that revealed small hand-held devices, "This," she said holding up a pen-like laser, "is for your teeth. Don't be scared by it. It's a laser and requires no soap. It cannot hurt you." She turned it on, and a thin blue light was released and she showed the women how to use it. Then she picked up another device from the drawer and it was a laser to remove hair, "This is permanent hair removal. You can choose to do as you wish, but just in case you didn't know, Alliance citizens have no hair on our bodies except for our eyebrows and hair on our heads. Your future husbands may also prefer you have the hair on your bodies removed. I make no judgements about what you choose to do. I just want to give you this information and you can do what you want with it." Everyone was too tired to care about body hair and just wanted Madame Bai to move on with the tour so they could shower and go to sleep. "One more thing about hair, we don't cut our hair as it goes against the gods. If you are caught doing it, you will be punished. And so, we are clear, when I say you, that means every one of you. We expect you to work together to integrate and conform."

"The women downstairs had cut their hair," Rebecca commented as she had dark brown hair which she kept cut just above her shoulders.

"They're slaves, the closest to the gods. They're allowed to have the look of the gods. That is why they cut their hair and dress in green," Madame Bai explained as if this was the most common of knowledge.

"But if we remove our body hair won't that be going against the gods?" Jane asked.

"No, because I don't think the gods intended you to ever live on Earth. You're the Lost People and your bodies have mutated through natural selection to suit that inhospitable planet you were forced to live on. Removing your hair will bring you closer to the gods."

"Should we paint our skin grey then and dye our hair black? We're not your Lost People. We're human. We're meant to look this way," Jane defended them, everyone could hear she thought this whole situation was ridiculous.

"I'm not going to have a religious debate with you. It's a fact that we are 160 trillion in the galaxy and you are only 12 billion, but we are genetically identical. Do you think that is a coincidence? No, it can't be. You're the Lost

People. You were the unfortunates in our early space exploration that became stranded, but now you have returned to us in our time of need through the will of the gods. The sooner you accept this the better it will be," Madame Bai looked at them all sternly then and added, "Have I made myself clear? I don't want to start punishing you on the first day."

"Clear," said Jane sarcastically. *Isn't this whole thing a punishment?* she thought.

Dru smiled at Jane having heard her thoughts.

"Now, on to the clothing. In your wardrobes are four simple Alliance dresses for everyday and one more formal dress for special occasions. We had your measurements from your human fleet records and the dresses were made especially for each one of you while you were enroute to the Capital Planet. You'll also find appropriate stockings, shoes, coats, hats, scarves and gloves as well. The dresses have been made especially warm for you so that you will not suffer from our cooler temperatures even now. Don't worry, it won't be long now before you can change into one of these warm dresses," she looked with sympathy at one of the thinner human women, who's teeth were beginning to chatter again. "When I looked through your human fashions to make sure we made clothes that would be comfortable and keep you warm, I noticed that you like to wear undergarments. In the Alliance, we don't wear any undergarments as they are unhealthy and unnecessary. I'd suggest that you stop wearing them as well, especially for those of you who were just pierced. Your bodies should be free underneath your clothing, to do otherwise goes against the gods. You will also find a couple outfits for practicing with your swords in your wardrobe as well. Those must never be worn anywhere else, but the gymnasium and gods forbid if you are challenged to a duel, you'll wear one of those then. Your human clothes will be recycled. I realize that you might be tempted to keep them for a memory, but we believe that'll only hinder your acceptance of your new life here. Instead, after we finish our short tour, I'll take a picture of you all together in these clothes so you can look at that and have the memory of your old fleet uniforms and of this memorable day."

Just fantastic, Dru thought, *What a clever reminder. Here is a memory of how terrible you looked when you were brought here from the war and we took you in.*

Then Madame Bai brought them over to the desk in the bedroom and opened the 3D computer, "For the moment, your computers are all locked. They will be unlocked for you tomorrow after your universal translators are changed for one of ours. Also, tomorrow you all will be able to send video messages, VMs, to your families on Earth to let them know that you are alive and well. No doubt they'll be sorry that you'll not be returning to Earth but rejoice that you are now Alliance citizens and the privilege that brings in the galaxy. Don't get any ideas about escape or sending messages to your fleet to rescue you. These videos will all be monitored, of course. Your Earth social media accounts have all been locked. When you are settled here with a husband and a child they'll be unlocked. The same goes for all human culture, music, books, dramas are all blocked for you until you are married with a child. Also, you may have no visitors from Earth until you are married with a child. You may send VMs and messages to your friends and families on Earth or on your human colonies, but these will be limited to five a week. This is all done so that the processes of integration will go both quickly and smoothly. Now moving on," she instructed the women to continue following her.

Madame Bai began walking downstairs to the large

drawing room and everyone followed quietly. In the drawing room, they all sat on the circular black sofas surrounding the large medieval looking fireplace and Madame Bai motioned to one of her assistants who brought forward a large black wooden box. Madame Bai opened it and began calling each woman's name, giving each one of them a silver necklace with a small round charm on it. The charm had Alliance hieroglyphics engraved on it. As Madame Bai took the necklaces out of the box, she explained, "In the Alliance we wear jewelry that represents our status and our family names. You can't read these yet, but each necklace says your name and your designation as a part of House Human. I'll explain more in detail about our society tomorrow, and the place we have created for you, but just so you all know, you must wear this everyday over your dresses at all times except when you are sleeping. Now that you all have your identity necklaces, let's take the picture for your keepsakes. Please all line up there," she indicated against a yellow, stone wall. "I know this isn't what any of you imagined, but it truly is the best thing that could have happened. To be saved from your backwards planet and now to be Alliance women. Embrace this gift."

Dru and the rest of the women from the *Dakota* lined up and a picture was taken. It seemed almost surreal to Dru that they would even bother with this, but then she reminded herself, *It's all for a purpose, that a feeling of gratitude would haunt us every time we look at the picture.* Dru shuddered to think that a day might come when she actually thought that was true, that there would be a day she would be as grateful to the Alliance as they wanted her to be. She brushed the thought away. All she wanted to do now was have a hot shower and go to bed. She was in pain and exhausted. Now that she knew what their new prison was like for the foreseeable future she just wanted to collapse.

Madame Bai ended her lecture by reminding them all that the guards outside, the forcefield and the slaves were there to serve them and that they were no longer prisoners but members of Alliance society. Then she and her assistants left with the promise that their cultural classes would begin tomorrow after the midday meal. To give them a chance to rest from their long journey. All the human women just looked at each other in silence after Madame Bai and her assistants left. Although the city was buzzing around them through the windows, the room was silent. Everything was still.

Jane ran a hand through her short brown hair, "I feel like this is the calm before the storm," she said to them all. "I suggest we all find our rooms, bathe and then sleep. I can't remember what time it's now but since it doesn't look like mealtime is happening anytime soon, I'm going to skip that today so that I can just sleep."

Everyone agreed and so they went upstairs to their designated rooms, which were ranked according to age. The only noise they made was the sound of their footsteps on the stone hallway floors. Outside each door was a small screen with their name in English and Alliance on it. Dru found her assigned room and went in, closed the door and immediately took off her filthy uniform. She winced as she took off her bra and cursed the Alliance culture. Then she went into the black stone bathroom and said, "Computer, raise temperature to 23C." Suddenly she heard warm air filling the bathroom and felt a bit better. She pressed the blue button on the toilet and then sat down. She had never considered herself a private person, but after spending over a week using a toilet in front of the other women, she was happy to have some privacy now. She sat on the toilet for longer than she needed to, in a daze, half-thinking half-not, letting the warm air surround her. The toilet seat was warm too and she thought in that moment, *Maybe the Alliance isn't so bad? At least my butt is warm, and I have some privacy at last.* She couldn't help but smile at her own joke. She hadn't realized how cold she was until she began to warm up. Her fingers and toes were tingling as the small bathroom warmed. After many minutes of just sitting on the toilet, she finally got up and turned on the shower by simply stepping into it. It had never occurred to her how warm the water should be so after many minutes of telling the computer to go warmer she finally settled on 42C and stood there letting the hot water roll over her skin. Then she unabashedly let her tears fall with huge cries and this time she couldn't help but kneel down from the sobs her body was producing. After countless minutes, when she felt like she had cried enough over everything that had happened, she got control of herself and stood up again. She asked for soap and the shower produced both shampoo and soap for her skin that she couldn't help but think smelled overwhelmingly like petrichor with a touch of an unfamiliar sweet scent that she wondered if it came from a native flower to the Alliance. As the water ran down her body, she looked down at her ruined nipples and began to cry again, but then scolded herself, *This can all be completely healed. It's not permanent.*

Dru took a deep breath and said out loud to herself, "Be strong now and not such a cry baby. You've just been taken prisoner, don't be confused by all of this. You're probably not staying," Dru felt comforted by this new thought of either escaping or being saved, both for some reason felt like a possibility in the hot shower.

When she ended her shower, she was subsequently dried with pleasant gusts of warm air. Dru had long red hair with a bit of curl to it and obviously the dryer was designed with Alliance people in mind, who had heavy, long black hair, so when she looked at herself in the mirror, she could not help but laugh at her appearance and the absurdity of all of this, pierced nipples and big hair, "Is this what you think passes for beauty in the Alliance?" she asked her reflection jokingly.

When she spoke, the mirror lit up and asked her if she would like some hair styles suggestions and immediately the mirror began showing her images of herself with different style options, *All of which must be popular in the Alliance*, she thought.

She dismissed the mirror and enthusiastically used the laser to brush her teeth. Then she looked down at the hair removal laser. She had no intention of using it. She knew in human history at different points in time men and women had both mutilated their bodies with tattoos, piercings and hair removal. Everything humans did now was temporary, cutting their hair or wearing makeup. To permanently change your body went against human nature and if someone did it, it was understood they had underlying psychological issues. She suddenly envisioned what it would be like to be intimate with a man with no body hair and decided that it would feel too strange, as if she were with a lifelike robot, *Or an alien*, she thought, *because that is what they are, aliens*. But she did have the tugging notion that what she had heard about humans being the Lost People might actually be true. It was almost impossible that there would be two species located across the galaxy that were genetically compatible. However, she didn't want to think about that just now because that would mean in a way that she had come home. Home to a foreign planet. She frowned at her reflection.

Dru banished the thought of the Lost People for now

and walked out into her room naked. She quickly went to the wardrobe, opened it and looked for pajamas. When she couldn't find any, she examined the four identical dresses of various solid colors. The fifth dress was made of a different kind of material that seemed to shimmer like water in the light, she had no idea what kind of formal occasions that dress would be for, but hoped she would never have to wear it, as she feared it might be a wedding dress. She took out the plain black dress. It had been machine made. She had never seen a machine-made piece of clothing before. On Earth, everything was handmade, even their uniforms. This also meant that most people owned very little clothing as it was expensive to buy. Most humans put great thought into what they wore and owned. She didn't want to put on the machine-made dress now, it seemed to her like a prisoner's uniform, but she put it on anyway, without any undergarments because her nipples hurt, and her underwear was disgusting having not changed it for over a week. She looked at her bare feet and looked back in the wardrobe for the 'appropriate stockings' and wondered, *What do inappropriate stockings look like?* She found a pair of thigh high soft black stockings, again machine made and said out loud, "Really? The most advanced civilization in the known galaxy and women are wearing these?" Dru put on the stockings anyway and then looked at herself in the full-length mirror that she activated from the menu next to the bed after pushing almost all the options and then realizing she could just request it from the computer vocally and muttering, "I'm such an idiot some-times," as she looked at her reflection.

Her usually curvy figure was eclipsed by the loose fabric of the standard Alliance dress. The top closed nicely with a cross-over mandarin collar but the rest of the dress had too much loose fabric and just hung on her down to the floor, making her appear much bigger than she really was. The three-quarter length sleeves did nothing to help the appearance of the dress either. She couldn't help but wonder, *How did this dress ever become the fashion in the Alliance? Thankfully, the rest of the galaxy has seen it and said, 'No thank you,' to this ugly grandma dress.* And then she thought, *Why am I insulting grandmas the galaxy over, they wouldn't wear this either?* As she ran her hands down the sides of the dress, pushing the extra fabric down to expose her figure, she wished fervently that Alliance women wore undergarments. She was completely naked underneath, which didn't make a difference in her overall appearance in the dress, but her breasts, once they healed from the piercings would feel better supported by a bra, *I'm no A cup like these Alliance women,* she thought, *The gods will have to understand that.* After looking over herself in the dress for longer than she should have she resigned herself to it and decided at least no man would want her as she looked like a fat goose in it with red hair.

She had overheard some of Madame Bai's assistants' thoughts about her red hair and she now knew that red was the color of instability in the Alliance and that is why they thought her so out of control in her medical exam.

Dru sighed and picked up her dirty bra and her filthy underwear from the floor, the latter she had turned inside out too many times to count and washed them in the sink. She left both of her undergarments to dry overnight in the bathroom. The mirror tried to talk to her while she was washing out her undergarments, but she told it three times to turn off. "I'm already tired of this technology," she muttered.

"Drusilla, let me…"

"Turn off stupid mirror," she said again.

After she finished, she went back into the bedroom and

with great gusto, threw the fur blanket off the bed and got under the covers. However, she realized that she might be cold without the fur so then she got out of bed and put it back on top and then got back into the large bed with her dress on. She tried to make herself as comfortable as possible under the smooth yellow sheets. This was no easy task as the sheets kept trying to conform to her position which would have been nice if she had not had on the large dress. Once Dru was settled and the sheets comforted her she realized that she had not felt this warm in over a week and she was so happy just to be warm and clean.

Dru kept the shade to her floor to ceiling window up so that she could fall asleep looking at the busy alien city outside. She suspected it was late afternoon now and there were thousands of transports silently flying through the forest of tall rectangular stone buildings surrounding theirs. Tears were silently rolling down her cheeks again. The confidence she had found in the shower had been short-lived. She was sad having to start all over again. She had only had four short years outside the Exterior and she had finally felt like she was beginning to belong to something on the *Dakota*. Now, if they weren't rescued, she would have to start all over again on an alien world, having to relearn and integrate. However, unlike on Earth, she had doubts as to whether or not she could ever integrate into an alien society. But again, the thought crept back into her mind, *But what if we are the Lost People?* She shooed the thought away again and closed her eyes, trying to think of nothing but it didn't work. She cried so much she shook. Her grief in that moment was overwhelming. She didn't know how long she cried, but when she took in the city again, the afternoon sun faded into blurred darkness. Her last thought before she drifted off to sleep was, *Tonight is the last night*

I'll allow myself to cry like this. I'll conquer this too... and find pajamas.

Ket of House Vo was onboard the Alliance Alpha starship *Tuir*. He was the Chief Medical Officer under the command of Admiral Ver. He was in his private circular glass office in the center of sickbay and was reading the Day, the daily news report from the High Council. An article caught his attention, *Admiral Tir Rescues 27 Human Women*. He opened the article and began reading about the 27 human women that were now Alliance citizens. It was no secret that the Alliance had a demographics problem and the only stopgap they could think of without using medical technology was to integrate human women into the top tiers of their society. The Alliance had no separation between its religion and its government. As such, it was heresy to alter embryos, as it would be seen as interfering with fate and the gods' wills. As a result, the Alliance was now relying heavily on their Lost People myth to bring human women into their fold to balance out the uneven numbers between the sexes.

Ket smiled when he saw that it was Tir who had taken the human ship in his last encounter with the Jahay and their allies. The last time they were all having drinks, Tir boasted that he would do exactly this. He had told Ket, 'Someone needs to jumpstart this thing. We've been all talk about the humans for years now.' In front of him, Ket flipped through the faces of the 27 human women and their biographies. He flipped past one with shocking red hair and then went back to the picture. Ket stared at the official human fleet picture, it was a standard galaxy image of her whole body. The woman was looking directly into the camera wearing a fitted uniform, her long red hair pulled up messily in a distinctly human fashion and she had the curviest figure he had ever seen. Of course, he had seen humans before and his opinion about them was, as most in the galaxy, that humans were the most beautiful and enchanting creatures ever created, but deeply misguided. They spent too much time making things beautiful and pondering the meaning of life, rather than working hard to better their civilization and quality of life.

Ket looked again at the picture of the red-haired human, he couldn't deny the woman was gorgeous. He loved the way her big green eyes were serious and that she had plump pink lips that were almost turned up in a smile, the kind of lips that were perfect for long sensual kisses. He wondered if her nipples and the folds of her labia were also the same color pink. He almost got an erection just thinking about it. He tapped on the picture and the computer began reading out all the known information about the woman, "Drusilla Anne James, 22 Earth years old, human, birthplace, unknown, mother, unknown, father, unknown, siblings, unknown, marital status, single. Most recent post, Junior Doctor in the human fleet on the *Dakota* under the command of Captain Kara Rainer, both now Alliance citizens. Captain Kara Rainer now Captain Kara of House Zu by marriage to Admiral Tir of House Zu. Drusilla Anne James now a part of House Human, Residential Ring Four, Capital City, Capital Planet, Alliance Empire. Do you wish to see the details of her Space Port One medical exam?" the computer asked.

"Yes, I'll read it myself," he quickly read the report and he knew that the Space Port One doctors had kept a lot of the information confidential. But from what he could piece together, Drusilla was very healthy and had a lot of spirit. The only thing that troubled him was her young age and her sexual inexperience, he wondered if she was a virgin because they had to perform a sexual qualifying test.

He said her name out loud then, "Drusilla," letting it roll across his tongue. "Strange name," he said quietly to himself, but then thought, *She is human after all. They have strange names.*

He smiled when he saw that she had resisted having her nipples pierced. He couldn't help but think, *And I'd love to show you how pleasurable it can be to have those piercings and your breasts adorned with the finest jewelry.*

He read through the rest of her file and was satisfied, not only was she a doctor, which was convenient as he must marry a doctor as he was a part of the First Imperial Medical House, but also that her telepathic levels were some of the highest, he had ever seen. He pondered then if her lack of sexual experience was due to her being able to read her lovers' thoughts and being turned off. He remembered his own first sexual experiences and how difficult it was for him to block the other person's thoughts as sometimes it was terrifying to know what the other person was thinking in those intimate moments.

The only thing that made him pause was the Chief Doctor's note,

Obstinate human. Failure to comply. Failure to understand her situation. Strict routines. Punishments.

However, Ket had the advantage of actually knowing Chief Doctor Anu and that she was not an understanding woman. She was the kind of person who would expect these humans to arrive and be thrilled to be in the Alliance. *She would have no sympathy especially for one so young,*

Ket thought. He compared Drusilla's reaction to what his own sister's might have been in the same situation and decided she would have reacted in the same fiery way. No one wants to leave what they know, unless they absolutely must or are forced to.

Ket looked at Drusilla's human fleet picture again for some minutes weighing out the pros and cons of pursuing this woman. He couldn't decide in his office, so he left sickbay and went to the *Tuir's* common shrine. There he lit a candle and prayed in front of the goddess of fertility for many minutes thinking about Drusilla. When he finished praying, he returned to his office and opened the Alliance Ban Application and logged in. He found her name and cursed; three men had already put a ban on her. Thankfully, he was higher ranking than them all and could pay the most so he would out rank them and outbid them. Then he wrote:

Ket of House Vo claims the ban on the human Junior Doctor, Drusilla Anne James of House Human, for one year from this day, 4th day of the 33rd week of the year 18904.

He paid the exorbitant fee in the amount of 2,000,000 UC as she was counted by the ban committee, a group of older men who review all the eligible women. The committee reasoned that she was the most desirable of the 26, still single, human women traded for by Admiral Tir. It was no surprise Drusilla was expensive to keep to himself, she was the youngest among them and a doctor. She was the most likely to assimilate to Alliance society, if that was possible. The humans' ability to assimilate had been what had kept the Alliance from formally moving forward with the human government to begin with.

After Ket placed the ban, he was assured that no single men could speak to her or court her for an entire year. If a man below him in rank tried to do either, he would challenge him to a duel and Ket was good with his sword and had a reputation of never walking away when a duel could solve an issue. Most men would think twice about talking to Drusilla while the ban was running. Then when he returned to the Capital Planet after the war, he would pursue her. He thought to himself that it was a good omen from the gods that the ban would end, and she would come of age on the same day a year from now.

Ket looked back at the picture of Drusilla, saved it to his IC and said quietly to himself, "And let's hope you are just as enchanted by me as I am by you my fiery human beauty." Then he left his office to attend to a patient who had just come in.

Later that evening in his quarters, Ket received a VM from Tir, "Ket, I just saw the ban. I told you this would be a good thing. I'm sure you know that I already married their human captain. When I saw Kara, I had to have her. Although I must admit it has been more difficult than I imagined it would be to tame Kara into our culture. Perhaps things will be easier with yours as she is on the planet and other women are helping her. I only have slave artists here and I feel like they hinder more than help sophisticate my wife. I expect I'll see you soon when we decide about reparations with the Jahay and their allies, this war won't last too much longer. Our enemies are weak. And you know what I will ask for from the humans. May the gods light your path and the Empire always rise," Tir signed out.

Ket smiled to himself and then said to the open screen,

"Gods Tir, we are friends, but I'm nothing like you. I'll give this poor woman an opportunity to say 'no'." Everyone had been shocked at what Tir had done, pressuring his wife to marry so quickly. Even though it was obvious she liked him, it was still something that was not done, well had not been done for centuries. But Tir was that kind of man. He just pushed everyone and all the rules all the time. He always made people slightly uncomfortable, making people wonder if he was really laughing with them or at them.

Ket was really nothing like Tir. He was a telepath from a family of telepaths. Where Tir was gregarious and popular, Ket was reserved and some would call him arrogant. Both men were from Imperial families dedicated to the Empire and deeply religious. Both were tall, muscular and handsome, but where Tir had big green eyes and a congenial face, Ket had strong symmetrical features and a strong jaw with sharp grey eyes. People easily warmed to Tir but were cautious around Ket. His reputation as a superior swordsman who wasn't shy to duel didn't help his ability to easily make friends either. However, people should have been more fearful of Tir, the next in line to be Emperor, than Ket, who would always be a doctor onboard a starship.

Ket opened a message from his father. He had no doubt that this was also about the ban. Every time a ban was made; all men received a message about it so there could be no misunderstandings.

Ket,

I am surprised you put a ban on the young human woman. Her telepathic abilities are desirable, but humans are feral. They are a people of pleasure and nonsense. Earth is voted the Best Party Planet every year by the Galaxy Court, they are not a serious species. It is good that you have the year to observe her. That being said, when your mother read the article about the human women the other evening after dinner, she stopped at your Drusilla's image and said to us all, 'Ket should marry this one,' and you know your mother is very rarely mistaken so maybe I am wrong and it is possible to tame a human. I guess we will all see in a year's time. Also, the sword from your last duel arrived. I put it with the others in the storage room in your house. Your mother suspects you and Tir have something planned. Write to her and calm her otherwise she will be in my head every waking moment and I can't have that. May the gods light your path and the Empire always rise.

Juh

Ket sighed, his father was so prejudice he would rather watch the Empire crumble than bring in human women. This message's content came as no surprise. Ket was much more of a risk-taker than his father and Ket recognized Drusilla's potential in the Empire outweighed her being human, so she was worth the risk. His sister was unlikely to have many children. If his family was to remain First Imperial Family, either he or his brother needed to marry and have daughters who were also telepaths. Although, his older brother Kio had said on many occasions that he wanted to die fighting for the Empire rather than take a wife. Ket on the other hand, had always imagined himself as a husband and father. Never had he imagined it with a human woman, but now he saw the opportunity and opened his mind to it.

Ket brought up the picture of Drusilla again and said, "And you. What can I do for you?" he thought about it for a minute and then brought up an Alliance storefront on one of his screens. Then he chose a beautiful black wooden comb and organized it to be sent to Drusilla anonymously. And so, began the game; women always knew when a ban was put on another woman by a high-ranking man as no men would talk to her. Then, it would become a game between the sexes to figure out who and why and when it would end. It would be speculated about all year and then at the end of the year, the ban would be made public. Ket smiled to himself wondering if anyone would be able to figure it out before the year was up. Then he took off all of his clothes and got into bed thinking about the black comb sliding through her long red hair. He thought she was so perfect. Red represented modernity and the future in the Alliance and black, longevity and stability, *Red also represents instability*, he reminded himself, but he brushed that thought from his mind.

2

A New Life

Dru woke up the next day and realized that she had been
so exhausted from the last weeks that she had slept for over
16 hours. She got out of bed and went straight to the bathroom. She took off her dress but left her thigh-high stockings on and went to the toilet. She looked at the top of her
stockings as she sat there thinking how odd it was that
Alliance women still wore such old-fashioned clothing, but
she had to admit that the stockings were both warm and
comfortable. After she finished, she stood up and looked at
her reflection in the large oval mirror. She was naked
except for the black stockings, and she took in her body, she
was thinner than she had ever been in her life. If she raised
her arms, she could easily see her ribs, but otherwise she
looked healthy. All except her nipple piercings that were an
angry red and still hurt. "Mirror," she said, and the mirror
turned on. "Do you have any painkillers? My nipples
hurt." Dru figured she might as well start by asking the
mirror. She had no idea to the limit of Alliance technology.
Human bathrooms did have some of these same functions

but very few, and they didn't usually work well enough to be reliable. The mirror turned itself on, "Good morning Drusilla. I do have a wide variety of medicine. However, you are still being punished, therefore I cannot provide you with any pain relief until your guardian allows it."

Dru looked at her reflection in the lit mirror and asked angrily, "Who is my guardian?"

"Jane Johnson."

"May I help you with something else? A new hair style?" asked the mirror congenially.

"No. Turn off mirror," the mirror's light went out and Dru couldn't help but ask out loud, "Punishment? What am I? A child?" she questioned as she walked out of the bathroom. Despite all the shame and embarrassment from yesterday, she didn't feel so defeated anymore. She felt emotionally more stable today and angry at not being able to seek pain relief.

She opened her wardrobe and took out a navy-blue dress and put it on over her stockings with no bra or underwear. She winced when the fabric touched her nipples and muttered some curse words. Then she went over to her desk and brought up the computer. She couldn't use it. It was locked in the Alliance written language. Then she saw her identity necklace, put it on and went out to find Madame Bai and Jane and get this sorted. She knew that there was no way Jane was holding this punishment over her.

She passed a slave in green in the dark, yellow stone hallway, "Where is Madame Bai?"

"She isn't here. She will be here after the midday meal."

"I'm hungry. Is there breakfast?"

"You missed the morning meal. The midday meal is in

65

three hours. Bless the gods for organizing our days," the slave said flatly and walked away.

Dru just stood there alone and said sarcastically, "Bless the gods, indeed."

Dru found her way to the drawing room with the circular black sofas surrounding the large fire. It was strange to see all the familiar faces, clean and now all wearing Alliance dresses of various colors sitting together with the Alliance Capital City sprawled out behind them. Dru came in quietly, sat down and began listening to their conversation.

"I'm sure that our government will negotiate for our release. The Alliance can't just take us. We can't be traded away like possessions, we're people. This must go against some galactic laws and the Galaxy Court can do something," one of the women said confidently.

Another laughed, "What do you imagine our government would negotiate our release with? The Alliance doesn't want anything Earth has to offer, except for women apparently. We should feel lucky that they actually went through the charade of making it look like a trade, they could've just taken all human women and there is no one in the galaxy to stop them. Humans don't even have a seat on the Galaxy Court. No one takes us seriously. I've not got high hopes for a rescue or anyone caring that we are here except for humans, who can do nothing and Alliance who feel they are giving us some kind of gift by abducting us."

"It's true, no one cares what happens to humans but humans and the Alliance in a strange way, I guess. The Jahay were constantly using us as fodder. It's only because of Captain Rainer that we are even alive."

"Being a slave isn't life," another said.

"But we don't know what our fates are yet, so let's just

take each hour as it comes ladies," Jane said authoritatively as she entered the room in a black Alliance dress. "I must admit though; I don't have high hopes of being rescued. But who knows? The Alliance may decide that introducing human women into their precious society is too difficult and end up releasing us all after a few months or a year. We can always hope," she smiled. "Alliance culture seems to be very contrary to our own and they may find that it is better to use medical technology to fix their demographics problem, and risk angering their gods," everyone smiled at her as she sat down. "I miss my family too and this is tough on all of us. We need to just concentrate on each thing as it comes."

Dru could at least be grateful then that she had already left her loved ones behind willingly when she left the Exterior. She had already cried those tears. What she was most upset about now was being stuck on the Alliance Capital Planet and being married to an alien for the rest of her life. And this punishment thing, she was just about ready to bring it up with Jane when the women began talking again and she decided to wait. She didn't want to remind anyone of her examination yesterday. It was mortifying that they all watched her orgasm with a robot that way.

"Does anyone know much about the institution of marriage?" Jane asked the group. She was hoping someone had an interest in archaic mating rituals.

Dru spoke up, "I only know what we all probably know, that women were owned by men. Forced to change their names with no control over their lives." She knew that some people in the Exterior considered themselves 'married' and she had read some old books about it, but like slavery, it was just in the past. No one on Earth was really married in the traditional sense anymore, not even in the Exterior.

"Yes, that's about all I know too. Does anyone know anything about Alliance marriages?" Jane asked. "The doctors on the space port didn't look owned, nor does Madame Bai or her assistants and presumably, they all must be married since there are so few women. Maybe marriage isn't what we think it is," Jane was trying to be positive and get a good conversation going about this so they all wouldn't dwell on what was lost, whether it be temporary or permanent.

"They call those three women who live here with us 'slaves', except they don't act like slaves. One of them aggressively batted a piece of bread out of my hand this morning with very strong words and threatened to beat me if I was in her kitchen ever again without permission," Rebecca admitted, her beautiful golden eyes serious. "I have seen slaves before on Beta 56 and they were in chains, beaten and didn't make eye contact. They did what they were bid to do by their masters, broken. These women," she gestured towards the kitchen, "are telling us what to do. So, it's possible that 'marriage' in the Alliance is the same as 'slave', neither is what we think it is."

"It could be our translators," Jane suggested, and everyone grimaced. Human translators were notoriously bad. Humans were just too creative for most languages in the galaxy that were solely focused on efficient communication. Humans just had too many words to describe emotions and different aspects or scenarios in life. "I agree with you; those slaves don't really seem like slaves and Madame Bai definitely doesn't act like anyone owns her."

"Marriage and slavery could just be different in this culture and we don't have words for what they really are," Dru thought out loud. "I'll be very surprised if our new Alliance translators have different words for them, but I suspect we just don't have the cultural words for them as we have never had these kinds of relationships on Earth ever."

Everyone considered this quietly, but the truth was no one remembered anything about human marriages except what had already been mentioned. Slavery, marriage and religion had been abandoned a long time ago on Earth in exchange for equality and acceptance of everyone regardless of sex or color. Being confronted now in the Alliance with what they considered the most negative aspects of humanity's history had them all worried.

"Did Captain Rainer look owned when we saw her?" asked Rebecca. "I was so overwhelmed with what was happening I couldn't really take anything in."

Jane laughed, "No and judging by the amount of security laid on us she had given her new 'husband' a lot of trouble already. If I had to make a snap decision about this, I'd say, that we hear the word 'marriage', but it is not a correct translation or as Dru suggests we don't have the word for what this really is. I hope when we get our Alliance translators later today, we'll understand our situations better. It's possible we are worried for nothing. Maybe they want us to have a child, donate some eggs or DNA and then we can go home."

"The doctor yesterday told me women can't leave the planet according to something called the Contracts," Dru said. "I think when they say 'marriage' that is what it is, but I agree there is something not right about it if we think of it in the human way because Captain Rainer was definitely not harmed by her ... husband," Dru had to pause before the word 'husband' because it was strange to say. She smiled when she thought, *It's a strange as calling someone 'Knight Lancelot'*.

"Do you think she had sex with that zombie?" another

woman asked, newer to the crew than Dru, and obviously didn't know about Captain Kara Rainer.

"Have you met our captain? She is just as wild in her personal life as she is professionally. The answer to that question is 'Yes, without a doubt.' The real question is if she would ever allow herself to become pregnant and have a child. She isn't really the mothering type and it seems that's all the Alliance wants us for, to be breeders for them under some guise of marriage or whatever marriage is here."

"Captain Rainer will do whatever she needs to do to survive and I've no doubt she has a million plans to get herself free and rescue us, none of which I can even imagine or speculate about, but I'm sure she'll implement one of them to make sure she ends up on top of all of this. She's like a cat, never dead and always happy, weirdly enough," said Jane. She had served with Captain Rainer for years and nothing surprised her about that woman anymore.

Rebecca smiled, "You're right. Remember that green guy? The smuggler we took onboard last year."

"Don't remind me," complained someone else, "I could hear their screams in my quarters. I was so relieved when we had to turn him over to the authorities at Europa Space Port. That was the longest week of my life. I just couldn't imagine; he was so green and with a tail."

Dru couldn't help but smile, she knew about their captain's more experimental sex games as it was not that uncommon that Captain Rainer would occasionally drop by sickbay and want something healed privately and quickly. Dru was always easy to accommodate the Captain as she could read her mind and they never needed to discuss anything. There were no awkward questions between them, not like when she saw John their chief medical officer. She wondered where he was now. She knew that he had stayed onboard the *Refa* with the Captain.

"Life is short, each to their own," said Jane. She couldn't help but think about her partner and her children then. She was happy that at least they had had almost two decades of happiness together and that the children were almost adults themselves. She knew Jim would miss her greatly, but she also knew that he would rather have her alive here than dead somewhere in space.

The conversation then changed to the dresses they all had on, the warm beds they had slept in and anything else they could talk about that was not too emotional. It was an unspoken feeling that no one wanted to continue their conversation about marriage. Either for fear of working themselves up to something that was all a miscommunication, or for the worse, that it really was marriage and they would all become a forced breeder to a zombie.

Finally, at 13:00 they were told by one of the slaves that refused to give them their names, that the midday meal was ready, and they all walked very quickly into the dining room with the unreadable banners and the long tables. Individual plates were set out and platters full of white vegetables family-style were placed in the center of the table. There was a white hard bread on each individual plate and there was red wine in their cups. No one spoke as they all ate ravenously at the mediocre food. The slaves replaced the food numerous times as they continued to eat. The vegetables were served at a luke-warm temperature which Dru thought was probably considered piping hot for Alliance people and the wine was closer to vinegar than wine, but she didn't care. It all was delicious compared to what they had had over the last weeks. They had been on low rations for the entire war and then even worse dietary conditions when they had been taken prisoner. Dru wanted to warn the other women not to eat too much too quickly or it could make them ill, but she didn't want to be the Junior Doctor now. She just wanted to eat. She was so hungry herself she didn't even abide by her own advice and after the meal was finished, she felt a little ill.

When they had just finished drinking some luke-warm herbal tea, Madame Bai came into the dining room beaming and instructed them all to come out to the drawing room. They finished their tea immediately and joined her on the circular black sofas around the fire. When they were all seated, she introduced two doctors who had accompanied her and her assistants. "These doctors will change your translators from human ones to Alliance ones. As I understand it, it's not a difficult or painful procedure, but it's best, if you're all laying down while it's done. I'd like to ask you all to return to your bedrooms and the doctors will visit you to perform the procedure in good time. Jane and Mary," Madame Bai searched Jane and Mary out with her eyes, "They'll begin with you two and Drusilla will be last. As everything in the Alliance, we do it according to rank," Madame Bai reminded them and then she dismissed them.

Dru went back to her room and just laid down on the soft yellow fur on her bed. One of the slaves had obviously cleaned her room while she was downstairs. She knew that because she never made her bed unless she was in fleet accommodation. She definitely had not made it today. Dru closed her eyes and relaxed. She didn't mind being the last as she thought she might vomit from all the food she ate if anyone tried to change her translator now. Unlike many of the other women, she had only gotten a translator when she joined the fleet. So, she, unlike the others who would have gotten their translators after puberty, remembered the dizzy fuzzy feeling that lingers with a new translator quite vividly and she imagined that this would probably be worse because they were exchanging one for another.

She closed her eyes and relaxed on the bed. She couldn't hear anything. Everything was completely silent. Her mind wandered. Dru was looking forward to being able to read everything around her and have a better understanding of what people were saying. Alliance translators were the best in the galaxy. She decided that even if she were rescued, she wouldn't give back the translator.

Dru wondered if she would ever leave this planet. She thought about escaping but realized if she did and Earth had not negotiated for their release, she would be a fugitive. She thought about returning to life in the Exterior, but then decided that she would rather be a pirate in the galaxy than return there. She was almost dreaming about what her life would be like aboard a pirate vessel when she heard her door chime.

Dru opened her eyes, sat up and said, "Come on," and then mentally berated herself for sounding so casual.

The doctor entered and gave Drusilla a smile. She mentally greeted her, *Hello young one.*

Dru was still unaccustomed to this kind of communication and struggled to respond so she spoke out loud, "Hi," then after a minute of silence while the doctor set up her things she said, "I'm looking forward to getting a better translator."

"Oh, human translators aren't that bad, you should hear some of the others. It's just that human technology is everyone's favorite to make fun of in the galaxy."

"Charming," Dru said.

The doctor looked at her and smiled, "We all can't help ourselves," she explained indicating Drusilla should lean back. "Humans are adorable."

Dru leaned back and looked up at the doctor in her navy dress with the white trim and before she could ask the doctor answered her.

"Yes, it's a doctor's uniform. The men's look different, of course, but when you are an Alliance doctor you will wear the same."

"What if I don't want to take that path?"

The doctor smiled at her again, while picking up her instruments and moving Dru's head to the side. "I can read your thoughts and besides what else would you do? You have been a great gift to the Empire."

"You mean because we are human women and good for breeding?"

"No, you because you are strong, young, clever, tele-pathic and good for breeding. The rest of the human women are standard, you are special Drusilla."

Dru didn't know how to reply so she didn't. She closed her eyes and let the doctor begin the procedure. After a few minutes, the doctor began talking again, probably to take her mind off what she was doing.

"Your Captain Kara is quite happy with Admiral Tir aboard the *Refa*. There are so many rumors about their sex life. I've no doubt that the Admiral will be able to convince other human women to join you here when he goes to Earth for the war reparations."

"I can't believe that. Why would human women choose to come here to be wives? I'm sure that my government will not only deny the Admiral his wife back but negotiate for our release as well."

The doctor shook her head, "I'm sorry, but I must disagree. In this galaxy we are the strong and you are the weak. And just because you oppose this doesn't mean that all human women oppose this situation. I've seen the reports from Earth. You're poor. You make strange decisions about population control and you're severely disadvantaged in the galaxy."

"That's all a choice," Dru corrected her. "We're true to our home. Every planet is born with a perfectly balanced ecosystem and most of you have destroyed yours in the quest for technological and military gain. We're as we are meant to be."

"Misguided, poor and backwards?"

"I don't see it that way. Earth is beautiful. Our nature is beautiful."

"And humans are beautiful but misguided," the doctor said with a hint of a smile. "Listen, I don't mean to make you irritated. I'm just being honest. We all think humans are interesting and attractive. But we don't think Earth is beautiful. Your sun is too bright and your nature too strange. We believe you are us but somehow many years ago you were lost in the galaxy. Maybe an early space exploration ship or an experiment that went terribly wrong."

"What's your point?" Dru wanted to ask her about the 'experiment' but was too cross to do so.

"My point is that you shouldn't be so proud of a place that is so low. You are truly Alliance now, not just one of our myths."

Dru didn't really understand everything the doctor was referring to but just said defiantly, "I'll never think this is better than my home planet."

The doctor gave her a sympathetic look, "This is your home planet. And I know from your initial medical report that you were not vaccinated for anything until very recently. Your body showed signs of broken bones that were set improperly only to be corrected years later. You were ..."

Dru interrupted her, "I know my life. I don't need a

recap."

The doctor then got images of poverty, ignorance, pain and suffering from Drusilla. She knew it was an unintentional share, but she still could not help but be moved by such vivid memories of needless suffering. "You might not have minded such a life, but many women from your planet, would rather move to the Alliance and become wives than live in galactic poverty." Then when she realized that Drusilla thought marriage was some kind of punishment she said, "Marriage is not what you think it is. But I will leave that topic for Madame Bai to explain."

"Please stop reading my thoughts," Dru said looking up at the doctor.

"You're projecting them in your anger, Drusilla. You might as well be saying them to me." The doctor brushed her hair away from the side of her head preparing to change the translator, "Just relax now, I'm going to remove your human translator. "The doctor made some adjustments, removed her human translator from above her ear and then said, "Now, you will feel some pressure and some heat. It shouldn't hurt."

Dru nodded and her eyes remained closed. She remembered getting her first translator right before she joined the fleet and she had a bad headache for days.

After a couple of minutes, the doctor asked, "Can you hear me clearly?"

"Yes," Dru said opening her eyes tentatively. "Wait, I cannot turn it on and off. Is it broken?"

"No, unfortunately our translators, as most in the galaxy don't have that function, only human translators. I know that you humans value your diversity in languages so this will be a loss for you. Maybe in the future the Alliance will make special translators for you if everything works well between our civilizations." The doctor gave her a sympathetic smile, "Now please look at the bedside panel and read it to me."

Dru sat up slowly. She felt a little dizzy. She looked at the panel and read everything out, "Lights, shades, internal communication, mirror, bed. Bed? What is that?"

"Every one of you have asked that question. That's for your personal pleasure. You're alone here without a man. It …" Dru interrupted her.

"Oh, stop. I understand," she said blushing and thought, *I'm definitely not going to push that button. It will remind me too much of what happened at the space port medical exam and other memories I'd rather not relive.*

"I can hear all your thoughts," said the doctor. "Now it's time to send a message to your family. Let's move over to the desk to make sure you can read and operate everything correctly. You shouldn't feel too much discomfort, just a little dizziness."

Dru slowly moved over to the desk and sat down.

"Do you speak to your family in your most dominate language? I noticed you had a couple of languages. I hesitated before selecting the strongest one."

"Yes. Did no one in the Alliance ever think it was boring to only speak to each other in one language?"

"No one has used a different language in the Alliance Empire for thousands of years. It's practical to have one language only. Humans are the only ones in the galaxy that waste time on making things more complicated because you think it's beautiful," the doctor was becoming impatient now.

"What's the point of life if there is not some beauty to it?"

"Some beauty is desirable, of course, but you humans take it too far. That is why your civilization is so far behind the rest of us. You waste your time on love, art, food and I don't even know what else, but I'm sure there is a long list of nonsense."

"I don't know if humans can survive without the beauty of life, what you call nonsense," Dru admitted quietly and it seemed like the doctor ignored her, but she still continued. "What do people in the Alliance live for?"

"Honor and the knowing we are the best in everything. You're one of us now. You must relearn what to prioritize in life. I can already tell some of your crewmates are actually enjoying the few modern conveniences they have seen so far. You're the only one who has questioned any of this. Don't be difficult, just accept this and learn how to be a good Alliance citizen so you may have a good life as the gods' intended. Now come, it's time to send a message to your family."

Dru sat at the desk and the doctor stood beside her. She could easily read the menu now and unlock her computer with facial recognition and her unique Galaxy Court code. Soon she brought up her messages, she had a lot obviously as it had been weeks since she had logged in, but she ignored them. She opened a new line to send a VM to her family.

The doctor moved out of the way so that Dru was alone in the video.

"Mother, Jesse, Jimmy, Barbs," she hesitated as she had not spoken to any of them since she left the Exterior. "I bet you never expected to see my face again. You probably don't know, but I was in the war in space. Our ship was saved by an Alliance Empire warship, you know the grey aliens, and now they are making us stay here on their planet. Just the women." Dru paused then and then said what she had gone over in her mind countless times if she ever saw her mother again. Her voice changed then and almost became accusatory, "And just so you know, I don't regret leaving. That life wasn't for me, you always knew that. I'm here now, so I am just as dead to you as I was when I left before. If you want to reach me, this account will still work, but I don't expect it and don't expect me to reach out again." Dru closed the message and cried. She didn't cry because she missed her family. She cried because she realized that she was very much alone in this galaxy.

The doctor put a hand on her shoulder, "Thank you for acquiescing to send the message." The doctor had gotten images from Drusilla's childhood while she sent the message and unlike the other women, her childhood was filled with darkness, hatred, violence and poverty. It wasn't very difficult to summarize that she had run away with no intention of ever returning. "At least you have let them know where you are now and that they never need be concerned for your welfare again."

Dru wiped away the rest of her tears and replied, "They don't care. They don't even have a computer, there is just a communal one, it maybe months or years before they see that message if ever." Then she smiled through her tears, "And I'm sure if they did care, they wouldn't feel too comforted that I was here among aliens."

The doctor hesitated only for a second, "You're right, they probably don't care. We care though. You are valuable to us in so many ways and not just for breeding. Drusilla, you represent the hope of a dying Empire. No more tears now. Be strong for your new family. We may be clumsy in welcoming you, as the doctors on Space Port One were, I apologize for them, but we desperately want you."

Dru was overwhelmed. She had never been important to anyone before. She didn't know how to respond.

"You don't have to respond. Give this opportunity, this second life, your Alliance life, a chance." The doctor gave

Drusilla one last look and then packed up her things and left.

After a few minutes Dru composed herself and went downstairs where everyone else was already seated at an assigned seat at the circular table in the classroom. One of Madame Bai's assistants handed her an IC and a tablet as she sat down.

"Now that we are all here, I'd like to go over some practical matters and then we are going to begin our first class on Alliance culture. First thing," she looked down at her list, "You all have an IC in front of you. It's monitored so don't try to plan any escapes." She looked around at the women who seemed disappointed, "You didn't honestly think we would just hand out IC's for you to plan your rescue? Be serious ladies. Let me remind you again, Alliance citizenship is a gift, and you are no longer prisoners, but you must earn your independence. Now, if you would each turn on your IC, I want to point out two important functions to you. The first, is what we call the Day. This is a summary of everything of importance that has happened in the galactic day specifically organized by the High Council. You must watch it or read it every day. If you don't you will be punished by the government. You cannot cheat either, the IC has sensors to see if you are really paying attention or not."

Jane raised her hand and Madame Bai nodded at her, "What kind of things are covered in the Day?" She wanted to ask if it was government propaganda, but of course, even if Madame Bai thought that it was, it was very unlikely, she would admit to it.

"The Day covers anything from great military achievements to new schools opening on colonial planets. It can be anything. When you were brought here there was a short mention of you all in the Day."

"I want to see that," said Rebecca. "How do I search for that?"

Madame Bai brought up a 3D screen of her IC and showed the women how to search the database of Days. There they watched the 30 second clip of a stern Alliance woman with banners behind her that said the 'Day' report the following, 'Yesterday, 26 human women from the human starship *Dakota* arrived on the Capital Planet. The women were rescued by Admiral Tir of the *Refa* and chose not to return to Earth but to come to the Capital Planet and become Alliance citizens. Their wellbeing and introduction to society will be executed by Madame Bai an anthropologist. Let us all pray that they are our redemption.'

After it was finished Rebecca said, "We didn't choose to come here. We were taken."

"You mustn't remember it that way. You chose to be here," Madame Bai said looking at all the women very seriously. "You must always remember that. Is that clear?" The women just looked at her in astonishment. "I imagine that on Earth, it's easier to have different accounts of events and many varying opinions, but the Alliance Empire is vast and therefore the Days are often simplified so that people can remember the important part of the events more easily. The important part of your event is that you are all here and will marry and hopefully have daughters, not how you came to be here."

"That is exactly what I thought," commented Jane. "And our punishment if we don't watch?"

"Thirty public lashings for the first time and then the punishments increase with every day."

"I see," said Jane. "I think we'll all be able to find the time to watch the Day every day."

"Good," said Madame Bai, "Now moving on to the

other important part of your IC, the 'Prayers'. If you open that application, you'll see that this monitors how often you pray to the gods. You must pray, either in the private shrine here or at one of the city temples at least once a day."

"And if we don't, we will be punished?" Rebecca asked.

Madame Bai nodded, "Yes."

"How do people find the time for so much praying?" asked Dru.

"You'll find the time," Madame Bai assured them all.

"Now, moving on," Jane interrupted her.

"Are all Alliance citizens made to pray every day too?"

"Of course, you are now Alliance citizens and have access to the same freedoms that we enjoy."

"We have to watch the government sponsored news every day, we have to pray every day and we can never leave the planet, these are the freedoms?" Dru asked for clarification.

Madame Bai smiled sympathetically, "Yes, these are just some of the freedoms you now have, access to the true religion of the galaxy, access to the best information about what is important to Alliance citizens and the privilege of never having to travel through the galaxy yourself but living in the best part of it."

Dru frowned, "This is all so contrary to what I think about when I hear the word 'freedom'," she said and others around her agreed.

"Maybe on Earth you were using the word 'freedom' incorrectly?" Madame Bai suggested sharply. "Now, moving on, you all have been given universal credits into your own individual Alliance accounts which can be accessed with your fingerprints, facial recognition and for larger purchases your Galaxy Court code. This will help you to begin assuming a more normal life here on the Capital Planet. These credits reflect your age, skill and what you have left behind at home. Jane, you've been given the most, 3,000 UC, as you are 37 years old and left behind three children and a boyfriend on Earth. Dru you have been given the least, 250 UC, as you are the youngest and have left behind no children or boyfriend. The rest of you are somewhere in between. The Alliance hopes that you will see this as compensation for the drastic changes in your lives."

None of the women said anything about this as they were in a state of shock, 3,000 UC was equivalent to being one of the wealthiest humans on Earth.

"You are free to do what you like with the money; you can send it home. Whatever you would like. Let me remind you again, as you were all so tired yesterday, that as long as you are unmarried, the Alliance will provide your living, food and clothing. You can remain here in this building indefinitely and you will always be looked after." Madame Bai looked them all over to make sure they understood this and when she was satisfied she continued, "As for earning money, from this day forward, you all will begin to earn 5 UC per month for just being here and that will continue until your death. You will all receive the money, regardless of work or marriage, as an understanding between yourselves and the Empire." Madame Bai knew this was not a lot of money in the Alliance. But the Alliance would provide for them everything else they needed, and the idea was to make them feel welcome, but give them some incentive to get married as well.

Again, the women were silent, 5 UC a month was more money than any of them had ever seen at once.

"As for work, we all work here in the Alliance, you will be trained for what you are most suited for and hopefully it won't be long until you are all happily employed again. I don't want to get your hopes up, but your captain, now

married to Admiral Tir, who is a very important man, has
pushed the High Council to allow you all to be allowed to
serve in the Alliance fleet. This, of course, would change the
laws about women in the military and leaving the planet,
which is part of the ancient Contracts between the sexes
that keeps us all equal, but if Admiral Tir wants it, he has
enough power in the Alliance to make the High Council do
it. Don't think though this would be a means of escape. You
wouldn't be alone on the ship, it would be integrated with
Alliance officers and no doubt you would be a part of
Admiral Tir's fleet, but I thought it was right that I should
tell you that your captain is trying to make the best of this
situation, as you should too." Madame Bai saw the excitement in some of their eyes and she was pleased that she
could give them something to look forward to. "Now, I'd like
you to switch on your tablets and look at the first page.
Today we are going to begin studying Alliance culture from
a nuclear family perspective. Our culture is much older than
human culture and it's very strict as it's more complex, and
this strictness first begins at home. That is why, I thought it
was best to begin our lessons there. As you know from the
mealtimes, we try to avoid disruption to the order of things
at all times. I hope it won't take too long for you to adjust to
our way of arranging our days and nights, our families and
our relationships. You are all one of us now. If you turn to
chapter one, we will begin with home life." Madame Bai
looked out onto the human women, "Jane, I think it's fitting
you begin reading as this affects you the most here."

Jane found her place and began reading, "Ideally,
Alliance people all belong to a hereditary House which
provides for them their identity and subsequently their
occupation. All three of the social classes are represented
in each House, maximum, middling and slave. Only

84

women move from House to House when they marry and can retain membership in both if merited. A man will forever remain in the House he was born. The eldest woman of the maximum class is always head of the entire House and if possible, will represent her House, at least annually at the High Council General Assemblies."

Madame Bai interrupted Jane then, "Jane that's you. Now listen ladies, this means that if you want to get married, take a job, anything outside this House, your Human House, you must ask Jane's permission." Madame Bai looked at Jane then and said, "And you have a great responsibility to all of these women that they make the right decisions. In your IC you have the ability to restrict their funds and issue punishments when needed. For example, Drusilla is still being punished for resisting the piercings yesterday. It's up to you to decide when her punishment will end."

Jane got out her IC immediately and asked, "How do I do that?"

Madame Bai went to Jane's side and showed her how to access each woman's account and make adjustments.

Jane looked at Drusilla and said, "James, the punishment is over."

Dru nodded, "Thanks."

Then Jane asked, "What about if I marry?"

"You can choose to still be Head of House Human or pass the responsibility on to the next oldest woman, and so forth."

"And what is your role then Madame Bai?"

"I'm only your cultural guide. I've no legal responsibility over you."

Everyone was stunned, most of all Jane, of course, but she spoke confidently, "At least nothing has changed then except I'll have to be more curious about your ladies' love lives," she tried to make a joke.

"What class are we then?" asked Rebecca, already moving on.

"You are the lowest of the maximum class. It was thought it was best to replenish the top with human women first," Madame Bai explained, "and then over the centuries the healing blending of Alliance and Lost People would trickle down."

"What class are you?" Dru asked.

"I'm upper middling," Madame Bai explained pointing to some of her jewelry. "There's a section in your handbook dedicated to ranking jewelry which we'll go over in detail in the next few days. We know everything by our jewelry. The most important part of socializing in the Alliance is knowing your place."

Madame Bai looked out on her students who were just waiting so she continued with her lesson. After many hours they began to discuss relationships between children and parents. "There is nothing more sacred in the Alliance than family. Daughters live with their families until they are married. They look to their mothers for guidance in all things. The relationship between a mother and daughter and sisters is unbreakable. Conversely, sons are sent away to school from eight years old and even after marriage will not live with the family until they retire from the military or pursue another occupation after their minimum military requirement has been met."

"All these poor, young boys sent away from their families at eight years old, forever?" Rebecca asked horrified.

"Boys leave to be trained to serve the glory of the Empire. They form strong bonds with the other boys and men so that when they are gone for long periods of time, they feel like they are with family, a family of fighting brothers. And when they are on leave or anytime on their home planet they can return to their familial home. And when they marry, they bring their wives to live with their families. Men, unlike women, always call their familial home, 'home' and just like women have two families. Women have the family that is genetically theirs and the family they marry into. Men have their genetical family and the military," Madame Bai explained.

"When do young men and women meet and begin a family then if the young men are always away for such long periods of time?" Dru asked somewhat confused. And couldn't help but wonder, *And maybe you wouldn't have a demographics issue if men were around more?* Even though, she knew the two probably weren't linked, she couldn't help but think it. The man she suspected was her father only came around once every six months or so, and she thought it was a terrible way to have a romantic relationship, if she could call her mother and probably-father's relationship, 'romantic'.

"Men are eligible to marry from 30 years old and women from 20 years old, only if they have finished their education and have begun working. However, those are our Alliance years so in Earth years they are slightly older. Young men and women can meet through friends, family or at official functions just for these purposes called 'Assemblies'. You each have a formal dress that was purposely made for these Assemblies. Once a couple has courted for at least one month, but no longer than one year, they can get married and then begin having children. The woman stays here and works, and the man sees her when he is on planet or in our territory depending on the arrangements and rank. Minimum age of retirement from the military is 150 years old, but very few leave then. It's an age that should be moved to 250 years old as that is the typical age a man retires." She paused then and added, "And this is only for maximum class, the other classes differ in requirements and ages for marriage because their lives differ so greatly from yours. We will discuss those later as it's not important now as it doesn't affect any of you. You," she looked at them all seriously, "aren't allowed to court or marry anyone that is not from maximum class. Is that understood?"

All the women nodded and then Dru asked, "Why do you marry so young if your lifespans are so long?"

"It's not only our ancient tradition, but we don't interfere with fate either," Madame Bai answered as if that made all the sense in the world.

"What do you mean, by not interfering with fate?"

"We don't use medical technology for the procreation of children. Therefore, we must marry young."

Dru was intrigued, "How old is the oldest recorded mother in the Alliance?"

Madame Bai looked up trying to remember, "I think about 55 or 60 years old. It's not old." She looked them all over then, "That's why you all have come here to help us, now moving on."

"What is courting like?" Rachel asked. "It sounds complicated given that the planet is just full of women, boys, and old men. Are we all just waiting for men in their primes to return at random times and then we jump on them like dogs in heat, or have I missed something?"

Dru looked over at her and thought, *Of course you would ask.* Rachel was striking. She had, cream colored skin, green eyes, blonde hair, and was tall and strong. Every time Dru had seen her off-duty she had been surrounded by men smiling.

"I wasn't going to talk about this today, but maybe it's right we should just jump in and start here given that you are all of marriageable age. Except for you Drusilla, you must wait a year and I assume you will attempt to become a doctor here as well which will also set you back. As for the rest of you, I've no doubt that Alliance men will find you all very attractive," Madame Bai said. "Please turn to chapter five, 'Courting and Marriage'. Courting is when a man and a woman begin to see each other privately. Under no circumstances does this imply sex. Or even too much physical contact. It's for the sole purpose to get to know one another intellectually and emotionally. During this time, you might go on dates, for example, walks in the park, the morning or midday meal at a restaurant, yes, I see your faces, we do have restaurants here even if you do not like our food," Madame Bai frowned. "If you like the man you continue to meet him privately and then after some time you decide if you would like to be married. If you decide to marry, you'll have a small ceremony with some of your closest friends, exchange bracelets and then you'll be married."

"What about unmarried?" Jane asked pushing a hand through her brown hair.

"You mean not married yet?" Madame Bai tried to confirm the question. "Yes, you are all referred to as 'unmarried women' right now."

"No, I mean when the marriage dissolves," Jane clarified.

"If you run away from your partner you will be brought back and put to a very painful death either by your husband's hand or the court's. That's the only way a marriage is dissolved, by death. In some rare circumstances, if you have married a man who is uninterested in you sexually, you can dissolve the marriage that way. But this is even rarer these days with a shortage of women, many men who don't enjoy women don't have to pretend to be interested in them as they did in the past."

"Must we marry then? And if so, how long do we have to find someone?" asked Rebecca.

"Women should all be married by 40 years old. Some of you have only a few years to meet someone and of course we are not barbarians, we understand that some of you older women may not be able to meet a man to marry. If that's the case, you'll be adequately compensated. The rest of you that are below 30 years old must marry and you will be punished just as any other Alliance woman would be for not marrying. Traditionally, all men should be married by fifty. Unfortunately, with the demographic issues we have now, many men are unmarried and will never have an opportunity to marry and so many of them have chosen to remain in the military permanently," Madame Bai said regretfully. "But I guess if you cannot marry there is no greater honor than to die for the glory and expansion of the Empire. Thanks be to the gods' who light our paths in these dark days."

"Is this why the Alliance has been waging wars on the entire galaxy for the last 100 years or was that just for expansion, power and profits?" Jane asked coolly.

Madame Bai gave her a nasty look and answered her just as icily, "Jane, let me remind you that you are no longer considered a human in this galaxy. Your allegiance stands with the Alliance now, so you ought to have some sympathy for all those men who died for the Empire, never having a chance at a family of their own. If you ask another sassy question, you'll be punished. And let me remind you all, that means you'll all be punished. Understood?"

"Understood," said Jane fiercely.

"What if your husband dies?" Dru asked to change the

subject. She didn't like the angry emotions flying through the room and she didn't want another punishment today.

"You can remarry, but you don't have to. However, if there is any hint of foul play it will be investigated, and you will be put to death if found guilty. Marriage is the most sacred contract two people can make together. My advice to you is to not marry anyone lightly." She sighed and then began again, "Now, to continue, when a man is courting you, he'll give you jewelry to mark how he perceives the attachment. No matter what happens in the relationship, you're able to keep this jewelry, but usually women don't accept or wear any jewelry from a man they aren't very serious about."

"I don't want a man I don't know well giving me anything," interjected another woman. "We're human women we're equal to men."

"This is the Alliance, not Earth, and men and women have strictly prescribed roles. This kind of gift-giving has nothing to do with being equal or not." She sighed, "Now, where was I?"

"We were talking about courting, but what about marriage? Do we become the property of our husbands'?" Jane finally asked. Everyone had been thinking it since they received their new translators and the words 'slave' and 'marriage' had remained unchanged.

"Absolutely not. What a preposterous idea!" Madame Bai looked at them all and felt sorry for them that they had come from such a barbaric place to even think they would not be equal to men. "Rest assured ladies that your husband will have no control over you in mind, body or spirit. This is the Alliance Empire."

"But Admiral Tir just took our Captain and married her, how is that if men and women are equal?" Dru asked.

She felt there was something not right, but she couldn't read Madame Bai's thoughts, so she had to ask.

Madame Bai frowned, "It's difficult to explain all the circumstances that led to your captain's hasty marriage being legal as you are so new here. However, it seems as though your captain agreed to the marriage freely and subsequently has agreed with witnesses. Although, there was no courting, Admiral Tir didn't break any laws in marrying Captain Kara so quickly. I'd advise you all to not go down that route though, long courtships end in the happiest of marriages in my experience."

Madame Bai continued talking about courting and marriage for another hour. All Dru really took away from it was that there were lots of rules that must be followed including what they could and could not discuss with men. Thankfully, all of these rules were clearly outlined in their chapter about courting and marriage. What she found most shocking was that women under no circumstance could ever discuss anything to do with female reproduction, including periods, with men. She thought that was so odd. She wanted to ask about it, but was so overwhelmed with everything else she decided she would just save that question for another time. She did not imagine herself ever going through the process of courting with an Alliance man any time soon, so she wanted to focus her attention on things that mattered now, like understanding what was expected of them for the rest of the day and tomorrow without a punishment.

Later in the afternoon, they were told about the Alliance's religion which was made up of a pantheon of gods. In their tablets they had a picture and synopsis of each god or goddess and their role in life. "The Alliance has two major religious festivals every year which all citizens must attend. The next one will be in two months, by which time you will be well-acquainted enough with the temple and its routine to not make fools of yourselves. I'm well aware that you think you all are above us because humans gave up religion centuries ago, but let me share with you one myth that will be of interest to all of you,

Long ago, when the Alliance was still an infant and ships got lost, a fleet of explorers and scientists were pulled to the other side of the galaxy by an unknown force. Unable to come back, they found an almost inhospitable planet, too bright, too hot, but uninhabited except for some small animals. They sent a message back to the Empire explaining their situation, begging to be rescued. The message took over one-hundred years to arrive. When it was received, the Alliance had already counted those in that fleet for dead. The Empress and Emperor then were very greedy and did not want to waste time and resources to go look for some citizens who may or may not be still alive and waiting to be rescued. The Imperial Family decided to conceal the information about the Lost People. They had the message destroyed. From that point forward, everything only got better for the Empire, technology, military, colonies and Alliance civilization in the known galaxy soared and no one thought about the rumored Lost People again, until we discovered a species almost like our own. They called themselves 'humans. We sent ships to investigate them before they had the technology to understand what we were doing. We believed that these humans were most likely the Lost People. However, since the Empress and Emperor of past had all the original documents destroyed, no one remembered the exact location of the Lost People. So, it was decided, conveniently, that humans were not the Lost People and the Alliance continued to expand and to almost completely ignore humanity. But now, the gods are punishing the Alliance for not retrieving the Lost People when we were twice given the opportunity to do so. They are making us suffer with low-female birth rates and catastrophic disruptions to our perfectly ordered society. We have been given a third chance now, to accept humans back into the fold or die from our pride.

Do you see now?" Their religious teacher all looked at them and smiled, "You are the Lost People. That is why in a galaxy filled with thousands of different species we are the only two genetically identical. It is not luck. You are us. That is why it is only natural that you return to us now."

Dru and the rest of the women did not know what to say. None of them had ever met someone so zealously religious who was trying to convert them before. They sat bewildered. For the rest of their religious class, they had to learn all the basic prayers and practice saying them and lighting candles in the small shrine. This reminded Dru so much of home and growing up with her mother it almost seemed natural to her, but she shrugged off the feeling. *This is an alien world and an alien religion, this has nothing to do with Earth or me,* she reminded herself. And when she opened her mind to the other women around her, she knew they were just repeating the words but thought it was all just empty beliefs of an empty people with no beauty to live for, so they had religion.

"I don't understand why you, coming from such a tech-nologically advanced civilization, still believe in mythical gods?" asked Jane, echoing what all the women had thought in private. "Why can't you just say, 'You are a group of Alliance people who became stranded long ago and now we need you back because we have messed up our demographics somehow?' Or why can't you just use science to fix your problem?"

Their religion teacher thought for a moment and then answered, "Think of religion as a road map for life. A set of vows and rituals with a spiritual belief that may or may not be strong for you. To live in a galaxy without these road maps would be to live a half-life, a life reinventing the wheel. The gods provide for us clear guidelines how to be good and efficient in our lives, without them, we might as well just program computers to continue the Empire and do nothing ever again. We might as well not exist at all."

"Is it then the struggle of life which motivates the Alliance?" Dru asked. "The knowing you'll never be as perfect as the gods and that you will always disappoint them and suffer the consequences. The pain to remind yourselves you are really living?"

"Or just plain social control, James" said Jane.

The teacher ignored Jane's comment and answered Dru, "I guess, in a way, you may say it's the suffering. We do place a great deal of emphasis on rewards and punishments. I find it very difficult to believe humans no longer have a place for spirituality in their lives," the teacher placed one finger over her heart to indicate her deep sincerity in what she said, while looking directly at Dru.

"Why do you pray?" asked Rebecca.

"I pray because it's impossible to know everyone at once, but I wish them all good lives. Only the gods can know everyone, their hopes and temptations. I pray for the gods to provide for all." The teacher looked around the room, feeling pleased that she had at least explained one thing that seemed to resonate with these women. "Please begin memorizing the first three prayers from your prayer book. I'll expect you to know them without hesitation by tomorrow. Dismissed."

After the evening meal, the women were allowed to do what they wanted and most retired to their rooms to sleep. The next day would be another day of classes. However,

Dru was asked to remain in the classroom with Madame Bai and a woman that Dru now recognized as a doctor by her blue uniform and medical jewelry, a silver circle with three horizontal lines going through it.

"Drusilla, this is Doctor Jina. She's here to help you prepare to enter the medical school."

Dru looked at the middle-aged woman, she wore her hair in thick braids that were wound up on either side of her head and she had large sympathetic green eyes. "It's nice to meet you," Dru said but did not extend her hand. Alliance people did not touch each other unless you were family or very good friends.

Jina smiled at Dru, "I look forward to introducing you to Alliance medicine. If you're ready to begin, we can dismiss Madame Bai." Dru nodded and then Madame Bai smiled and left. "Now, I've seen your medical reports from Space Port One. The first thing we must do is teach you to use your telepathic ability to its full capacity. Whatever they taught you on Earth, clearly, is not working at all."

"My mother was a telepath and she taught me how to use it, but when I wanted to figure out how to use it more, I basically was only using the trial and error method. I had never even met another telepath until I came here.

"That makes sense why you have trouble replying telepathically then. It's like learning to speak, it's natural but you must practice. You must learn to do this as you'll want to have private conversations with people using telepathy. You must also be able to shield your thoughts from others too, to become a truly proficient telepath." Jina saw the look of concern on Drusilla's face and added, "Don't worry, only a small percentage of the population is telepathic, it's a recessive gene and most of us are doctors, so you will always have a good guess who heard you if you found you projected a thought or two."

Dru looked at Jina and said honestly, "I can't tell when I am projecting."

Jina smiled at her, "Okay, let me show you. Do you mind if I touch your hands?"

Dru kindly held out her hands to Jina, "Please."

Jina took Dru's warm hands in her own and showed her what projection felt like by sharing her own perception of it, "It feels like a thought greater than your own."

"I can barely feel that," Dru admitted.

"But you can feel it and that is the beginning. Your sensitivity to telepathy will grow the more you use it. Now, let's practice. I want you to ask me questions telepathically and then I'll answer them. I want you to say the answers out loud so that I know you heard me and that I understood your question."

Dru looked into Doctor Jina's warm green eyes and agreed, *First question, Are you married?*

Jina smiled, *Yes.*

Dru said out loud, "You are married." And then telepathically, How *long have you been married?*

Ten years.

Dru commented, "You've been married for ten years, a long time."

Jina smiled, "Not long. We're practically newlyweds, you'll see. Keep going, you are doing well."

Dru asked another question, *How many children do you have?*

Doctor Jina smiled again, *One son,* and she projected an image of her son to Dru.

After about an hour of practice Dru was getting better. "It's invigorating to speak telepathically," she admitted after Jina said that it was enough practice for today.

"It is," Jina agreed. "How were you and your mother using this skill at home? Your ability to project and manipulate is very strong. Whatever you tell me remains between us," then she put one finger over her heart to indicate her sincerity.

Dru looked into Doctor Jina's eyes and decided she might as well say some of the truth as it might help her get better at using telepathy. "My mother is a traditional healer. We used it to calm patients and make them see what they wanted to see and feel what they wanted to feel."

Jina nodded, "I see, that is a bit like influence, but manipulation of another's mind goes against the gods and carries punishments with it if not used in the appropriate situations."

"I won't do it here."

"I didn't say that," said Jina. Then Dru heard her say through telepathy, *In the Alliance we can say one thing while doing another. Don't ever let your guard down, but don't get caught either.* Then out loud she said, "And now there is one more thing I must discuss with you. Drusilla, we need to talk about the rape."

"I wasn't raped," Dru said evenly.

"Will you share with me the memory then so I can change your record? The doctor who examined you on Space Port One believes you were and that is the root cause for your sexual inexperience. She wants you to begin a monitored mandatory sex routine. Putting you through a monitored sex program here, I think, would only make matters worse."

"Monitored sex with whom?" Dru was in complete shock.

"A slave who does these things for a living. It's a controversial theory that has taken over in the last years. As we've had issues with our demographics, women who've not been inclined to be with men, have been put through it. As a result, these women, have only learned to tolerate a man's touch. It's not a healthy program."

Dru didn't want to have to have sex with therapy men in front of other doctors regularly so she said to Doctor Jina adamantly, "I'll show you the sexual encounter, but on the condition that I'll not be punished for it here or on Earth. And that you will change my record so that I don't need to be put through any monitored mandatory sexual routine." Dru had just learned from Madame Bai that in the Alliance you could make formal deals with people that bound them to you. And it was so common that there was a function on everyone's IC to do it, from the very simple to the very complex.

Doctor Jina nodded.

Dru took out her IC and made up the small contract. Doctor Jina put her finger to it. Then Dru asked, "Now, how do I show a specific memory?"

Jina smiled sympathetically and began guiding her through the procedure.

When she was ready, Dru took Jina's cool hands in her own and focused on keeping both of them within her mental bubble, in case there were any telepaths nearby. Then, she conjured up the memory from four years ago.

It wasn't difficult to remember and set the scene to share it. It was always with her, lurking close to the surface of her consciousness. That night she was sweating. It was summer, hot and humid. Some of her hair was sticking to her forehead as she walked through the overgrown trees on the muddy path. She was walking just along the border of the green forcefield that separated the modern world to the Exterior. She saw the lights of the guards' box and continued to walk, one foot in front of the other, shaking with fear, all the time telling herself, *This is the only way out. You can do it. It'll be a long time before another opportunity presents itself when Mother is away so long.* When she approached the guards' box, she was dismayed to find five men there instead of two. She could have manipulated the minds of two but not five. She still tried, but it just led to confusion among them and then some of them began asking if she was an Exterior witch. She then changed tactics. She lifted up her sweaty cream-colored dress that was already stuck to her curves and asked if sex would change their minds. They all hungrily agreed and immediately let her through the forcefield and were on her like men fighting over water in the desert. They circled her and one grabbed her hands with one hand behind her and let the other hand begin to caress her breasts over the thin fabric of her dress, while the others watched, all making lewd comments. Then a second man joined the first and he began stroking her vulva over her clothing. It was not long before they had taken her dress off and had her on her back on the guard house's rough wooden table. She had some splinters in her back as they pushed on her naked body. One man hovered above her with his penis in her mouth almost choking her, his large sweaty stomach over her head, she worried she would be suffocated in his sweaty fat. While he used her mouth, the others used her vagina and slapped her breasts aggressively. Then they flipped her over and put her on her hands and knees on the wooden table, she could feel tiny fragments of wood piercing her. She was scared, the table shook with her trembling as she didn't know what to expect next. Suddenly they began beating her bottom with a piece of wood. It hurt so much she cried out and the men laughed at her. After the spanking they began putting themselves everywhere, into her mouth, her vagina and her anus. She was in so much pain. She was crying and choking and everywhere hurt. She wished at the time that she could have blacked out from the pain, but she couldn't and what was worse is that she remembered every second of it. Their hairy, fat sweaty bodies all thrusting their penises into her in wild animal-like motions. It was a depraved act. All five of them used her in every possible way they could. It seemed to go on and on. Not only was it the pain of men roughly putting their penises into every orifice she had, but it was the disgrace of what they said to her while they were doing it. They called her vile names and she had been unprepared for the psychological aspect of sex. When she offered herself to them, she didn't know people could say these things about a woman. These words would haunt her for years afterwards, worse than the sex. She was so young and naïve. Thankfully, when they were finished, they let her go. They threw her clothes at her, disgusted by their own animal-like behavior now that they looked at her, bruised, bloody and crying. They slapped her a couple of times, hard, and told her angrily that if she ever told anyone what they had done to her, she would be put in prison for escaping the Exterior. Two of the men wanted to push her back into the Exterior, saying, 'She'll be back and then we will have her again.' But the oldest of the men, who looked like he felt the guiltiest, held a gun to the other two men and said, 'It was a fair deal, she is walking out of here.' Dru got up slowly. Blood, semen and excrement ran down her thighs from her mouth, vagina and anus, but she was free. In that moment, she rallied herself, *It's over. I just need to put on my clothes and walk away. This was the price for freedom.* She tenderly put what was left of her dress on, picked up her small bag with her few belongings and walked towards the nearest encampment, what she later found out, was called a 'city' in the outside world.

Dru released Jina's hands then, "It wasn't rape. I let them do it. It was a trade."

Jina was completely in shock by the repulsive human behavior she had just witnessed. If Alliance men were ever to behave in such a way, they would be put to death no matter what the situation or what the woman had offered. "Drusilla, you had no idea what you were offering as you were a virgin and those men acted barbarically. In the Alliance this would be considered rape. You were not old enough to consent and they used you in a way that had no purpose but to satisfy their own beastly needs."

Dru just looked at Doctor Jina. She didn't believe her. In her mind, she had been old enough to offer herself and she had done it to escape. She was still traumatized by it to be sure, but she knew like everything else that had happened to her, this pain too, would pass in time.

"This is why in the Alliance, men are not given much responsibility when it comes to women and children. Without the guidance of women, they revert back to their most primal instincts, just using brute force for everything without logic." Jina took a deep breath, trying to clear the images of the rape from her mind. This memory would always be with her now, unless she had it medically erased, which she considered doing at this moment, as the memory had been so horrific. "I don't know what to do now. Obviously, this first sexual experience has scarred you, but the sexual monitoring program would definitely make this worse. Could we decide on something between ourselves now to help heal this wound?"

"I agree that I need to heal, but I think that will just happen in time."

"That's not for certain and you don't have the time. You'll be of age next year and men will want to marry you, and, in the Alliance, we know that sex is just as an important part of your life as eating and shelter. You need to begin to align yourself with a routine."

"You mean a sexual routine?"

"Yes."

"Is that what you have? A sexual routine?"

"In a matter of speaking, yes. When my husband is home, we have sex frequently, when he is not, I have other means. It's an important part of a healthy life. I think you should begin with yourself and no one else first. You must start all over from the beginning. You must separate your experience with those men from what your body truly desires."

"Are you talking about masturbating?"

"Yes," Jina said as if this was the most common thing in the world.

Dru just looked at her and wondered what else she was going to say.

"I could help you if you don't think you can do it alone."

Dru immediately shook her head, "No, I think I can figure it out by myself."

"You need to know your body sexually and in a healthy way. If you don't know yourself, how will you ever know which husband will be right for you?"

"But you don't have sex before marriage, or?"

"No," Jina said, not confidently because quite often people did. "But you do get close to one another and you talk about sex beforehand quite extensively to make sure it will all work out. If you don't know how to satisfy yourself sexually, you can't talk about your sexual expectations with a partner and this can lead to problems in the future."

"Just to clarify, a man courts you and you don't have sex, but you touch each other in all other ways and talk a lot about sex before actually getting married?"

"Yes."

"Why not just have sex?"

"Because it is a custom, part of the Contracts. And it builds the desire over the weeks and months before marriage. One of my most memorable sexual encounters was the first time I had sex with my husband and we finally did things we had been talking about for months before," Jina said wistfully.

"I can't even begin to understand what the point of that would be," Dru commented.

"That's the problem. You have shut yourself off from sex because your first experience is still an open wound. It makes sense. Now you need to rebuild yourself. Maybe it's for the best you are in the Alliance. Whereas the other human women might struggle with the physical differences of Alliance men, you can begin focusing your sexual desires there. Their bodies look nothing like the men who raped you and their behaviors will be quite the opposite."

"You want me to fantasize about Alliance men?"

"If it helps."

Dru shook her head, "I don't know."

"It's okay, you're not supposed to know. It's fortunate that you are still young and there is still time to save your sexuality almost completely. You will always carry these scars, as it is too interlinked with other very important memories to erase, but you will overcome this."

"What if I wanted this memory erased?"

"No, we can't."

"Do you erase other rapes?"

"Yes, but usually those have no purpose to them. They were just random acts of violence. Yours had a purpose, one of the most important challenges in your life, leaving your home. If we were to erase it, not only would you be a completely different person, but we might alter everything else about you. So much is linked to memories, it's playing with fire to do too much."

Dru nodded, she had read about a lot of human memory programs going seriously wrong. "So, you want me to begin masturbating and then tell you about it?"

"I don't need play-by-play details, Drusilla. What I want is to discuss it afterwards. Where your mind goes when you touch yourself and to make sure that you are able to move forward. I want to help you heal this wound, so that when the time comes to marry, you are ready. I don't want you saying 'yes' to the first man who shows you any kind of good sexual attention. You represent our hope for a dying people, we want you to marry and have children with a man you enjoy. Not someone you suffer through."

Dru could not help but remember the medical exam on Space Port One and those orgasms. As humiliating as it was to do that in public, if she could look at it without emotion, if she had experienced that with a man, she liked, she would want to be with him all the time. She would crave his sexual touch. "I understand. I just feel..." Dru trailed off. She didn't want to say 'embarrassed' because that was not exactly the word, 'ignorant' was probably better. She just didn't know where to begin.

Jina gave her a sympathetic smile, "Your bed upstairs has many different options. Start trying them. Next week, we'll talk about this again. The most important thing is that you take this seriously. If you marry a man who does not please you sexually, it will ruin your life."

Dru thanked Jina for tutoring her, but not specifically for which topic.

Doctor Jina turned to her before leaving, "And Drusilla, one more thing, don't read other people's thoughts or influence them in any ways without their consent. There are secret police everywhere monitoring this and the punishment for unlawfully reading someone's mind is quite terrible. The Empire values us as much as they fear us."

"What's the punishment?"

"I don't want to give you nightmares," Doctor Jina stated as if she were talking to a child, but technically, in the eyes of the Empire, Drusilla was still a child, "Let's just say it is a fate worse than the longest death you could imagine."

Drusilla nodded not wanting to know more but had to ask, "And if I accidently project things is that punishable too?"

"Not yet. Not if it's clear it's an accident. The problem is with these secret police is that it is their word against yours. Just be careful."

"I'll do my best." Dru returned to her room and sat at her desk, she opened her messages. There was one from Madame Bai. It was the picture of the female crew of the *Dakota* in their uniforms that she had taken yesterday. She had sent it with the message that said,

Remember where you come from.

Dru looked at the picture as it appeared in 3D on her desk. She looked at her crewmates and herself, tired, dirty and blank. She thought about Madame Bai's double meaning in her message. The message being, to always be human, but to be Alliance as well. Dru suddenly felt overwhelmed. She wanted to be rescued. But at the same time, already she was beginning to feel some sympathy for her Alliance hosts. She couldn't help but remember Doctor Jina's words, not an hour ago, 'you represent our hope for a dying people', and Dru felt a betrayal at wishing she would be rescued and, at the same time, betrayal that if she remained, she might not be able to be everything the Alliance hoped she would be. She wondered again, *Are we the Lost People?* She shook her head in denial. But she couldn't deny the Alliance women on the planet had already shown her more concern and sympathy than anyone had on Earth. No one had cared what she had been through, but she defended them to herself, *They didn't know what had happened and they weren't using me for breeding.* With those thoughts, she closed the picture and decided to go to sleep, despite it being early.

Dru slept in her dress again. No one had asked about pajamas so she just assumed hers were missing as an oversight and she would need to ask Madame Bai or Jane about it tomorrow. She kept her shades on her window open again to watch the city move all around her. As she lay in her warm bed watching the transports whiz around, she wondered what Alliance people did in their spare time. If they socialized like humans socialized. Madame Bai had told them that people tended to meet their friends in the evenings after dinner with their families. Dru wondered if there would be a time that she would have some grey Alliance friends. That they would meet for drinks and all the hands at the table would be grey except for hers. This image made her feel very homesick for Earth again, but she held back the tears and thought, *No, add some human hands there, I am not the only one here.* Then she tried to change the image in her mind with her make-believe Alliance friends, but she couldn't add another human friend there and she knew why. When she had left the Exterior, she had had to give up all of her friends and family to start over. She couldn't help it then and the tears began to fall, she wiped them away and thought, *But this is different, we are all in this together. It's not like starting completely over again, not like that.* She cried for herself and her bad luck at being in the Alliance now. She felt like she was back to square one, again

Dru woke up in the middle of the night and was unable to go back to sleep. Her mind was racing with everything that was going on in her life. The unknowingness of whether they would be rescued or not. The weight of the Alliance culture with all of its rules and the expectation that not only would she need to become a working member of Alliance society, but that she must marry and bear a hybrid child. With the thought of marriage and a child on her mind, she thought about what she and Doctor Jina had discussed about her sexuality and needing to know herself. With that in mind, she turned to her bed's control panel and began exploring some of the options under the heading of 'bed'. There were so many options she really didn't know what most of them were. She decided to first choose the option that said, 'basic,' she thought, *I am a beginner to these people after all, who knows what they have in here?* Then she laughed out loud at the thought of what this bed might actually be able to do. *Can it conjure a man?* she wondered. When she looked at the panel again there was another long list of options. A lot of them did not make sense to her and so she just decided to choose the first option that said, 'orgasm five minutes.' Then she quickly got out of bed and took her dress off, then she got back under the covers and waited for the bed to begin, in those seconds, she wondered if whoever monitored their building was going to enjoy watching her too. She wondered if they were male or female. She guessed they were probably female as the only men she had any contact with were the guards that just nodded to her when they all passed.

It was not long before the bed became warmer to her

skin. It seemed to come alive with warm air touching her skin at random and not so random places at different intervals. Finally, after some minutes getting her very aroused, hot air seemed to swirl around her nipples, intermixing with cold pinpricks, making them hard and the bed gave her a similar treatment over her vulva and then clitoris. It was so much pleasure, but with an edge she really liked. And it was so different from the medical exam orgasm, this was sensual where that had been medical. This was warm, gentle and most importantly private. Just as the bed had promised it brought her to a climax by shooting hot air in and out of her vagina and anus, never stopping with her clitoris or nipples. She had never felt anything like it in her life. The hot air felt like large warm, firm feathers caressing her but as her need grew the feathers began to feel like gentle, warm water caressing her in all the right places with all the right pressure. After she climaxed the bed returned to just a normal bed and Dru drifted off to sleep again, thinking that was a good but strange sexual experience.

The next morning, while Dru was in the shower, one of the slaves came into the bathroom with no shame at all that she was showering and said, "You have received a package. I will set it on your desk." Then instead of leaving she looked at Dru's body and asked, "Are you going to keep all of that fur?" indicating Dru's entire body.

"Yes," Dru said shocked.

The slave shrugged then and said, "Some men may like that fire fur, I guess," and walked out.

Dru looked at where the slave had gone and said to herself, "'Slave' is really not 'slave'." She looked down at her body hair. There was an average amount on her body. Removing it had been something unequal women had been forced to do in Earth's history. She felt to remove any of it now would be signing herself up to be subjugated in the same ways as those historical women. She shook her head and thought, *I would never remove any of my natural hair for a man. I am an equal.* She finished her shower and when she was dry went to her desk to see what was sent to her without dressing.

She saw the small black wooden box on the desk. She looked at the note attached to it. It had her name written on it.

Drusilla,

Welcome to the Alliance.

She flipped the small note over, but there was no sender. She opened the fine silver clasp to the box. Inside was a small beautiful black comb. She picked it up and investigated it. Then she ran it through her hair trying it out. It wasn't like any combs she had ever used before, it glided through her hair as if her hair was silk that never snagged or got knots. She looked at the comb again and said, "Well thank you mystery person." But when she thought about it, she suspected the gift was from Madame Bai and she had given them all combs.

When Dru went downstairs for class and then breakfast everyone was seated as they had been before. Even at the dining room table there were assigned seats in their ranking order. Dru didn't mind being the last as she was the youngest, but already even after a couple of days, she felt the other women began treating her more like an inferior than an equal, or a superior as they had done before they came to the Alliance, and she was sure this had to do with the ranking. She decided if it continued, she would have to show some dominance because in the fleet she still outranked most of them and she was a doctor. *I'm not the lowest among us, even if I am the youngest,* she thought as she sat down.

The next days and weeks were all the same, Madame Bai came to their building and they had a cultural class from five to seven in the morning then they ate breakfast together. At eight their religion teacher came and taught them for one hour. From nine to eleven they had sword training. Then they had a break until after lunch. At two in the afternoon, they were led out on the town with Madame Bai. They went to cultural sites, mostly military monuments or religious temples. Sometimes they went to shops so that she could introduce them to different products and how to pay, which was with your fingerprint. In the evenings, they all ate dinner together and then could do what they wanted. Once a week, Doctor Jina came from the Capital City Hospital to practice telepathy with Dru and talk about sex.

One evening Rachel and Dru were in the drawing room, looking at Rachel's Alliance social media feed on the large 3D view screen that could be projected over the fire. She was the most active of them all and had already made some Alliance friends both men and women through social media, so her feed was the most interesting to them all. They were looking through the various articles trying to figure out what Alliance people were interested in. "Here is one for us," Rachel said with a laugh. "The most eligible bachelors now," she read the title and opened the article. Unlike a human article that would have probably shown pictures of the men with their clothes on, this Alliance article was shocking as the men were pictured with nothing on. And the pictures were intentional. The men had proudly posed for these in various positions showing off their best angles. And even more surprising to the women was that most of the images had been taken in various areas of starships to reflect their specific professions and duties.

The women were dead quiet for about 30 seconds, in shock, and then looked at each other and burst out laughing. They laughed so hard they cried and were so loud, everyone who was practicing swordplay in the gymnasium came out to see what all the noise was about. When Rachel and Dru tried to explain, they only began laughing more. They just pointed at the 3D screen above the fire and then the women from the gymnasium began asking them why they were looking at pictures of naked Alliance men, which brought on more fits of laughter from Rachel and Dru.

Finally, Rachel composed herself, wiping the tears from her eyes and explained, "We opened an article about the most eligible bachelors in the Alliance, expecting to see headshots, biographies and maybe a video but this is what came up."

Then all the women started laughing. They could not control themselves. It was all just so strange, everything about the Alliance and all their hypocrisies, but this was the best yet, no sex before marriage, but then these men had proudly posed for these nude pictures.

The women started looking through the pictures together with great interest. All the men were grey with long black hair that was worn in different styles of braids and some loose. None of them wore any jewelry or anything on their bodies at all. Some had tattoos which they knew were a kind of ranking, but they had not specifically studied tattoos with Madame Bai yet, so they meant nothing to them. One thing all the men had in common though was muscle. The women had already realized that

Alliance people took great care of their bodies, but it was becoming even more obvious that they were actually obsessed with their bodies, every muscle had to be toned and not an ounce of body fat. Most of the women felt very intimidated by this, worried that Alliance men would find them repulsive because they were not as fit as Alliance women. Dru had already given up on that as she had large breasts and there was no way she would ever be as lean and muscular as a typical Alliance woman.

"Oh, here is one for you James," remarked Jane dreamily. "Ket of House Vo. Imperial Doctor. Currently serving onboard the *Tuir* under Admiral Ver of the Imperial Family. Doctor Ket's favorite time of the year in the Capital City is blooming season. What he is looking for in a wife, a doctor who is just as dedicated as he is."

Dru laughed as she looked at the picture of the undeniably handsome naked man, in what looked like a sickbay, and asked, "Dedicated to what? Working out in the gymnasium all the time?" Everyone laughed and then they looked through more pictures, but there was something about the doctor that she liked and Dru decided that she would look back through his profile alone in her room later. She thought, *This was what Doctor Jina had suggested wasn't it? To begin fantasizing about Alliance men.*

"Oh," said Rachel. "This must be old, look there is the Captain's husband."

They all went quiet. Their hearts beating faster. He was absolutely a god of a man with tattoos running down the length of his body and then they all stopped laughing when they read the bio.

Next in line to the Imperial Throne.

. . .

Jane started, "I don't think..."

Rebecca who had always found fault with their captain interrupted her, "You don't think she sold us to be Empress of the Alliance? Well looking at this, I think she absolutely did. And I'm disgusted."

Dru didn't know what to think. But it was difficult to put it out of her mind that she might have been betrayed. Then she reminded herself of Captain Rainer's thoughts as they were being escorted off the *Refa*, "No," she said quietly. "Captain Rainer didn't betray us. Can a human even be Empress? With all their rules and racism towards humans, I doubt it. She's just as much a victim as we are."

"And even if she hadn't married him, do you think the Alliance would have just let us go? No, they had this planned from the beginning. Captain would be right here with us if she wouldn't have married him. Now let's see this as a positive thing, if she's in a position of power, that's good for us all. As Madame Bai said, she was pushing Admiral Tir to get us in the fleet," Jane said persuasively.

"The wrong fleet," Rebecca commented bitterly.

"But a better fleet," Rachel said.

Jane nodded, "A better fleet indeed. Let's not be too hasty with judgements now. We don't know what happened between the Captain and her husband."

There were lots of nods around the room. The conversation died then. Rachel closed the screen and they all went off to bed.

After six weeks, Madame Bai announced that they would all go to their first Assembly and that they should wear the formal dresses provided for them. They had a special class the morning of the Assembly as Madame Bai wanted there to be no misunderstandings about what to expect and how to behave. Madame Bai came into the classroom and it was obvious that she was very excited for them. Unfortunately, her excitement was not contagious. They had all become closer in the last six weeks and they had found learning about the Alliance culture interesting, but now to actually go out and live it was not something any of them really felt they wanted to do.

"Tonight, will be your first Assembly. This will be the first opportunity for you to meet with eligible men who you might marry," Madame Bai was beaming. "As I mentioned before you should all wear your formal dresses and I would prefer you wear your hair in Alliance styles, but I'll leave that up to you. As for what to expect," Jane interrupted her.

"Will there be alcohol there?"

"Yes, but I expect you all to act in a civilized way. Alliance citizens do not drink to get drunk." Then she looked them all in the eye and said sternly, "And if any of you drinks too much or acts inappropriately, you will all be punished. This is your first outing and all the eyes in the Alliance will be on you." She took a deep breath, "Now as I was saying, this will be your opportunity to meet eligible men."

"How will we do that? Will I just say, 'Hi, I am Rebecca do you want to get married?'" Everyone laughed at Rebecca's comment except Madame Bai.

"No, you will certainly not say that. As a part of the Contracts, women may not approach men for social conversations, that was outlawed thousands of years ago. They have the right to choose us and we can decide to accept or decline without prejudice. And please remember that you must dismiss them, or they won't leave you at the Assembly." All the human women looked at her in bewilderment, "You will wait for a man to approach you, and if you like the look of him, you will have a conversation. When the conversation is over, you must dismiss him. If the man likes you, he will contact you again to meet him on another day. If you meet again and get along well, he will probably ask to begin courting. Ladies, please read your cultural handbook. We have gone over this."

"But no sex?" questioned Rachel.

"No, definitely not. Ladies I have explained this many times, you do not have sex with an eligible suitor until he is your husband."

"I just cannot believe that is true," said Jane. "You know on Earth we have this wild idea to follow our bodies urges and our hearts."

"We are more civilized here so keep your bodies and hearts under control until marriage bracelets have been exchanged."

"Is marriage not for love then at all?" asked Dru.

"Marriage can be for love, but it should also be for respect and similar position in society as well."

"What is our position in Alliance society again?" asked Jane sarcastically and everyone laughed because Madame Bai had made it clear on many occasions that they were in many ways second class citizens despite their official ranking as maximum class.

"Order," Madame Bai said and clapped her hands to stop the laughter. "It's true, as humans you are below us all, however, as women who can potentially breed other females, your status is higher. You're all also very beautiful and brave so I have no doubt you will be able to marry above your station. Please do not embarrass yourselves tonight. Remember what you have learned and behave in accordance with the Contracts."

"I feel like we should all be reading Jane Austen," Jane said quietly and there were more smiles.

"Jane, if you don't stop with this nonsense none of you will go to the Assembly. You may find this funny as an older woman, but think of your younger crewmates, they must marry or be punished. Now act your age and live up to your position in your House. Do not forget you are responsible for everyone's behavior."

Jane met Madame Bai's eyes with defiance but said no more, she knew that the other women wanted to go just to get out of the building. "Good, now if there are no more questions, I'll leave you free for the day and then one of my assistants will accompany you tonight. If a man asks to see you another day, you may say 'yes' in the moment, but you must let Jane know who he is and where he wants to meet you. Jane will not permit you to go off with any riffraff and I expect there will be many who will try just because you are human. Keep your guard up and follow your instincts. And ladies, don't drink too much, I don't want to read about any debauchery in the Capital City gossip columns tomorrow."

Later that evening, after dinner, Dru put on her formal dress which was the exact same cut as her other Alliance dresses, boxy. But this formal dress had the appearance of water moving at night over the entire fabric. So, when she walked it was as if she were wearing water that glimmered in the light of the two nearby Alliance Planets that were always visible in the Capital City's sky. Dru investigated the material but could not figure out how the illusion worked. She looked at her hair and decided she would just wear it loose. It fell becomingly down to the middle of her back and curled nicely at the ends. She had no doubt this was a direct result of the fine comb she had been given weeks earlier and her tinkering with the dryer in the bathroom.

Once she was satisfied with her appearance she went downstairs to 'the great fire room' as they now all called it.

Jane was handing out drinks, "I don't know if this is any good, I bought it from a nearby shop. It's called Zota. Apparently, it is a kind of hard alcohol. I'm sure Madame Bai would have a heart attack if she knew we were drinking this before our first Assembly," Jane said, handing Dru a drink. When they had all arrived, Jane made a toast, "To Madame Bai and our first Assembly. May we all find zombie husbands and have many hybrid babies."

"To Madame Bai and the hybrid babies," they all said and drank and then choked because the alcohol was so strong and disgusting.

"Wow," said Rebecca coughing, "Well, I don't ever need to taste this again in my life."

Dru had had much worse homemade moonshine in the Exterior and finished her glass of Zota and then took another. She didn't know how she felt about tonight. On one hand, she was curious to see what an Alliance Assembly looked like, but on the other hand, she didn't want to meet any Alliance men with the idea of marrying and having hybrid children. But then she reminded herself that she still had a year's reprieve, as she was not considered of age yet, unlike her crewmates who would all be expected to find a man as soon as possible. She drank another glass of Zota and looked at the other women, they all had the expression of people who were lost in their own thoughts, like people who knew they would die soon, and wanted to live their last days as well as they could.

After a few drinks of Zota, all the women were chatting happily as they made their way to the Assembly in the transport with one of Madame Bai's assistants. Of course, the assistant was upset as it had taken longer than she had expected to corral the human women into the large transport.

They were 30 minutes late. And everyone turned when

they entered the room. The Assembly was being held in a very large yellow stone building that seemed to be just one large rectangular room. There were some statues of the various gods and goddess scattered around, but otherwise devoid of any decorations or beauty. The room itself had very high ceilings and was lit entirely by candlelight.

"Look at all the men," commented Rebecca as they entered. There seemed to be twenty or more men to every woman.

"And these are just the ones who happen to be on planet tonight," said Madame Bai's assistant. "This is a lesser Assembly. At the Year Assembly, you will struggle to see other women as there will be so many men."

"Can anyone attend?" asked Rebecca already eyeing some men up.

"No," replied Madame Bai's assistant. "It's by application and this is only for maximum class as well."

"Where is the wine?" Jane asked. Their escort pointed out the bar and they proceeded to all get a cup of wine. With wine in hand, they settled into a corner to watch this Alliance ritual.

All of the Alliance women were dressed in dresses with patterns not unlike their own, with the illusion of moving images on them. And most of the men wore their black military uniforms proudly with all of their status jewelry so that nothing would be left to guessing. The women from the *Dakota* thought that they wouldn't have been affected by seeing so many eligible men tonight, but the truth was it had been months since they had seen a man besides their guards and here were many good-looking eligible men of all looks and ages looking to marry and they were taken in by it. And most of the women did long to be spoken to but were dismayed that a lot of the men were looking but no one coming over to talk to them. And they knew that they were not allowed to approach any men, so they just stood there in a deadlock.

Dru was dared after a cup of wine to walk around the room and see if any of the men talked to her privately. "You are the youngest and they all stare at your red hair. Go on, James," Rebecca said playfully.

"But I'm not even old enough to begin this ritual with them," she protested. She didn't want to saunter around by herself among all these men. There were so many of them.

"Even more of a reason, just go," said Rebecca giving Dru a slight push with a smile.

Dru walked away slowly. She didn't turn around but just focused on walking through the crowd. They parted for her without actually making eye contact. This made her feel like a queen or the ugliest person in the room, she couldn't decide which. She wanted to open her mind to hear their thoughts, but she remembered Doctor Jina's warning and resisted the urge.

After walking around for about five minutes, she decided to stand in a random place where she could see the other human women across the room. When she found her place, she was shocked to see that none of her crewmates were looking at her, but they were surrounded by hundreds of men. Her heart sank, she was so repulsive no Alliance men would approach them while she stood with them. Tears welled up in her eyes, *Don't cry. You're fine*, she told herself. Then she turned away from the scene and went out into the garden where again, the few men that were there, didn't look at her directly and some actively avoiding her.

She walked in the symmetrical garden until it was time to leave. When she rejoined the group at the entrance, waiting for Madame Bai's assistant, everyone was buzzing about their conversations with the men, both the good and the bad, and no one brought up that Dru had been completely left out.

It seemed that everyone had offers to begin courting, even Eve who had one eye and Jane who was almost too old for courting. Some, like Rebecca, even had multiple offers. Dru smiled for them. She would feel the same in their position, they had been so bored and now they had been out and met men who were attractive, well as attractive as grey people can be, and courting would give them something to do besides Madame Bai's classes and being cooped up in the Human House building all day. Even if they all still held the thought that they may be rescued, it was still a very interesting perspective to spend one-on-one time with a man from the Alliance Empire.

Late that night, Dru looked at herself in the mirror for a long time before going to sleep. She wondered what it was about her that made her so distasteful to Alliance men. In the end, she resigned herself to be a spinster forever and decided to look up the punishment for not being married tomorrow. She was sure it would be something ridiculous, as most punishments were in the Alliance. She imagined having to wear an 'U' around for 'unmarried' like Hester Prynne's 'A'. She went to sleep even being jealous of Hester as at least she had had her fun before her punishment.

Ket normally did not read the gossip columns from the Capital City, but today he had good reason to check them out. He wanted to see a picture of Drusilla. Their guardian watched over them so closely they were rarely let out and because of that, there were rarely any pictures of Drusilla. The Assembly, which by law they must attend, would be the first opportunity for the Alliance to view its newest citizens and everyone was curious.

. . .

With so much speculation about the human women and what their behavior would be like at their first Assembly I must admit we were all disappointed that their behavior was impeccable. Madame Bai can feel no shame about her charges today. Junior Doctor Drusilla even had the courtesy to move away from the group so that suitors could approach the eligible human women. Of course, there have been many rumors circulating that a ban had already been put on Junior Doctor Drusilla, but it wasn't until last night that we could confirm this. Despite being the most eligible among the human women and the most beautiful, not a single man spoke to her. We must summarize that whoever put the ban on Junior Doctor Drusilla is high ranking. The ladies in the office and I have come up with a list of men who might be behind the ban. Here are our top five candidates:

1. *Admiral Zo of House Huot*
2. *Doctor Kina of House Loa*
3. *Doctor Ket of Imperial House Vo*
4. *General Piun of House Bose*
5. *Doctor Rea of House Edda*

We look forward to your suggestions in the comments. However, we realize the list may be long as this Assembly was not the Year Assembly, so countless suitors were missing. Our heads are spinning with all the possibilities.

Ket smiled at the article, women loved to wonder about who put a ban on whom, and the men loved to watch the women guess. He then flipped to the pictures from the night, there were pictures of the human women arriving, they looked in good spirits. Then he flipped through more, there were many of the other human women talking to potential suitors and then finally at the end he found another picture of Drusilla in the garden, she was stunning, even in her cheap dress. He looked at the picture and wondered though, *Why is she so sad? Doesn't she realize she was already spoken for by someone greater than anyone there?*

Madame Bai was so pleased with the outcome of the human women's first Assembly the next morning when they were all in the classroom for their cultural class, she announced happily, "Because you ladies all performed so well last night, today we will skip our usual morning classes and I'll take you to the Earth Store. I've arranged transports outside."

Everyone was excited by this. They had been out in the city, but only under the watchful eyes of Madame Bai and her assistants and so therefore not allowed to go into the off-world ring of the city nor do any shopping for familiar things from home. According to Madame Bai, they had not earned the right, not until now.

Dru was not surprised that Madame Bai had also hired guards to accompany them. She was always talking about how dangerous off-worlders were to them and Dru always wanted to point out that they were off-worlders themselves.

On the way there, Madame Bai was answering some questions, "Oh there are less than 100 humans that live on the Capital Planet. They're almost all men. There are a few that work in the Earth Store, some traders who claim residency here but are not here often and, of course, most of the humans work at your embassy."

"Why haven't we met our ambassador yet?" Jane asked.

Madame Bai looked at her and said condescendingly, "Because you are no longer citizens of Earth but Alliance citizens."

"I'd still like to meet the human ambassador. How would I arrange a meeting?" Jane asked.

"You can make an appointment at the embassy. However, I doubt that he will be allowed to meet with you until after the war. You do realize that we are all still at war with Earth?"

"Then why is the ambassador still here?"

"I suspect because the human government is too poor to send him and his staff back and forth. And because the Alliance Empire does not see humans as a threat."

"That's odd," Rachel commented, "that there are so many human men working here and so few human women."

"It's not odd, it's natural. We wouldn't allow women to live here away from their home planets, it goes against the gods."

Jane had to hold her tongue not to point out the hypocrisy of that now, but she did roll her eyes which made a lot of the women smile. "What about the one other human woman?"

"She is married to the Earth Store owner," replied Madame Bai. "A deal was struck that they were allowed to open their store and live here if they married just like the rest of the Alliance."

"And what about the other human men? Are they married? Or do they have lovers?"

"I believe some of them are married, but not to human or Alliance women," Madame Bai didn't want to say anything more about it, she didn't want her charges seeking out human men, so she changed the subject. "I hope you all will enjoy shopping today. The Earth Store has been operating for about 150 years, it opened when the humans sent their first ambassador. Apparently, he couldn't stomach our food. Since then, it sells much more than food for humans and other people who like human things."

It was not long before the transports set down and the guards escorted them into the large shop. Frank the owner, a middle-aged balding man with a long grey beard and dark brown eyeliner around his light blue eyes, came out to greet them. He wore human clothes of brown trousers and a white shirt. He looked so pleasantly human and the women felt drawn to him like meeting an old friend, "Ladies," he had a big smile, "It is so nice to finally meet you all. Please come in. I have closed the store especially for you. Please come and ask me anything. My wife Zelda is not here now but I know she will be sad she wasn't here to meet you all today. Don't just stand there, come in."

When they had all entered the store and were looking around at all the familiar items and smells of Earth things, Frank pointed to a small console, "I've a lot on display, and of course, a lot in the warehouse and most things can be ordered. Madame Bai has made me aware of your restrictions until your marital status changes, however, aside from specific cultural products, I can offer you comfort products from home, such as food and drink. I've nice things such as Swiss chocolate, Canadian maple syrup, Thai sriracha, Indian spices, Chinese tea and French wine, all of which I just sent off to your captain aboard the *Refa*. I also run cooking classes for your slaves, if you think you could get them to cook human food?"

Everyone laughed and Jane replied for them all, "Unfortunately, I'm sure our slaves would never condescend to learn to cook human food, but we will keep it in mind if our situations ever change. Thank you."

Frank smiled, "Yes, they aren't really slaves, more like trolls of mischief roaming our houses. Apart from food, I of course, have clothing from Earth. I stock pajamas with extra prayer candles for the gods," all the women laughed at that. "Yes, I petitioned the High Council some years ago to begin making the prayer candles for wearing pajamas. You should light them in front of the goddess of home." He looked at all the women smiling and said joyfully, "And much more, please look around, take your time and ask me anything."

Dru smiled at Frank, she couldn't help it. It was a relief to see a human man. To hear someone, speak to them as they were accustomed to. Dru wandered through the large store. First, she went to the food section. She was so excited when she found apples and strawberry jam, she put one of each in a small basket. The cost of an apple was 3 UC and the jam 1 UC. It was highway robbery, but she still wanted it. Alliance fruit was texture less and tasteless. Next to the outrageously expensive spices she noticed a small advertisement for a cookbook written by the owner, called 'Cooking in the Alliance with Earth Spices'. It cost 5 UC. Dru thought that she should remember that for when she had more universal credits to spend. She thought perhaps it would be a good book to have when she married. She didn't understand why Alliance food had to be so bland, as it could have a lot of taste without being unhealthy and most Alliance people had more than enough universal credits to buy delicious spices. She sighed, this was probably going to be an Alliance mystery that she never solved. As she wandered around more, she found herself in the makeup section. Alliance people didn't wear makeup, but humans liked it and she wondered, if maybe, she wore some makeup Alliance men would find her more attractive. She couldn't help but remember last night and how no one spoke to her, no Alliance man or woman. It was humiliating. She looked at the black eyeliner and mascara. She was relieved to find that unlike the fruit and jam; this was much more reasonably priced, and she put both in her basket. Then she went to the clothing section and found the pajamas section. The store had the most beautiful set of blue silk pajamas with a matching robe, but it was way out of her budget. She ended up having to settle for cotton pajamas with little pink flowers on them. She also picked up the accompanying prayer candles. Then she saw some underwear and picked up five black lace pair, also with the accompanying prayer candles which she noticed were to be lit in front of the goddess of fertility not the goddess of home.

Then she looked around and as they were barred from anything cultural like music or dramas, there was nothing else she really wanted. She had never been a huge fan of chocolate and although she wanted to buy a bouquet of flowers from Frank's greenhouse, she couldn't bear the expense of it. She would have purchased Exterior coffee in a heartbeat if it were available though. Exterior coffee was a mixture of coffee, chicory and milk and was difficult to find outside the Exterior, she doubted Frank would have it here.

Dru was the first to check out. She put her items up at the register and Frank asked her name.

"Dru James," she answered with a smile. "You can call me either."

"Okay, James. And did you find everything you wanted? I can get almost anything you know."

"Do you know about chicory coffee?" Dru couldn't help but ask as they were the only ones in earshot and if she was going to be here forever, she reckoned better to ask now and know than wonder only to be disappointed later.

"Chicory coffee," he repeated looking directly at her with an unreadable face.

Dru couldn't help it, it was taking too long for him to reply and she wanted to know what he was thinking, *Did he hate Exterior people?* So, she jumped into his mind, hoping he was not a telepath and that there were no secret police around. When she did, she found that he was innocently trying to figure out where he could get some chicory coffee and she felt guilty for invading his privacy. "It's okay. It's unusual I know."

"Do you know how to make it? Chicory can be gotten, and I have coffee of course. I aim to please, and I reckon you and I will be friends for a long time to come."

"Chicory as in the root of the blue-flowered perennial plant not the lettuce," she had made that mistake when she was first out of the Exterior.

Frank smiled, "I've never grown chicory myself, but I have a greenhouse here. If you would like I will look into getting it and then you can buy it with the coffee and make it how you like."

"How much do you think that will cost? It will need milk too," Dru needed to know, she didn't have a lot to spend on frivolities. But she reckoned at this point, she would pay at least 20 UC to just have some coffee that tasted like home, just one more time.

"Since you are going to be my customer for as long as we both live, we will work something out," Frank winked at the young woman. He had read about her in the Day and felt so sorry for her, so young and to be thrown into the Alliance like this at full force. He had come here to make universal credits and for the prestige of living in the Alliance, but he didn't like the culture here and he felt sorry for all these women, especially this one.

Dru gave him a grateful smile, "Thank you Frank."

Frank just nodded and tallied up her apple, strawberry jam, underwear, pajamas and makeup. Then she paid with her fingerprint. The store already had her facial recognition.

When they all entered the transport to return home, everyone was buzzing with what they had bought, most of it was food. Jane delighted them all by saying, "I have a surprise for you all tonight after the evening meal, so don't be late. Two surprises actually and if you want to wear your makeup to dinner," a lot of them had bought makeup, "then tonight is the night to do it."

Again, everyone was excited, Dru reflected that for some reason now things began to feel real for the first time since they had arrived in the Alliance. Really real.

That evening Jane surprised them all with champagne. Real champagne. It must have cost a fortune. When everyone had a glass, she made a toast, "To our new lives and to Frank who is a small light in this dark world and will give us the liquid courage to continue."

"To Frank and small lights," they all repeated and drank with smiles and a bit of laughter.

Dru couldn't help but be a little pleased. They had very little to celebrate but Jane was right in doing this. It was a bright point. And it was nice to see everyone with a bit of makeup on too, as a reminder that they were all human.

Jane asked one of the slaves to take their picture, "I want a better one than the other one." She didn't need to say more, they had all, except for Dru, been approached by men at the Assembly and no doubt one of them would be married and gone, sooner rather than later, or that they would be rescued and return to their lives and separate naturally. Jane wanted a picture because she felt like they had conquered something by making it this far and she wanted the women to have a nice picture of them all, because if they were staying, they would be like family for one another and have many more hurdles to jump together.

It occurred to Dru then for the first time, that maybe some of these women wanted to escape their lives on Earth, as she had wanted to escape the Exterior. That maybe they welcomed this new adventure, as the doctor who had given her the new translator had suggested. Then Dru had the most cynical thought of her young life, *Maybe it doesn't matter where you are in the galaxy, that as long as there is a minimal base point of food, shelter, stability and society, you will feel the same levels of contentment and happiness regardless of location.* But as soon as she thought it, she dispelled that thought because if it were true, she should have never left the Exterior or she should just be content here. She hated to think the latter, that she should just resign herself to her new Alliance life, without a fight. She looked at Jane, "Do you think this picture is any better in these clothes? We're all still here."

Jane knew that James was the most reluctant to accept their situation and she had sympathy for her. James would probably never have human children, a human life, everything that more than half of them had experienced. Although the Alliance didn't see her as giving up much, to all the human women, James was giving up the most, a human life she would never have. "It's different," Jane said gently. "We are progressing. It doesn't matter that we didn't choose this. We are moving forward as we must one way or another. To survive we must enjoy these small moments when we can. To stay in despair over things we cannot change doesn't make sense."

"I'm not despairing," Dru replied.

"No, I don't think you are when you are working on learning about Alliance culture or something that you can justify that you must do. Now you have no justification for enjoying yourself here and you are despairing over it. This isn't a black and white situation. Just because we are enjoying ourselves now and I want to have a picture of this moment doesn't mean that I have given up on leaving or on the people I left behind."

"I don't want people to find this picture after we are rescued and think that we are spies or traitors to our own people. We should be doing only what we have to do."

Jane was old enough to know that that wasn't all that was bothering James, "And just sulk the rest of the time? That's unnecessary. And it's not wise to dwell on the what ifs. We should just do what moves us forward here, with the situation as we see it from our perspective now. What we learn now will make us more ready for whatever happens in the future, whether it be returning to Earth or remaining on the Capital Planet or joining the Alliance military. The worst thing we could do would be to remain stagnant or become depressed. We must maintain our morale. So, we are here, in our Alliance clothes having a little fun, a little reprieve from thinking about our situations for the moment, right James?"

Dru gave her a half smile that didn't reach her eyes, "Right."

Jane squeezed James's hand, "Let's talk later." Jane worried about her the most. She was all over the place emotionally. She was by far the cleverest of them all and took to learning all the prayers, social codes of the Alliance fervently, but then in social situations like this, she was apathetic at best. Jane didn't know how to reach her. Speaking to the other women, she had discovered that

James had never had a boyfriend and almost seemed afraid of men. Jane felt that James's issues were more about what was expected of them as women than their citizenship or political situation. However, when she tried to have private conversations with James, she was brushed off, once it turned personal.

The next day, the Day, reported that the human government did not consider the women from the *Dakota* to be prisoners of war, but to have given up their fleet positions and human citizenships to pursue a life in the Alliance Empire. Everyone was in despair when they read that. Even more troubling was that their captain was to be put on trial for treason on Earth in a few days' time. The Alliance was on Earth now for war reparations. None of the women thought it boded well though that Admiral Tir, Captain Rainer's husband led the envoy. They knew he was powerful, and he wanted their captain, his wife, back. And they knew that whatever happened to their captain would influence their own futures too. The next days would be anxious ones and already many of the women had given up hope of ever being rescued after seeing the article.

Dru was alone the next evening after dinner in the great fire room. She was flipping through articles from her IC over the circular fire. She was trying not to think about what was happening on Earth. Everyone else was out with a man they had met at the Assembly. Dru wondered, *Why did no one like me? What will I do if no one wants to marry me?* She had looked up the punishment for being an unmarried woman and it wasn't pretty. If she could not find someone for herself the High Council would arrange a match. If no man would have her then, she would be forced into a kind of convent where she would be punished physically daily. So, she was here waiting for anyone to return to pick up any tips on meeting an Alliance man.

She was surprised that Rebecca was the first to return. She walked into the great fire room, "Dru, are you alone? What are you doing?"

Dru gave her a half smile, "Nothing. How was your date?"

"Oh, you know," she said sitting down, her golden eyes bright with excitement, "I never thought I would like an alien man, but Kole is so tender and thoughtful. Tonight, he asked me to marry him."

"But you've only known him for a couple of weeks, marriage is forever."

"I know, but it just seems like the right thing to do. He is perfect for me, good-looking, sweet and he meets all the ranking requirements. He has a small house and if this is going to be our fate, I figure I might as well get on with it and go with him."

"You don't want to wait and see what happens with our captain's trial? Maybe we can go home."

"I don't think we are going home. I don't have much faith in our government rescuing us. I believe the Alliance when they say we are here for the rest of our lives," Rebecca said adamantly. "So, I might as well marry someone nice."

"I suppose you're right. I don't think we are going to be rescued, but I wouldn't make any hasty decisions before we know for sure."

Rebecca looked at Dru and felt badly for her that all the Alliance men seemed to be repulsed by her appearance. None of the other human women could figure out why. She had even asked Kole about it, but he just shook his head and changed the subject. Rebecca didn't want to point out that Dru would probably never marry so she said, "But don't you want to go to the medical school here? I'm sure you'd love to learn about their medicine with all their technology. Maybe someday you could bring some of that to Earth? Since we are all genetically the same."

"Maybe," Dru replied and then asked, "You're really going to marry an alien? Do you love him?"

"Love or lust," she smiled, "I don't know, but maybe I do love him. And I miss my family back home. I want to be able to talk to them and my friends. I can't do that unless I am married with a child. And Kole will treat me well. I figure they will all be able to visit in about a year and a half, if we move fast."

"So, you said 'yes'?" Dru still couldn't believe what Rebecca was telling her.

"I did."

"When will you get married?"

"As soon as possible. I have to talk to Jane about it obviously, but I can't imagine her saying 'no'. She already looked over everything about Kole before we began courting."

Dru looked at Rebecca in disbelief.

"Don't look so shocked. I didn't have a boyfriend or anything at home."

"And if we are rescued will you stay here?" Dru asked.

"I don't know. I figure Captain has something worked out. She is married too."

Dru thought that was one thing she could agree with Rebecca about; the Captain would have a plan. But she didn't want to point out that the fact the Captain was willfully married to Admiral Tir might seal all of their fates to not be rescued.

"I guess, I should say, 'congratulations'," Dru smiled.

"Thanks. I'm really happy," Rebecca said without too much enthusiasm.

Dru just gave her a look.

"I mean, I'm waiting for the really happy part to happen. I know it's coming."

Dru just nodded in understanding, "I'm sure it is." Then she rose and said, "I'm tired and I'm going to bed. Good night."

Rebecca remained on the sofa, "Good night. I think I am going to stay up and wait for Jane."

Dru walked back up to her room wondering, *Will I just live here all alone until I'm forced to move to the gods' convent and be whipped every day?*

3

A Choice to Remain

All of the women from the *Dakota* sat on the black sofas in the drawing room around the fire to watch the clips from Captain Rainer's trial on Earth. No one spoke as the beautiful Alliance woman reading the news unemotionally reported, "Over the last week, Admiral Tir has led the diplomatic mission to Earth, located in the Orion Arm of the galaxy, to collect war reparations and ask if any human females of acceptable health and age would like to return to the Alliance Empire with him to be granted Alliance citizenship. In a surprise, Admiral Tir's new wife had been abducted from his ship, two weeks ago and then accused of espionage by her own people. Admiral Tir had no choice but to offer a million UC, 50 model 15 laser weapons, 20 eternal batteries and two Alpha starships for her return. However, in a stroke of luck, many human females were moved by his actions and not only is he returning with his wife who is expecting their first child, but 1,000 more human women. Thanks be to the gods as they shine their light upon us today."

They all watched the clip three more times just to makes sure they had heard it all correctly. Now it was definite, they knew that they were never going to be rescued. Not only was their government not going to attempt to liberate them, they had just sold their captain and 1,000 more human women to the Alliance Empire.

Dru thought the Alliance was archaic for practicing marriage rites, but she didn't even know what to call her own government right now. They had just been sold like slaves. And 1,000 more women coming to the Alliance in the deal. All sold. Dru went back to her room without saying anything and went into the bathroom and threw up in the toilet. She looked at the vomit for a minute wondering what she was going to do now. She flushed the toilet, stood up, took a deep breath and looked at herself in the mirror, "This is your future, forget Earth, they have given up on you so you should give up on them." She splashed some water on her face and made sure she did not look like she had been crying and went to sit at her desk. Before she could open her own computer to watch the news clip again, there was a knock at her door. She thought it must be one of the other women, so she just said, "Come on," and was surprised to see one of the slaves walk in holding a small parcel. The slaves usually didn't even knock these days, they just burst in. She thought, *They must feel some pity for us today, being sold by our government.*

"This just came for you, Drusilla."

"Who is it from?"

"No one knows."

"Should I open it?"

The slave just looked at her in disbelief as they often did, and she realized she had said something stupid.

"Do you think it is dangerous?"

"No, I think it's jewelry from a man. A suitor."

"Oh," she said surprised and a bit excited by the prospect of a man taking an interest in her. Any man. Especially now that she was here for the foreseeable future. She took the package, but before Dru could ask any more questions, the slave was gone. Dru looked at the parcel. It was wrapped in black shiny paper. She unwrapped it. Inside was a black wooden box with a silver clasp. Inside was a striking silver necklace. It was a beautiful silver, single-strand necklace with 28 blue-rounded stones completed by silver engravings of some kind of Alliance mythological beasts on the large clasp at the back. The necklace looked gorgeous with her plain dress as she took it out of the box and held it up to herself in the mirror. She put it back then and picked up the black card with a silver script note.

Drusilla,

I hope that you find this pleasing enough to wear often.

She flipped the card over and looked for a name. She couldn't find one. Dru then went to her computer and opened her messages, but before she could message Madame Bai and question her about the parcel and what she should do, she saw she and the rest of the women had received a message from Captain Rainer. Her hands shook as she touched the written message to open it.

· · ·

Sisters of the Dakota,

Plans have changed. I am on my way back to the Capital Planet to get you. We will now serve in the Alliance Fleet. I hope you are all still with me. I will come to your building in a weeks' time. Be ready.

Captain Kara

Dru didn't know how she felt about this. Her first choice would, of course, to be to go home to Earth, but that was no longer an option. *Was it better to serve with Captain Rainer in the Alliance fleet or learn about Alliance medicine on the planet?* She had already been told that she could start attending classes soon by Madame Bai and Doctor Jina. She decided that she would decide in the week as Captain Rainer traveled to them. Dru suspected that all the other women would join their captain with great enthusiasm.

Dru VMed Madame Bai in real time then.

"I'm assuming you saw the news about your captain's trial?" Madame Bai said sympathetically.

Dru nodded.

"I just want to reiterate, as painful as this might be for you, that your government sold your captain and you all. We are your future."

Dru nodded again, of course, Madame Bai was never one to sugarcoat anything.

"I understand this must be truly upsetting for you all to know that now you really are here forever, but if I can give you some good news? Admiral Tir has pushed for you all to be back on a starship. Apparently, he adores his wife so much he cannot deny her anything. The law is going to be passed by the High Council within days and then you all will start being trained as Alliance officers, that is, if you want to be back on a starship? However, you, Drusilla, still have your place at the medical school. You can start anytime from next week. I assume that is why you are calling? The choice will be yours. For the other women, returning to the fleet will be the only option for them to have reasonably successful lives. As unorthodox as it is for women to be on starships and as much as I disagree with it, I think it will be the best for them."

"I understand," she could not think of a better way to punish the human government for this than by serving with the Alliance fleet. "I've another reason for calling though," she held up the black box and the necklace. "I received this today with no mention of who sent it. I think this is the second present I have received. Some weeks ago, I was sent a black comb, I thought it was from you and you gave one to each of us. But when I began to ask around, I realized I was the only one. How do I find out who sent these things to me? I thought only men who were courting me could give me jewelry or gifts."

"Oh, dear Drusilla, someone has put a ban on you. Didn't I tell you? It's been on you for a long time now."

"What does that mean? No, you never told me. I don't understand."

"It means that someone has paid a lot of universal credits to make sure that no other man that is lower-ranking than he is can court you or even converse with you while the ban is running."

"When did this begin? How do I find out who it is? Why would someone do that?" Dru was in complete shock. *How medieval was this civilization?*

"Women are not privy to the details of bans until they are over and revealed to both sexes. I would speculate that the ban was put on very early and will probably last until you are old enough to be properly courted or longer. I would also guess that whoever did it is very high ranking as no men have spoken to you at all since you arrived, have they?"

"No," tears began to fall, and relief overwhelmed her. She wasn't as revolting as she had imagined, "I was beginning to think that everyone was horrorstruck by the sight of me, because of my red hair." Dru wiped at the tears, "I'm overwhelmed." She began crying in earnest then and could barely speak, "Captain Kara's trial and now you tell me about the ban."

"This is obviously a lot to take in. I apologize for not mentioning the ban earlier. I thought you knew. Do you want me to come there so I can discuss all of your options face-to-face and we can talk about all of this?"

Dru shook her head, "No, tomorrow is fine."

"Are you sure? I'm worried," she said with a concerned look. Madame Bai didn't like that Drusilla was crying and she didn't understand why she was not happy to learn someone high ranking put a ban on her. She felt it was her responsibility to make her understand what a good thing this was.

"I'm fine. I'm just in shock," she took a minute and composed herself, then she looked down at the necklace again and asked, "Do I wear this even though I don't know who gave it to me?"

"Yes, as you don't know who the giver is it cannot be taken as a token of his affection. This is more a token to your beauty as you have never met. There are no strings attached."

"Would you wear it if you were me?"

"Yes. Absolutely. It's a beautiful piece. You should definitely wear it."

141

"With my day dresses? And with my ID necklace?"

"Yes," Madame Bai hesitated and then asked, "And, if I can offer one more piece of advice?"

"What is it?" she asked quietly.

"Let our culture in and silently let Earth go," said Madame Bai gently.

Dru knew that Madame Bai was right. She needed to let Earth go, just as she had let the Exterior go four years before. But knowing what needed to be done and allowing her heart to catch up were two different things. Dru knew very well that emotions didn't respond well to logic. "I'll wait to hear what Captain Kara has to say before accepting my place at the medical school." She knew if she decided not to go with the Captain, she was really making the choice to stay in the Alliance and really become one of them.

"Of course," said Madame Bai. "I'll see you tomorrow. In the meantime, I'll send you a list of the men who are the most likely to have put the ban on you, if you would like?"

Dru agreed and then closed her computer. She didn't want to think about anything anymore. She went into her bathroom, had a long hot shower and then went to bed even though it was still early. She closed her shades for the first time since she had arrived and slept in complete darkness. Hoping that the darkness would also stop her mind and heart from fighting with each other about what her next move should be. To stay or go.

Captain Kara arrived the next week as promised. They all met in the great fire room. Dru was surprised that their captain was now wearing a black Alliance fleet uniform with her husband's family name around her neck and there was no question about whether he was imperial or not or whether or not he was the current Emperor's successor. It was all right there in front of them on her ranking jewelry. That and the slight bump in her normally slender figure of a pregnancy.

"I'm glad to see you all healthy," she began. "When I sent you here, I blamed myself for not being able to protect you from this, but now I blame our government for not being able to resist the universal credits and other trivial things the Alliance offered for us. They sold us like slaves. Now we are destined to be a part of the Alliance forever and I'm not one to wallow in misfortune. I have accepted the Alliance into my heart."

Dru thought, *And into your uterus as well.*

"And I've accepted a new destiny here with these people. We are their Lost People. These Alliance people are *our* people," Kara emphasized the word 'our'.

There were gasps all around the room.

Had Kara become religious? Jane questioned but then reversed her thinking, *No, she is just putting on a show.*

"We are here to help the Alliance even out their demographics problem, but we will not do so without bringing something of humanity to them as well. They cannot cherry pick what they want from humanity. I have an Alliance Alpha ship," she said the two 'A' words with emphasis. It was a big deal. These were the best warships in the galaxy. It was unprecedented that a human would command one. "I'll need a loyal crew, but mind you, an Alliance crew. You must all pledge your oath to the Alliance Empire. We aren't going back to Earth. This isn't an escape mission." She looked them all dead in the eye, "And if we come across any human fleet ships, we will fire on them and offer them no quarter. If you're comfortable with that, I would like to invite you all to return. I will need your answers by tomorrow, and we will depart next week."

Many of the women made enthusiastic replies affirmatively.

Kara smiled and then said casually, "There is one last thing I must mention according to the new High Council Order that allows us on ship, I must also tell you that if you accept these positions, your position in the Alliance will fall. It will be more difficult for you to find husbands if you haven't already," she looked at Rebecca. "As this will be the first integrated crew of human and Alliance as well as for men and women, Alliance courting rules will be different. If you begin courting someone you must marry after two months and share the same quarters after the marriage has taken place. Rebecca has already asked for her husband to be transferred and I have granted it. For the rest of you, I am waiting to hear your answers."

"Do you share quarters with your husband, Captain?" Jane asked.

"No, he is on the *Refa* and I will be on the *Zuin*, but we are in the same fleet. We may visit each other from time to time."

"And the child? Where will it live?"

"Between both I imagine. I will bring a slave onboard to look after it."

"Doesn't that go against Alliance protocol?"

"It does, but I refuse to leave it here without me and I refuse to be here. The options to the rest of you because we must have children will be to leave the children with your husband's families here or take a year's leave of absence and then come back when the children are one year old."

They all knew better than to question why their captain got special rules.

Dru could sense that most of the women were happy with this arrangement given the circumstances. In the human fleet even if people were long term lovers they could not live together and would not be given any special treatment for children. Women who had children did get the same year off, so Dru suspected that Kara had added that bit herself. Dru felt that this was a decent arrangement and was considering it.

Jane interrupted her thoughts, "It's difficult to choose when your life is going so well here, isn't it?"

"You think my life is going well here?"

"You've learned everything that Madame Bai has set out for us to learn and you've learned it well. And you've been invited to attend the prestigious Capital City Medical School to learn some of the most advanced medicine in the galaxy. Yes, I would say your life is just beginning to go well here."

"I haven't been fully accepted yet. It's conditional on my passing some exams."

"And you'll pass. You're the cleverest person I have ever met James, and I have met a lot of people in my life, and that is including the captain. You're destined for something greater than dying with us in space. If you stay here, you can be the first human to wield Alliance medicine and be an insider into their culture. Part of the reason they want us onboard a ship is to keep us separate from their precious society. I think they have found us," she motioned around her to the other women, "and the Captain, too strong to keep here. That is also why they have replaced us with more docile humans who weren't in the fleet. Captain told me that most of the 1,000 women just brought from Earth did actually volunteer to come, if you can believe that? You are strong and could become influential here. If Madame Bai is right and your Mr.

Mystery giving you gifts is high ranking, which he must be because no one speaks to you, just close your eyes, marry him and then see how far you can go in this new world. Don't waste your time with us in the galaxy playing cowboys and indians. No one will remember any of our names after we die, but you have a chance to do something meaningful for both the Alliance and humanity. Don't throw this opportunity away."

"I hear you. I just don't want to be all alone here."

"You won't be alone. This building is going to be heaving with 1,000 more women."

"You know what I mean."

"I know what you mean, but listen to me as your House head," they both smiled at the joke, "I'm actually taking away your right to go right now. You must begin the Alliance medical school."

"You're kidding, right?"

Jane nodded her head, "Of course, I'm kidding. I haven't gone all Alliance on you yet," she said with a smile. She put a hand on Dru's shoulder, "But James, I think you'll thrive here. Give it a chance. You can always message me. You will never be alone. Do you understand?"

"Yes."

"Are you going to do the right thing?"

"I'm going to do the human thing."

"Good answer," Jane laughed quietly, "See, you're the cleverest woman I've ever met."

"Besides me," said Kara coming up between them. "James, I need you tomorrow. Admiral Tir is doing this ridiculous punishment at the Grand City Temple. I don't want to be the only human there but the only way I can bring someone else is to bring a doctor, so that is you. I don't want John. I'm tired of looking at his face as we've had too many meals together on the *Refa*."

"Yes, Captain," Dru said knowing about the punishment as she had read about it in the Day.

"Good. I'll see you tomorrow. Dismissed," Kara said and then turned to Jane and began talking about crew integration.

Dru went up to her room to consider her options. She laid down on her bed. She was sure that Captain Kara Rainer, Zu, was as wild as she had ever been and now the woman had an Alpha Alliance Warship. Not to mention, a powerful husband who seemed smitten with her. Going with the Captain could be the wildest adventure of Dru's life, and she couldn't deny that a part of her wanted that adventure. However, she also wondered about her life here. If she were to stay. What the other human women would be like and what kind of expatriate community they could build here. *Do I want to be a part of a community more than have a grand adventure in the galaxy?* She didn't know, she had chosen to go into the human fleet because it had been her only option. Now she had a choice and she had to search her soul to figure out who she really was. Something that she had never really considered before. She had never had a choice like this before, a choice between two good options. Dru wished she had someone to tell her the future, but then she laughed thinking what a bad idea that would be as in every story, anyone who ever asked what happened in the future ended up with that bad future because they asked.

Dru looked across the room at her desk. She got up and sat down and brought up the picture of all the women from the *Dakota* that was taken the day they arrived. She looked at herself in the picture and then went into the bathroom and looked at herself in the mirror. She thought about Jane's words downstairs, 'You have a chance to do something meaningful for both the Alliance and humanity.' Dru asked herself quietly, "Are you willing to risk a brilliant future for an adventure? Or stay here, and ride out the unknown, to see who this Mr. Mystery is and become an Alliance Doctor? What's it going to be?" She looked at herself seriously in the mirror for so long she began to see herself differently, but after 20 minutes she knew what she had decided. She was going to stay.

The next morning, Dru took a hired transport to fly her to the Grand City Temple as it was across town. She was alone in the transport, which was uncommon for hired transports, and when she arrived, she paid with her finger-print. She wondered if she could ask the Captain for reim-bursement for the trip as it cost her 3 UC and technically, she was working, illegally, but working on the Captain's orders, nonetheless. She had never been overly shrewd with her money but her 250 UC were slowly dwindling down and she had only been in the Capital City for a couple months. As she exited, she was surprised by the crowds lined up outside the temple. She pushed through the people that were lining up to get a glimpse at Admiral Tir's punishment. People moved aside when they saw that she was human and that she was on her way in. When she reached the massive antique gates, which were closed, two guards asked her where she was going.

"Captain Kara has asked me to accompany her today as her doctor."

The large guards looked at her ID necklace and nodded. They let down the forcefield and opened the antique gates. Inside, Dru walked towards the main temple building. There were very few people in the temple courtyard today, just some slaves and religious devotees that probably worked at the temple. Dru reckoned it must be because of Admiral Tir's punishment that there were so few people here today.

Captain Kara had described this punishment to Dru as some ridiculous Alliance thing so that he can be granted forgiveness for her escaping because he didn't treat her well enough onboard the *Refa*. Dru didn't know anything else about this particular punishment, but she had read a lot about punishments in her cultural handbook. She knew punishments were a large part of Alliance culture and the fact that this was taking place publically at the Grand City Temple, she could only assume that it was going to be bloody, painful and difficult to watch.

As Dru approached the large yellow stone temple, she saw Captain Kara and Admiral Tir as well as what she suspected was the rest of his family and Imperial Entourage there. Dru noticed that Captain Kara and Admiral Tir were in a heated conversation, so she held back with the rest of the Alliance people just watching them.

"Tir, you don't have to do this," Dru heard Kara saying. "It's absolutely barbaric."

"Yes, we do. Things will never be right between us without the goddess's blessing. You would have never been taken if I had been a better husband. I must make this right before you, my family," he touched her abdomen, "and the gods."

Then the High Priestess appeared and cleared her throat to get everyone's attention. She was an older woman with silver hair that she wore in many braids down her back. She also had on so much jewelry Dru wondered how she could move. When everyone stopped talking, she ceremoniously bowed to the statue of the goddess of marriage, which they all did in turn, and then the High Priestess addressed them all.

"Admiral Tir has put his name on the temple wall to amend for his actions concerning his wife's abduction. I have prayed to the goddess for many days concerning this issue and it has been decided that his punishment will be The Bloody Tears Until the Candles are Lit."

Dru had not realized that by Admiral Tir saying he put his sins on the temple door that it meant the High Priestess decided his fate. She had read about this punishment. The one seeking penance will kneel praying while he is cut by the one he wronged to fill a sacred chalice which is then poured through the back of the goddess's eyes, as if she is crying bloody tears for the sins committed. And as the priestess indicated, 'until the candles are lit,' that meant until the sun set which was hours from now as it was only mid-morning.

"I freely accept the punishment. Thanks be to the goddess," Admiral Tir said formally as he began taking off his shirt and handing it casually to a nearby slave. He then took a large black chalice from the High Priestess and a silver ornate dagger with a purple sashed tied around it. He handed the dagger to Kara.

"What do you want me to do with this?"

Admiral Tir gave Kara a look of annoyance, "I will kneel in front of the goddess and you will cut me across my chest until this cup is full. Then you pour the blood through the spout behind the statue of the goddess, so she cries blood and we will repeat this until the candles are lit for evening prayers."

"That's hours from now."

"It wouldn't be much of a punishment if it were easy. Now, please proceed, Wife."

Kara looked at the chalice and at the dagger. Tir was

kneeling before the large statue of the goddess of hearth and Kara had no choice, she began making small cuts across his strong grey chest to try and fill the cup. It took a long time as she didn't want to accidently cut too deep or hurt him too much. She hated this.

Dru watched as her captain cut Admiral Tir, it took at least 30 minutes for her to make enough small and shallow cuts to fill up the chalice. Dru wished that she could have guided her captain's hands telepathically, but there were two other doctors there and they would notice. And of course, it was forbidden to help either of them in a punishment scenario. Before Captain Kara poured the blood down the spout, which would slowly make the goddess statue cry Admiral Tir's blood, all the witnesses had to light some candles and say some prayers, all while Admiral Tir knelt, blood running down his body and onto the yellow stone around him. Dru had seen a lot of rituals in her life, many involving blood, but she was still shocked to see it in such a technologically advanced society. It almost seemed surreal, this ancient temple with the ancient punishment going on in the most modern metropolis around them.

Zol, the First Imperial Doctor to the Empress, had been sent to oversee the punishment as Admiral Tir was next in line to be Emperor. She was pleased that the Admiral had made his wife bring the young human doctor along. She knew her son Ket had put a ban on her. It was supposed to be a secret, but her husband Juh was bad at keeping secrets. Zol didn't mind that Ket might be interested in this human. She was healthy, young and had more potential to have daughters than any Alliance woman at the moment. The only thing that worried Zol was the question as to whether or not human women could become civilized. She had read Anu's report from Space Port One, 'Obstinate human. Failure to comply. Failure to understand her situation,' which gave Zol serious pause. She knew that Captain Kara struggled with the most basic of rules, so she wanted to see this young doctor for herself and to see if she had the same obstinate disposition as her captain. People had speculated that Captain Kara's bad behavior could be blamed on Admiral Tir, and that human women brought directly to the planet, surrounded by other women, as they should be, probably could be taught to appreciate Alliance ways.

Zol watched the woman with red hair and she could not help it, she was charmed. Drusilla came appropriately dressed, wearing a necklace she assumed that Ket had bought for her, it looked like his taste. When she arrived, she quietly stood back with the rest of them. When the prayers were said, she knew all the words and said them without hesitation. When Admiral Tir was cut, she gave a telepathic shout of disgust that only Zol and the other doctor there, Siu, could hear. Then closed her mind off again, realizing her misstep. Zol knew from her reports telepathy was somewhat new for Drusilla and so she gave her some leeway as it takes children years to control themselves especially when they have strong emotions. Zol thought is showed good character that she was disgusted by seeing this punishment. As any normal person should be, this was barbaric, and it was only men who liked to do these things to prove themselves.

Drusilla half wished she would have eaten more for breakfast and then half not, as the blood, even though she was a doctor, was disgusting to watch run down from the statues' eyes, down the body of the statue and onto the floor. They repeated the punishment twelve times before it was time for the candles to be lit for the evening ceremony. It was a good thing too as Dru noticed Admiral Tir was almost ready to pass out.

When it was finished, Captain Kara was holding Admiral Tir in her arms with no thought at all to the blood all over him and now all over her. She was whispering something in his ear, and he replied something back which made her hug him even more tightly and then he groaned. She moved away after some moments and his doctor and the Imperial doctor, dressed in navy blue with silver trim began to see to him as Captain Kara stood aside.

Dru moved up, "Do you need anything, Captain?"

"No," Captain Kara replied not taking her eyes off of her husband. Her face and hands covered in his blood. "Do you know about these punishments?"

"Some, we have a cultural handbook. I can send you a copy."

Captain Kara waved her hand, "No, I shudder to think what I would find in there after what I already know from living Alliance life onboard a ship. What life here must be like?" she shook her head. "I already have document upon document to memorize about Alliance fleet regulations and I prefer to make Tir teach me cultural things, then I know what is really done in practice not just in theory. The rest, I'll have Jane fill me in on when she can on a need to know basis."

"The Alliance likes the idea of order," Dru remarked and Captain Kara smiled.

"Yes, and that will be their downfall," she said cryptically.

Dru didn't ask what she meant by that. At this point she did not want to know. "I'm sorry I'm not going with you."

"You aren't sorry James, so don't say it. If I were you, I wouldn't go either. You've a lot of potential here on the planet. And we might be dead by the end of the year."

"True," Dru said and then after a couple minutes

added, "If things don't work out well here, could I join you later?"

Captain Kara turned to Dru then and said genuinely, "There will always be a place for you on my ship, but don't you quit here James for any frivolous reason. And if you do end up returning to me, don't bring a husband, already too many of the women are now trying to get their husbands onboard and I don't need that. For the first time a human has an Alliance Alpha Warship and my crew is trying to make it a love boat."

"I can promise you; I won't bring a husband."

"Do you know who this mystery man who put the ban on you is? Tir won't tell me. He says it is forbidden for women to know. What medieval nonsense."

Dru shook her head, "I don't know, but it is assumed he is high ranking."

"I've no doubt about that. I know he is one of Tir's friends. I overheard a VM the other day, but I couldn't find out who it was."

Dru was excited by the possibility that Tir knew who put the ban on her. She wanted to read Tir's thoughts, but she imagined the penalty for reading someone as grand as Admiral Tir's thoughts was probably quite severe, so she resisted. "Please try and find out, it's driving me crazy not knowing. Do you think he is here now? Does he serve on the *Refa*?"

"I don't think he's in Tir's fleet. I think he is an old friend."

"Old?"

"I mean they grew up together. I'll message you if I find out anything else. It's such a ridiculous custom." Then Admiral Tir got up and Captain Kara said to Dru quickly, "You may go, James."

"Yes Captain," she replied not moving and just

watching everyone to really make sure she could leave. She guessed that there would be one final prayer and she was glad she didn't walk away because she was right. Captain Kara had not been on planet learning about the Alliance culture like she had. *She doesn't know or just doesn't care,* Dru reflected. And then she thought, *Gods help the Alliance if she ever becomes Empress.*

4

Alone

All the women from the *Dakota,* except for Dru, left one
week after Captain Kara, as she was now called in the
Alliance, as surnames were worn on their ranking jewelry
and generally not spoken, had come to see them and
offered them a place aboard her Alliance Alpha Warship,
the *Zuin*. Now it was only Dru and the three slaves in the
entire building. The additional 1,000 human women that
returned with Admiral Tir were stuck in quarantine for the
foreseeable future as they had caught some kind of galactic
flu on the way to the Alliance from Earth. The Chief
Medical Officer Anu on Space Port One, said she did not
want to risk any contamination. Dru did not envy those
women having to be under the care of that woman. She
absently touched her cheek remembering how she had hit
Dru after the humiliating medical exam.

Dru banished those thoughts and tried to concentrate
on the good things that were happening. Tomorrow would
be her first day of medical school. Doctor Jina had supervised a cognitive download of all the Alliance medical
knowledge she would need over the last week. All which

would be dormant until integrated and activated through actual study, then it would become her own knowledge. It was the most technologically advanced way to learn in the galaxy. Humans had just begun to discover how to use similar technology, but so far it wasn't in use for the general public. She had also had an interview and assessment with the Capital City Medical School a couple days ago. The school only admitted women. She knew she shouldn't have been surprised as she had already come to realize that almost everything was run by women on the Capital Planet. Older men of maximum class were consultants to the government or military. Male doctors that retired from the military were also only consultants on Alliance planets, they were only allowed to practice on ships or on colonies.

Dru had been assessed both by written examination and orally by a panel of Alliance doctors. Doctor Jina had been one of the doctors on the panel and Dru knew that she had been her biggest advantage. The test was all day and they only broke for the midday meal. The next day she returned and was told her results.

"You have quite a talent Drusilla and we think you will do well here. Obviously, you lack a lot of technical knowledge, but this, we have no doubt you will easily pick up with some study, especially with the aid of the downloads. It's amazing how far behind human medicine is and yet you are all still here. As for your age, we want to put you with women almost the same age as you, so we will place you in the final year of structured classes. You will have to do a lot of studying to catch up, but we think you can manage this. After this year you will begin your practical training based on your results and when your practical finishes you will be an Alliance doctor. Do you accept this opportunity?"

Dru was surprised they were offering her so much,

"Yes," she had to catch herself from saying 'thank you.' Instead she replied, "The gods have given me so much. I am grateful for their grace."

Dru was so happy she almost skipped on her way home. The first thing she had done when she returned to the quiet apartment building was to visit the private shrine. She went to stand in front of the goddess of home and said the standard prayer to the black statue and then added, "And don't think I am leaving this building because I don't like it. I just want to work again and be a part of something." Then she lit a candle, bowed and left. She reckoned she was beginning to talk to the statues because she was so bored. The slaves refused to talk to her other than a couple of necessary words. They said, 'It's not proper we speak to you more than what is necessary,' which disappointed Dru. She was so lonely. She followed her crewmates through social media and sent the occasional message back and forth, but they were embarking on new adventures and had little time to talk to her. Also, in the past week she had had little to say other than she was going to medical school which didn't interest them at all. John, who was now the Chief Medical Officer on the *Zuin* did send her a nice message about it and shared what little information he had picked up from serving with Doctor Siu on the *Refa*. And she was happy for his long informative message.

Dru ate her meals at one of the large tables, always with one of the slave women watching her eat, as it went against the gods to eat alone. The slaves rotated who would sit with her because whoever it was also had to skip their meal if she took too long to eat. Dru thought it was all ridiculous, but she always ate as fast as she could, anyway. As she left the table tonight though and said the standard phrase, "Thank the gods for they have looked after us," she felt a shiver run through her and she had the strangest feeling that maybe in a parallel universe she actually believed in the Alliance religion. She shook off the feeling and assumed it must just be her tiredness making her feel peculiar and went up to her room.

Not long after, a slave came into her room unannounced and gave her another parcel from her Mr. Mystery. It was the same kind of black box she had received before but this one was smaller. She unwrapped the black paper and opened the black wooden box. Inside was an ornate silver ring with a light blue jewel on it. She tried it on, and it fit perfectly on her ring finger. She extended her hand admiring it and said out loud to herself, "A bit gaudy, but this is the Alliance, I'm sure it is considered demure given the amount of jewelry they all wear." As before, there was a note and she took it out and read it.

Drusilla,

Good luck tomorrow on your first day at medical school. Please wear this and know you belong with us.

She looked at the ring again and sighed. She wished she knew who her suitor was. Madame Bai gave her a list of over 500 possible candidates, she looked through them, but in the end, it gave her a headache to think about, so she gave up and resigned herself to the fact she was just going to have to wait. Madame Bai said that he would probably make himself known when she came of age or at the Year Assembly which was only months away.

. . .

Dru got up at five o'clock in the morning. She showered and then put on her navy-blue dress, black everyday stockings and her black boots. Then she looked at herself in the mirror and put on the small ID necklace and the necklace from Mr. Mystery and the ring he had given her as well. She wore her hair down as she always did unless she was working. She went downstairs and ate a kind of porridge with an Alliance tea while a slave watched her and then said 'goodbye' to the guards as she began the 45-minute walk through the city to the capital's medical school.

Dru felt good on her walk. The city was coming alive around her and for the first time here she had a purpose and was beginning a routine. She ignored the stares that she got as she was becoming accustomed to them and hoped that in a couple years, no one in the capital would be surprised to see a human woman with red hair walking among them. She always wanted to stop people staring and ask, 'What is the difference between me and that other alien?' as there were other aliens that lived and visited the Capital Planet.

Of course, Dru knew the answer to that question, humans were different. They were, to the most religious people, the Lost People, and to the most secular Alliance people, they were the stopgap to the demographics issue. She wondered then if they would ever be able to figure out why their female numbers were dwindling, and she hoped that it would not affect her. Unfortunately, she had the suspicion that whatever was affecting Alliance women would soon begin to affect the human women as well after a generation or so of living on the planet. She thought about this as she entered the medical school gates. The guards did not need to check her identity as they knew exactly who she was and waved her in.

Dru found her classroom easily. It was a good-sized

auditorium. There were 123 women in her class including her, all of about the same age. Every day the students were ranked by the teachers and had to sit in that order. Rank was so important in the Alliance it was always the first thing people seemed to think about when considering people for anything. Dru checked the electronic display outside the classroom and found her name. As Madame Bai had told her to expect, she was last in rank because it was her first day. She went in and then found her name again, displayed with light on the back of the chair to the far right in the very back of the auditorium. She took her seat and got out her tablet and waited. She was the first to arrive, but not soon after the other women began coming in, some silently and some chatting to each other and they all looked at her. Some gave her curious looks and others looks of disdain, Dru ignored them all and just sat with a passive look on her face. *I'm not here to make friends. I am here to learn and make a future for myself,* she thought to give her strength. She couldn't help but look at the ring and be reminded of her Mr. Mystery's words, 'You belong with us.' She warmed to this Mr. Mystery for the first time now, his words and actions had made her feel confident in this moment when she was all alone in this room full of aliens.

Soon the instructor appeared. It was one of the more senior doctors Dru remembered from her oral examination. The instructor waited for everyone to settle down before she began teaching that day's lesson. Throughout the class she would randomly call on students to answer questions and if they could not answer the questions, Dru assumed, they would move down the rank in where they sat tomorrow. Dru was called on three times, which she thought was quite excessive as some had not been called on at all, however she was able to answer all the questions easily, so again she assumed that she would move up tomorrow.

The rest of the morning proceeded like this. Classes were approximately 40 minutes long with ten-minute breaks between them. There was an hour break for the midday meal. Dru went to the canteen however they had only bread as a vegetarian option so that is all she was able to eat with some water. She sat alone in the crowded dining hall, everyone mostly ignoring her now. Dru didn't reflect too much on that. She thought if it were reversed, she would probably not go out of her way to talk to an alien if she had been on Earth and she also reminded herself that being ignored was better than being bullied.

In the afternoon, she had two more classes and then she had an appointment with the head librarian at the library and adjacent study hall in a massive building next to the even more massive Capital City Hospital. As she walked into the grand entryway of the library, she was quickly met by a middle-aged woman in a black dress with greying hair who introduced herself as the Chief Librarian Zola. She spent 30 minutes showing Dru around the library. Including, showing her how to access information, the rooms for past, present and hypothetical medical holographic simulations and finally the study hall which was composed of long tables with many chairs in front of massive windows, beautifully overlooking the urban sprawl below.

The Chief Librarian ended her private tour by saying, while opening a door to a good-sized room that had a window with a nice view of the city, "And this is your private room to study, any time of day. The library is open all day and night. All we need to do is set up the locks with your fingerprints and voice activation."

Dru was surprised. Madame Bai had told her that she

did not have a private study room at the library and when she heard the cost, 10 UC a week, she decided that she could not afford it either. "There must be a mistake. I don't have a private study room."

The Chief Librarian pulled out her IC, checked and then said, "You do. It has been paid in full for the duration of your studies. Two years. I have the receipt right here and as you are the only human and the only one with a human name at the medical school, there can be no mistake."

"Who paid for it?" Dru tried to ask innocently.

Chief Librarian Zola checked and Dru was excited to think that she was suddenly going have a name to who put the ban on her but was disappointed when the older woman shook her head, "I'm sorry, it was an anonymous purchase." Then she smiled at Dru, "An anonymous suitor? Or it must be a ban as you are not old enough for a proper suitor."

Dru gave her a tired smile, "It's a ban, but I find it difficult to accept things from someone I have never met, who I don't even know his name."

The Chief Librarian closed the door to Dru's study room, so that they could have some privacy and said, "Drusilla, do you mind if I give you some advice?"

"Please do," she said.

"Just accept the gifts. Whether this man has the intention of really courting you or not, no one knows. It may just be someone who really believes in the Lost People and wants to make your transition into the Alliance as smooth as possible to pave the way for others. These gifts come without prejudice. You owe this benefactor nothing but to do the best you can with what is given to you. Does that make sense?"

"It is just so difficult, on Earth…"

The Chief Librarian cut her off, "You are an Alliance citizen. Forget what you knew before. Live this Alliance life now. Constantly comparing the two will only make your life more complicated."

Dru was taken aback by the Chief Librarian's abruptness but she knew she shouldn't have been. This is what everyone kept saying to her, 'Forget Earth, you are Alliance now.' But she would always be human and have a place for Earth in her heart, even if her heart was shattered now. "I understand, but it's still difficult for me to do that," she placed one finger over her heart to show in the Alliance way she still very much-loved Earth. Then she hesitated and said after a couple seconds, "Thank you for your advice."

The Chief Librarian smiled sympathetically, "We are all in this together. I'm a true believer in the Lost People and I, just like your benefactor and many others, want to see you do well. More than any of the other women."

"Why me more than them?"

"You're the youngest, you're a doctor, you've the most potential to learn our ways. To see if you can become civilized. And I like the color of your hair."

Dru smiled at her little joke, "Thank you for showing me the room."

The Chief Librarian nodded and said on her way out, "If there is anything you need don't hesitate to ask. May the gods continue to shine their light on you."

"Let the gods be praised," Dru said automatically as she sat down at the large desk. She opened the computer menu and began to study, forgetting all about Mr. Mystery, her racist classmates and all her other worries in the Alliance. However, every now and then she would look at her ring and think, *You have really outdone yourself with this study room.* And again, she was warmed by Mr. Mystery's thoughtfulness. She hoped he wasn't a grotesque old man wanting to marry her, but as the librarian hinted at, only someone who wanted her to do well.

Ket sat at his desk in his quarters aboard the *Tuir* and opened the VM from his sister Dera. Dera knew that Ket had put the ban on the human doctor. Everyone knew that there were no secrets in Alliance families, even though, on the outside they all played to the tune that they kept to the Contracts and that men and women kept to the strict codes that separated their worlds.

"Brother, as requested I'm reporting to you about your human," she gave her brother a big smile. "As you know, today was her first day in our class. She arrived on time, with her red hair shockingly loose, down her back. I guess, just like Captain Kara, she wants to show us that she is not afraid of us and is proud to be human. However, besides her hair being unbraided, her clothing was very appropriate, and she was wearing both the necklace and ring you gave her. She sat in the last chair as she is the newest to the class and therefore in the last position. When she was called upon to answer questions, she knew the answers without hesitation, but didn't over answer any questions in an attempt to show off like others are known to do. After class she went straight to the library and I don't know how long she stayed because I'm not a stalker and I went home. My recommendation to you is to give her some hair clips or something so she gets the message to wear her hair braided. And please Ket, take my advice on this one. Your old flame Rez already hates Drusilla for being human, she'll hate her even more when she finds out you have put a ban on her." Dera paused for a few seconds and then added, "You know, it's so strange having a human among us. She's the same but so different, her pale skin and red hair. Are you sure you want to really pursue this? Nothing else is new here. Mother is constantly busy at the palace; the Empress says she has trouble sleeping as she wakes up obsessed with what Admiral Tir has done and the very thought that a human may be the next Empress sends her into bouts of despair and anger. We all know that will never happen, but the Empress cannot be consoled on the matter. When are you home next?"

Ket hit reply and began a message to his sister, "Dera, it's always good to get your advice," he said a bit sarcastically. "I'll send Drusilla some kind of hair pin just so she does not open herself up to unnecessary ridicule. Would it be too much to ask you to speak to her? As for the Empress, I cannot imagine that Admiral Tir would ever be Emperor now with his choice of wife. Why is everyone so afraid of humans all of the sudden? We have nothing to fear from them, they can hardly make it out of their galaxy and are so easily distracted by beautiful things. We've brought them here to help us have children, they're not going to change everything." Ket looked into the screen and smiled, "And I know what you are saying to my image now little sister, 'Oh Ket, you're a man, what do you know of real politics on the planet?'," he laughed a little. "And I'll reply, I know enough of what goes on in men's minds and having dealt with humans enough to know we have nothing to fear. Speak to Drusilla and you will understand." He paused thinking, "I don't know when I'm next back, possibly in six weeks, there is a conference and I have been asked to speak about applications of new technology onboard. I'll let you know. Please keep an eye on Drusilla," he hit send.

Ket took off his necklaces and unbuttoned the mandarin collar on his black uniform. He opened his social media account. There was nothing of interest there. He searched for any new news about Drusilla from the gossip columns and there was only a small article he had seen before about her starting medical school. Every now and then the gossip columnists would write something about her, there was still large speculation among the women who put a ban on her. He smiled to himself, he loved this Alliance game between the men and women. He wondered if Drusilla had any idea. He went to his favorite ornamental hair jeweler's shop then and bought a barrette and two hair pins with some fragrant hair oil. Dera was right, it was enough that she was human. When it came to the message, he hesitated on what to write. He did not want to be condescending.

It was late when Dru returned home after her second day of classes. She had moved up five seats in the ranking. She was pleased with herself and her upgrade urged her to study even harder so that she could move up again. Dru had missed the evening meal, as she had been studying in her private study room, so she just went up to her room. She knew the three slaves were already asleep. The whole building was completely quiet. The lights turned on for her automatically as she made her way to her room. When she entered, she noticed another small black parcel for her on her desk. She went directly to it. Her heart skipped a beat and she opened the box quickly and found the black card with silver script.

Drusilla,

.   .   .

I hope these will only add to the beauty of your fiery hair.

Dru was annoyed he still didn't say who he was. She sighed and then looked in the box at the two simple but beautiful hair pins, a silver barrette and a small glass vial of hair oil. She took them all out and investigated them. The only thing she had ever worn in her hair before was a simple hair tie. She had no idea how to braid her hair or use these hair pins as the Alliance women wore them. Thankfully, she remembered that the mirror in the bathroom could do it for her. She had noticed that all the other women in her medical school always wore their hair up and it had been on her list to ask Madame Bai about it. She thought, *It must be so shocking I don't wear my hair up that even Mr. Mystery interfered.* She wondered then who was spying on her in the classroom to tell him, but then realized she couldn't even guess as it could be any of them. However, if it was a sister then her Mr. Mystery couldn't be too much older than she was, and this thought made her stomach flip.

The next day Dru wore her hair up with one of the hair pins. She noticed that she got less disdainful looks from her classmates. As the weeks went by Dru moved up the ranks and after two months, she was number five and had become accustomed to her new life which was primarily made up of only learning and studying. Sometimes, one of her classmates would speak to her, to offer her salutations or another pleasantry, but she still ate the midday meal alone and no one invited her to spend time with them on any days of rest.

However, during her twelfth week, one of her classmates asked to join her for the midday meal.

"Drusilla may I sit with you?"

"Yes," she was so surprised that one of her classmates wanted to sit with her, she almost knocked over her water as she looked up.

"My name is Dera. I assume it must be more difficult for you being new to remember all of our names."

"Yes," said Dru a bit nervously. She really wanted a friend but did not want to seem desperate even though she was desperate. She knew Dera was number eleven in the rankings but not much else. "Have you all known each other for a long time?"

"Since birth. You know if you are born into a family of doctors, you usually become a doctor. Especially if you are a woman. And we can't leave the planet, so we all know each other very well. On Earth don't you know the same people your entire lives?"

"It depends," she didn't want to talk about the Exterior. "I wanted to see the galaxy, so I left my hometown to join the fleet."

"Is your family all doctors too?"

"My mother is a doctor," this was no lie, Dru's mother was a medicine woman of sorts in the Exterior and Dru had been her apprentice, just as her mother had apprenticed with her grandmother and so forth. However, she broke with tradition by leaving and she had sometimes wondered if her mother's curse, she knew her mother would have put a curse on her for abandoning her, had reached her here, across the galaxy. And that is why no one wanted to socialize with her.

"And now that you are here? What does she think?" Dera looked straight into her soul.

Dru knew she could not block these strong emotional feelings from Dera's telepathic sensitivity, "I imagine she is disappointed," which was putting it lightly.

"You haven't spoken to her about it? Does she know you are here?" Dera was shocked. Her mother was her closest confidant and her guide in life. She would never want to keep anything from her. She couldn't imagine being separated from her for a long period of time and even worse not speaking to her.

Dru knew she needed to tread lightly now as Alliance people valued their family life above all other things. "No, she only saw one path for me." Then Dru took a deep breath and said something she knew to be true but had never said out loud to another person before, "I knew it was my destiny to leave." She specifically didn't specify the Exterior and knew that Dera would assume she meant Earth. It didn't matter, both were true, although her urge to leave the Exterior had been so great, she couldn't have ignored it.

"The gods have been kind to you bringing you to us," Dera commented. "I'll be honest with you, we laughed when they said a human would join our class. We didn't think much of humans before we met you. And now look how wrong we all were to doubt you. You are doing so well…"

"For a human," she finished the sentence and before she could excuse Dera she continued, "I have a lot of time to study." She wanted to change the subject, "Are you married?"

Dera held up her left wrist, "No, are you?" she asked with a smile.

"Sorry, I keep forgetting that you can tell when someone is married or not by their bracelets. A lot of the other human women are already married, but they are away so I don't see the bracelets and therefore I'm not reminded regularly"

"I understand. It must be so different. I hear that

170

humans don't marry. I find it so difficult to believe. How do you organize yourselves and keep track of everyone?"

Dru smiled, "Well, to begin with, we only have a population of 12 billion. And then I guess we use our names and databases to keep track of everyone."

"And no incest problems?"

Dru was shocked by her question, "No. Twelve billion is small but it's not that small and we know who we are related to even if we don't marry. We still have familial relationships."

"It sounds so confusing," Dera commented. "Are you courting anyone?"

"No," Dru smiled, "I haven't even spoken to an Alliance man yet."

"Haven't you been to an Assembly? I read in the Day…" Dera was thoroughly enjoying this conversation now. She thought it was adorable that Dru didn't know who put the ban on her.

"Yes, but unfortunately someone put something called a ban on me, so no one would talk to me."

"He must be very high ranking if no one spoke to you at the Assembly. Doesn't that make you feel special?"

"I feel excluded. And at the Assembly no one told me what was going on so I thought I must be the ugliest woman ever for so many people to ignore me."

Dera felt she needed to defend her brother now, "I'm sure the man who put the ban on you had absolutely the opposite reaction in mind. You know for us, it's charming when a man puts a ban on us. I think it would be so romantic," Dera said wistfully.

"Has anyone ever put a ban on you?"

"No," she said sadly. "But maybe someday a man will look at me and want to court me but for whatever reason he has to put a ban on me. Maybe he is away fighting in a war or on a long expedition, but he sends me things to let me know he is still thinking about me. It's dreamy."

Dru looked at the young woman talk about the ban and tried to be respectful of their culture but right now it just felt too different. "I don't like the mystery. I want to know who he is. It makes me uncomfortable to accept gifts from someone I've never met."

"But you wear his jewelry?" Dera pointed out. She knew she could say this as there was no other way Drusilla could have Alliance jewelry.

Dru looked down at the ring, "I do. He has good taste and I must admit, these pieces of jewelry have given me some comfort, but I wish I knew who he was."

"That is all a part of the fun, Drusilla. You must speculate. Do you have any clues other than that he is high ranking?" Dera had to watch herself now, it was forbidden for her to talk specifically about Ket to Drusilla by the rules of the Contracts.

"No idea at all," Dru said with a small smile, "I just hope he isn't old and ugly."

"I don't think he is old and ugly," Dera said, "Old and ugly men usually don't care about marriage and only want slaves."

"What do you mean?" Dru didn't know what she meant by that as she thought the social classes were not supposed to interact with one another on a personal level. But the bell chimed, and it was time to get back to class so she never had the opportunity to ask and had forgotten about it by the next day.

The days passed, Dru woke every morning at five, ate breakfast with a slave on rotation watching her, went to her classes all day. Ate lunch either with Dera or alone. The medical school canteen now provided her with a selection of Alliance vegetables which the canteen slaves were actually friendly enough to set aside for her every day. In the afternoon, she had classes and then she studied late into the evening and sometimes missed the evening meal.

Now that Dru had spent many months studying she was first in her class. And she felt that many of her classmates respected her for it, but there were still some who were openly prejudice about having an alien among them. One in particular was named Rez. She had hated Dru from the beginning. She had spread rumors about Dru, nothing true or serious, but rumors nonetheless about how no one wanted the red-haired woman, not even her own crew who had abandoned her here in the Capital City.

Dru was usually able to just ignore the insults and hold her composure, but today she was extra sensitive because she knew her period was going to begin in a few days. So, after class Dru had planned to quickly check her exam results and then get to the library without speaking to anyone. All she wanted to do was shut herself inside her private study room and lose herself in study. Away from everyone else.

Rez saw the results and was angry that Drusilla scored higher than all of them again. She couldn't help herself and said loudly in front of everyone, "Oh look, the red-haired, hairy human must have cheated her way to the top. How did you do it Drusilla? Witchcraft? I heard humans still believed in such things. Wanton barbarians that have come here to steal our men. You all should be of the slave class. Disgusting any men would want you."

Dru looked at Rez passively and tried to walk away, but Rez followed her, continuing to say demeaning things while some other students laughed. Then Dru turned her, "Rez, you ignorant woman. The only barbarian here is you. Shut your mouth and try studying and then you might not always be so ignorant, but then again, maybe you are just plain stupid and no amount of studying will change that."

Rez was in such shock from Drusilla's words, she stood there and was about to slap Drusilla but then saw Ket out of the corner of her eye. She pined for Ket. They had courted last year, and her heart still ached for him. All thoughts of Drusilla were lost now, and she let the human just walk away.

It was snowing and Dru had her head down walking through the courtyard to the gates of the medical school. She was going directly to the library. She kept her head down to protect herself from the cold, as she didn't have her hat on she had left in such a rush, and to keep her face hidden form the tears that were about to fall from Rez's cruel words. Then she ran right into a man. She looked up; it was a handsome man. Their eyes locked and Dru felt like she couldn't breathe. His sharp grey eyes seemed to see right into her inner most thoughts. She excused herself and tried to continue walking, but he gently held her arm.

"I'm sorry. Are you all right?" Ket could not believe that Drusilla had walked right into him. He noticed there had been something going on between her and Rez. Drusilla looked so lovely with her red hair and pale skin, but she was obviously distraught. He wanted nothing more than to comfort her in that moment. He hesitated, his voice had disappeared when their eyes locked. He wanted to say something, that he had put the ban on her, that he was in awe of her accomplishments, that she was the loveliest creature he had ever seen, but all he could do was apologize for running into her and used his influence while touching her arm to comfort her. Then he let go after half a minute. He watched her go, her red hair moving gloriously with her steps and the wind and the snow towards the library and he felt like a fool.

Not soon after Dera came out from the medical school. "Ket, I didn't expect to see you here." Then she smiled, "Or if I would have thought about it, yes, I would have expected to see you here. Did you see her?"

"Yes, but she seemed very upset."

"Rez and her friends were giving her trouble again. Don't worry, Drusilla is resilient."

"And you don't defend her?"

"She must find her own way and earn her right to be with us. She will always be human, and some will always hate her for it. Rez is going to be livid when she finds out you have put the ban on Drusilla."

"Rez is the worst kind of person."

"I told you that, but you still insisted on courting her last year. Now, Brother, where are you taking me? I would like to eat dinner at Leld." Leld was one of the best restaurants in the Capital City.

"I was thinking the Earth Store first."

Dera laughed, "Oh dear, are you that worried for her? I'm sure she is fine and I'm not sure if it's safe to go to the off-worlders' ring."

"Are you afraid of off-worlders?"

"Yes, aren't you?"

"No, since I'm in the fleet, I meet them quite frequently and not usually the nice ones, who are fully vetted before being allowed to come live on the Capital Planet. Come on, I'll protect you," he said jokingly.

Ket and Dera took his transport to the other side of the Capital City to what was called the Immigrant Ring, although it was more of a full circle than a ring around the palace as the rest of the city rings were. The Immigrant Ring was an afterthought and therefore not a ring, or that is what the Alliance people liked to say. Immigrants from other worlds who lived and worked there would say the Alliance did it on purpose to keep them as separate from Alliance society as possible.

Ket parked the transport in the Immigrant Ring, and they found the Earth Store quite easily, it was a large glass building with a sign that said, 'Earth Store' and a moving image of what Ket and Dera assumed to be Earth under it. They went in and it was reasonably busy.

"I didn't realize off-worlders liked human things so much," commented Dera.

"Humans make most of their universal credits from selling food, wine and beautiful objects without any other functions," Ket explained.

"Greetings Alliance customers. How may I be of help today?" Frank the owner of the Earth Store asked.

The man looked so friendly, Ket could not help but smile, charmed by his blue eyes defined with paint, "I'm looking for something for a friend."

"A human friend?" Frank asked with some humor to his question. He had already had many Alliance men frequent his shop for gifts for the human women that were taken from the *Dakota*. He thought it was adorable the way they were so shy about what to buy for these women.

"Yes, one of the women who Admiral Tir rescued."

"Do you know what she misses from home?" The shopkeeper hazarded. He knew Alliance people usually did not even consider this. They thought everything they had was far superior to anything Earth would have to offer and couldn't readily understand a human could miss something from Earth. When his customer gave him a blank look, he offered, "Many of the human women who live in the city shop here. I could check the woman's account and tell you what she likes?"

Ket thought for a minute and then looked at the man, "Do you know who I am?"

Frank looked at Ket's ranking jewelry closely for the first time and then it dawned on him, "Of course, yes. I know who you are and who you are buying for. I can help. Follow me."

Ket was relieved that the owner of the Earth Store followed the Contracts and knew about the ban. It wasn't too difficult as she was the only human who had a ban on her which would make him take interest, but he was still impressed the man did and that he didn't have to put his trust in blindly choosing something for her or revealing himself to the shopkeeper who could ruin all the romance by telling Drusilla it was him.

Ket and Dera followed Frank back to an area of the shop with lots of flowers from Earth all arranged beautifully.

"Human women like to receive flowers from Earth. I know the woman in question would like to receive them."

"Which ones are her favorites?" Ket asked.

"I don't know, she has never bought any for herself. She always admires them though."

Ket had never been without universal credits. It didn't occur to him right away that she wouldn't have enough to buy herself flowers. "Maybe something else then?"

"I think she doesn't buy the flowers because they are expensive," Frank said directly. "If she doesn't like them, I'll give you a full refund. But trust me, I know this young woman and she would be so pleased to receive flowers."

Ket looked at Dera and then at the flowers considering, "What do you think Dera?"

She shrugged, "I don't understand it. They are flowers that will die in a matter of days. How is that romantic?"

"I don't know," admitted Ket, "but let's try it." He nodded to Frank and wrote the card to her himself.

Dru had just put on her pajamas and was about to turn her light out when one of the slaves burst into her room with a huge bouquet of flowers. The bouquet was made up of peonies, scabiosa, sweet peas and lilac in a gorgeous ceramic vase that must have come from Earth as it had two swans beautifully painted on it.

"Are these from Earth?" the slave asked.

Dru sat straight up, *Am I dreaming?* "Yes, these are from Earth. How did they get here?"

"They were sent to you. There is an envelope," she was handed the small envelope. It was written on thick cream paper and was also from Earth. Before she opened the note, she looked at the flowers, closed her eyes and inhaled their soft fragrances. After a minute, she opened her eyes and opened the card. In the most precise and straight writing she had ever seen was the following note,

Drusilla,

I hope the tears in your eyes never fell today.

She turned the card over and again there was no signature. She wondered if this was from Mr. Mystery or from the man she bumped into today or another man who saw what had happened. All this mystery was beginning to give her a headache, so she decided to finally begin to take everyone's advice and just accept the gifts without thinking too much about them. She reached out a hand to touch one of the purple lilacs and felt loved for the first time in a long time. Even though the feeling was ridiculous, she didn't even know who sent these to her, but they cared enough to send her something from Earth, something that meant something to her. She left the swan vase with the flowers on her bedside table and fell asleep looking at the bouquet and dreaming of Earth.

"Snap," Dru said as she jumped out of bed. She was late. She had been so excited by the flowers that she had forgotten to set her alarm. Today was a day of rest, but there was a symposium at the medical school about practical medicine onboard the warships. Dru wanted to be prepared if she ended up joining Captain Kara on the *Zuin*. As such, she had completed many of the military medical simulations with the hologram programs in the library that were most likely to happen onboard the warships in her spare time. Today some of those men would be at the medical school to talk about the changes that they had made to different procedures when actually used aboard a starship.

Dru quickly threw on her black dress and the necklaces Mr. Mystery and Madame Bai had given her and ran out the door without eating breakfast. Because it was a mealtime, there were considerably less people on the streets, and she figured if she walked quickly enough, she may still have time to eat with everyone else at the medical school. She could have hailed a shared transport, but she didn't want to spend the universal credits for her own mistake.

By the time Dru arrived there was only one-minute left of the shared morning meal, so she quickly drank some Alliance tea and then went into the large auditorium.

When she entered, she was momentarily shocked by all the men in their black uniforms, strong, tall and handsome, standing around talking with one another. Many gave her glances as she sat down, but no one spoke to her. It had been a long time since she had been to an Assembly and she had gotten used to seeing mostly women in every part of her life. She couldn't help but feel a rush of excitement with so many young men in the room and suddenly she felt alive again. She of course was sitting in her assigned seat, which was close to the front, all the women were sitting close to the front, but if she would have had the choice, she would have rather sat in the back so she could have taken in all the men. For just an instant, she felt some remorse she was not onboard the *Zuin* with Captain Kara and the rest of her crewmates, naturally serving alongside men, as it was supposed to be. Then she probably would not feel like a schoolgirl who has been let out of the nunnery, as she did now.

Two of Dru's classmates were talking behind her and she could not help but listen to their conversation. One said, "The only reason I came was to hear Doctor Ket."

The other one laughed, "Let me correct that for you, to see Doctor Ket, and I think most of the women came to see him, especially Rez."

The first one replied quietly, "But he won't court her again. I hear he has a put ban on someone."

"Who told you that?"

"My brother."

"Oh well, your brother isn't a reliable source and we know most of the reasonable eligible women and I don't know anyone who has a ban on them, do you?"

"Hairy," the other said loud enough for Dru to hear and then continued, "But I doubt he would contaminate himself with a human. Admiral Tir has always been an enigma, but Doctor Ket, no way. He is true to the Empire through and through."

"But Dera," the other continued and then they stopped abruptly.

Dru wished they would have continued but they halted when Dera sat down in a seat, not her assigned seat, next to Dru and smiled. She whispered, "Hello friend, I know Zuna isn't coming so I thought I would sit here with you."

Dru smiled at her friend in reply. She knew Dera could do what she wanted. She outranked everyone in the room and she just followed the rules when she felt like it.

Dera turned around to look at the women behind them, "And if my brother had a ban on anyone, I doubt the woman would be so low that either of you would even know her."

The women just smirked at Dera but didn't dare to say anything back to her insult.

Dera turned to Dru and asked with a smile, "New hair pin?"

Drusilla couldn't help but touch her hair then, "It came with the other one and the barrette," then she mouthed the words, "Does it look okay?"

Dera smiled at her sweet human friend, "I can't read your lips because you are speaking a human language, but I know what you were asking. Yes, it looks good. You look like one of us. Is that why you were late?"

"I wasn't late. I made it in time for tea," Dru smiled back. "I forgot to set an alarm."

"Did something distract you last night?"

"Mr. Mystery saw me yesterday or someone who knows him saw me in a distressed state and sent me flowers. Flowers from Earth," she blushed. "I was so touched, I put them next to my bed and fell asleep looking at them, not realizing that I hadn't set my alarm."

"Do you remember seeing anyone yesterday?"

"I ran right into a good-looking man outside the school gates, but he didn't say much to me, only apologized."

"But all the men know who put the ban on you so, no doubt, he told the other man. Maybe they are friends? Who did you run into? Did you recognize him?"

Dru shook her head, "I don't think so, but something did seem familiar about him."

"Is he any of the doctors here today?"

Dru scanned the panel and then stopped on Ket, "Yes, third from the left."

Dera followed her eyes and then briefly described her brother, badly, "One long plain braid in the back, strong jaw and little grey eyes."

Dru nodded, "I wouldn't describe him that badly," she smiled at her friend and then added, "And I just realize I recognize him from a holographic simulation I did last week. He is on the *Tuir*."

Before Dera could reply the presenter came out and they had to stop their conversation.

Ket had felt eyes on him and then looked at his sister and Drusilla and wondered what was going on. He could not help but look at Drusilla. She was just as beautiful as she was yesterday, and he was pleased to see in a better mood today. It was taking all his control not to stare at her through the others' lectures.

Dru could not keep her eyes from Ket. She knew him from the holographic simulations and from yesterday, but she kept thinking something else was very familiar about him too, but she couldn't remember.

When he stood up to give his lecture, Dera wrote on her tablet and showed it to Dru,

· · ·

182

That is one of my older brothers. I see you two looking at each other. I will introduce you after.

Dru blushed at what Dera had written but she could not deny that she had been looking at this man as much as he had been looking at her. Dru's heart had begun to beat faster when she read Dera's note. Then Dera wrote something more,

Control your thoughts, friend.

And Dru blushed again but put her complete mind on lockdown. She had forgotten for a moment and then everyone who was telepathically listening heard that she was excited to meet Dera's brother. Embarrassing. But then she thought, *Oh but he won't talk to me, the ban.* She wrote,

The ban.

Dera shrugged in response.

Dru knew this was either because her brother would probably outrank whoever put the ban on her or because maybe her brother, like Dera, cherry picked when he would follow the rules. Madame Bai had lectured them again and again, 'Know everyone's rank for they will know yours and treat you accordingly.' She knew that Dera was of the Imperial House so her brother was obviously equally high ranking and so if he spoke to her, she knew her Mr. Mystery would be below him.

183

Now she focused on Dera's brother, taking in his good looks and confidence as he took a lot of cutting questions from some of the doctors here who had come up with the procedure to only have it changed by him and his team in practical use. Dru suddenly felt that she was in elementary school again and it was the boys versus the girls, except in the Alliance, it seemed to her that the girls always seemed to win, and she could not put her finger on how the boys really felt about that, yet. It made Dru uncomfortable the way some Alliance women immediately assumed men acted on instinct alone and needed to be directed at all times. Equality between the sexes and the Contracts was constantly talked about on the Capital Planet, but in practice, Dru saw very little equality.

Ket almost lost his train of thought when he heard Drusilla's thoughts about meeting him. He was ecstatic. He didn't even care that the head emergency doctor was cutting his ideas and methods down, even though, he knew they worked better, *What did she know about being in a war? How long these men stayed at their posts and what could and could not be expected of them when they finally arrived in sickbay.*

When the questions were finished, Ket took his seat again and looked over at Drusilla. She was making some notes. He tried to hear her thoughts again, but she had completely closed herself off. He must have looked at her too long though because it was not long before she looked up at him and they held eye contact for some time, too long. Enough for Dera to whisper something to Drusilla to break it off. *Curse younger sisters,* he thought.

Drusilla was curious about Dera's brother and she found herself wanting the lectures to end so she could talk to him. She had not felt this way about someone in a very long time. Her mind began to wander then, *Do I want to speak to him so much because it had been months since I have seen any eligible men? Or have I finally become so accustomed to Alliance people that I find them attractive? Or was this really what they called love at first sight? Or lust at first sight?*

When the lectures finally ended, and people got up to talk to one another. Dera and Dru stood up and before either could say anything, Ket was standing in front of them. "I wanted to come and speak to you before I missed the opportunity," he explained looking at his sister, but the words were meant for Drusilla.

Dera did not miss that, "Drusilla, let me introduce you to my older brother Ket. Ket this is Drusilla." Then she looked at them both looking at each other dreamily and said while walking away, "I will see you at home, brother," but she doubted either one was listening to her.

Dru was surprised Dera just left like that. She looked at Ket, to see if he was surprised, and if he was, he didn't show it. His face was unreadable to her. But she couldn't stop looking at him. He was tall, she barely came up to his shoulder, strong and she found his strong facial features very handsome.

Ket found Drusilla so attractive. Her hair was braided today and held back with one of the pins he had given to her. He longed to remove it and unbraid her long red hair. After a long minute of just looking at one another, Ket said, "I've heard a lot about you from my sister. It's impressive that the first human to attend medical school is also the best in her class."

Dru blushed, she didn't know why, "I've a lot of time to study."

Ket smiled thinking about her studying in the private room he provided for her, "But when you finish school, you'll stay on planet and not join your captain?"

"For the moment, that is the plan, but I can't say for certain."

"What would change your mind?"

Oh, gods did he really just ask me that. I need to stop my mind from running away, he is not my Mr. Mystery, although I wish he was. He is just making conversation. I need to put my panties back on. "A good position here, I guess."

Ket had no idea what panties were but picked up that thought from her and almost smiled that she was flustered enough to accidently project it. He would look that word up later in the database. "Well, I hope you find a good position then." *With me in a bed,* he thought. She smelled so divine and her pink lips looked so inviting.

"Are you on planet for long?" *You god of a man. I'm sure you have naked pictures of yourself on social media which I will definitely be looking at later,* she thought.

"Only until tomorrow. However, I'll return for the Year Assembly. Do you attend the Assemblies?" Ket didn't think that he could talk to her much longer without running his hand down the side of her face. She looked so soft. He longed to touch her smooth creamy skin and see if she felt as soft as she looked.

"Of course, I wouldn't want to risk any punishments."

"You don't like being whipped?" He enjoyed the surprise in her big green eyes that changed to desire at the thought.

He asked her that in such a seductive way she thought he was offering to do it himself and if that were the case she didn't know if she would say 'no'. Then she thought, *Get a hold of yourself. You are so starved to talk to a man you are just pouncing on the first one. Hold back.* "I've never been whipped so I can't say, but it seems like something to avoid."

"Possibly," he said purposely with a lilt of seduction.

She looked into his grey eyes and thought, *If you ask me to just leave with you I will. Oh, snap did I project that?* She was searching his face.

He stood so close to her that his hand briefly touched hers at her side and sent shivers down her back. Then he whispered in her ear, "You did project that, but I don't mind. I feel the same."

Dru's lips parted. She wanted this man. He just came out of nowhere and suddenly she couldn't imagine not knowing him.

Everyone was watching Drusilla and Ket. All the men knew that Ket had put the ban on Drusilla and for the women they were still guessing, because of Ket's high status he could talk to almost anyone, but bets were now in favor of him having put the ban on her. And everyone, except for Rez and a few others, found their interaction truly romantic. It was obvious that it was love at first sight for both of them.

Then Ket said, "Unfortunately, there are many people I need to speak to here, but another time I'm on planet, I'd like to get to know you better."

Dru was completely charmed, even though she was disappointed their conversation had to end now, "Of course," she didn't want to say, 'I have only one friend and live alone so I am quite free,' so instead she said, "I can make time for you."

Ket smiled, "Good and goodbye for now Drusilla." He was reluctant to walk away; she was more enchanting in person than he had ever hoped to imagine she would be. And her reaction to him was more than encouraging.

When she arrived home, she skipped dinner and looked through all the information she could find about him, which there was a lot. He was considered an eligible bachelor and he, of course, had a naked picture of himself and she blushed and berated herself for not recognizing him before when she realized she already had a nude image of him saved. He was the doctor from the article she and Rachel had found of the Alliance's Most Eligible Bachelors. And because of that, she did not think he was her Mr. Mystery. He was high ranking and that is why he was able to speak to her. She decided if he had been her Mr. Mystery, he would have acted differently or completely revealed himself as such today. Dru was disappointed but consoled herself in that at least she had a new friend.

That night Dru had trouble sleeping and so she turned on the self-pleasing function on her bed. She had the option of adding a holographic man and she thought about it for just a minute, thinking about adding Ket, but then in the end decided against it. She didn't know who watched her and she didn't want her embarrassment to be any greater than it was that she needed this release. It had been so long since anyone had touched her and months since she had met any eligible men and today, she had not only been surrounded by them, but one had actually spoken to her and he had been gorgeous.

She set the function on her bed and closed her eyes imagining Ket. She imagined him in his uniform stripping it off and then wait, *Did they take off their jewelry first or always wear it?* she wondered. Then went back to her fantasy where all the jewelry was just gone, and he was there naked, tall, strong, muscular with a fantastically large cock with ridges across the top just waiting to take her. He approached her on the bed, *No wait,* she thought, *on the medical bed, yes.* And then he began gently removing her clothing while asking, "What seems to be the problem Dru?" Then she stopped her fantasy again and thought, *Oh no, he calls me by my real name. 'What is the problem Drusilla?'* She was getting so wet just thinking about him calling her by her real name with his deep voice, she wondered if she even needed the bed function to bring her to climax. Then she imagined him touching her breasts, just as the bed was doing for her and asking, "Does it hurt when I touch you here?" And then as the bed function moved up and down her body with the soft hot air that mimicked the feeling of a moist tongue on skin, she thought of him licking her up and down. And then finally the bed began to work on her inner thighs and clit, and she imagined him touching her there too saying, "I want to see you come for me." Then he brought her to climax and after a couple minutes she opened her eyes alone in her bed and everything was calm now. She said out loud to herself, "Oh moon, I'm so naughty sometimes," thinking about him seducing her on the medical bed. Then she turned over and went to sleep with thoughts of the gorgeous man who was completely out of reach for her, *But a girl can have her fantasies.*

The next morning, Dru couldn't help but smile when she saw that Ket had added her as a personal contact on social media. She accepted him and looked at his personal profile. In complete Alliance style it had all his information there, including his nude portrait pictures. She sighed and said out loud to herself softly, "And only if you weren't so high-ranking Doctor Ket." Madame Bai had told them all repeatedly, that even though they were of the maximum class, because they were human, they should keep their expectations for husbands somewhat humble. She gave examples of what they should aim for, Captains of Beta ships, lower ranking officers on Alpha ships or government consultants. Rebecca's husband was a lower ranking officer on an Alpha ship, now they were both on the *Zuin* together and Dru wondered again if she should join those women. But then she remembered Jane's words, 'No one will remember any of our names after we die, but you have a chance to do something meaningful for both the Alliance and humanity.'

Then she thought about Mr. Mystery and went back to the list that Madame Bai had given her, looking through the names. Ket's name was there, number 116 on the list. But she dismissed him, he was Dera's brother and too high ranking. They were attracted to each other to be sure, but just as her classmates had said as they sat behind her, he wasn't one to stray from Alliance women. She wondered then if her Mr. Mystery could see if she had become connected to Ket and what he felt about that. Jealousy was a big problem in the Alliance, and she had discovered that most duels, among women as those were the only ones, she had access to check in the Duel Database, were fought mainly because of jealousy. Dru found it odd in a civilization that had everything they could ever want they killed each other over personal relationships or trivial material goods. She didn't think she would ever understand certain aspects of Alliance culture and dueling was one of those.

Dru was surprised to receive a VM from Ket that next week. She opened it with a big smile on her face.

"Drusilla, the gods be good I hope you find this message well. It was so nice to meet you the last time I was on the Capital Planet. I'm sending you this message today because something has been at the back of my mind since we met. You projected a word to me, and I don't know what it is and it's not in the database. What are panties? May the gods continue to shine their light on you."

Dru laughed out loud. She remembered what she was thinking at that moment that she had thought that. It was a phrase her best friend in the Exterior used to say to her, 'Keep your panties on.'

Dru hit the reply button when she stopped laughing, "Ket, May the gods be blessed. Thank you for your message. I find it difficult to believe the word wasn't in the database," she couldn't help but smile at his lie. "And the definition may or may not be exciting to you, I don't know. 'Panties' is a colloquial term for women's underwear on Earth. May the gods guide your way."

Ket received the notification Drusilla had responded and looked forward to watching it all day. After the evening meal, he declined playing a gambling game with cards with his Admiral so that he could look at the message. He went into his quarters and watched it, thinking when she smiled, *You are the loveliest creature I've ever seen.*

He hit reply, "Drusilla, the gods be thanked. As to the word and the item of panties, I hope that you have given those up as you are an Alliance woman now and soon an Alliance doctor. You must realize how terrible that is for a woman's health. It's, of course, not something you and I should be speaking about as we are neither courting nor married, but I am curious. Are you still wearing panties? May the gods continue to shine their light on you."

Dru received Ket's VM the first thing in the morning and she laughed when she watched it. She took a shower before responding, thinking of all the different ways she could reply.

"Ket, may the gods be blessed. Thank you for taking such an interest in my personal habits. I do still wear panties as I find them comforting, despite the health risks. But don't fear, special prayer candles have been made for the goddess of sexuality to beg forgiveness for my panty transgressions. Thankfully, you're not my husband and I'll be sure to find one who understands all my womanly human needs. May the gods guide your way."

Ket couldn't believe the sass of this young woman. He

loved it. "Drusilla, gods be great. You must be sure to add your panty requirement in your questions before you begin courting then, as many men will not accept it. I wouldn't accept it except under another extreme condition. Again, we should not be discussing these things as we are neither courting nor married, but I look forward to your reply. May the gods continue to shine their light on you."

Dru received his message and knew he was referring to the questions a couple would ask each other before they began a courtship. Usually a couple would meet once for the sole purpose of asking each other these questions, about 20 or so, all very personal having to do with everything from working and life expectations to children and sex, in order to determine whether or not they were a suitable match. In her cultural handbook there were many examples of typical questions men and women would ask each other. Also, examples of how compromises would be struck already at that first meeting if they wanted to begin courtships. Dru thought it was, as was most things in the Alliance, very well-thought out and logical. If you were going to spend 300 years with someone, it was best you knew what you wanted, what they wanted and what you were willing to compromise on and what you were not, before any strong emotional attachments were formed. She had heard already that Rebecca had run into some issues with her new husband as she *had* not compromised well. However, Dru had no doubt that would be easily resolved between them as Kole adored Rebecca. Dru didn't think she would be lucky enough to marry a man who would adore her. No, she knew she would marry a man who would probably make her fight for everything and she would do the same to him. If she were honest with herself, that is how she wanted it really.

Dru decided to reply with a written message as she

thought she would have a better chance of getting a sexy answer in writing,

No, we shouldn't be discussing my panties, but since I'm already on my way to the temple, I can spend some extra time there and ask forgiveness for this conversation. What extreme condition would you agree to? I'm asking as a friend, of course, so I can be prepared if I am ever in a position to court someone.

Ket was disappointed that she didn't send a VM as he loved the sparkle in her eyes when she was so playful. He was at work, but he took a minute to go into his office and reply to her straightaway.

No doubt, you will court someone who worships you and allows you everything, so you need not worry what I would demand of you for a panty's transgression.

Dru read Ket's reply over the midday meal.

Dera looked over her shoulder and said, "I've never seen you message anyone before." She couldn't mention that it was Ket by the rules of the Contracts, even though she saw his name at the top of the message.

Dru looked up and smiled at Dera who had just joined her, "I've a new friend in your brother."

Dera just began eating while she watched Drusilla smile as she messaged Ket.

Dru replied back to Ket,

.   .   .

As you are the only man who has spoken to me since I arrived in the Alliance, I think I should be prepared for a man more like you. Please inform me of your compromise about the sinful panties.

Ket laughed when he saw her reply and showed the message to his Admiral, who he was having tea with, and of course knew about the ban.

"Universal credits well spent," the Admiral commented. "I remember when I put a ban on my own wife," he said dreamily remembering, "it was so romantic. She had no idea it was me, of course, until I revealed myself. And then she jumped into my embrace and we had to pay a hefty fine for that night."

Ket smiled, he enjoyed this game. And it pleased him greatly that while he was away, he had no competition. He wrote her back,

I see your point. If you insisted on wearing panties as part of your questions, then I would make you completely loyal to me at least one day out of every week whether I was on planet or not.

Dru received Ket's message and looked at it as she was still having the midday meal with Dera. She didn't know what he meant by being 'completely loyal'. She knew this must be an Alliance thing, but she didn't want to ask Dera as she assumed this was probably sexual. So, she put her IC away.

Dera noticed Drusilla's look of confusion but was relieved that she didn't ask her anything. She didn't want to reveal Ket as her 'Mr. Mystery', as she called him, because she would then have to specifically say she couldn't talk about him with her which would lead to more questions.

She would message her brother later to make sure he didn't message her while she was at school so the chances of Drusilla talking to her about him would be less. *He is uncharacteristically thoughtless today,* she thought and then with a smile realized, *He is in love.*

The weeks passed and Dru and Ket messaged each other frequently. Her heart would skip a beat whenever she saw his name in her relatively quiet inbox and he felt the same when he saw anything from her.

One evening after a long day of classes and studying, Dru sat down at her desk and smiled as she opened the VM from Ket. He was in his quarters and she was surprised to see had undone the collar of his uniform, so it was open. She could see half of his very muscular chest and his long black hair was undone. She had never seen him this way. She had of course seen his manicured nude portraits, but this was different, this was real. *This is the way his wife would see him,* she thought but then corrected herself, *or a friend, like me. I will never be his wife, I need to get control.*

"Drusilla, gods be great. I began reading your favorite book this morning. Of course, this is my first time reading a fictional book and a human one at that. The world described on Earth is very foreign to me. I find the lead character's desires somewhat confusing. Why she is looking for love and companionship that she should have already through her family? But I guess it will make more sense when I get to the end. Maybe? Is it because I'm a man I don't understand or because I'm an Alliance man? I feel sorry for you that you are banned from all Earth culture until you have married and have a child. I've read more about Earth lately to help me better understand you and the world you come from. All I can really take away is that it's so different and vibrant, despite its inefficiencies. I hope the pain of never returning dulls with the knowledge that you are somewhere where you are safe. So safe on the Capital Planet."

He paused then and Dru knew that he wanted to say something more but caught himself, so she said out loud to the screen, "Good man, control saying that racist thing you were going to say about humans wasting their time on frivolous things or me being grateful to be in the Alliance." Then she looked at him hesitating and said, "No, this is something else, you are not just disheveled, you are also upset about something. What's happened?" She stopped the video and opened another window and looked for any information about the *Tuir* and there had been nothing reported for the last 48 hours. She kind of knew this already as she had signed up for updates about his ship, as all Alliance women did, to follow their friends, brothers, fathers and husbands around the galaxy. But turbulent events were shielded from the public until the High Council would deem it appropriate to share or not. So, it wasn't difficult to summarize something bad had happened, but he was not allowed to talk about it.

"When I'm here, and I think about you and my mother and sister at home and know you are safe, I thank the gods."

Dru paused the message again, *Did he just put me in the same category as his mother and sister? Is he just being polite, or does he think of me so closely?* "Ket, I want you to be as close to me as two beings can be," she said out loud to the screen wishing that she would have the courage to say that to him in real life if the opportunity ever presented itself. She resumed the message then.

"I'll be back on the Capital Planet for the Year

Assembly and I'm very much looking forward to seeing you then, panties and all. Gods be blessed."

Dru looked at his image. *Gods he was handsome even when he was preoccupied,* she thought. She didn't know how to reply though. He was obviously upset by something but couldn't mention it. *What is the correct Alliance response?* she wondered. Their culture was so counter intuitive sometimes. She just went with her instincts.

"Ket, gods be good. As much as I love seeing you with your hair down and collar unbuttoned, I didn't like the distant look you had in your last message. I've not had an update from the *Tuir* in over two days and having served on a starship myself, I've an idea of what kind of trouble that means. I also know that in the Alliance we aren't supposed to speak about these things that we are all thinking, until the High Council says it's okay, so I'll say no more and maybe I've already incurred a fine for even acknowledging this? But yes, I am very safe here. The safest place in the galaxy." She paused then thinking, *Gods, did lots of people die?* "Thank you for taking the time to read my favorite book. I don't know if you will ever understand Sasha's desire to fit in as in the Alliance you all seem to be born into your positions and that is it. Even I feel, as an outsider and a human, I still have more of a settled place where people put me than I did on Earth. Human culture is just so fluid." She paused then not wanting to add what he always said about humans, 'Never knowing when to be content.' But she had to admit she was beginning to see where he was coming from. At the same time though, she thought, *But this is what makes humans special, we are always searching and looking around the next corner. Not because we are prepared or ready, but because we are curious.* "I'm looking forward to seeing you too. May the gods guide you."

5

Understanding the Alliance

Dru looked at herself in the mirror. She had just showered, and she wondered if she should wear her hair up tonight. It was the Year Assembly. Madame Bai had told her that this was the largest Assembly all year and that most eligible men of the maximum class would be there. She also hinted that her Mr. Mystery would also probably be there and reveal himself to her tonight. Dru certainly hoped so, she was tired of being ignored. Last night, before she fell asleep, she decided that she didn't even care if he was ugly or old, if he was someone to talk to, she would take him for courting at least when she came of age.

She looked at herself again in the mirror and decided to leave her hair down, she thought she looked better this way. Dru also put on some of the makeup that she had bought so many weeks before from the Earth Store. It just made her feel better. She wanted to look her best, not Alliance best, her human best, if she were finally meeting her Mr. Mystery tonight. And if she wasn't meeting him, even more reason to look her best as it would be a long night not talking to anyone, standing in a corner.

But then she reminded herself, Dera and Ket will be there so she will at least get five minutes of conversation or more. She hoped more when she thought of Ket, but she didn't get her hopes up too much. She knew he was popular among the women and Dera never spoke to her about her brother and she couldn't think of a clearer sign indicating that she shouldn't put her hopes for a courtship or marriage there.

Dru's door opened and without acknowledgement a grumpy slave sauntered in with a small package. Dru was naked and took the package without question and then the slave left. *I'm almost enjoying the rudeness of my slaves,* she thought with a smile. Dru set the package down on her desk and then went to her closet to get her one formal dress. She put it on and then the necklace Mr. Mystery had given her and her ID necklace. Once she was ready, she sat down at her desk and opened the present. She assumed it was from Mr. Mystery. She took out the black card with the meticulous silver writing and read it,

Drusilla,

I hope this will help us find each other tonight.

Dru wondered what could be in the small package. She quickly opened it to find a silver ring with a small clear stone in the middle. However, when she put the ring on her finger, the stone quickly began to change color in the most fascinating and beautiful way right before her eyes, as if it were filling with a different color smoke that was constantly moving like rain clouds shifting above the ocean. She was fascinated but didn't have a clue as to how this ring would bring her any closer to Mr. Mystery.

She looked at the card again, no name. But when she opened her desk drawer to add it to the other cards, she noticed that the handwriting on this one and the last one that came with the flowers was the identical. She took out all the cards and spread them out across her desk. She saw that only these two matched. She knew the flowers came from the Earth Store and that this ring today was from a completely different store, so Mr. Mystery must have written these two himself. She was charmed by that and thought, *His handwriting is impeccable, I hope he isn't overly religious.* In the Alliance, one's handwriting reflected their closeness with the gods.

Dru wondered then if her Mr. Mystery had been a doctor at the symposium, as he had to have been on planet both then and now. She didn't have the energy to get the list of potential Mr. Mysteries out again and cross examine it, as she had gone over it too many times already and in a couple hours, she would know who he was anyway. But first things first, she had to figure out how to work the ring, so she opened a live VM to Madame Bai.

"You're not wearing your hair up?" was the first thing Madame Bai said when she saw Dru on the screen. "And human face paint?"

"I think I look better this way," she defended her appearance. "That's not why I am calling. I've a question. I just received this," she held up the ring that now instead of being clear was midnight blue, "but I don't know what it is or how it works. How it is supposed to help me find the man who put the ban on me."

Madame Bai looked at the ring and smiled, "It's a location ring. The man who has given it to you is on the planet or in orbit, that is why it is midnight blue. The closer you come to each other, the lighter the colors will be. When you are in the same room, it will be clear again and will become very warm. It is symbolic that there is nothing standing between you anymore but the warmth of your hearts."

Dru looked at the ring, "Nothing except I am not of age to be courted yet and I don't even know this man. How can there be warmth in our hearts?"

"That doesn't matter, he is revealing himself to you tonight and you can choose whether or not you would even enter a courtship with him after your birthday which is not too far away. Everything he has given you is without prejudice," she reminded Dru. Madame Bai had realized with a lot of the human women that they felt obligated to men who gave them things and she always needed to remind them that the men did that with the knowledge they may be rejected. And that they need not cater to any men's feelings that they don't naturally return. "You can't have a relationship with a man you don't feel attracted to. Everyone knows this. You'll know when you meet him how you feel. Trust in the gods."

"I will," she said knowing full well she still didn't believe in the gods. Every day she went to the shrine in their building and said her prayers, but they were still hollow for her.

"Enjoy this evening as much as you can," Madame Bai said warmly to Drusilla and then ended the conversation.

Dru looked at the ring and asked herself, "Who are you Mr. Mystery? And do you already love me?"

Ket entered the Imperial Meeting Hall. It was filled with many more eligible men than women and everyone who could be there was in attendance as this was the Year

Assembly, the grandest of the Assemblies. Ket had arrived with his sister, but she had already left him for some friends. He scanned the great room, looking for Drusilla. He looked down at his location ring which was connected to hers. It was now a light pink color almost white and showing signs of transparency; she was here somewhere. He thought, *She is the only human here and she has red hair, this shouldn't be difficult.* He decided to move through the crowds and begin looking for her. He didn't want to talk to anyone else. He wanted to find her and spend all his time with her, as tonight would be the only night they would have to spend time together, alone, until she was of *age*.

After 20 minutes of looking around the spectacularly crowded grand hall he finally found her. She had been at the complete other end of the building. He was only ten meters from her, they made eye contact and his heart stopped. He had been waiting for this moment for so long. His mind reached out to hers, *Stay, I'm coming to you,* he projected. He began walking towards her and then Rez addressed him completely out of line. It was uncustomary for a woman to stop a man. It was supposed to be the other way around so Ket was annoyed. And she was the last person he wanted to speak to, but he was too polite to just walk away and if anyone noticed it would make him look terrible, even though she had been the one to step out of line and stop him.

"Ket, it's so good to see you here."

"Rez, I've to see someone."

"Not so fast," she said *sweetly* and by protocol he could not leave her side, otherwise he would be breaking the rules just as she had done in stopping him.

He stopped, mid-step, waiting for her to speak and when she didn't, he said, "If I may go?"

"No."

"Rez, this has nothing to do with you," he said impatiently.

"I know that and that's why I am not letting you leave yet. I want it to have something to do with me," she was half pleading, but she couldn't help it. She was looking up at his handsome face wondering why he didn't want her anymore. Her mind reached out to his, *We can still be together.*

Ket was uncomfortable and ignored her telepathic comment by speaking to her out loud, purposely creating distance between them, "What I said to you last year still stands and my feelings are still the same. I've no doubt the gods have someone perfect planned to be your husband."

"And that person is you. I know it is you. Why don't you see that?"

He touched his chest over where his heart would be with one finger, signifying sincerity, "Because I think about another. Trust in the gods for your own fate and stop chasing fantasies. Goodnight."

She said nothing and so after a couple seconds he left. He had forgotten about Rez. He truly wished she would move on. He knew that there were lots of men interested in her. He let those thoughts slip away though as he realized he had lost track of Drusilla again. He scanned this whole area of the room and went to stand where she had been standing. He was so confused they had made eye contact he had reached out to her. *Didn't she know I was coming to speak to her? Didn't she notice her ring?*

A beautiful older woman Ket had never seen before standing nearby said unsolicited, "The human woman went into the garden. She looked upset when you began talking to that other woman. If I were you, I would go and make amends before she gets herself too worked up about it."

203

Ket nodded, "Thank you." He walked quickly into the garden determined to find her and not be detained by any more people.

The goddess of home smiled then as she watched Ket go and said to herself, "What would these mortals do without us?"

Ket cursed in the garden, he couldn't see Drusilla anywhere and the grounds around the Imperial Hall were massive. The garden encompassed 45 hectares and had dozens of paths both large and small and some very dimly lit for privacy. He feared he wouldn't find her, and he couldn't take that chance, so he pulled out his IC, even though it was forbidden, and he would be fined, and brought up a view of the whole garden. He asked for an overview of the occupants of the garden, also forbidden, and immediately all the names appeared. He found hers and then walked in her direction. As he approached her, she was oblivious to him, standing in front of the pond, leaning on the ornate railing, looking at some fish. He could hear her sweetly talking to the small creatures as he advanced.

"What kind of little fish are you?" Dru said rhetorically to the red colored fish thinking they looked remarkably like goldfish with larger fins. "And do all of you ridiculously marry as well? Is it always Assembly night in your pond?"

"They are simply called 'red fish'," Ket supplied as he walked up next to her, their arms just barely touching. "And these are the Imperial Halls which are used for many different functions throughout the year, so I doubt the fish are always at Assembly, but who knows?" He loved being close to her, there was an electricity between their arms, and he wished he could touch her more directly. She smelled divine, she was wearing the perfume he had sent her for her hair, and it mixed well with her own unique fragrance. He wanted nothing more than to run his fingers through her long red hair which she had the boldness to wear loose tonight. Any Alliance woman would have worn her hair in a braid to signify her humility at meeting the man who put the ban on her. He loved that Drusilla did the opposite. *She wouldn't feign humbleness for anyone*, he thought.

"Ket," Dru said happily as she turned. She hadn't heard him approach. She spilled some of her wine on her hand and his, but smiled up at him, nonetheless. Taking in his formal uniform, thinking how handsome he looked in it with his copious amounts of ranking jewelry, *He is an Imperial Doctor after all*, she reminded herself. His hair was pulled back and braided more intricately than she had ever seen it before, and his formal uniform was much more fitted, so it showed more of his muscular physique. Not that she needed to wonder, she had memorized some of the pictures of him without clothing.

"I didn't mean to startle you," he said while looking down into her big green eyes and then after a second his eyes couldn't help but drop down to look at her perfect pink lips. She looked so beautiful tonight, so exotic with her human paint on. So exotic, but so familiar at the same time. It was taking all his self-control not to reach out and stroke her face.

"I was hoping to see you and Dera tonight." She noticed the location ring was warm and tingley but didn't want to look at it now and be reminded that there was another man, besides Ket, looking for her. She wanted only the man in front of her, even though, she knew she couldn't have him. Madame Bai had discounted him and said that he could speak to her because he was above most others in social rank. But she wanted to speak to him now

205

and pretend, even if for only these minutes, she could have him.

"Would you like me to get you another glass of wine?"

"No, I wasn't really drinking it. I was just biding my time with these fish before I could leave."

"I'm surprised. I thought you would be waiting for someone."

She laughed a little, "Yes, the man who put the ban on me was supposed to reveal himself tonight, but I haven't seen any sign of him. And all of the other humans are in quarantine or onboard the *Zuin*. Until the ban ends, I'm like an apparition at these Assemblies, women ignore me, and men don't speak to me, well, except you."

"I'm here now, Drusilla." he said most seriously, looking deeply into her big green eyes.

"Thank you Ket, but it seemed like you had a lot of people to talk to besides me," she resisted adding, 'like Rez.' "Please don't feel that you have to stay with me. I'm sure someone else will turn up as I've heard that there are a lot of high-ranking men here tonight, so maybe someone else will be curious and want to talk to the human. If I become too bored, I'll find Dera. You can go," it was the last thing that she wanted him to do. She reminded herself, *He is not for me and I must dismiss him, or I might lose my friendship with him over my own rudeness at wanting to keep him to myself.* She didn't have much, but she still had some pride.

"Drusilla," he said her name with such fierceness she almost jumped, but simultaneously she had butterflies in her stomach. Then his tone softened, "I came out to the garden to find you."

"Oh," Dru said a bit breathlessly, "I just ..." she trailed off when he reached out and caressed her cheek with his open hand. It had been at least a year since a man had touched her in any romantic way and her body responded in kind. Dru leaned into his strong, cool hand and made a small sound of pleasure. She knew it was forbidden for him to be touching her, but she didn't care. And she knew that Mr. Mystery might throw her off completely now and she could never be with Ket for real, as he was too high ranking, but she didn't care. She wanted him to touch her now.

When Dru leaned into his hand, the most perfect and pleasurable sound he had ever heard escaped her lips and then she closed her eyes, reveling in his touch, he felt as if he was in a dream. He couldn't resist leaning down and kissing her perfect pink lips chastely. When he drew back, she looked up at him with desire in her eyes and he almost forgot that she still didn't know who he was to her. He made an even bolder move then and gently and very slowly, with some pressure, ran his hand from her cheek down the side of her exposed neck, to her shoulder, past her elbow and took her small hand in his. He then raised her hand so that the location ring was clearly visible in front of her eyes between them. It was clear and shimmering as it should be. They were matched and standing right in front of one another.

Dru looked at the ring astonished, "It's clear!" Then looked into his piercing grey eyes for acknowledgement and he nodded. All kinds of emotions were bubbling to the surface now. She was elated, but cross at the same time. She couldn't' help it, some tears began to fall down her cheeks. She wanted to wipe them away, but he was still holding her hand and she wanted him to never let go. She was frustrated and upset he had put her through so much but overjoyed at the same time. "It's you," she said. "I can't believe it's you."

He saw tears fall from her beautiful green eyes and he couldn't help himself, he let go of her hand and cupped her face and wiped the tears with his thumbs, getting some of her black face paint on his thumbs. He looked around then and realized that they were mostly alone in this area of the garden, so he just brought her into his embrace and stroked her long soft hair, her face against his chest, hiding her tears there. Her little form felt so good next to him, but he didn't understand why she was crying," Why does this make you sad?" This was not the way he had imagined this going. He had never put a ban on any woman before, but everything he had heard about the experience from other men was that it was romantic at best and ended in friendship at worst.

Dru was so comforted by his tender embrace that it took her a minute to regain herself, she didn't move but asked into his fitted uniform, "Why didn't you tell me at the symposium? When we first met? Why didn't you tell me in all the messages we sent back and forth?"

He didn't stop stroking her long red hair, so different from his own, "It wasn't the right time."

Dru allowed herself to enjoy his touch for just a few minutes longer, while she decided if his answer was enough, if this was enough for all the heartache she had been through. Finally, after deciding she couldn't forgive him yet, as much as she liked him, she couldn't, she suddenly stamped on his toes, hard, and began walking away without a word. She needed time alone to think about all of this. She knew she was being childish in not articulating her feelings to him, but she was just too overwhelmed with the entire situation. She was trying to regain control of her emotions as she walked back into the grand hall, wiping away the tears. *How could he not tell me? All the times we talked, was this a joke to him? I feel so foolish,* she thought over and over again as she walked aimlessly in the room.

Ket's toes did not hurt as much as his pride. This was

not the way he imagined this happening at all, and he definitely did not want this to play out in front of an audience. Unfortunately, Drusilla was walking fast to the great room of the Assembly and entered before he could stop her.

"Drusilla, could we please talk privately about this?"

"I can't," her eyes were glittery with tears again. "I need to be alone to think about all of this before I can discuss it. I'm sorry about your foot," she added the last statement very quietly.

"I don't understand why you are upset. Most women would have been flattered by the ban," he also spoke quietly as they were drawing a crowd.

"I'm not most Alliance women, if you haven't noticed" she said agitated by his ignorance. "You put me on display, by myself in this alien world and you didn't even tell me it was you who had done it when you had the opportunity. Countless opportunities."

There was an audience growing around them but Ket knew enough about humans from Tir to know that if he didn't act now and tell her, audience or not, she wouldn't forgive him. He took a deep breath and spoke the truth, knowing that her telepathy was good enough to know if he lied, and already cringing at this being all over the gossip columns tomorrow. "Drusilla," he took her elbow and she looked up at him. "When I saw your picture as one of the women rescued by Admiral Tir, I was spellbound by you and desperately wanted to meet you. However, as I was still on the frontlines of the war with no end in sight, I needed to make sure that you wouldn't already be emotionally involved with someone else by the time I was able to come back to the Capital Planet. So, I did what any Alliance man would have done in that situation, I put a ban on you. It didn't occur to me that it would make you feel so isolated or negatively showcased. That was not my intention.

However, I take responsibility for being so thoughtless about your ignorance of Alliance culture and I apologize." He was not going to discuss why he didn't mention it before in front of everyone. If she wanted to know, she would need to speak with him privately.

Dru looked up at him and then at the crowd around them watching quietly. All the grey faces that seemed commonplace to her now. She realized that she would look ungrateful if she did not accept his apology. She knew if she had advice from Jane or Madame Bai in that moment, they would both advise her to be polite and to deal with the real issue later, *Not to embarrass the rest of the humans just because I feel slighted.* "I accept your apology." She could feel the crowd breathe a sigh of relief for him and she was surprised. She could not help but look at their audience, all watching them as if they were watching a romantic play. Obviously to Alliance people this was all very romantic. She didn't understand. He had made her life miserable for months and the ban had not made her feel special, but more like an outcast. But when she looked back at him, it was unmistakable, despite what he had done, she did like him, intellectually, emotionally and physically. And she didn't think those three came together often when looking for love, so she didn't want to just cast him aside because he had adhered to his own culture, as hurtful as it was to her. She would give him a chance to apologize and make it up to her.

"Drusilla, would you accompany me to a table?" he asked formally.

Dru knew that there was a special area, sectioned off from the grand hall with numerous tables for two, so couples may sit and talk with one another more discreetly. To possibly already ask each other their prepared questions that they would ask before courting. Dru looked away from

Ket and at the crowd of people all still watching them and then back to Ket. She wanted to be with him, of course she did, but she was still irrationally cross with him and wanted to make him suffer a little, so she waited a full minute before answering. Then she said, "Yes," loud enough for their audience to hear. Satisfied the crowd around them dispersed as Ket led her towards the back of the building, through corridors she would have never thought to go down

They walked for a couple minutes through empty hallways before stopping in front of an impressive door guarded by two Imperial Guards. Ket didn't say anything but they released the door lock for them, and they entered side-by-side.

Inside, the room was filled with warmly lit bubbles that encased tables for two. The bubbles resembled something out of a fairytale, they shimmered like soap bubbles with occasional rainbows reflected in the light, but more importantly they kept the occupants' appearances and conversations blurred and secret. Ket scanned the room for an empty one and they went to it. They entered silently and then he closed the enclosure for privacy with the wave of his hand. Inside, there was only the soft glow of the rainbow bubble light, a small table with two chairs and each other.

Dru's heart was pounding. She was so overwhelmed with happiness, that it was him all along, but simultaneously, a strong feeling of distrust that he had not revealed himself the first time they met lined her joy.

Ket took in Drusilla's countenance now. Her big green eyes were just staring at him. They knew each other from across the screen but this was different. If he wanted to, he could reach across the table and stroke her cheek again. He could smell her sweet human scent mixed with Alliance hair oil. He could feel her strong energy that was a mixture of happiness, confusion and anger. He wanted to reach out and touch her, to calm her, but it was inappropriate, he would be fined, and he couldn't bear it if she rejected his touch now.

Dru watched Ket, his face and grey eyes revealing nothing about what he was thinking. She looked at the matching location ring he wore, his large hand resting on the small black table, "Why did you keep this a secret from me?"

"To have had said something to you before, at a less formal occasion, where we couldn't be alone together would have lessened the seriousness of my intentions and my respect for you." He said earnestly, "But let me assure you, I've wanted nothing more since we met, and I've been looking forward to this night for so long."

"Does your sister know?"

"It's forbidden for me to tell any woman, except for you, until the ban has run its course."

"So that is a 'yes'. Is that why she befriended me?" Dru felt very sad suddenly that Dera might have only pretended to be her friend because Ket asked it.

"I'll admit, I asked Dera to speak to you when you first began medical school, but you must know my sister well enough to know she would've stopped speaking to you if she didn't like you."

Dru thought about the conversations she had had with Dera and none of them had ever been about Ket, so she nodded satisfied with that answer. "And the ban why did you do that in the first place? I heard your previous answer in the grand hall, but I want the real answer."

"My answer in the grand hall was my real answer," he said slightly exasperated. "From the moment I saw your picture, I wanted to meet you. I knew that would not be possible for many months, so I wanted to make sure you hadn't begun courting another before I had the opportunity to see if there might be something between us." He hesitated, "And I would say that my instincts were correct, there is a strong connection between us," His eyes bore into hers as he spoke. "You are so clever and intriguing. I enjoy every message and conversation we have. And on the few occasions I have been lucky enough to be physically close to you," he reached out a hand to touch her hand now, "I just want to be even closer." He was pleased she didn't move her warm hand away from his. "I'm sorry the ban made your start in the Alliance difficult, but I won't say I wouldn't make the same decision again."

"And it didn't occur to you how this might make me feel? You talking to me and not telling me that it was you who put me in this position?"

He shook his head slowly, "Alliance people like a mystery. I don't know how else to explain it. Most Alliance women would've felt special that they had caught someone's eye, to be so singled out, even if it didn't result in courting or marriage. Then, if it turns out that the couple has mutual feelings for one another, it's considered romantic when a man reveals himself." *And that is how I thought it would be tonight, romantic*, he thought but didn't say. He didn't want to blame her for misinterpreting the situation and he still had hoped this night could turn more romantic.

Drusilla needed to get this off her chest to fully accept his apology, "The first Assembly I attended no men would even look at me. I thought I must be so revolting to Alliance people that I would never find a husband, which, as you might imagine was a terrifying thought for a human woman who had been brought here for the sole purpose of breeding. I imagined being imprisoned in a medical facility for the rest of my life. I was losing sleep over my inability to attract even one man to come and speak to me, let alone court me or marry me." She didn't want to mention that she cried herself to sleep or bought makeup in hopes of making herself more attractive. "What made this situation even worse was that all the other human women met Alliance men almost instantly, even Eve who has one eye. One eye Ket." She looked at him while pointing to one of her eyes.

"Yes, but that can be repaired," he countered.

"I know, and she has two eyes now, but still. I mean, I thought I was so repulsive that she got a man with one eye, and not a great personality either I might add, and no one would even look at me let alone speak to me. Nor do they now. It's like I'm a ghost."

"An Alliance woman would have felt honored a man so high ranking had put a ban on her so that no man would speak to her."

"They don't even look at me," Dru said accusatorily.

"Good," he replied without thinking too much. He had paid good money to have that ban put on her and he was good with a sword and not shy to a duel. He liked that many feared him. A lesser man would have been challenged to a duel over this ban.

Dru lifted her hands up, "You can be insufferable. It wasn't 'good'," she emphasized the word 'good'. "I felt terrible. No one told me the ban was on me until you sent this necklace," she gestured to the necklace with blue stones that she was wearing. "I had to ask Madame Bai why I was receiving jewelry from an anonymous sender. The comb I thought was just from Madame Bai and that everyone had received one, it was very confusing in those first days."

He was going back through his mind now, counting out

the weeks she hadn't known about the ban and when he realized it was quite a few, he did feel a bit sorry for her then and backtracked on his strong position a little, "I only meant to say 'good' because everyone should respect the law and the ban. I'm sorry again for putting you in a situation you didn't understand. Madame Bai should have explained it to you earlier."

"How could she have known if only men are notified of the ban while they are running?"

"It was obvious to every Alliance person in the Empire that someone had put a ban on you. You should be just as upset with Madame Bai as you are with me." Then he asked, "Drusilla, don't you read any gossip columns?"

"No, I don't think so. Why?"

"Because you are in them and that is how you would have known as well."

She scoffed, "I don't believe you."

He sighed and brought out his IC again wondering how much this night was going to cost him in fines, but he needed to make this right. He searched and easily found the article from the night after her first Assembly and handed her the IC.

Dru scanned the article and didn't hide her emotions. Her eyes had tears in them again, "Why didn't I see this?" She looked at him and took out her own IC, but he put his hand on hers.

"Don't, you'll be fined a great deal of universal credits."

She didn't feel guilty about him being fined, but it did make her realize all that he was doing to try and backtrack now. She handed him his IC back and then asked telepathically, *Do you think my IC is blocked from these things? I'm on social media, I read the Day and the regular news.*

Ket was surprised and pleased she used telepathy with

him. Her mental voice was strong and loud, and it felt natural she would speak this way even though she had only learned how to do it a few months ago. He replied, *I'm sure your IC is blocked from everything about you and the other humans if it's not news in the Day.*

"It makes me wonder what else has been shielded from us?" she asked rhetorically and Ket didn't answer. "I can't blame you for that, but I can blame you for all the worrying about my future, especially after it was made clear we would not be returning to Earth after watching Captain Kara's trial. It was a heartbreaking betrayal. When Captain Kara returned, and everyone joined her onboard the *Zuin*, I thought the other 1,000 human women would be joining me, but they are, even now as we speak, still in quarantine. And the slaves in my building must be the worst slaves ever, they are rude and refuse to speak to me more than a few sentences," she realized she was babbling and so got back to the point, "I've been so lonely; you've been one of my only friends and now I find out you lied to me about this thing that has been such a thorn in my side ever since I arrived. Why didn't you write, 'I have put a ban on you for such and such amount of time because I want to meet you,'? In all our conversations, why couldn't you have told me? Didn't you notice how lonely I was?"

Ket had sympathy for her but wanted to defend himself, "Because my actions said all of that and more." He paused trying to think how to articulate this cultural practice, "I didn't realize you didn't have a family or friends to guess with. I didn't realize the isolated position I put you in and how difficult that must have been." Then he reflected on her sadness, "You never seemed lonely to me when we exchanged messages. If you would have mentioned to me, you were upset by the ban I would have told you it was me. As I said before, it was never my intention to hurt you. I'll try to do better in the future, if you think you could still consider a future for us?"

"I do think there is a future for us. I'm just so cross with you for not telling me. It's just all so different and overwhelming. Now are you going to ask me to begin courting you? Is the ban over?"

"The ban is on you until the day of your birthday, the converted Alliance date, of course, as it is the only one that matters in this case. After that, you will have many offers of courtship, including mine. Between then and now, I'm one of the few eligible men you can speak to. I'm not lifting the ban early," he hesitated and then added, "I still want these weeks to have you to myself. Besides our messages, Dera talks about you so well, and I just feel all of this is so right, as if the gods have arranged it all."

Dru didn't want to add a religious and fatalistic layer to their conversation, so she ignored that aspect of his answer. "Dera never talks about you to me," she said flatly, purposely wanting to hurt him. "And I did really like you, until I felt like you had been keeping secrets from me. Now, you've fallen in my estimation," Dru almost smiled to herself, she knew that was something that would hit him hard as Alliance people always ranked everything and to fall in rank on anything, they cared about bothered them.

Ket knew that she mentioned the ranking just to be hurtful and he let her have that, "Your innocence is endearing and a reminder to me that you have just arrived and don't understand all of our ways yet. Let me be your teacher in this, it should have been a big clue to you that it was I who put the ban on you because Dera never mentioned me to you even after she introduced us, and it was known to her that we often messaged each other privately. She never mentioned me to you because she is not allowed to talk to you about me unless we are married. Family members of the person who applied the ban are not allowed to discuss with the person to whom the ban is directed, in the same way, if we are courting, Dera cannot mention me to you. It is to keep you from being influenced by my family members. Your decision to be with a man must be yours alone. That is also why Dera didn't seek you out tonight. It is forbidden." He could see the tears in her eyes, and he cupped her face again and wiped away the tears, he knew that his fines would be great if the surveillance cameras were picking this up, but he couldn't watch her cry and know that he was the cause of it and not comfort her with his touch. Words were not enough now.

She looked at him through the tears and admitted softly and honestly, "I don't know what I am supposed to be doing now, Ket."

He made the Alliance shushing sound that had more 'z's than 'sh's and she actually calmed a bit at that and then said gently, "Right now, we are supposed to be getting to know each other better. I'd like to do that very much." He waited and then when she didn't speak, he hazarded a little joke, "I have my questions if you have yours?"

When she didn't answer he asked, "May I share some memories with you?"

She looked at him blankly.

"So that you might better understand how I feel and understand what is going on now. Do you consent?"

She nodded.

"My memories of these events will become intermixed with your own memories. It's a very personal thing to do, but I feel right now, we have so little time and I don't think even if we talked the whole night, we could resolve your confusion and doubt, without me doing this. I'll show you two memories, the first, when I saw your picture in the Day

and put the ban on you. The second, when I was introduced to you for the first time. Will you permit me?"

"Yes," she stopped crying, moved by this truly intimate
action.

He leaned closer to the table and said quietly, "Please
give me your hands." He held her hands in his, just for a
couple seconds, squeezed them and then turned them,
palms up, and placed his just above hers, so that they were
almost touching. Ket found that almost touching was better
when he wanted to specifically share certain memories. If
he actually touched the other person, it would be too easy
to share too much, and he didn't want to show her everything about these memories.

As the cold air swirled around her palms, she could feel
his hands hovering and moving closer to hers, so close but
not exactly touching. Her heart was beating so quickly she
could hear it in her ears. Mentally she felt like she was
tumbling into darkness, like that dream where you are
suddenly falling.

After what seemed like an eternity of falling, she was
him. She was Alliance, thinking like an Alliance, so logical,
strict and spiritual. It was almost unsettling to be in his
mind, to feel what he felt. As he looked at her picture, she
experienced his overwhelming curiosity for her, his strong
belief that humans were the Lost People and that she was
meant for him. That the gods had given him a sign and
that is why he immediately was drawn to her. She was
moved that he didn't take the decision lightly either and
that he had left his office and gone to the shrine to pray
about it. Then he returned and put on the ban, and she
couldn't believe how much he paid. She could see that she
had been valued as the highest among all the human
women from the *Dakota* and this did, even though it
shouldn't have mattered, make her feel better. It almost

made up for all the nights she thought she must be the ugliest most vile person on the Capital Planet. Then he skipped the memory to the next, it shook and twisted, which she wished he hadn't because she was curious as to what Admiral Tir had said, but that began but then quickly disappeared. Then she felt like she fell down another hole and she found herself looking at herself at the symposium at the medical school. Next, she was overwhelmed with desire. It was so intense and wrong because she was looking at herself sitting next to Dera talking. His excitement and nervousness about talking to her for the first time was all-consuming. How he thought she looked even more beautiful in person and how he hoped she liked him. Dru experienced his great hope that she would message him when he was away and his doubts about his own control to wait until the next Year Assembly to talk to her and reveal himself. And then he was backing away, she was climbing up and up and the memories were now hers and he was gone.

Dru opened her eyes and looked into his grey ones. Surprised to be back at the table and nowhere else. He was searching her face for a reaction, no doubt concerned that he had shared this, and it had not changed her mind. "You paid a lot of money for that ban," was the first thing she could think of to say. Her mind was still a little muddled.

He frowned.

"That was a joke. What I mean is, thank you for sharing those memories, it meant a lot for me to understand how you perceived everything. I believe you completely now."

"Good." He could see her thinking about something, and he was self-conscious. He had just shared his most personal memories with her, he had never done that with a woman before who was not his mother, "What is it?"

"I didn't realize how religious you were until now."

"We are all religious."

Dru didn't answer that. She didn't feel anymore religious than when she left Earth. She believed in spirits sure, but deities that controlled her fate, she was unsure. She could see that he needed reassurance of her favor though, "Let's ask our questions then. What is your favorite color?" She wanted to ask this question for frivolousness, to see how far the Alliance seriousness went in the man. She didn't want to spend the next 300 years with someone who was too serious.

"Is that one of your questions?" he smiled a little thinking how strange humans were with their minds obsessed with making things beautiful.

She nodded for him to answer the question, pleased that he had smiled, meaning he had more emotions than just being logical and serious all the time.

"Unfortunately, it is ka, one of the two colors humans have trouble distinguishing."

She put her hand up to the silver necklace with the blue stones, "Are these stones ka colored and not blue then?"

He nodded, "Yes, but they look beautiful with any color dress and suit you."

"Next question, what is your favorite food?"

"I don't have one," he replied honestly.

Dru wasn't surprised, Alliance people really only looked at food as sustenance, so she was not going to press him. Then she just jumped to a very serious question, which would be more what he would expect in this situation, "What do you expect from a wife?" She could tell from his bewildered look that she had caught him off guard and this pleased her.

Ket took a minute to think about his answer. If she had

been an Alliance woman, he knew what he would have said, but given her reaction to the ban, he needed to be careful now about how he explained himself, to make sure she understood his intentions and expectations properly. "I would like a wife who is a doctor, with strong telepathic skills, and who looks forward to my returns. A wife who smiles at me when I've been good and frowns at me when I haven't. And a wife that has a special look reserved only for me."

Dru had not expected that answer. The example answers to that particular question in her cultural hand-book were very different, they were more detailed about exact responsibilities and nothing about emotion. She asked more, "And where would your wife live?" She honestly wanted to know, and this was the second question women asked men they were considering courting, if she were going by the book.

Ket answered this one without hesitation as though he had done it a million times, which made her feel a bit sad that she was not the first one asking this. "I've a house suited to my rank in my House's compound, near my parents' family home. It is a 15-minute walk between them in the Imperial Ring of the Capital City. I think you would be very happy there. I'd allow you to decorate the house as you wish, with some things from Earth. I've heard that this has been a difficult compromise between Lieutenant Kole and his human wife, but I would welcome the diversity you would bring." And to be honest he was a bit afraid of denying her as Admiral Tir had done Captain Kara and now the Admiral's whole house was painted red, both inside and out.

Dru knew that once a couple was to be married that the wife to be could make considerable changes to a house, all paid for by the husband's family. Some of the women who had already been married had done that. Dru had grown up in rustic circumstances and then had rooms either at the fleet academy or onboard ship. She wouldn't know how to decorate a house especially not a large or grand house.

Ket noticed her change in demeanor, "Is there a problem with the house I mentioned?" He wondered if the proximity to his family put her off. Her captain had actually taken her sword to her mother in-law the last time she was on planet and Tir brushed it off saying, 'Humans don't live with their families like we do. This will just take some getting used to.'

"No, I just realized something about myself for the first time. It's only a triviality." She could feel his mind searching and looked into his sharp grey eyes and easily made him forget what he wanted to ask her then. And then she gently reminded him of his courting questions. She knew she was flirting with danger by doing this as she didn't know the extent of his telepathic skills, but what better way to measure his skills but by testing them.

"What would you want from a husband?"

Dru had thought about this question a lot. It was a typical question before courting according to her cultural handbook. She had prepared an answer for Mr. Mystery, but she had expected him to be a stranger, not Ket. "I've a prepared answer, of course, but that's not fitting now. I never expected a man I already knew to be asking this question, and definitely not you."

"Drusilla," his tone strict, "tell me what you would want from a husband."

She looked directly into his eyes, "I don't know now. Knowing you, changes everything. I would forgive you so many things. I can't believe I have already forgive you for the ban and now my prepared answer for this question is useless. For you, it would be a completely different list."

"Try."

She thought for a moment, "I would want you to be more honest."

"I'm always honest."

"No, you're always Alliance honest. You only tell the truth when asked. I want you to be more forthcoming with things and not keep so much hidden from me."

"I don't know if that's possible, as I don't realize I keep so much from you."

"Really? The word 'ban' mean anything to you?"

"That's different."

"That's exactly what I mean. I would like you to start telling me things. Try to understand that I don't know what is always going on and that sometimes I need some help."

"But that's no fun Drusilla. You'll figure it out. No one is judging you and it's adorable to watch you navigate the Alliance."

"Adorable?" she asked quietly.

He stood up, leaned over and whispered in her ear, "Absolutely adorable." He kissed her ear lobe and then sat back down, "Tell me, when did you first know me then? When you ran into me outside the medical school?"

His warm breath on her ear sent shivers down her spine and when he kissed her ear lobe, she almost moaned. She was so aroused. He sat back in his chair and she blushed thinking about the naked picture in the article. That was the first time she had seen him.

"You just projected that," Ket told her with humor. "I love the lovely shade of pink in your cheeks over it."

"I'm glad it doesn't bother you."

"Why would it?"

"I can't explain it," Dru admitted.

"See, explaining your culture is difficult. Now please tell me the next time, I'm curious."

"I wanted to know what specifically would be talked about during the symposium about new procedures on warships and went through a lot of the holographic simulations in the library. Thank you for the private study room by the way. It has been invaluable to me," she said, and he nodded. "You were in a couple of the simulations I did. At the time, as I didn't look up the names of the doctors, I didn't put two and two together."

He was looking at her blankly.

"That those beautiful nude images and the impressive doctor on the warship were the same. I never checked the names."

He smiled at her inexperience.

"In the holographic simulations, I was impressed with your skills and confidence. I've been in war and in the moment keeping a clear head isn't easy, I don't think I could have done what you did. Then when you were berated for it on planet, I was again impressed with your demeanor as you defended your amendments to the procedures. I think you were right."

Ket had never been so complemented by a woman before. Most women just assumed because he was a man, he had some special skill that made it easier to deal with violence and emergencies. And that because he was a man, he cared more about his appearance than his work and therefore should never presume to amend a woman's procedure. Now, he realized what Tir had been trying to tell him the last time they met, 'Humans see the sexes as equal; I mean really equal.' Ket had never thought of himself as a man who wanted to be equal to a woman, but being here with her, he didn't know what he wanted anymore. He always thought that he would leave the actual mating and shaping of human wives to the other men, until he saw Drusilla. Now he realized that she was his greatest tool in the change Tir wanted to bring about. A change that he was apathetic about before, but now suddenly he was almost passionate about. He would guide her to become exactly what he needed, what they all needed. *It is the gods' will*, he thought.

Dru couldn't make out his reaction to what she said. She wasn't sure if she should compliment his looks instead, as her handbook had instructed her to do, but the truth was, his being handsome was secondary to his mind and manners.

"You have caught me off guard with your praise of my skills. Most women compliment me on my appearance and rank."

"Would you prefer I do that?"

"Of course not."

"Good. If we are going to spend 300 years together, I want a husband I respect not a vain man."

"But you do like my appearance?" he couldn't resist asking, in the end, he needed to make sure. He was still an Alliance man after all.

"Of course, you are very attractive to me. I thought that was obvious," Dru was surprised he wanted this confirmation. *Wasn't he attractive for an Alliance man? It doesn't matter as he is attractive to me*, she thought looking at him.

"Another time we should discuss attractiveness. I'm curious as to which humans are considered attractive and why. Obviously, in the Alliance you were the most attractive out of all the other humans taken from the *Dakota*."

"On Earth I am not," she admitted. "Rebecca is considered to be the most attractive among us."

"I guess it's a good thing you are here then where you are the true beauty," he smiled. "Now back to questions.

This is not one of my usual questions obviously, but I must ask it. Will you abide by the ancient Contracts?"

"I feel like you are asking me something specific, but I don't know what."

"Will you ever want to leave planet? Join Captain Kara?"

"It's not illegal anymore for human woman to do that. The High Council changed the law regarding human women."

"I'm aware of the law change. However, I'm not Tir. I can't have my wife off planet."

"Why not?"

"I'm old fashioned. I wouldn't be able to sleep. I would need to know you are safe at all times. You are only safe on the Capital Planet. I would never want you to leave."

Dru didn't know whether to be charmed or scared by that admission, "You're not going to imprison me in your house or anything?"

He was horrified, "No. I just don't want to risk you dying needlessly. The Alliance is powerful because we always protect our most prized possessions at all costs."

"But you..." she countered, and he interrupted her.

Men and women are not equal, he projected as it was forbidden to say it out loud. "Without women the Alliance would fall and more importantly if we had children, they would need you more than me."

"I'd say any children would need us both equally."

He ignored her comment. He wanted to tell her that she was straying into a forbidden topic but was afraid it would trigger her to talk about it even more, so he asked the same question again, "Would you join Captain Kara?"

She looked in his eyes deeply, "If I have a good job here, I wouldn't consider joining, but I can't say, 'never'. I know the human government sold us, and I'm probably

227

seen as just as much of a traitor as Captain Kara but it's difficult for me to say that if I had the opportunity to return to Earth that I wouldn't. I think though, it is unlikely that I would ever do either."

"I don't think anyone in the Alliance Empire was surprised by Captain Kara's trial except the women from the *Dakota*. I'm sorry for that, but even you must see what a great opportunity we have given you all by making you Alliance citizens." He didn't react to the flash of annoyance on her face, "If it makes you feel any better, the amount paid for you all, was an offer the human government couldn't refuse. The full details were not disclosed as I know Tir used a lot of his own universal credits and connections in the deal," Ket admitted.

"That doesn't make it better."

"No, not from your point of view, but I must admit that I was relieved. We are meant to be Drusilla. Before the trial, I was slightly concerned that I would have to come to Earth to find you."

"What do you mean?" Dru had just assumed he would have given her up if she had returned to Earth and the human fleet.

"One stipulation of the ban is that I must present myself to you before or within the week of the ban ending in person."

"Would you have really come to Earth to do that?" Dru had forgotten his condescending words about a better life for them all in the Alliance and was a little charmed now.

He gave her a look of disbelief, "Yes. You know in the Alliance we take our commitments very seriously."

"Even with humans?"

"With everyone."

"And then what would you have done?"

"I would've taken an extended holiday to convince you that we are destiny. We are the gods' will."

"What if I wouldn't have believed you? I want details Ket," *Didn't he understand that this would have been very romantic for me? More than having a ban being placed on me or receiving jewelry or any of the other rituals,* she wondered.

He brushed the side of her cheek with the back of his hand, shockingly, instantly showing her mental images of him kneeling before her naked form licking her sex. His strong hands cupping her naked bottom and her hands intertwined in his long and loose hair.

Dru closed her eyes, so aroused by the scene, but then opened her eyes in surprise when he took his hand away and the fantasy was gone.

"I'm sure we would have found a compromise. This is the gods' will. But if we were to enter into a courtship, I would need your word that you wouldn't join Captain Kara or return to Earth."

Dru was still reeling from his telepathic skills to convey such a sensual feeling, so real, with just a momentary touch it took her a couple seconds to answer him, "Not an official compromise?"

He shook his head, "I want to trust you, Drusilla, and I want you to trust me. I know, it's very modern not asking for a written compromise."

She was momentarily stunned by this. She thought that all Alliance people needed everything in writing. "Good. If you ask me to court you, we will discuss it again." She could tell he wasn't satisfied with that answer, but she wasn't prepared to compromise on anything now.

"I'll accept that for now," he agreed. "Moving forward, how often would you imagine we would have sex when I was home, if we were married?" He tried to casually stand at the edge of her thoughts with his own mind to see if he could catch any stray reactions. He still didn't know if she were a virgin or had had a very bad sexual experience for her to have had to undergo a sex test in the medical exam on Space Port One. She was so young and clueless in Alliance culture to begin with the last thing he wanted was that she was clueless in sex as well. He didn't find the idea of having to teach a woman about sex arousing at all, quite the opposite.

"Is that really one of your questions?" Her cultural handbook had mentioned that this could be a question but stated that it usually came after a couple had decided to court unless one of the parties had a specific or unique reason for bringing it up. She wondered then; *Does he have access to all of my medical file? Surely not, men were forbidden from knowing anything about women's reproductive or sexual health.* She had been told by Doctor Jina that, 'The birth of children is a miracle to men. It's best to keep them at an arm's distance from it. Men have no understanding of what it feels like to bring life into the galaxy and their minds are not equipped to understand. Therefore, they are kept ignorant of women's bodies, except for what is expected in the sexual act.'

"Yes, it is an important question. Everyone is different."

"Is there a specific reason you are asking it now though? Do you have something you want to tell me?"

He liked that she was turning this back on him. He smiled, "We can come back to it another time," he felt her shame in not wanting to answer and picked up a sight of Doctor Jina with her and then her bed functions. He was satisfied that, even if she was a virgin, she was working on it with a professional.

"What would your answer be?" Dru honestly wanted to know. She'd never been in a relationship with sex. In the

Exterior, she had been too young to do more than kiss or hold hands with a boy and at the fleet she had been too jumpy to go further with anyone because of what had happened with the five guards.

"After a couple gets married, they have a months' honeymoon alone at one of the designated resorts on planet. I would imagine we would have a lot of sex then. Afterwards, for the first ten years of marriage, men are allowed to take months off at a time to be home with their wives. During those times, I would say I'd like to have sex three or four times a week, maybe more. But I would also like to talk to my wife too." He wanted to add but resisted, 'But, I'm not like Tir, who apparently has met his match in interspecies sex games onboard the *Refa*.'

"That sounds reasonable," Dru replied not having a clue as to if it were reasonable or not and wondering if the months, they took off were to make sure children were sired.

Ket could tell she didn't even begin to know her mind on the issue of sex and so changed the subject, "One more thing I must flag up to you."

"What's that?" Dru asked wondering if this was going to be another sex related question.

"In my family, we are all telepaths. It's very difficult to maintain privacy. Many people are unable to live like this, but this is also why we have maintained our position for so long. Even some of the slaves are telepathic."

Dru was relieved they weren't talking about sex anymore, "I thought reading minds without consent was illegal."

"Inside a House it is not. Often not a sound is heard in my childhood home as my mother prefers all the slaves in her home to be telepathic as well. There are few secrets."

"There are few secrets in the Alliance for me anyway. I

think just one family monitoring me instead of a government would be a step up."

"I'm not joking Drusilla."

"Neither am I. You realize where I live, House Human, is basically a prison."

"The forcefield is to protect you all."

"Okay," she said unbelievingly.

He ignored her sarcastic reply because he knew she was right, but he still had to tow the government line, "Do you think you would be able to live with my family?"

"Yes, my mother and siblings were also telepathic, although we didn't use it to communicate in the same way. We always knew each other, if you know what I mean?" That was why it had been so difficult for her to escape; she had had to pick a day her mother had gone to serve as a midwife in a faraway encampment and Dru had to remain home to tend to a patient there. It rarely happened that she was allowed that kind of freedom and so she took the opportunity, packed a small bag with everything that mattered to her in life and left in the night while her siblings slept.

"I understand. I can't believe I've never asked you this before, do you miss your family?"

Dru gave him a surprised look.

"I'm sorry," he realized that this was not something she wanted to share with him.

"It's fine. I was just surprised you asked. My childhood was not a tender one and I've moved almost directly from the human fleet to here and I feel I've been alone enough in my life now. I long for a place to belong. My only worry is that your family or any Alliance family would not accept me." She had already heard negative stories from Rebecca and Captain Kara in regard to their Alliance in-laws.

"You are first in your class; you are healthy and a

woman likely to have daughters. You are clever and respectful. They would accept you. Dera and my mother already approve."

"Your mother? I've not met her."

"Yes, at Admiral Tir's punishment. She's the First Imperial Doctor. She observed you and was pleased you weren't anything like your captain."

Dru grinned, "No, I am nothing like Captain Kara." Dru was trying to remember the day, it was so long ago, and she couldn't remember much except Captain Kara cutting Admiral Tir in all the wrong places and then putting it into the statue's eyes. She would never forget the statue crying his red blood into a pool on the stone floor.

"She said that you weren't a barbarian."

"Are her standards that low for a human woman? Don't answer that. Is that what she thinks Captain Kara is?"

Ket didn't answer.

"So, the answer to that is 'yes'. But she is meant to be Empress."

Ket didn't answer that either.

"Never mind. I don't even really care. I like you. I want to be with you. I just don't want your family to hate me especially if they are living right next door and you're away a lot."

"They won't hate you anymore than they would any Alliance woman."

"Wow, that is not what I want to hear, Ket."

"I was joking."

"No, you weren't."

"No, I wasn't. But it's always tense bringing women together."

"Why?"

"The power struggles," Ket felt he was just going forever the wrong way with her.

"Never mind. We will cross that bridge if we come to it. Let's focus on the here and now. I still have some questions."

"Here and now sounds good," he agreed.

"I want to know about Rez, you were talking to her before you found me in the garden. What was that all about?" she tried to keep the anger out of her voice.

He looked into Drusilla's eyes seriously, "I know it's difficult to believe, but she stopped me and then I couldn't leave. Finally, I did just go. As to our history, there isn't much to tell. We courted for only two short weeks last year. I ended it quickly. It was a mistake. We were not suited in any way, but she still thinks that I may come back to her even though I have made it more than clear that will never happen. You know the rules at an Assembly, I had to talk with her until she dismissed me. I was coming to talk to you. You and I made eye contact, but then you left, and I had to find you in the garden."

"Oh," said Dru thinking that Rez must be fuming now that she realizes Ket is with her. "I hope she saw that it was me you were coming to talk to."

"If she didn't know it then, she knows it now," he commented.

"Good," Dru said. She had never known herself to hate someone as much as she hated Rez and to be so pleased that she could hurt her in this way by having Ket. She knew it was wrong to enjoy it so much, but she couldn't help herself. "Now tell me, what's home life like between a married couple in the Alliance? We don't marry anymore, what should I expect?"

"What do you mean?"

"Do you sleep in the same bedroom? Do you love each other? Do you eat the morning meal together?"

"As you know, we typically eat the morning meal with colleagues or friends, however, when men are home, yes, they always sleep in the same bedroom as their wives unless for some reason they are not allowed, and I would definitely hope for love between myself and my wife. I could marry many women for position alone, but I want more." Then he looked into her eyes and said softly, "And we should absolutely not be talking about love. You are still underage, and we're not courting. It's forbidden." Then he said, even softer, "But I think I would love you in every waking moment I was able to spend with you in our home and long for you so much it ached when I was away."

Dru looked into his grey eyes, filled with sexual desire, no doubt matching her own. Images of his naked body flashed through her mind and then she said boldly, "I think I could love you very much both in and out of our home. I find it odd that it's appropriate to ask how often we would have sex but to not speak about our strong emotions for each other."

He took her hands and squeezed them as a small reprimand, "It's forbidden to speak of love if we are not seriously courting or married. We shouldn't get too emotionally involved until all of the practical details are settled. But I look at you and I forget all the Contracts made about it. I touch you when I am not supposed to, and you make me feel like everything is more real than it ever was before. Let me take you home. The Assembly is almost over. Our night has almost come to an end and I want to savor every minute of it as we won't be able to meet again like this until you are of age." When he saw her indecision, he assured her, "My guards will be with us, so we will never be alone."

Dru was disappointed at the mention of his guards but then agreed. She rose from the chair realizing her underwear was soaking wet from her desire and wondering when and if they would have sex as she walked out with him. She wanted him but she didn't know if she was ready to have sex with any man yet, but she smiled and thought, *But if I had to choose to do it with one man right now, it would be Ket.* She wished he would take her hand as they walked so closely together, sometimes his hand would touch hers lightly, but he never got any closer. When they reached his transport, she got out her IC to call Madame Bai's assistant to let her know the change in plan. Then she and Ket entered his transport but his guards remained outside at his signal.

"Aren't we going?"

"Not yet. I want to speak to you for a few more minutes in private," he couldn't help himself; once the door of the transport was closed, he sat down and pulled her onto his lap and ran a hand through her long red hair. She smelled amazing and her softness next to him was so alluring. "This isn't enough time," he said absently, "I want to know everything about you and I'm so reluctant to let you go."

Dru was so overwhelmed with his presence and the way he was holding her, running his hand through her hair, she never wanted this to end. "I feel as if time is standing still."

"It's gods' time."

"I've heard that before, but I don't understand."

"It's this," he said and then he leaned in and gave her the most gentle and chaste kiss. Her lips were so warm and her skin so smooth. He caressed her cheek and then pulled away and looked in her eyes brimming with desire and said gently, "It's gods' time. This is meant to be. It's their will that is why we feel this way. They are guiding us now."

"Suddenly, I'm religious," she said quietly and put her arms around his neck and drew him back to her. He was cooler to the touch than a human man, but not so much so, that it detracted from the sensual feel of his strong lips on hers. It had been so long since a man touched her and never in such a simple way that actually made her tremble for more. She kissed him chastely once, twice, and then without warning, took his bottom lip between hers, sucked gently and pulled away with her teeth. It was not long before his tongue was tantalizing hers and his hands were holding her so strongly against his large, muscular body she could feel the pinch of his ranking jewelry through her formal dress. It should have been uncomfortable but instead it just made her desire him more.

After many minutes of kissing, Ket pulled away, "We must stop, although it is the last thing I want to do. But we are not even courting," he said as if that gravity would mean as much to her as it did to him.

"Ask me then."

"You know it's not that simple."

"I know it can be, there are exceptions."

"There are," he agreed, "but there is no need to draw any more attention to ourselves. We can wait." He was searching her face wondering if she really could wait or if the human barbarian genes were too strong to ignore.

"This, now, you, have been one of my only pleasures since coming here. I don't want it to end, but if you promise me you will ask me when I come of age, then I can wait," she looked at him, biting her lower lip.

He touched her cheek to try and satisfy her, "I'll ask you." He kissed her again, "I'll always ask you."

"When?"

"When I am back on the Capital Planet and you are of age. Now, I should get you home before we become the next Kara and Tir," Ket said regretfully and began to release her from his embrace.

"Just a little longer, don't let go," Dru said trying to move even closer to him. She put her head against his chest again, closed her eyes and breathed him in. She reveled in the feeling of someone holding her. *Of him holding me*, she reminded herself and pushed other negative thoughts about her situation down.

He expertly ran his hands through her long red hair, down her back, and down the side of one of her legs over her dress all the way down to her ankle. Then he remembered something and dared running his hand up her stockinged leg under her dress.

Dru felt his hand moving up her leg and without opening her eyes or moving asked, "Ket?"

"Yes?" he answered mischievously.

"What are you doing?"

"Just checking something, if you will permit me?"

She sat up a bit and looked at him, "What?"

His hand moved ever so slowly as it climbed up her stocking. She continued looking at him and said nothing, so he didn't stop.

She had decided, when his hand touched her knee, that she wanted to have sex with him. As long as he remained this sweet and gentle, she wanted to feel him inside of her. Dru searched his eyes and wondered if she had missed something and they were going to have sex now. *Please gods reward me with sex with this man*, she silently prayed.

When Ket reached the top of one of her stockings, he moved his fingers even more slowly over her soft skin at the top of her thighs, making little circles as he climbed closer to where her human panties would begin, that is, if she were wearing any. He only needed to move his hand a couple centimeters, but he felt like it took an eternity while he held her gaze. When he reached the fabric of her panties, he asked, "Panties?" And couldn't help himself and ran a finger up and down the slit in her vulva over the wet fabric. He loved the sound that escaped her when he did that and so he didn't move his hand away but continued to stroke her wet sex over the fabric.

She had closed her eyes when he reached the edge of her underwear. *Gods, touch me everywhere and specifically there,* she thought. He stroked her while asking her about her underwear. She replied breathlessly, "They're comforting to me, especially in these times of uncertainty."

"Unnecessary. Give them to me."

"No," she knew her panties were drenched from all her strong emotions for him that night and she was definitely not giving him these.

"Drusilla."

She almost jumped with the strict way he pronounced her full name and a bolt of fear and excitement passed through her. She jumped up quickly and declared, "You'll have to take them from me by force."

He jumped up after her and caught her wrists behind her back. Then brought his mouth down on hers for a long and sensual kiss. He held both of her wrists with one hand while he continued to kiss her and with his other hand, he bunched up the copious fabric of her dress to get to her panties. When he reached them, he couldn't help but pull away, still holding her hands, getting far enough away to admire the black fabric covering her sex. The fabric had become so wet it clung to all the details of her vulva. He ran a finger over the fabric again and she made another sound of pleasure. His penis was so hard it took all of his self-control not to continue stroking her, but then he remembered his one goal with this, which was not sex or to bring her to orgasm. He began slowly removing her underwear to reveal her sex.

Ket knew that she would have hair covering her sex, but he was unprepared for how erotic that would be for him. He had imagined it might have the opposite effect, but no, when he saw it, he wanted nothing more but to grind his naked body next to hers and feel her barbarian hair next to his body. But he couldn't now. This wasn't the right time. He tried to gently remove her panties, saying, "Your sex is the most beautiful thing I've ever seen, and I look forward to running my fingers over that soft fur, licking and sucking every centimeter of it the next time we meet." When she refused to step out of her panties, he slapped the back of her thighs. "Drusilla."

Again, ripples of pleasure ran through her at the sound of her name being called in such a formal and serious manner. She wanted him to slap her bare thighs again. She wanted him to touch her everywhere. She purposely tried to squirm to feign escape. This was so different than her first sexual encounter this was fun and at every turn he was different than those other disgusting guards. He was fit and strong. He had grey skin and he called her pubic hair 'fur'. Nothing was the same and she was so happy for it.

He held her away from him, her eyes open now and filled with mischief. He increased his grip on her wrists and leaned down to kiss her. As his tongue entered her mouth, he slapped her bottom hard. Then he pulled away looking at the panties halfway down her thighs and her exposed sex, he touched it. "I love this fur," he said seductively in her ear as he continued to stroke her.

Dru couldn't believe he called her pubic hair 'fur' again. If she hadn't been so aroused, she would have laughed, but under the circumstances she thought, *You can call it whatever you want as long as you do what you promise. Touching, licking and sucking.*

Ket was looking at her beautiful sex hardly able to control himself. He wanted her panties though. He was not going to lose focus. He was not a brute. He knew if he slapped her thighs or bottom again and heard the little whimper again, that was more from sexual desire than pain, the chance that he wouldn't take her right now was low, so he did the only thing he could think of, he took his sword and quickly cut the panties off of her. Then he just as quickly sheathed his sword and put the wet panties into his pocket.

She wanted him to continue touching her, but when she felt the tug of her panties and then their release, she opened her eyes as he let her go and she watched him put her dirty underwear into his pocket as the hem of her dress fell back down to the floor, "You're really taking my panties?"

He nodded, "And they are so fragrant with your arousal for me. I think that makes them partly mine anyway."

"That's embarrassing. Please give them back."

"Why is that embarrassing?" He took her hand and put it over his hard penis. "I'm equally as aroused. I want something of yours and this is one of the most intimate things you can give me. Tomorrow don't wear any panties and tell me how your beautiful sex feels free as it should be. Send me a VM describing it. I want you to think about me when you don't wear these." He took out her panties and held them up for her to see and then put them back in his pocket.

She laughed, "What?"

"Will you do it? Will you be loyal to me tomorrow?"

It dawned on her then what he meant by 'be loyal' to

him. "You mean like a dominance role where you tell me what to do and I do it?"

"Yes. One day a week. That is the compromise for the underwear."

She laughed, "We're not married, we are not even courting. I didn't think I had to do anything until then."

"Call it a warm-up to see how it feels. I know from other men it is difficult for human women to give up their panties. I want a formal compromise for this. Something that comforts me equally. I've heard that loyalty days are difficult with humans."

"And you would like me to be loyal to you for one day every week?"

"Yes. You'll either be able to comply, or you won't."

"I don't know exactly what you are looking for," she admitted.

He brought her into his embrace, kissed her and said, while running his hands through her long red hair, "You will know when we begin. One day a week."

"Tomorrow then."

He nodded, "And every 4th day of the week from tomorrow onwards, you will be loyal to me, whether I'm here or not." He was so aroused by the idea of having her doing his bidding once a week. It was a common request among men, and so Alliance women knew how to play the role. However, now he had a human who would have to be taught which in some ways was a turn on in itself. Something that he had not considered would come with her sexual inexperience.

"We will try it, but I don't like it you need to come up with something else."

"Fine," he said and then reluctantly let go of her. He took a deep breath to calm himself and opened the transport door to motion his guards to join them. They flew the

242

short distance to her building. He walked her to the door, "I meant to tell you before, all slaves are rude and ill-mannered in the Alliance because it's just a name, they aren't really slaves anymore. If they were overly nice then you should be worried that they are spitting in your food or something."

"You're not serious?"

He nodded, "I'm sorry our night has to end."

"I'm looking forward to my coming of age day even more now. I'm afraid the days will pass even more slowly."

He touched her cheek with the back of his hand, "At least tomorrow you are not even allowed to think about anything without my permission. I want complete loyalty."

He spoke so softly she thought it almost sounded like a prayer. She looked up into his grey eyes, "Tell me what you want me to do," she couldn't help but smile.

He wished they were in private so he could wipe that smile off her face. Later, he told himself. "I want you to wake up, shower and wear your navy dress and no panties. During the morning meal you will eat the food I arrange for you. After your classes you will go to your private study room and send me a message from there and describe to me how it felt to not wear panties all day and all of your naughty thoughts about me."

"Not from my study room," she protested, and she liked the momentary annoyance she saw in his eyes. *Oh yes, you are a little controller when you get the chance.* Thankfully Alliance men rarely had the chance to control women and she realized that this was his day, what he was asking for and then she replied, "I'll do it."

This satisfied him and then he brought out his sword again and without any explanation took the bottom of her hair and cut a very small piece some off. "I want this too."

Dru was dumbfounded. If she were in the Exterior, she

would kill him to get that back for fear of a spell. *But this was the Alliance and they didn't believe in spells, did they?* she questioned looking at her hair in his hand. "I thought it went against the gods to cut our hair. Why don't you give me some of yours to make it equal?"

"I'm taking this for a purpose. You'll see and you'll be pleased, I think. It's a surprise. Trust me."

"Trust you?"

He took her in for a kiss, knowing they would both be fined and then pulled away long enough to say, "Yes, trust me," then kissed her again. He was reluctant to let her go, "May the gods shine their light on you my little fiery one."

"May the gods guide your path," she replied. She watched him go and was surprised he took out his IC as he walked away. She was even more surprised that he had messaged her, instead of just telling her something.

Leave the fines to me.

She smiled wondering what had they done that would be fined? Kissing yes, she knew that, but what else besides his IC usage at the Assembly?

That night Dru fell asleep looking at a naked picture of Ket from his profile wondering what it would be like to be with him. To feel his cool hairless body next to hers. The next morning, she woke up with a fine on her phone.

Drusilla Anne James, House Human, Fines for 3ʳᵈ day of the 13ᵗʰ week of the year 18905:

. . .

Year Assembly, holding hands with Ket, House Vo at 20:45, 21:04, 21:55, 22:19
   Fine: 50 UC per citation.

Year Assembly, kissing with Ket, House Vo at 20:45, 23:06
   Fine: 50 UC per citation.

House Human, Residential Ring Four, kissing with Ket, House Vo at 23:57
   Fine: 250 UC per citation.

Total: 550 UC
   Disputes can be made publically only.

Triple charge- underage public display of affection.

Dru looked at the numbers and felt sick. So many credits, way more credits than she even had. *What was I thinking last night?* she wondered. What was even worse was that Jane had been sent a copy of this as Head of House Human. And sure enough, she also had a message from Jane waiting for her.

"James," she sounded a bit annoyed. "I'm not sure what is going on in the Capital City? Was this really you? Do you have money to pay this or are you going to dispute it? You know they double the fine if you dispute and lose. This just isn't like you. If this was you and you don't have the money, we will find it somewhere as we are all responsible for this. Get back to me."

Dru hit reply, "Jane, I'm so sorry. I knew, but I didn't know it was going to be so expensive. I'm under the impression that Ket will pay the fines. I'll be more controlled in the future."

Dru looked at the bill again and then noticed that she was charged triple for being underage. She didn't know what to do. She went back to his message and thought it was clear he was going to pay it. She got in the shower. Afterwards when Dru was about to put on her underwear, she remembered with a smile, this was supposed to be the day she wore nothing and was 'loyal' to him. She put the underwear back and thought, *I have to report to him later about the no panties day anyway so I'll ask about the bill then.*

Ket looked at his IC and sighed. *I was reckless last night,* he thought. He simply paid their fines by facial recognition and voice confirmation from his IC, "I, Ket of House Vo, agree to pay the fines of 1,550 UC." Then he hit another button, "I, Ket of House Vo, agree to pay the fines of 550 UC for Drusilla Anne James, House Human."

"That's a lot of universal credits," his mother reflected. "I don't know if you've ever incurred so many fines in one night with one woman." Ket had had some interesting nights when he was younger and would go to Assemblies, but nothing like this had happened in about a decade.

"Apparently Drusilla didn't know that I had put a ban on her until many weeks after the fact. I think all of the humans' ICs are blocked from most news about them."

"Of course they are," his mother replied. "How welcome would they feel if they could read what people thought about them before they understood us? Before they could put it in context? And those weren't the specific fines I was referring to."

"You know exactly what they are for as you received a copy as well."

"Move slowly Ket, she needs to be approached with patience."

"Are you recommending that to me because she is human?"

"No, because I've seen her full medical exam and I've talked with her doctors in comparison with the other humans. There is something different about her."

"Yes, she is not old or ugly and she is telepathic. She's perfect."

Zol gave her son a condescending look and then without words began, *You know it is more than that. She was not raised like the rest of them. The human government has rejected any enquiries into her past. They tell us her lack of parentage, hometown, medical records are a clerical errors, yet supply no more information. Her former Captain lies for her. Her former superior lies for her. Something is not right.*

Ket nodded. He was also told the lack of information was a clerical error and although he had meant to ask her last night, with everything else, he had forgotten. He wondered then if she drove the conversation subconsciously, so he wouldn't ask. He half projected that thought to his mother.

"Yes," she said out loud. "She is far stronger than you telepathically which is why you should marry her, but also not be so accepting of everything she does or says. Had the officers on the supply ship that brought them to the Capital Planet not been protected by a the anti-telepathic forcefield on their room, their captain is certain the humans would have gained control of the ship. She can easily influence a couple men without telepathy at a time and probably you too if you are not vigilant."

I don't have the impression she is hiding anything important from us, Ket projected.

"No," his mother said and then projected, *But she definitely wants to keep something from being made obvious to the human government. The sooner she is under our protection the better.*

She is Alliance now.

Yes and no, don't be so naïve Ket. If they found, her guilty of a crime that somehow called her fleet status into question before Tir traded for her she could be extradited and replaced. When she marries you, she will have chosen to marry you of her free will and then it would be the human government against our family, and I don't think they would bother for whatever crime she committed.

I don't think she committed a crime, Ket projected.

I don't think it's a crime in the traditional sense but something humans are ashamed of and are hiding and that is why so many protect her. Whatever happened they feel it was wrong, Zol projected, the thoughts she had been chewing over for weeks. She had begun to study Earth and its culture to better understand Drusilla and the other human women. She had been disappointed to learn nothing from the official records as to why Drusilla suffered from childhood diseases, primitive surroundings and suffered rape. But she could not talk about these things with Ket, so she simply said, "Go with the gods," as she left to go to the Imperial Palace.

"May the gods keep you, Mother," he replied now replaying his whole night with Drusilla in a different light. He reviewed everything trying to remember if at any point he had felt she was leading him. *She was leading me by the swell of my penis,* he thought. And then his thoughts ran to her panties that were still in his pocket upstairs. He returned to his room and retrieved the panties. They were black, soft and smooth and smelled of her. He closed his eyes and remembered her beautiful sex beckoning to him.

He imagined how exotic it would feel to thrust inside of her, her sweet scent covering his penis and the feel of her fur, wet with her scent, against his skin. He took down his trousers and started pumping himself thinking about Drusilla. He would go to the shrine later today for this sin.

Dru went down to the dining room for her morning meal. As she walked in, seeing her, one of the slaves walked into the kitchen and then walked back out with her food, but instead of her usual human breakfast of Alliance bread with strawberry jam and chicory coffee, today she had a complete Alliance breakfast of bland porridge with small pieces of meat in it and water.

Dru looked at the slave and the slave looked at her.

"What's this?"

"Your requested morning meal," replied the slave impatiently. She couldn't eat until Drusilla was finished and if Drusilla took too long, she would not be able to eat until the midday meal. "The message was sent through Doctor Ket of House Vo."

Dru suddenly remembered and blushed.

"Some loyalty game, no doubt? The maximum class is so childish," the slave commented to no one but herself. "Eat it Drusilla. Eat it all."

Dru picked up her spoon and took a bite. Unlike the rest of humanity, people in the Exterior had never given up eating meat. As such, she had only been a vegetarian for the last four years of her life. She didn't mind the taste of meat nor the thought of eating it. Dru didn't mind the porridge although it was so bland and filling, she couldn't finish it.

"Finish it," said the slave.

"I can't."

"I have instructions that you are to finish it. Just do it. You can throw it up after," the slave suggested helpfully.

"Barbarians."

"You're the one making me play this stupid loyalty game."

Dru picked up her spoon and finished the rest of the porridge feeling ill afterwards. She did actually think about making herself vomit but didn't want to give the slave the satisfaction. She was pleased with the knowledge that this loyalty day was a normal occurrence in his class and that he was not deranged in this way.

Then she went to school and went about her day. She only remembered she wasn't wearing underwear when she sat and could feel the fabric of her dress against her naked sex or when she went to the toilet, and there was nothing to pull up and down.

By the time she was in her private study room that afternoon though, she had butterflies in her stomach with the thought of calling Ket and saying what he wanted to hear about her day of being loyal. She checked all of her other messages first, putting off the VM for as long as possible. She had received a message from Jane, "James, your fines were paid this morning by Ket of House Vo. I'm assuming everything is going well, but please don't do that again. I know I am going to sound all 'Alliance House Mother' now, but it makes us look bad. However, as you could have guessed, Captain wanted you to challenge it, so thankfully it was paid before she convinced you to fight for your right to kiss in public and promised to pay for the fines herself." Jane gave her an exasperated look that Dru reckoned had more to do with the Captain than her. "Please be more vigilant of their rules, these fines are expensive, and you know House Human is as poor as the poorest House in the Alliance can be."

Dru sighed and smiled at the thought of Captain Kara wanting her to dispute them and said out loud, "Of course she would want that." The Alliance might have gotten more than they bargained for with the Captain, she reflected.

Then she received a message from Ket.

I am waiting little tabi.

.

"What is a tabi?" she said out loud and then the computer answered her.

"A tabi is a small winged-mammal found on the north-west continent of Alliance Planet Two. Tabis live ..."

"What about as a term of endearment?" Dru interrupted the computer.

"Tabi is a term of endearment referring to a girl or woman, especially one exhibiting characteristics such as slyness, attractiveness, or playfulness. Originally used as a term of disapproval, in later use, from 8904 onwards, 'tabi' morphed into a pet name or term of endearment."

Dru smiled, then decided she would VM Ket in real time as she could see that he was available for a real time message. He answered on the second chime.

"Drusilla, my loyal one. I thought you needed a little push."

"What made you think that?"

"You have been in your study room for 45 minutes and hadn't messaged me."

"How do you know that?"

"It's registered. I can look it up if I search for you. Don't humans have this on Earth?"

"No, we like the idea of not knowing where everyone is

all the time. Using technology that way is forbidden on Earth."

"Oh," he smiled, "That's a conversation for another time. Now, tell me about your day without panties."

She blushed.

He looked directly into the camera and held up her panties which he had cut off the night before, "Were you missing a pair of these?"

"Yes," she said almost breathlessly.

"Show me that you are not wearing any today."

"No."

"Yes, you said you would be loyal to me today."

"I'm not doing that here."

"Why not? No one can see you. This is a secure channel, and no one would ever invade my privacy," he stated confidently. He would challenge them to a duel, and he had already won enough this year that he doubted anyone would risk their life angering him over something like this.

"I study here."

"I know, that's what makes it so sexy."

Dru looked at his handsome face considering. It was true no one could see her, but she remembered Jane's words about making House Human look bad. She shook her head, "If you were here I would do it, but not like this."

"Oh, how I long to see your beautiful vulva again. I've been dreaming about that red fur and your smell," he smelled her underwear in his hand again. "I'm going to lick and suck on your clitoris until you see stars. Does that make you wet with arousal imagining that? Are the top of your stockings wet now? The inside of your dress?"

There were many things that she found shocking about his statements of desire, the first which she had noticed before, that the direct translation of her anatomy was not nearly as sexy as the colloquial words for it, but she guessed she would get used to it. The second, that everything else he just said had really turned her on. She wanted to show him her pussy now. If he asked again, she would do it. "The top of my stockings and the inside of my dress are wet."

"Show me," it was a command.

Lust had taken over her and she stood up and pulled up her dress slowly. She purposely went very slowly. Once she had raised it high enough for him to get a good look at her hairy pussy, she began to put it down again.

"Stop, I want to memorize your sex. I love how your clitoris has become stiff and peaks out between your furry folds, so beautiful Drusilla." He wanted to continue. Had she been an Alliance woman he would have asked her to touch herself for him, to spread apart her sex. To lick her fingers, but he remembered his mother's advice and backed off.

She dropped her dress and then sat down at her desk, her cheeks flushed, not with embarrassment but with desire. "Was it how you remembered it?"

"Better."

"Will you ask me to do this every 4th day?"

"Yes, and more," he was trying to read her expression.

"I look forward to it," she said and then added not wanting this conversation to end and to take some of the control back, "Tonight I will touch myself wishing you could reach through the screen and be here with me now."

"No," he said.

She was not surprised by his answer and tried not to smile when she asked, "What do you mean, 'no'?"

"It's still my day. You don't touch yourself without my permission on 4th days."

"What if I do? You'll never know."

"In the future I'll know. But it's true tonight I won't. I hope that you would want to please me today as this is your day to be loyal."

"I don't know," she said coyly. "How would you punish me if I disobeyed you?"

"As I'm not there I would have to have one of my slaves come and whip you while I watched over VM. Would you enjoy that?"

"Naked?"

"Yes."

"And would that get you aroused? Watching me get whipped naked by a slave?"

"Probably, but only on the 4th day." Ket imagined her then getting whipped by a slave artist, maybe a woman, who would then bring her to climax if only she repented.

"And every other day?"

"I want you soft and tender."

"Is this normal?"

"I don't know. It's fun." He gave her a considerate look then and reminded himself to back off. "What do you think?"

"I want you to lick my pussy and then pound into me so hard I forget where I am. That's all I can really think about right now to be honest."

He smiled, "Fair enough." He didn't want to push her. He already felt he had pushed a little too far today.

"When will I see you again in person?"

"The 4th day of the 34th week."

"Several weeks away."

"You'll be of age then and the ban will be over."

"Less fines?" she commented, amused.

"Less fines," he agreed.

She wanted to thank him for paying them but knew that would be disrespectful in Alliance culture, so she said instead, "I enjoyed the actions that led to the fines. Will we do that again?"

"That and more. Now unfortunately I must go. Do not touch yourself until tomorrow. May the gods continue to shine their light on you."

"May the gods give you strength."

Dru was officially an adult today. She woke up with a smile on her face, thinking, *One more thing to cross off the list.* After she showered and put on her black dress with her jewelry, she had the mirror braid her hair and put a hair pin in it. The mirror told her, as if she were unaware, "Today you are an adult in the Alliance."

"Mirror off," she said.

Dru went to her desk and opened her messages on the computer.

She opened a message from Ket. It was written which was not like him at all. Then she realized that this was the formal release of the ban. She assumed this was probably automated as she could not imagine him writing something so cold to her.

Drusilla Anne James, House Human, the ban I put on you, 4th day of the 33rd week of the year 18904, ends today. May the gods light your path. Ket, House Vo

Dru was disappointed that that was all there was but then she reminded herself he had messaged her about a special day when he returned next week so she shouldn't be so demanding. Next, she opened a message from Captain Kara which she was surprised to see. She and the Captain had never really been close, she didn't think the Captain was close with anyone. It was also a written message,

James,

Be aware the ban Doctor Ket placed on you ends today. Tir mentioned it yesterday and said that if he was Ket he would have made them for two years and hinted that Ket can be a bit foolish about these things. The way Tir made it sound, be prepared for a lot of unsolicited atten-tion. And if you kiss your man again and are fined, dispute the fines. I will pay. I will be more than happy to pay.

K

Dru did not believe for a minute that she would have men approaching her in droves. So, she moved on to her next message from Jane.

James,

You are finally of age. I hope you are feeling confident and good about the future. Your instructors send me your grades and I am so impressed. You are doing so well in the Alliance despite everything. I know it must be difficult to be the only human. I wish you the best today. I have sent you some flowers from Frank's store, but I am not sure if you have received them already? Congratulations on all your accomplishments so far!

. . .

Jane

PS. There is, of course, some formal paperwork if you begin courting someone. Just let me know. Thanks.

Having no other messages, Dru went down to the dining room to eat breakfast and was surprised to find Dera there waiting for her.

"Good morning friend. The gods' welcome you as an adult."

Dru smiled broadly, "I will let the gods' guide my way," Dru replied in the set response. She was surprised, *But this was a very special day for Alliance people and maybe she felt sorry for me that I would be alone.* "Will you have the morning meal with me?"

Dera nodded, "I hope there is more than just vegetables here."

Dru laughed and then blushed it was a 4th day, "There is, in fact your brother would have arranged my breakfast today."

Dera gave her a look of surprise, "You two are moving quickly."

"It seemed good to try some things out first," Dru replied not wanting to discuss this with Dera. She was happy that she did not have to eat breakfast alone with one of the slaves looking at her. She was sure the slaves were pleased too. She and Dera discussed their final exams and who was doing their practical where. Dera of course was going to the Palace to train under her mother, the First Imperial Doctor.

"Thanks for coming over today," Dru said after they had finished eating.

"Of course. It's an important day, most of us have this meal with friends and since all the other humans were gone, I didn't want you to have the morning meal alone."

Then, surprisingly, one of the slaves brought out a small cake with a candle on it. Dru looked at Dera and asked, "Did you arrange this?"

"Of course, I did. Since we have become friends I have looked occasionally at human customs," she explained. "To understand some of your more eccentric behaviors," Dera smiled.

Dru was beaming, she almost began to cry. The slave set the little cake with white icing down in front of her and she closed her eyes, made a wish and blew out the candle.

"It's from the Earth Store so it should be like home."

Dru smiled as the slave cut the small cake in half and then proceeded to give each woman half. Even though the cake was small, the pieces were larger than twice the size of a regular piece of cake. Dru shrugged and then she picked up her fork and tried it. It was chocolate cake and it was delicious. "I love this so much. You're such a good friend to me."

Dera didn't want to eat the cake at all especially not the large piece in front of her. Alliance people took their health very seriously and did not eat unhealthy food ever. She looked over at Drusilla clearly enjoying this and wondered if humans had evolved differently to enjoy unhealthy food and not get fat from it.

"You don't have to eat it if you don't want to," said Dru seeing Dera's uncomfortable face.

"I want to try it. I just don't want too much," Dera said not making any kind of move to eat the cake.

"One bite will not make you overweight."

"I know. It's just that I have never tried anything like this, and I am worried about becoming addicted."

Dru just looked at her bewildered. She would have thought Dera was talking about a narcotic. "I don't know anyone addicted to chocolate. Okay, no that is a lie, Captain Kara loves chocolate and eats it every day."

"She is not fat."

"No, try the cake. You probably won't even like it."

Dera took a bite of it made a face and then spit it out, "I'm sorry. I cannot eat this." Dera couldn't help but think of all the bad things the ingredients in the cake would do to her body when it was in her mouth. She had no idea why humans would actively seek out such unhealthy food.

Dru smiled and said, "This just means there is more for me." Dru reached across the table and pulled Dera's plate in front of her. "I'll eat the rest for the evening meal."

"You're not worried about getting fat?"

Dru laughed, "No, I think that would be impossible here. Your food is too healthy, and I can't afford to eat cake every day."

"But after you marry?"

"I'll marry a poor man then." When she saw the concern on Dera's face she continued to explain because obviously Dera thought she could be a sugar addict or something. "I'm going to shock you now and tell you that on Earth, humans eat whenever they want and whatever they want. Some of us do get fat, but very few. I eat every-thing like this in moderation. I will not become fat just because I can afford to buy chocolate every day. I'm already way too thin here anyway."

"You need to eat more meat," Dera said. "I agree, you are too thin for your body shape. You looked better before, eat the cake."

"I don't disagree," she smiled at her friend, "So now, I will happily eat this cake."

When Dru finished her piece of cake and left strict

instructions she would eat the other for dinner, they walked to school. Today they had exams. Dru had studied and was confident that she would do well. She felt happy as she and Dera talked casually walking into school. This was the first day since she came to the Capital Planet that she felt like she really belonged there and had a life. That some people would miss her if she were to suddenly disappear.

Throughout the day, Dru was greeted by some of her classmates with the same set phrase Dera had used that morning, 'The gods' welcome you as an adult' and she would say the set reply. She was touched that some of her classmates remembered today was her special day. When she mentioned it to Dera at the midday meal, Dera explained, "Ket's ban on you ended today. He purposely ended them today, a bold move to set you free and the gossip columnists are going mad for it. Everyone is watching now to see who will pursue you and if Ket will also continue to show interest. Some of our classmates have recognized that you are here to stay, and they need to start taking you seriously."

"Because of a man?"

"No because you caught the attention of a man who will raise your status which will put you above them because everyone recognizes how clever you are. And you might be able to have daughters. A man would only provide you with the correct platform to propel yourself." Dera brought out her IC and brought up an article and showed it to Drusilla. Ket had told her that the humans' ICs were locked out of a lot of information.

Dru read the short article and laughed, "I'm not going to throw off your brother for a man I've only met today. And I've not met any men today and we have exams all day anyway."

"But here's the thing, there is nothing between you

and my brother now. Not until he is back on planet and formally requests it. He cannot do that when he is away, and you are surrounded by men that are here now. I think they are just biding their time; no one would be dumb enough to approach someone during exams, but trust me, they will send you things and seek you out afterwards. And, no one knows that you and Ket actually know each other quite well. All they know is that you met at the Year Assembly briefly, and no matter how romantic that was, romance can fade when someone is away and there is someone new and exciting here and now."

"Do you think Ket's romance has faded for me?"

Dera smiled, "I have never seen two people so enamored with one another. Even now when you mention his name your eyes go a bit darker." She paused, "We have this week where you can ask me anything about Ket and I will tell you. When you start courting, I won't be able to talk to you about him."

She didn't need to tell Dru twice, she jumped right in with some questions, "Has Ket courted many women?"

"Yes."

That was not the answer that Dru wanted to hear, "So he falls in love a lot?"

"I don't know. We've never talked about it." She whispered then, "Drusilla, we don't talk about love."

"Do you think he will ask me to begin courting?"

"Yes."

"Do you think he wants to marry me?"

"I think he thinks he does now."

"But he has courted many women before?"

"Yes, but I think it's different with you."

"Because I'm human?"

"No, because you surprise him like no woman has and

261

as much as he enjoys the order of the Alliance way of life, he likes your disruption of it."

"Hmm, that's not exactly comforting. Is that why we are friends?" she motioned between them, "Because I'm disruptive to you?"

"No," Dera smiled, "You're not disruptive to me. We are friends because you liked me before you knew who my family was and then you didn't act any differently when you found out. You saw me as an individual and if I hurt you, I know you won't be my friend anymore." She motioned to the rest of the women in their class, "Most of these women will always be around and the others are so nice they would let anyone walk all over them, especially me. Not you, you are real to me and I am to you. It's a true friendship which is rare."

"I don't know how else to be," Dru admitted. "I don't see this as an advantage. I see a lot of games going on here that I don't know how to play."

"Interesting that you say that, as I would say you have done surprisingly well, even though, Rez and her friends have done their best to thwart you at every turn."

Dru gave her a little smile, "I did take pleasure in knowing that she still likes Ket and was jealous that it was me he was talking to and not her. But on the other hand, I can't believe he ever courted her in the first place."

"I know, me neither. I told him, but he never listens to me. But, she's not ugly, and she comes from a good family. Don't forget though, he broke it off very quickly and has never wavered on that decision, despite her advances."

"He was courting her because of her position?"

"Yes, we don't marry for love." She said the world 'love' very quietly.

"Really?" Dru said sarcastically, "Because that is the only reason, I like your brother."

Dera wanted to tell her she was a fool, but held her tongue. Then she decided to say something she would have never said otherwise just to caution her friend into what she was getting into, whether she understood it or not would be no longer on Dera's conscious. "You know women aren't supposed to know why men duel," Drusilla nodded, "but I know that Ket has been in quite a few this last year and the one most recently it was rumored he fought one for Admiral Tir. My brother is loyal to the Empire." She was looking into Drusilla's eyes most seriously and then decided at the last minute to touch her hand and show her the memory she had overheard in her house of her brothers talking.

Dru wasn't prepared for Dera to share a memory with her. She almost threw up from the sensation of falling through the darkness, but suddenly she was there in what she supposed was their home. It was sparse and mainly made of smooth yellow stone. Dera was standing in a strangely lit hallway and then Dru realized, *Not strangely lit, this is how Alliance people see in the dark.* Then she heard the conversation between Ket and another man. Ket said, 'I fought Joux because he directly threatened Tir's plan.' Then the other man asked, 'Is this really our fight? Why can't we just deal with the demographics issue and separate the two.' Dru didn't know what the other issue could be. Ket spoke again, 'Why not do both at once? Human women don't know the difference.' Then Dera brought her out of the memory and Dru kept her eyes closed to keep herself from vomiting. When she opened them, she looked a Dera.

"I'm sorry I should have warned you. It was a quick decision."

Dru nodded, "You are telling me he is only thinking of courting and marrying me to have daughters nothing more?" Her mind was racing with this information though. She had felt something from Tir when they were removed from the Refa. *What were these men thinking and would it be better or worse for human women?* she wondered. *Alliance women had been more civil than expected to their human sisters, what could Alliance men offer them that was better for both of them?* She thought about the Contracts and the inequality of men in the Empire. *Do they want their equality? Or more?* This was a frightening thought to Dru. She didn't want to be part of a catalyst that flipped Alliance inequality from women ruling men to men ruling women. And if she were being honest to herself, she did like the way the Alliance was set up, things were easy for her even as a human.

Dera shrugged, "Possibly or something more."

"What more could I bring? Humans have nothing the Alliance doesn't have."

"Really?" asked Dera feigning ignorance. "I don't want to discuss it anymore, but as your friend, I encourage you to always keep this in the back of your mind. You have an advantage over Alliance women, Alliance men are letting their guards down with human women."

Dru looked at Dera and her seriousness, "I understand. Is that why they were given permission to serve in the Alliance fleet to spy?"

Dera shook her head affirmative but said, "No, it was to give them fulfilling careers alongside their husbands as many humans would be used to."

Dru looked at her friend seriously, she didn't like it when Alliance people did this, said one thing while blatantly indicating the opposite. She didn't know which answer the real answer was. Madame Bai told her that usually the silent answer is the real one, but on some occasions, it was the spoken answer because of people who might be watching. Dru decided that she would have to consider this later, so she said what she knew Dera wanted to hear, "My loyalty will always be to my Alliance sisters who have given me this opportunity to live my second life, my Alliance life. May the gods always be blessed."

"Thanks be to the gods' who willed it to be," Dera replied in all seriousness. They were quite for a minute and then the chimes sounded, and the midday meal was over. All of their focus was now on their examinations.

After a full day of examinations, Dru went to her private study room at the library. She had completely forgotten it was the 4th day until she received a message from Ket.

Little tabi, even though the ban has finished you still have an obligation to me today. It is the 4th day of the week.

Dru looked at her IC and smiled. She opened a VM to Ket. It couldn't be in real time, but then she closed it and decided to write something instead. She wanted to unnerve him a bit.

Ket,

Today is the 4th day of the week and I'm not wearing any panties. All day I've been taking examinations and my little pussy has been completely dry until now. I'm thinking about you touching my clit with your fingers, softly running a finger up and down almost making me come while one of the other men that has approached me today pushes his finger in and out of my vagina. And then other two men suck at my large human breasts and I come so hard with all of my Alliance men servicing me. May the gods give you strength.

Drusilla

Dru laughed as she sent the message. She got a very quick response.

Today is the day you are loyal only to me. You think only about me. I give you permission now to touch yourself thinking only about me. Now. And I want you to VM it to me. Now.

Before she could reply he sent her one of his nude portraits. She smiled thinking; *This must be the one he thinks he looks the best in.* It was him with no background standing with his hands behind his head, looking down at the ground. In this position with the position of the light, all of his muscles were beautifully highlighted and his large penis clearly on display. Dru couldn't help but wonder what it would feel like to put her fingers around his cock. How soft it would feel at first until she brought him closer to orgasm. How it would feel in her mouth and then in her pussy, *Those ridges*, she thought.

She opened a VM to Ket. She set up the camera so that he could see all of her. She stood behind her chair and said, "As you can see, I'm in my study room. I have set the room to privacy and now I will be loyal to you." She smiled slyly at the camera and then bent over and slowly began lifting her dress up from the hem, but she didn't stop when she reached her sex she kept going and lifted the dress all the way over her head. She was wearing a sexy black lace bra that covered her nipples which she knew would annoy him too and that made her smile. Then she threw the dress to the floor, only wearing her black thigh high stockings, black bra and necklaces, she put one of her feet on the chair in front of the camera, to give him a full view of her sex and began stroking the top of her thighs and around her vulva. "Do you see how excited the thought of you makes me? I'm so wet thinking about you touching my little pussy. I wonder will you be gentle or smack it? Smack me for forgetting to be loyal today?" Then she did smack herself a couple times, not hard of course but for the dramatic effect. Then she began rubbing her clit in earnest. She took her other hand and caressed her nipple through the lacy fabric of the bra. "Ket, I'm thinking only about you," she said at the same time thinking, *I'm so naughty*. But after a couple minutes of touching herself, she didn't think about anything but her orgasm to come. And it didn't take long for the wave to roll over her. Less than ten minutes. When she finished, she licked her fingers for him, "I'm looking forward to seeing you next week." Then ended the transmission without thanking the gods for anything.

Ket hadn't necessarily expected Dru to send him a VM of her masturbating, so he accidently began watching it in his office. When he saw her begin to take off her dress, he paused it and said out loud to himself, "Gods Drusilla, a little warning next time," and then closed the message. He wrote her,

Good tabi.

. . .

Then went back to work. That evening he excused himself from playing a drinking game with Zota and a new puzzle jug another officer had recently acquired to watch Drusilla's message.

Dru was late getting home. She missed the evening meal and just wanted to go to sleep. Tomorrow she had another full day of examinations. While she was getting undressed one of the slaves entered her room.

"Drusilla, there are quite a few parcels for you downstairs. You need to come and sort them out, naked or not."

Dru frowned at the slave and pulled her dress back on and then went down to the great fire room and saw at least 50 parcels mainly all black boxes. "Who are they from?" she asked the slave who was standing with her.

"Obviously men who would like to potentially court you," the slave replied condescendingly. "What do you want to do with them?"

"Is there one from Doctor Ket of House Vo?"

"Your friend brought it this morning but said we should wait to give it to you this evening. We put it aside," the slave pulled out a large purple package and gave it to her.

"Good. I'll take this one and decide what to do with the rest tomorrow." On the way back up to her room, she shook the box a little bit, it was light, and she wondered what could be in it. She got a second wind thinking about what could be inside the box.

Once in her room, she set the purple box on her desk and undid the silver clasp, inside was a beautiful blue dress and a note written in what she now knew was Ket's handwriting. She was charmed realizing that this note was probably written several weeks ago before he left the planet.

Drusilla,

As an adult now, I want you to have something nice, but as you know, men are forbidden to buy clothing except for their wives, so I had to trust Dera in this. I look forward to seeing you next week please wear this. May the gods continue to shine their light for you.

Ket

Dru pulled the dress out of the box and held it in front of her. "Room, mirror," she said, and a full-length mirror appeared in front of her. The dress was made of a finer quality than her other dresses but did not have the movement or any pattern like her formal dress for Assembly. She wondered if this could also be a day dress. She had noticed that all of her classmates had a bit nicer dresses than the ones she wore. This didn't bother her as she had been poor her entire life and was always grateful just to have something decent to wear. Before coming to the Alliance, she had allowed herself one nice dress for formal occasions, although she had never had an occasion to wear it and now it was lost with the rest of her possessions from the *Dakota. Back on Earth?* she wondered. Anyway, she looked at this beautiful dress and wondered, *Will my wardrobe be filled with more dresses like these now?* Then she couldn't resist taking hers off and putting this one on. *Yes, it feels nicer and a bit more breathable.* Her other dresses had been made with more

269

fabric to keep her warm in the lower temperatures that Alliance people preferred however, this dress was just as warm but was made of something else to keep her warm, not extra fabric so it also gave her the feeling of being more free. She loved it.

She messaged Ket directly,

The dress Dera bought is perfect.

She knew she couldn't thank him as that was impolite and she couldn't say that he had been the giver as that was forbidden. After she took the dress off, she put on her pajamas and was about to fall asleep when she received another message, it was from Ket.

There was another package for you as well. No doubt, it was lost among all the others?

She smiled. Of course, he had also sent some jewelry, maybe to test out just how many other men had sent her something now that she was an adult. She smiled and replied,

There were too many boxes I didn't even begin to go through them now as I am busy. I knew this one was from you, so it was the only one I opened. I will look for the other one tomorrow.

. . .

"And decide how to return all the other men's gifts," she said out loud to herself. Then she closed her eyes and she had another message from Ket.

Will you send me an image of you wearing what I sent in the unopened box?

She was bewildered by the question and tired, so she just responded,

Yes, good night. I have my last day of exams tomorrow.

Then she heard no more from him and fell asleep.

The next morning Dru got up and quickly washed her face, had breakfast and then went to school. It was the last day of exams. She was confident but still nervous. After an exhausting day she returned home and then remembered she needed to look through the gifts for Ket's other gift. She employed one of the slaves to help her. When it was finally found, she opened it. There was a note,

Drusilla,

Your first true Alliance gift.

Ket

. . .

She was intrigued now. *What could be more Alliance than the jewelry or the dress?* she wondered as she opened the small box. There were two identical silver dangly earrings. She said out loud, "But only married women have pierced ears."

The slave who was helping her said, "Gods Drusilla, those are not for your ears."

Dru's cheeks turned red and she remembered telling Ket she would send him an image of her wearing them. She looked down at the jewelry and then thought, *No, I just can't.* She tried not to think about her nipples being pierced most days. It was something that still made her angry. Now the doctor's words came back to her, 'Your husband will expect this.' *You really are a barbarian aren't you Ket?* she thought. Without another word to the slave she took the jewelry and went upstairs to decide what to do. She couldn't call Dera as that just seemed too strange as Ket was her brother. She could call Jane, but she knew Jane would tell her to do what she felt comfortable with and that was not the answer she needed. She needed to know what an Alliance woman would do. Dru decided that although Madame Bai was more like a mother figure, she was the best person to ask and she needed to find out about what to do with the jewelry from the other men too, she didn't want to keep it and Madame Bai would know the answer to that too.

Dru opened a real time VM to Madame Bai, she answered and was surprised, "Drusilla, is everything okay? You have your exams now and it is late to be calling."

"I'm sorry. Today was the last day of exams. I'm just calling because I have a couple of questions."

"About the examinations?"

"No, not about that. That went well, I think."

"Good, what is it then?"

"I received many unsolicited gifts the day that the ban stopped, and I became eligible for marriage. I don't want any of the gifts."

"Not even the ones from Doctor Ket?"

"No, of course I want those."

"Good, you had me scared for a minute. In regard to the others, just hire a delivery service to return them all. You know why Ket chose to end the ban on the day you became an adult, right?" She thought she better ask, it always amazed her what the humans did and did not understand about Alliance culture. She had given up weeks ago trying to predict it.

"Not fully, to be honest."

"To give you a public opportunity to find someone else and that if you do choose him, it is public that you did that of your own volition. This is two-fold, first he wanted the competition to show you are sought after and second to show the galaxy that a human woman is choosing to be with him. The Galaxy Court has issued some enquiries into the human women's galactic equality rights here in the Empire."

"And if I didn't choose Ket would the Galaxy Court let me return to Earth?"

"Probably after some time, but you are all listed as traitors to the human government after Captain Kara's trial so you couldn't return there." She looked at Drusilla seriously, "Are you so unhappy here? I believed that things were going well with school and all?"

Dru nodded her head, "Things are going well. I just want to know all my options. As you are aware, our ICs are blocked from news about humans."

"It'll be unblocked after you marry. Drusilla, forget Earth. You can't ever go back. Just continue to focus on the future. You are building a good life for yourself here. I'm

273

so impressed with all of your accomplishments. And I heard from Doctor Jina that you earned a place for your practicals at the coveted Capital City Hospital?"

"Yes," Dru felt a surge of pride, this was the first time someone had mentioned it to her this way. None of her human counterparts understood and so they didn't even comment on her achievement and she hadn't mentioned it to Ket. Dera of course had given her a backhanded compliment about it, not because Dera had wanted to be rude, it was just the way Dera was. "I've worked very hard and I'm honored to have the opportunity."

"Who would have thought?" Madame Bai was beaming at Dru. "You're really flourishing here. Don't throw it away thinking about Earth." Madame Bai stopped herself from continuing and then asked, "Is there anything else you wanted to talk about?"

Dru hesitated and then reminded herself, *This is the only other person you can trust to give you an honest Alliance answer about this.* "Yes, it's something to do with some jewelry Doctor Ket gave me."

"Yes?" said Madame Bai curiously.

"They are adornments for my ..." she trailed off hoping Madame Bai would understand but she could see on her blank face across the screen she had no idea what Dru was hinting to.

"For your?"

"Nipples," she said finally getting it out and rallying herself, *You are a doctor just say it you weirdo.*

"And? Are they ugly? Too heavy?"

"No, I don't know," Dru was flustered by Madame Bai's casual questions. Then she took a deep breath and explained, "I've not even tried them on yet. I'm just struggling because he asked me to send an image of myself wearing them."

"Okay?" Madame Bai was still waiting for the problem and then after a couple seconds of silence she said, "Drusilla, I'm so sorry. I remember now. You resisted this being done. It's in your record. This is seen as beautiful here. Ket just wants to see a beautiful part of you. This is no different than a picture of your neck with a necklace on."

"What if I don't send a picture? Would he be offended?"

"Probably not, but it would be strange not to." She looked at this young human woman and tried to think of the words that would help her. "You're meeting him next week, right?"

"Yes, he says he has something special planned."

"Don't you want him to fantasize about you between now and then?"

He is already fantasizing about me from the video I sent yesterday I am sure, she thought but didn't dare say. Instead she said, "I never thought about it."

"You should think about it and you definitely want him to fantasize about you between now and then. As much as possible. You want him to think so much about you that he can hardly decide which of his known jewelry he will bestow upon you and when and how you will begin courting."

"What is known jewelry?"

"If only you would have paid as much attention to my lessons as to your medical lessons you wouldn't have to ask me this," Madame Bai stated exasperated. "Known jewelry is jewelry that a man has publically collected since he came of age for his future wife. Doctor Ket will have this listed somewhere in his profile on his social media page. Known jewelry says a lot about the man, his expectations for a wife and his expectations for a courtship. If he gives some of his

275

known jewelry to you, he has high expectations for the relationship, as known jewelry is considerably more valuable than other jewelry."

"Oh," said Dru now concerned about Ket's known jewelry and suddenly worried about whether or not he will give her some even though she just learned about this cultural practice a second ago.

"Yes, so if you want some of the known jewelry, send a good picture of yourself with the nipple jewelry."

"How do I make the image?" she asked quickly, Dru liked to win and she wanted some known jewelry. But when she saw Madame Bai's face expression as if Dru didn't know how to take a picture she quickly clarified, "I mean should it be all of me or just my breasts," she blushed a little and then told herself, *Calm down, this is not a big deal, stop being a prude. Be cool. Be Alliance.*

"Do it how you like. I would suggest low lighting and obviously not laying down. You've seen pictures of naked women before?" Madame Bai didn't know if humans had such pictures.

"Yes, I just never thought of taking one of myself."

"Maybe you could ask one of the slaves to help you?" Madame Bai suggested.

"No," Dru replied quickly. "I'm sure I'll figure it out."

"Good night then and good luck on the picture. Let's talk again next week."

Dru ended the call and then took off her dress. She looked at her nipples and the bars going through them. She gently took out one and expected it to hurt a lot, but it didn't. Then she took the jewelry out from the box and put it in the vacant piercing, she felt some pressure but not real pain. Then she brought up the mirror and looked at herself and said out loud, "Well, that looks anything but sexy." Her breasts were not small and taunt like Alliance women's breasts. Hers were full, but firm. She took out the other bar and replaced it with the matching nipple jewelry then looked at her reflection again. "I'll never understand their aesthetics." She looked at herself and tried to understand how this could be beautiful. She then decided to take off the rest of her dress wondering if that would help, which she thought it did a little. Then put on her black lace underwear, as she thought this looked better, and had the mirror take an image of her from the neck down. She looked at it and it looked terrible. *Think, there must be a better way. Sexy is not always wanton nudity.*

Dru then brought some of her long red hair forward and so it hung seductively next to her breasts, framing them and had the mirror take the picture from only neck to belly button. This was better she thought. Then she remembered Madame Bai's words, 'You want him to fantasize about you all week.' Then she thought about some of the most famous nude pictures she had seen and decided that she should look as she felt about this. So, she had the mirror take an image of her whole body, she stood against the blank wall. She put on the dress he had given her and pulled up the fabric quite dramatically and held it with her right hand at her lower hips so that her full torso was exposed. Then, she turned her head to the side and somewhat down, as if embarrassed, which was not difficult to show, as she was embarrassed. Finally, she put her left hand under her chin to emphasize the embarrassment and then she had her mirror capture the image. When she looked at it now, she was pleased, but then she made it even better by taking the picture again but with the lights dimmed. When it was exactly how she wanted it, she just sent it to him with no message.

. . .

Ket received Drusilla's image with the nipple jewelry and knew it was going to be a very long week. Already he had slept with his usual slave artist twice after seeing her pleasure herself in her private study room, but this was in some ways even better. This was her personal submission to him and the Alliance. Ket knew from Tir that human women didn't send images of themselves around casually and that Captain Kara had punished him for sending unsolicited pictures of his penis to her and that she refused to ever send anything to him. So Ket knew that Drusilla was giving him so much more with this image. He was relieved, proud and aroused all at the same time. He replied to her message,

I will have trouble sleeping this week. Your beauty speaks to my most primal urges.

Then Ket called for a slave artist to come to his quarters. He decided at the last minute for it not to be his usual slave artist. Ever since he met Drusilla in person, his regular just did not satisfy him the way she used to. He had had her twice yesterday and her body had done nothing to satisfy the lust he felt for Drusilla. She just didn't seem to understand how he wanted her to behave. He remembered Admiral Ver mentioning a new slave artist they had just taken onboard, Pera, she was older apparently but highly skilled and reassuringly expensive. Neither her age nor the expense bothered Ket. He was the kind of man who liked women who knew what they were doing and that usually came with experience. He summoned her to his quarters and then waited. As he waited, looking at the image Drusilla had sent, he reflected, *Gods, we are not even courting yet. It is going to be a very long year.*

Pera was surprised to be summoned to Doctor Ket's quarters. She knew that he had his regular and rumor had it, he was the kind of man who never strayed when he found something he liked. Pera gave his usual a shrug as she passed her in the common area of the slave artists' area of the ship and said, "Maybe his human began courting someone else today now that she is of age and the ban is finished. It could just be, he needs something completely different." Pera was trying to be sympathetic. She had been there, thinking you have a man in a high position and he will make you enough universal credits that you will be able to return to the Alliance on your own terms, but then it all comes crashing down the moment he requests someone else for no apparent reason. Pera suspected this reason had everything to do with what was happening on the Capital Planet though. It was no secret onboard that Doctor Ket had put the ban on the red-haired human, slave artists were above a lot of the laws of the Contracts that preserved the equality between the sexes. Pera was intrigued as to what Doctor Ket would request. *What does a man who seemed until last year, the last man who would ever stray from an Alliance woman, who has most actively pursued the most exotic of humans want from sex?* she wondered. This had been a question on many of the slave artists minds ever since the human women were granted Alliance citizenship. And there had been many rumors, Sera, had even become a regular with Captain Kara, but she wasn't giving away any secrets, nothing that could be directly traced back to her anyway.

Ket ushered Pera in, even though she was older than

he was, she was beautiful and as he watched her walk in, her green dress flowing behind her, he knew there was something special about her. He sat down and she went to go pour drinks. She looked at him and asked, "Wine Doctor?"

"No, but help yourself."

"I don't like to drink alone," she said and sat down across from him. Pera could see that he did not want to talk, or any ancient myths recited. She just reached out her hand to his and caressed him. He welcomed the touch. She saw the image of the human in his mind and knew then exactly what he wanted. This is what made her such a successful slave artist. She could read the minds of her clients: But she had to be careful with Doctor Ket as he would feel her doing it if she were too forceful.

Pera took Ket's hands and ran them over her small breasts so that he could feel the nipple jewelry under her clothing. He closed his eyes and she thought to herself, *There is something very meaningful about this for you today.*

Soon she was leading that same hand into his bedroom, she undressed him and he her, wordlessly. She could tell he wanted to imagine he was with his human, so there would be no words between them. This was just for the sex. Pera did not mind, Ket was very attractive and a good lover, she was a bit amused he spent a lot of time sucking and moving her nipple piercings back and forward. After they had finished, Pera quietly got her things and left, she said nothing to him to preserve his fantasy.

Ket watched Pera leave and was still not fully relieved. All he could think about was the image that Drusilla had sent to him. He opened his communicator and looked at it again. *No, nothing will sate this until I have her,* he thought and then went to sleep after transferring 500 UC to Pera. His Admiral was correct, she was good. He was so relieved she knew what he had wanted without words, but unfortunately, it still wasn't enough.

After her final examinations were complete, Dru immersed herself in her Capital City Hospital Handbook for Practical Students. Her practical, as they colloquially called it, would last for the next year and if she passed, there were no grades, just pass or fail, she would be an Alliance doctor. She had also found out that in the Alliance, where you did your practicals was usually where you ended up working as well. This pleased Dru as she didn't want to move from the Capital City. She had begun to think of it as her home. And even though you could be anywhere on the planet in minutes, she liked the idea of living close to where she worked, as most Alliance people did as well.

The Capital City Hospital was run differently than a human hospital as there was a lot to do with both rank of the patients and the doctors. In addition, people had to pay to use the hospital, which was unusual for her, not that she would be accepting anyone's money, but on Earth medical care was free and doctors were adequately provided for by the government. In the Alliance she would be making a salary that would increase with her experience and would triple if she married Ket just by ranking alone. Dru felt the system was unfair but not so unfair that she wouldn't take the position if offered to her.

And she would be happy for the money too. From the 250 UC that were initially given to her she only had 75 UC left. Of course, the Empire gave her 5 credits every month, but she would be happy when she was making a real salary and didn't have to cringe every time, she bought something. Frank at the Earth Store had told her he would offer her credit, but she didn't want to do that. Nor did she want to ask Ket for universal credits just because she wanted some comforts from home. Unfortunately, having little money also meant that she couldn't readily socialize with people who asked her to join them for tea at the popular tea houses, breakfasts or cocktails, but she rationalized all this by telling herself it was just more time to study.

She exchanged messages with Ket frequently and always on the 4th day. He would constantly ask her to show him her breasts in a VM and that was the one thing she wouldn't do as she wanted to save something for later. That would be new the first time they were actually together. Ket didn't agree with that at all and he thought it would make it even better when it was real. She also refused to send him another image with another set of nipple jewelry he had send to her. She felt that if she took another, she would detract from what he enjoyed so much about the first image. She was, of course, very pleased that he was so enamored with the first one. And of course, she was doing this all because she still had her heart set on some of his known jewelry. She didn't know why but it had become a mini obsession. In between reading the handbook for the hospital and following her old crewmates, now on the *Zuin*, on social media, she had casually looked through Ket's known jewelry on his social media page more than a couple times. She even berated herself, *Calm down, he hasn't even asked you to begin courting.* But she couldn't stop herself from singling out a couple favorite pieces from his known collection. She had also researched other men's known collections for comparison. And she began to believe that you really could tell if you were a good match by what the man had already chosen. Most of Ket's pieces were understated for maximum class but were subtly intricate or portrayed allusions to the Alliance's religious myths. Two of his pieces, that she noted, were bought after he put the ban on her, alluded to the Lost People myth.

The day that Ket was back had finally arrived. She knew he was on planet and probably in the Capital City because when she put on her location ring, the moving clouds inside turned a reddish color. She was so excited she put on the beautiful blue dress he had bought her for her coming of age present and all the jewelry he had gotten her except for the nipple jewelry as she didn't think it would feel right with her bra. And then went down to eat breakfast.

She had to eat what Ket had ordered, which surprisingly wasn't very much at all this morning. She questioned the slave about it.

"You are the one playing this game not me. He was very specific about the portion size today. Maybe he thinks you are overweight?"

"Do you think I'm overweight?"

The slave shook her head but said, "We all think you are overweight."

Dru resisted slapping her but instead said, "I feel sorry for you that you will never know the pleasure of a real human man, his sweaty chest hair rubbing up against your naked body."

That was enough to make the slave run for the toilet to vomit.

Dru smiled to herself and waited for her to return.

When she returned, Dru took a long time to eat the small portion of porridge. Long enough that the slave would have no chance to eat her own breakfast. Then she left the building and almost skipped on her way to meet Ket.

In the week prior, she had purposely avoided going to the large Promenade Ring, now lined with blossoming tress, on the outskirts of the Imperial Ring of the city so that the first time she would be seeing the blossoms would be with him. She arrived early to the South Gate where they were meeting. She enjoyed the excitement of the people around her and her own excitement at seeing Ket.

Dru looked up at the beauty of the blossoms on the tree directly above her. The blossoms signaled the warmer months were well on their way and this was a natural time for a short holiday for everyone. Most schools broke now, and many people took time off work to see friends and family. There were no set days for the blossoms as they bloomed at slightly different times every year.

Ket was happy to see Drusilla already waiting for him as he approached the gate to the Promenade. She had her hair braided which he was thankful for as if it were down all he would think about was the topless image she sent, and he would not be able to focus. As he approached, she didn't see him, as she was looking up at some falling dark purple petals in the breeze. "Drusilla," he said softly.

She jumped slightly, "Ket," she said excitedly and then said the accepted phrase she was supposed to say on their first and only meeting they could have without courting. "Today we will make a decision, let the gods guide us."

"Let the hours be blessed," he replied in the set response. "It's good to see you. I've thought about you a lot." He wanted to touch her cheek that had some pink to it but resisted thinking about all the fines he incurred the last time they were together.

Dru could see the desire in his eyes and thought, *I'm sure you have after the image I sent. Madame Bai, you were right, he has been thinking about me all week.* "I'm excited about today. I've avoided the Promenade so I could experience this for the first time with you."

Ket felt touched by this, "Let's not wait any longer

284

then," he motioned for them to join the other pedestrians and begin their walk around the ring. If they walked the whole ring it would take three and a half hours, but he had arranged for something quite special just over halfway through the ring. After a couple minutes of walking in silence, he commented, "You must feel satisfied now that you only have your practical left."

"Yes, I 'm just nervous about a whole new group of people who need to get used to interacting with a human."

"It's not that bad, is it?" He knew that Rez was a terror, but he assumed most other women would be decent.

Dru gave him a look, "Ket don't ruin this day by pretending to be ignorant of at least half your population's disdain for the human women who came here, and by half, I mean Alliance women, who I solely work with."

"Drusilla," he stopped walking and looked into her beautiful green eyes, he touched her cheek and she slightly leaned into his hand. The sensation was so sensual he almost forgot what he was going to say, "I believe there is only a small number of people who are still racist against humans now and least of all you. I know Rez and her ilk are still around and will cause trouble, but I would like to believe that most of us see you as our saviors."

She didn't want to speak she just wanted him to keep touching her and touch her everywhere. When he drew away his hand, she felt an ache to reach out to him. She had never had this strong connection with anyone, and she wondered if it was because he had been the only one who had touched her since she arrived on the Capital Planet or if this is what love really felt like. "Show me now that I am your savior," she said in what she hoped was a tantalizing way to lift the mood and as a way to say, *Forget these blossoms let's go somewhere private.*

He smiled, "Don't tempt me now. We are not even courting yet."

"We can be, just ask. Right now. I want to touch you."

"Don't rush me. I have things planned out," he said seriously. "You must be patient little tabi."

Dru smiled. He is such an Alliance man, *They plan to the end of their days*, she thought. "What have you planned?"

"You didn't try to figure it out when you knew where we were meeting?"

She felt foolish then that she hadn't. She had been doing nothing the past two days except thinking about his kisses. "No, I didn't want to ruin the surprise."

"You're a terrible liar."

"I know. It didn't occur to me to try and figure it out. I trust you."

He was charmed by that. Every Alliance woman would have had figured out multiple different scenarios for what he had planned and how they would react. This was refreshing, "We are going to the sky bath house, so we can sit and enjoy the blossoms in the warm water with wine."

"Without clothing?"

"What other way would there be?"

"Humans invented these things called swimsuits for going in the water in public places."

"Ah," he said, "It's because you have fur on your bodies. It can get places if not contained. Don't worry, I've booked a private bath and I don't mind if your fur touches me."

"I'm glad my fur doesn't bother you," she said because she couldn't think of anything else to say.

"The bathhouse is one of my favorite places this time of year and today is a beautiful day for it." The sun was shining, and the sky was dark blue with a few white cumulus clouds. "You cannot see them, but there are

286

floating tubs above us in this area of the park. They are camouflaged for privacy and muted for sound."

Dru looked up. She only saw the tops of the trees, runaway purple blossoms floating randomly through the air and the dark blue sky.

After walking for another hour, they walked into the bathhouse lobby. The building itself only appeared to be one floor, but it actually had an elevator up to floors beginning with fifty. Dru summarized the top floors of the building must also be camouflaged. From there, were glass rooms with large balconies. Each balcony had a small private infinity pool overlooking the park with glass bottoms to see clear down to the ground. The infinity pools separated from the balcony so that bathers could float above the pedestrian ring and take in the blossoms from above.

When they entered their room, there were already a few female waitstaff waiting there to serve them, all slaves judging by their hair cuts.

Dru walked in and was overcome with her gorgeous surroundings. The room itself was mainly mirrors that reflected their private pool and then the top of the blooming purple trees, the park and both the Imperial Palace and Capital City were visible as well. "I've never seen anything like this. It's breathtaking."

"Good," he said and then motioned to one of the women waiting to take her clothing, "She will help you undress."

Dru looked at the woman and then said to Ket seductively, "I'd rather you help me take these things off. I'm embarrassed by my fur." She didn't know what came over her to say such a thing to him, but she didn't regret it as she saw desire flicker in his eyes when she mentioned her 'fur'.

Ket just looked at her for a second, in shock, and then immediately dismissed all the staff with a wave of his hand. He walked directly over to her, took her in his arms and kissed her quite passionately. It felt so good to see her, smell her, hold her and yes, kiss her. He didn't care about the fines. He needed this and by her reaction she needed it too. They kissed for many minutes before he let go and said in her ear so softly, "I've missed you. I've missed this. Your sexy hot tongue in my mouth."

"That tongue can go anywhere you want. Today, I'm loyal to you."

He grabbed her bottom, a hand on each cheek and pulled her against him. Her curvy body felt so good against his and he wanted nothing more than to have sex with her right now, but he couldn't do that. After more than a few minutes of grinding and kissing, he put her back down and took a step back.

She protested when he moved away.

"Don't tempt me Drusilla."

She smiled slyly at him, "Are you going to ask me to begin courting now?"

"You're rushing. I've this planned."

"I've no choice but to wait. Help me undress then." She undid her coat, took it off and handed it to him. He took it and hung it up in a small wardrobe that was only a meter away from where she was standing. One wall was all mirrors and she enjoyed watching him walk to the wardrobe and hang up her coat. Before she could take off her dress, he came up behind her, pressing his whole body against hers and ran his hands down the length of her torso and hips. "Are we really going to do this and not have sex?" she asked in a whisper. She could feel his hard cock pressed up against her back. She wanted nothing more than to turn around and take it out of his trousers and greet it with a kiss.

He whispered in her ear, "We can't."

His breath on her ear sent shivers down her body. "Oh," she said, not wanting to move and not quite believing him. She hoped this was another case of an Alliance person saying one thing but completely doing another.

Ket dropped to his knees then, running his hands heavily down her body while he did so. When he reached the hem of her dress, he began slowly lifting it up touching her stocking clad legs as he went, the naked curve of her hips and the side of her breasts which he forgot would be covered with more material. She automatically lifted her arms and he pulled the dress over her head gently and then moved to hang it up.

Dru stood there in her bra, stockings and shoes looking in the reflection of the mirror at Ket but also out the large floor to ceiling window onto the beautiful landscape below. She could see the Imperial Palace just beyond the Promenade lined with the blossoming trees. And she could not help but think, *My life is so beautiful right now.*

Ket returned to her body after hanging up her dress and gently removed her shoes and put them in the wardrobe. He returned again and knelt before her, removing her hands from covering her sex, "No little tabi. You're loyal to me today. Show me your fur."

She moved her hands to her sides watching his movements in the mirror.

He took his finger and ran it along her labia and asked, "Do you want me to touch you here?"

"Yes."

"With my finger or tongue?"

"Either."

He did neither but put a finger inside her vagina.

Dru was unprepared for his quick movement and gasped at the sensation.

"So wet already. Let's get you naked before your reward. Be patient." Then he stood behind her and ran his hand up and down her back for some minutes, just watching her enjoy his touch. He then ran his fingers back and forth under her bra straps, kissed her shoulders lightly and whispered in her other ear, "What's this human contraption that is keeping me from viewing what is mine today?"

She smiled, "A bra." She answered him softly while holding his head against the side of her face, inhaling the nearness of him. He smelled of petrichor and something she couldn't' identify, but it must have been an aphrodisiac because she had never wanted anyone as much as she wanted him right now. His cool strong hands were still running up and down her bra straps, tantalizing her. She could feel his erection through his clothing against her back and she for the first time in her life was only thinking about what it would be like to be with him.

He kissed her neck and caressed the side of her breasts through the fabric. Then he moved in front of her to properly kiss her. As he kissed her, he ran his hands along the entire length of her bra working out how to remove it. In the end, he took out his sword and cut it. She thought with a smile, *He loves to use his sword for human undergarments apparently.* Then he gently slid it off her and took it to the wardrobe with her other things.

As he walked back, she was covering her breasts and he was reminded of the picture. He stood in front of her again and put his hands on her shoulders and then ran them down lightly to her wrists that were next to her body, holding herself, omitting his gaze from her breasts. He pulled her wrists back slowly to reveal her perfect large breasts. She was, disappointingly, not wearing the jewelry he got her, but he thought that was probably a good thing because if she had been, he didn't know if he would have been able to control himself. He looked her in the eyes and couldn't read her expression, there was desire there and something else. He reached out with his mind, but she didn't let him in. He didn't try again, not yet. Without speaking he put his mouth on one of her nipples and began to suck gently moving the piercing back and forth expertly with his tongue. He reached out to her again with his mind, *This is why we like them, beautiful and pleasurable.*

Dru watched Ket suck on her naked breast in the mirror while he held her arms out. His long hair was kept back in an intricate braid as he sometimes wore it down his back. She wondered how it would feel to have sex with a strong grey alien. He was giving her so much pleasure by just sucking and tugging at her breasts she decided she would let him do anything. No, she wanted him to do anything. His mouth felt so good on her nipples she was sure she was going to orgasm just from him touching and sucking them. She thought, *What irony that I fought against these piercings.* She squeezed her thighs together. Her pussy was practically melting with his touch and she wondered again if they were going to have sex because for her it was slowly becoming a necessity. She knew she was projecting her thoughts to him intermittently because she couldn't help herself, this was so intense. She had never felt like this before and she wanted it all.

Ket pulled away reluctantly and let his hands trace her arms back down the side of her breasts her hips and then to the top of her vulva. He ran his fingers through her red fur there and said casually, "Will you allow me to lick you here now?"

"I thought it was your day?" she smiled.

He had forgotten, *Oh gods yes*, he thought.

But Ket surprised her then by moving further down to her stocking clad feet. And he began kissing and licking his way up to her inner thighs where they were fastened. When he arrived there, he licked all around the top of her thighs making her shudder. His hands cupped her rear so she couldn't move away, and he began kissing around her vulva and licking, "You taste so good. I want to make you come so hard," but then he abandoned her again and began slowly pulling her stockings down while on his knees before her.

She watched him in the mirror and thought, *And then please come back.*

When he returned, she was completely naked, and he gently parted her legs again and kissed the top of her thighs where he could taste some of her wetness, *You are so delicious*, projected. He placed his hands back on her bottom, a hand on each cheek, to steady her and then began to pleasure her in earnest. His tongue was working on intervals of lapping at her clitoris like a fast breeze blowing through a fan intermixed with long steady strokes from her vagina to the top of her vulva. After a few minutes he put two of his fingers inside of her, slowly pumping in and out and said, "Today is your day to be loyal, come for me now little tabi." She loved it when he called her that and had noticed it was only on her days to be loyal to him which made it even better.

She came so hard and fast she didn't know what to do with herself afterwards. He was still patiently stroking her aftershocks. It was the first time she had ever orgasmed from a real person touching her and it felt so different. She was almost emotional about it, but she quickly pulled herself together thinking, *If I cry, he might not ever do that again and I want him to do it again and again and again. I'll cry later at home.*

Ket looked up at Drusilla, "Good tabi." He knew that he should take it very slowly with her now. He hadn't even intended for it to go as far as it did, but when she invited him to remove her clothing, he couldn't help himself. *I must control myself now. She might have never been with a man before.* Then he got to his feet and began removing his clothing, but Dru took over.

She began undressing him slowly, with kisses and being just as attentive as he had been with her. When she removed his shirt, she was surprised to see how muscular he really was. She thought privately to herself, *The pictures are really no comparison for the real thing.* She ran her mouth all over his chest and when she got to where there should have been a happy trail to open his trousers, he stopped her momentarily, "Do not put your mouth anywhere near my genitals today." It was a command and she smiled up at him.

"I promise," she said and assumed it must be a 4th day thing. She moved her head away and let her hands run down the length of his thighs and then back up to feel his erect penis. She even could feel the Alliance characteristic ridges through his trousers and thought, *Those ridges. I want to feel those ridges though.* Then she unclasped his trousers and pulled them down. She almost began kissing him again but then drew away at the last minute and used her hands to caress him. She looked up at his large erect penis and telepathically asked or begged, *Please... are we not going to do this today?*

He took a sharp breath, "No. Stop asking." Ket thought if she asked one more time, he would not be able to say 'no' and then it would all be up to the gods whether they would face the shame of a child born out of wedlock.

He couldn't have that, not for either of them. If things became too much, he would say that out loud to bring it all back, *There was nothing more unromantic than mentioning dire consequences in the heat of the moment was there?*

Little did he know, Dru would not have cared. No one had ever touched her like he did, and she was absolutely sure making love to him would be one of the most amazing experiences of her life. She wanted that more than the risk of getting pregnant. She wanted to be so close to him she couldn't even put it into words, but she didn't have to. She was projecting everything.

"I understand Drusilla," he brought her to her feet and took her into his strong embrace, their naked bodies against one another, "But we cannot risk this. We don't have to wait too long."

She was disappointed, but then smiled into his chest and asked, "Are we courting now?"

He laughed, "You know we aren't." He just held her then for countless minutes. After what she had projected to him, he realized that more than anything right now she needed to be held by him. He wished he would have realized before they were both naked though as he wanted nothing more than to plunge his cock into her incredibly tight hot folds that were dripping with her sweet human wetness. When he could stand it no longer, he took her hand and led her out to the infinity pool, "I don't want to spend all of our time in the changing area, come on, this is my favorite thing to do at my favorite time of year and you are my favorite person."

"Right now?" she questioned playfully.

"It's no secret that I have courted women before you," he said seriously. "But in all your research, you should also know that I never put a ban on anyone before, nor have any of those courtships lasted longer than six months." He came to the edge of the pool and put his hands on both of her cheeks and kissed her chastely, then his face only centimeters away from hers, "But I've never taken a woman here before and I've never cared about anyone the way I care for you. Even if we don't marry, I'll always look out for you Drusilla Anne James from Earth." He let go and backed away further not breaking eye contact and put one finger over his heart.

Dru couldn't speak because she wanted him so much. *I don't even care if these are playboy lies, I want him,* she thought. And she wanted to tell him the forbidden, to break a compromise in the Contracts. She wanted to tell him that the chance of her getting pregnant at this stage in her cycle was about nil. But it was one of the oldest and most revered compromises of the Contracts so she knew if it backfired, it would not only mean they wouldn't be having sex, but maybe that he would never see her again. Ket was a religious man and followed some aspects of the Contracts, as far as she could tell, quite closely.

When Ket realized she wasn't going to reply, he went back into the dressing room before returning again a second later to ask, "You can swim right?"

Dru laughed, "The water is only up to here," she said with the water up to her chin as she stood at the deepest part of the pool.

He gave her a smile then went back into the dressing room. When he emerged, he carried with him a bottle of wine and too champagne glasses.

"Are those from Earth?"

"Yes, I heard that human women like this drink over wine."

Dru didn't know what to think of that comment. She liked champagne and wine equally depending on the situation but then was she really going to tell him not to buy her champagne? No, this might be the last time she ever had champagne as it was so expensive. So, she let that slide. "I'm excited that you brought champagne. Are we celebrating our courtship?"

"Drusilla, we are celebrating a lot of things and no we are not courting yet. If you keep asking, I'll leave it longer."

"Do you always know the women you ask to court will say 'yes'?"

"I know you will and that's all that matters to me now."

"You have this advantage; I've not talked to any other men."

"Last week you had the opportunity."

"Oh, those men," she said. "Maybe I want to see one of them."

"Drusilla, I know you didn't even meet another man last week."

"How do you know that?"

"Every public place is monitored."

"You are such a stalker."

"No, I wanted to know my competition if there was any."

"What if I've been sending messages back and forth with someone who gave me a gift on the day I came of age?"

"True, you could have done that, but I know you returned all the gifts, so that would be unlikely."

"How do you know that?"

He laughed at her then, "You told me."

She smiled, "I did." A minute passed as she watched him arrange the glasses and figure out how to open the champagne. She was charmed by the serious concentration he had while opening the bottle and even more so when he jumped a bit by the popping sound. "Just so you know, it's going to be terribly difficult for me to control myself, sitting naked in a pool with you in such a beautiful environment drinking champagne. I'm going to keep asking you about the courting, just to keep my hands from roaming."

"Thankfully one of your hands will be holding this glass," he handed her a glass and then entered the pool. He pressed some buttons and then they began their course above the blooming trees and the Promenade. It was spectacular.

"This is the best day of my life," Dru said. "It is so gorgeous up here. It's difficult to believe that this patch of nature is the center of one of the largest metropolises in the galaxy."

"I never thought of it like that, this is just home to me." He looked at her thoughtfully, "And I hope it is beginning to feel like that for you too?"

"A bit," she admitted and then wanted to know more about him, "Have you always lived here? I mean when you are not off-planet."

"Yes, my family has lived here for countless generations. We have been a part of the Imperial Medical family for as long as anyone can remember."

"And you always marry other doctors?"

"Yes, otherwise the telepathy might be lost, it's a recessive gene, and you cannot be a doctor if you cannot read someone's mind. It's less important in modern times as we can rely on technology to tell us everything, but in the past when we did not have technology to reach into someone body with technology, to be able to understand their suffering as a doctor was essential."

Dru thought about the history of medicine on Earth, all the twists and turns it took and concluded it would have probably been better for most of the patients if doctors would have been telepathic. She frowned then because she didn't want to talk about this, she wanted to get to know him better. "And out of all the places you have seen in the fleet would you still choose to live here?"

He laughed at her, "Oh my little tabi, tell me, what other planets have you visited besides Earth and the Capital Planet?"

"None," she admitted.

"You don't know how uncivilized the rest of the galaxy is. Images and videos don't show the realities of other places. The Alliance Empire is the light that shines through the galaxy bringing order to the chaos. The Alliance Capital Planet, our Capital City is the brightest of them all. I would never want to be anywhere else. When I'm away I miss it. It's warmth it's sophistication. It's sky. It's a genetical reaction, we're all coded to connect to our home planets." He took in her countenance and then said, "You will feel it too. Humans were never meant to be on Earth. It was a mistake."

"A mistake by the gods?"

"Could be?" he mused. "Or an ancient ship that became marooned and passed into myth."

"What do you believe?"

"I believe you're the Lost People."

"By the gods or chance?"

"Does it matter?"

"It matters to me," Dru said. She wanted to have a measure of his religious beliefs.

"By the gods," he answered.

Snap, she thought, *religious fanatical. Come on there were some warning signs*, she reminded herself.

"But of course, the gods that control all of our destinies. There are records of countless ships being marooned around the galaxy from ancient times. One in what would have probably been your solar system if we would have had more accurate maps," he added.

Not fanatical then, good, she thought. "It's strange though we don't have any records of it though."

"But you do. We have studied humans for a long time," he didn't add, 'longer than you know and helped more than you know.' "Many of your ancient religions are similar to ours. Some of your most powerful empires were based on our same social structure, but you became lost and confused. Obsessed with your own beauty and easily distracted."

"Is that all you think of humans then, that we are lost and obsessed with our own beauty?"

"Now that I know you, I know that there is so much more to humans, but you know how most of the galaxy views humanity, it's no secret. Voted best party planet every year by the Galaxy Court."

"I wish they didn't have those silly categories. Who makes those things up anyway?"

"Mostly Alliance and Kuiu representatives, I imagine, as we hold the most seats."

"It was a rhetorical question," she sighed. "Well, I'm not going to change my species' reputation, so I'd rather not talk about it. I want to know about you." Although they often sent VMs back and forth, this was different. It was so real, and she wanted to push him, to ask him very personal questions and really get to know him.

"Ask me anything," he said openly. He could feel her brimming with curiosity. Her eyes shown with it.

"Have you ever been in a duel?"

He frowned, "On occasion." He didn't want to answer her honestly as women were not supposed to know about men's duels and vice versa. Also, because he knew that humans had a much greater appreciation for life and viewed the Alliance way of solving personal disputes as 'savagery', or that is what Captain Kara had called it according to Tir.

Dru knew he was lying. She could sense it, "Over what?"

"These things are extremely private and not for women's ears, you know?"

"I don't know. I have a cultural handbook, but it doesn't cover everything. Madame Bai, my Alliance mentor, said that somethings would have to be covered on a when-and-if-basis as there just wasn't enough time to explain it all."

He nodded placated, "You shouldn't ask people about duels or the reasons behind them. If the person is standing in front of you, they won and someone else died." He answered her as he would a child.

She drank some of her champagne then and thought, *How many people has he killed with his sword and over what? Petty disputes? He didn't seem like a rash man. How could she find out how many people he had killed in duels?*

Ket couldn't help but overhear her thoughts, "You are projecting. I understand that as a human you find our justice system violent. However, let me reassure you I'm not someone who enters into duels rashly nor do I end a life without beyond reasonable doubt they have committed the crime."

"How many?"

"You'll know that answer if we marry."

"What do you mean?"

"In, what will be our home, there is a storage room where all the losers' swords from the duels are kept. You can count them then."

Dru just looked at him in disbelief, *How could he be a doctor and a murderer?*

300

Not a murderer, he answered back telepathically. *Calm yourself Drusilla.*

"I've never killed anyone; I don't think I could."

"If they were going to kill you, I think you could. You don't give up easily." She had suffered childhood illness, poverty, a war, abduction and now being reshaped into an Alliance woman and most importantly his future wife. *I must be patient with her and teach her our ways though,* he reminded himself, *I must try to be softer.*

"Maybe, I just couldn't imagine it."

"It didn't cross your mind when you were first taken prisoner? To kill the guards."

"That was war."

"Ours is justice. The societal thinking is just as applicable."

She looked at him and decided that this was something that they would just have to disagree about, and she hoped to the gods and all her human spirit helpers wherever they were, that she didn't ever have to fight a duel.

"Tell me more about your childhood," he requested. He wanted to ask her this in person not over a VM because he knew from their last conversation her childhood had not been an easy one.

Dru frowned, "Grim. But it is over."

Ket was stunned by her reply. Family was important in the Alliance. "Do you mind if I ask what made it so terrible?"

"Is it so important? I'll never see them again."

"Are they dead?"

"No, but they might as well be. They'll never come to the Alliance."

"I'm asking this Drusilla because I want to know what makes you, you." He noticed her blank look and then he added, "Every woman I've courted before I've known her

301

and her family since birth. You are a mystery to me and as a human I can't even begin to imagine your childhood, what has shaped you."

She wanted to ask, 'And do I scare you?' but she resisted and replied instead, "I'm here before you. I don't want you to think any less of me."

"I can only applaud your strength at being here. I'm not immune to my privilege in the galaxy as both being born into a high House or being an Alliance citizen. Please. Show me some memories so I might put you in context." *And find out where you are really from,* he thought.

Dru did not want to share any old memories with him. Even humans were appalled by the way people in the Exterior lived. "Once I show you, you can't unsee it and I don't like to think of it myself, let alone give some of these memories to someone else."

"Drusilla," he moved over to stroke her cheek. "I promise you that it won't change how I feel about you. Whatever happened was a long time ago. Please, I want to understand you better."

She looked into his grey eyes searching. She knew he was telling the truth and she was on the verge of doing it, but she wanted something in return. "I'll do it for exchange for one of your memories of a duel."

He was shocked. He whispered in her ear, "It is forbidden."

She put her hands on his neck and drew him in for a kiss and then whispered a reply in his ear so lightly he could hardly hear it, "That is the price."

He leaned back and looked into her eyes seriously for some time before nodding. Then he took her in his arms and placed her on his lap. He stroked her hair as he shared the memory of his last duel.

Dru had the sensation of falling again, falling into

Ket's mind. She was more prepared for it now that she had done this before. When she arrived in the memory, she felt a strong surge of adrenaline mixed with fear. She was in the center of a large ring. There were men cheering all around. In front of her was a naked man with a sword and he was bloody. Blood was covering his face and his body. They had been at this for a long time. She took in her own body, Ket's body, and she was bloody too. Blood was dripping from her wrist, no Ket's wrist. It was serious. He needed to end this duel, or he would bleed out from all of his small wounds. Suddenly, he lunged at the other man, moving faster than she could keep track of, finally issuing the killing blow down his back. Lots of blood pooled around the body on the stone floor. So tired. It took all of his or her strength, she was getting so confused, this memory was emotionally strong, she had trouble separating herself from him, to rise and bow in front of who? Ket was blocking the identities of the men, but Dru could feel it. It was Admiral Tir. Then the memory was over.

Dru looked up at him and then put her arms around his shoulders and pulled him closer to her. That was the most violent thing she had ever witnessed, but instead of being repulsed by it she only felt glad that Ket had not died. She began sharing her own memories now. It was not as easy or as neat as his had been.

Ket was struck by the strong emotions that guided Drusilla as he eased into her consciousness. Her mind was organized so differently from his own. Then the memories began, she was sweeping through images of darkness, poverty, humans screaming in pain, blood, illnesses witnessing her mother perform medical tasks, religious tasks, the killing of animals, childbirth all these things that Drusilla was her assistant in. A man visiting her mother, possibly her father. He looks exactly like her. Violence.

Hunger. This was not the Earth he knew. Now a more specific memory of her mother telling her as a child, she feels about 8 years old, about having to let some people die no matter how old or young. Drusilla watching a woman die of infection they got to too late and then just giving the dead woman's child away to another. Drusilla was crying now, and her mother refused to comfort her. She ran away into the forest or is it a jungle, Ket cannot tell. She stays away for days, hungry, dirty and scared. When she returns her mother asks her if she is done being a spoiled child and ready to get back to the work she was born to do, Drusilla concedes because she is afraid to be alone outside the encampment. But at this point she swears to escape. Ket focuses on the word and the feeling, 'escape'. He knows now she was born into some kind of prison, possibly a colony gone wrong, whether she wanted to share that or not, he doesn't know yet. More memories of her mother both the master and abuser. There is no love between them. Drusilla doesn't know why. Ket can see what Drusilla's child's eyes cannot though, he highly suspects that Drusilla was a product of rape or coercion of some kind. That is where the coldness began, but her mother never reveals that but in not revealing makes the rift between them colder. Finally, Drusilla shares with him the day she walked into the fleet office to sign up. He is shocked now by the Earth he imagined from humans he had met before, it is clean and technologically modern, not like her home. She is dirty and everyone in the office is looking at her. She is embarrassed by her appearance and nervous they will send her back after all that she did to escape. What did she do to escape? Ket asks Drusilla to show him this and she ignores him and continues with the memory. She speaks clearly to the clean and modern humans in the fleet office and is given an IQ test and a physical to see if she meets the standards of the fleet. The only living person ever to score higher than she did was Captain Kara Rainer. Drusilla feels relief, she is given proper clothing, a room and discreetly; medicine, vaccines and a translator, every modern convenience the rest of the galaxy takes for granted. She sends a message to her family, they never respond. Fast forward, Captain Kara specifically requests her on the *Dakota* and Drusilla is scared. She didn't want to go into the heart of the war, but Captain Kara is very convincing. Drusilla goes. Eight months later she is in the Alliance and it's like a repeat of her joining the fleet but in the Alliance. She tries to pull away before she jumps into the vivid memory of her medical exam at Space Port One, but she can't, it just plays, but then thankfully before they were more than a couple questions in, she stops the memory by thinking of him. Her joy at seeing him today. Then she backed her mind away.

Ket held her and stroked her hair silently. He wanted to think about everything she had just shared and try to put it into perspective before he spoke.

"We don't ever have to talk about it," Dru said a little nervously as she had inadvertently shared more than she had intended. "I just want you to know that I'm not a bad person."

"I never thought you were. Some people are not meant to live good lives. Some people were born to be evil. The gods intended it that way."

Dru nodded.

"But just answer me one question, where were you living? Mars or Europa? It didn't look like the Earth I've seen in pictures."

"It is a small area called the Exterior on Earth. It's where people who refuse to give up religion and people who want to live without technology go. I was born there.

305

It is protected by guards and a forcefield. Not unlike the Human House here in the Capital City."

"You're not a prisoner here," he kissed the top of her head. "How did you leave? Are children given a choice to remain?"

"That's all a conversation for another time," she replied shortly, so he would not question her further on the subject, she knew she would not be able to lie to him about something so emotional. She never wanted him to know how she escaped. She never wanted him to think of her being used in that way by those men, even though she wouldn't be sitting here today if she hadn't done it. But then she reminded herself, *He has killed people in duels, you traded your body for freedom. It's equally ghastly.*

Ket now knew that this was her secret that she had left this prison called the Exterior. And that of course this was an area of Earth that humans were ashamed of. People living in a pretechnological age. That is why the other humans lied for her. He wondered what the punishment was for escaping. He vowed to himself that no matter what happened between them, that he would keep her safe in the Alliance forever, so she would never have to return to such a backward place. "I understand. You never have to tell me, you know? There can be secrets between us."

"You keep secrets from me?" she asked sarcastically.

"And you'll always keep some from me. I'm a man and you are a woman." He kissed the top of her head again and then moved away from her again, picking up his glass to drink some champagne. "The man that you resemble in your memories, is that your father?"

"Possibly, he is a traveling trader who would pass through the different encampments in the Exterior. He always stayed with us and he looks like me, but no one ever told me if he was or wasn't my father. Every time he would stay with us, he and my mother got along for about a day or two and then they would have an argument and he would leave until he was back again six months later. In between the years my siblings arrived. Humans don't marry anymore, but this was not really normal either. Most families do live together, especially in the Exterior where life is more uncertain." Dru didn't add that he would usually leave her mother with more than a few bruises and sometimes a broken bone when he left. In the Empire, striking a woman in anger or with the intent to hurt without it being a sanctioned punishment or a role-playing game carried with it a reduction in rank and ten years servitude on a colonial planet. She didn't want him thinking her father was a criminal, even though, Dru suspected he was, even by human standards, and that is how he ended up in the Exterior to begin with. She knew very little about him, but she knew, unlike her mother, he had not been born in the Exterior.

"I see," Ket looked at Drusilla thoughtfully. *And no doubt your mother was judged for this,* he assumed, *And you probably carry some of this weight still with you.*

Dru watched Ket, unable to read his expression and thought, *Please don't throw me off now that I have told you the truth.*

Ket gave her a sympathetic smile, *You are projecting my beautiful one. I would never abandon you because of your unfortunate circumstances earlier in life.*

"I'm sorry, I can't tell when I am projecting sometimes."

"I know," he said sympathetically. "It takes a lot of practice. And I find it endearing because I know it is partly because of how strongly you feel about me."

Dru blushed.

He touched her cheek, "I love that, when your cheeks

turn pink." Then he kissed her chastely, afterwards moving back just enough to look into her green eyes, "Thank you for trusting me with your memories. I'll never judge you by them. Your experiences make you exactly who you are supposed to be." He kissed her again.

Dru wanted this man so much now, she moved closer to him and pressed her naked body against his in the pool and put her arms around his neck. He pulled her close as he continued to kiss her.

After a few minutes, Ket pulled back. "We can't give into our desires now. There will be a time," he smiled. "We can talk about it, though."

"You want to talk about sex? Now?"

"Yes."

"I want to have sex now," she countered.

"But we can't. Tell me what you like." He picked up his glass and took a sip of champagne waiting for her to answer. He had heard many women's fantasies, but he was curious to hear a human woman's fantasy.

She smiled, "I like an Earth fruit called an apple and pajamas, clothes you wear at night. Sometimes I miss human food so much I fantasize about it."

"If I caught you eating your apple outside mealtimes and wearing pajamas, I would replace the apple with my tongue, my penis if you were pregnant, and rip off your night clothes. Then I would lick every inch of your naked body until you were hungry for only me and begging for me to satisfy you with my tongue on your clitoris or my large penis in your tight, wet vagina."

Dru just looked at him. She was getting used to his use of anatomical words through the translator and she was so turned on. She was sure her mouth was open, "I wish I had an apple right now."

He smiled at her and was waiting for her to tell him

what she wants. When she didn't reply he thought about her medical exam on Space Port One and then asked gently, "Please tell me what your fantasies are."

Dru took another sip of champagne. She was embarrassed to talk about this. She had only begun masturbating regularly this year and talking with Doctor Jina about sex and separating her terrible experience with the guards out from her true desires. Doctor Jina had warned her that Alliance men would ask her these things as their relationships moved forward, but she still didn't think she was ready to talk about this with him yet. However, she worried that if she didn't, he would think she was not interested in being serious. That she was just using him for fun. As was in her nature she decided to be honest, "I'm not as sexually experienced as most humans, as I grew up in the Exterior. Growing up in a small community, we were all more careful about who we were intimate with."

Ket wondered then if she really was a virgin, "Have you been to an Alliance spa?"

"No, what's that?"

He ran a hand down her arm gently stroking it, "I'm forbidden to speak about it, but it's an important part of Alliance culture."

Dru moved closer to him, she wanted to kiss him again. She didn't want to talk about fantasies or spas with him, but she realized something had changed. "What are you thinking?"

"I'm thinking that I wasn't thinking before. I had all the information right in front of me, but I still let my own desires get the better of me. I should be taking things much more slowly with you."

"No, you shouldn't," she countered. "I don't want to go slowly." She looked into his gorgeous grey eyes pleading with him. "Is this about the fines?"

"Drusilla," he said and touched her cheek and let his hand travel down to the curve of one of her beautiful full breasts. "This is absolutely not about the fines. I don't care about universal credits like that. No one follows the rules when it comes to kissing and touching before marriage, anyway, hence the fines." He kissed her chastely to show her, then held her face with both hands and said gently, "I read your medical report from Space Port One, I didn't see all of it, but enough to work out that you are for whatever reason, not as sexually as experienced as an Alliance woman of your age and I've been pushing you too much and in the wrong ways perhaps."

She was slightly offended, "Do you find my touch wanting?"

"No, that is not what I meant." He paused, "Your kisses and your touch are so pleasurable the only reason we are not angering the gods and breaking all the rules right now is that I would feel incredibly guilty for any illegitimate child brought about because we couldn't control ourselves." He was relieved that his honestly softened her mood a bit, "Let me get directly to the point about my confusion, if you have never orgasmed with a man before me, just now, how is it you had sex with a man before?"

Dru didn't know what to do with that question. She realized she must have projected her thoughts when he brought her to orgasm before which was embarrassing and then she thought about his question and asked, "Do you think I'm a lesbian?"

"No," he answered confused as how she could come to that conclusion. "Why would you... never mind. No, I just..." He paused and then said seriously, "You don't ever need to tell me details but if you ever point that man out to me, I will challenge him to a duel and kill him for you. Rape is a serious crime." Rape in the Alliance was of course a crime punished with death. It was the only time the sexes were allowed to duel one another if they so choose.

"I've not been raped," she clarified. "On Earth, women often have sex without reaching an orgasm."

"Why would women do that? Is it some kind of sex game? A punishment?"

Dru looked at him confused, "No, it's not a game or punishment. I guess we want to have sex too and men..." she trailed off not having a good explanation at all. She didn't want to say, 'I guess most human men don't think about the women's pleasure and we let them do it.'

"Both Alliance women and human women are meant to orgasm before sex otherwise it is not enjoyable for them. I would never enter a woman who hasn't found her pleasure first and then hopefully at least one more time while I find my one and only pleasure. Women's bodies are the embodiment of the goddess, complex. It is a pleasure to bring a woman to orgasm. Why would human men want to enter a woman who is not ready for him? That can't feel good, either emotionally or physically" he mused the latter more to himself.

"I don't know why, I guess it's more about procreation then enjoyment for women."

"How is that possible?"

"I don't know," she repeated. Then looked him directly in the eyes, "Thankfully, I'll never have to think about it again as I'm destined for an Alliance man, and right now, I just want the Alliance man sitting right in front of me," Dru said and thought, *Shut up champagne, you're embarrassing me.*

"If I could give into my desires there is nothing more I would want right now, to put you under me on the side of this pool and plunge in and out of your vagina, floating

311

above the busy Promenade and the blossoms, but as you well know, we can't."

"If we could, how would you have continued after you made me orgasm earlier?" She wanted to hear more. Dru wondered if his mind just jumped to these things as a possibility when he saw her somewhere as one of the alternatives; a. offer her a drink, b. make conversation, c. have sex next to the pool.

"I would have lifted you up against the wall and pounded into your hot and wet sex quickly, as I've been fantasizing about you for months now. However, afterwards, I would have taken things much more slowly now in the pool, casually pleasuring you again over these hours and then taking you sensually on the pool deck a couple of times. You riding me perhaps with only the sky and the blossoms around you. Me pleasuring your glorious breasts while you find your own pleasure again and again."

Dru was so aroused she didn't think she could speak. While he was talking, he was broadcasting those mental images to her intermixed with his own arousal and she was overwhelmed. "Can you do that now?"

"I promise you, in one year, if you want me to, I'll do that and more right here. We will come back and it would be my pleasure."

"I can't wait a year," Dru said breathlessly.

"But the guilt of an illegitimate child? We cannot do that to an innocent."

Dru knew that abortion of a healthy fetus was illegal in the Alliance, punishable by death, but she had never looked into a child born out of wedlock, no doubt it fell under one of those subjects Madame Bai figured they would cross that bridge if and when they needed to. "A child born out of wedlock?"

"Has no place in society and even if we were to marry

after, the child would be classless. Adrift. We could raise it but not claim it. If it was a boy, he could attend the academy but never serve in the fleet. If it was a girl, she could live with us but never formally be recognized as part of the House and thereby never marry."

"Is that so bad?" She moved closer to him and ran a finger down his smooth face. "And I'm sure it would be a girl and exceptions could be made. I mean, the Alliance has even let in humans now and we weren't born into any House. The Alliance is desperate."

He took her hand and began kissing her wrist and said in-between kisses, "Yes, no. You're making me confused. No, it'd be terrible and there is no reason for it. Most of those children grow up to be pirates or worse somewhere else in the galaxy. I could never live with the guilt."

He moved away from her then, gave her her champagne glass back and poured the rest finishing the bottle, "Trust in the gods and don't push the fates."

She drank her champagne and looked out at the beautiful scenery wondering if she could listen to his religious beliefs for the rest of her life. Then she looked back at him and decided that she could. It was so far the only thing that really annoyed her about him, and it wasn't that bad. She had some quirky beliefs herself.

Their pool was docking with the building.

"Do you have something else planned now?"

"The midday meal at Leld. Do you know it?"

"I've heard of it, of course, but I've never been. Is it nice?"

"The best, I think, and they have two vegetarian dishes. I checked for you, even though today is my day, I'll let you decide what you want to eat for lunch as usual."

"Wow, a whole selection of two vegetarian dishes," he

smiled at her little joke. Then she remembered, "Is this why my morning meal was so tiny?"

"Yes, I wanted you to enjoy Leld as much as possible. And it's your day to be loyal to me regardless."

"I want you so much when you say things like that. I almost want to be naughty so you will punish me, something you've talked about but haven't done."

"Gods, little tabi, don't talk about that. We've got to continue with our day," he got out of the pool and then came over to help her out.

She could not help but notice that his penis was fully erect, but he seemed to have no shame in this whatsoever and she reminded herself, *Why would he be ashamed? He's most likely proud of his big erect cock.*

"Drusilla, stop staring at my penis. It doesn't help me control myself," he said sternly.

She looked into his eyes with all the concentration she could muster and admitted, "I just want you."

He wrapped a big warm yellow towel around her, "I want you too, but we can't, not now. There will be a time. I promise."

He helped her dry off and then brought her clothes out from the small wardrobe and insisted on dressing her like a doll. One by one, first her stockings and she almost orgasmed again with the touch of his hand so close to her pussy. She grabbed one of his hands and said, "Please?"

He looked up at her, "Not now."

"Ket, please."

Ket looked up at her and decided he would give her another orgasm. His reasoning was that she had not been to a spa and must be desperate for sexual skin to skin contact. He had been with slave artists a lot since they had begun messaging, fantasizing about her and she had only her bed functions which were no substitute for the real

314

thing. Machines could bring on perfect orgasms, but without another person to share it with, it was a hollow feeling no matter how good the orgasms. "Tell me what you want?"

"I want you to lick me like you did before. To put your fingers inside of me until I orgasm," she said breathlessly hoping that he was going to acquiesce to her request.

"Do you want me to smack your vulva first for being such a naughty girl and not being able to control yourself?"

"Yes," *Oh gods, yes,* she thought.

He rose and went to stand behind her. His hard-naked body pressed up against her back. His large erect cock poking into her lower back. He moved her legs apart with his hands and then leaned forward and gave her a decent smack right across her vulva.

Dru winced with both pain and pleasure rippling through her. This is exactly what she wanted from him right now even though she didn't have any idea why.

Ket whispered in her ear, "My little tabi, so naughty," as he smacked her again. "My naughty human, begging for sex."

Dru closed her eyes and just waited for the next blow.

"Open your eyes and watch me in the mirror," he commanded.

She opened her eyes and made eye contact with him through the reflection in the mirror. It was so hot watching him. His large and strong body holding her tightly and his arm coming down on her wet sex.

After the next smack he began rubbing her vulva and then specifically her clit. "I want you to watch me make you come just like this. I want you to watch your whole body shake with the pleasure I'm giving to you right now."

It was only a couple minutes before he brought her to climax by rubbing her clit and she watched as much as she could before she had to close her eyes from the pleasure. She leaned back into him and he hugged her for many minutes afterwards. She reveled in his embrace and never wanted him to let go.

He loved touching her and he wanted more than anything to lean her over and sink his penis into her dripping vagina, but he couldn't, and it went against the gods to masturbate. They would already have enough fines today without that one as well, which also carried with it a formal punishment by a shrine nun. *I definitely don't need that again,* he thought with disgust and held on to the last time he'd been punished by a nun to get his penis and body to obey his mind. He rubbed the top of Drusilla's shoulders with his hands and then moved away to retrieve her clothes from the wardrobe. He heard her little gasp of protest and he thought, *I feel the same way.* Then he brought her bra to her, "I don't think this is wearable now."

"No," she agreed. "Next time just undo the clasps please." She didn't want to tell him that they were expensive as they were not nearly as expensive as all the fines he was going to have to pay.

"Your beautiful breasts shouldn't be restricted anyway," he admonished while casually stroking a nipple and playing with the bar through her piercing.

She closed her eyes from the pleasure of his touch and then said, "I find it comforting to have them secure against my body."

"I'll try to remember there is a clasp for next time."

Next, he brought her dress and put it over her head and brought the hem down to the floor. She looked down at him and then began lifting her dress up to him, he was on his knees, so close to her sex, "I want you Ket. Just don't come inside me." She could see that he was so tempted. He ran a finger down her inner thigh, he looked at her sex and licked his lips deciding. He ran another finger along the tops of her thighs that were wet with her desire.

He thought of the shrine nun as she whipped his penis for masturbation and was able to resist Drusilla. "We can't, please don't tempt me anymore," he brought the hem of her dress down again and then came up and took her in his arms and kissed her passionately. Then he left her abruptly and quickly got dressed himself while he said, "It's good to know that you are just as uncomfortable as I am right now, even after you have orgasmed twice. I'm glad to know that I am not alone in this. It'll be a dreadfully long year but a pleasant end, perhaps."

She smiled. They were going to one of the fanciest restaurants in the city, she was wet all down her thighs and was like a dog in heat. Not the way she imagined doing this. "My coat?" she asked.

"Just one more thing," he motioned to the black sofa behind her. He went into the wardrobe and brought out a black box. He sat in the chair across from her and said, "I thought you might like this."

It was the first time he was giving her jewelry in person and she was almost emotional about it. She opened the box and inside was a gorgeous three-tiered silver necklace made of interlocking rectangles encrusted with blue stones. It went perfectly with the dress and she knew this was from his known collection. Her heart started beating faster and she said, "This is magnificent."

He didn't say anything but picked it up to put it on her. It hung handsomely on her and fell heavy enough now to see the curve of her breasts through the dress as Alliance dresses were meant to be.

She stood up and looked at him, "How does it look? Is this what you intended?"

He stood up and looked down at her with a serious

look, "You look how I would expect my wife to look now," then he kissed her while rubbing one of her nipples through the dress. "And I like that you have no bra."

When he pulled away, Dru couldn't speak. This all felt so right she didn't want to ruin anything by talking.

Ket broke the silence, "If you would agree Drusilla Anne James of House Human," he said quite formally, "I would like that we begin courting for a year from today with the idea that at the end of this year, or before, we either marry or decide to pursue different romantic paths."

"Ket of House Vo, I accept your offer of courtship and give you a year of my constancy, "she was ecstatic. "I should tell you something," she said.

He looked at her expectedly and slightly concerned.

"I'd prefer it if you called me 'Dru'."

"Dru," he said the name testing it out. "Why not Drusilla? I like Drusilla. It goes against the gods not to go by the name given to you."

"'Dru' is just a shorter version. And 'Drusilla' is, well, people will know where I was born, other humans."

He looked at her seriously and then said, "No, I'll continue to call you 'Drusilla'. And you are my Drusilla now. It's a good name and you should never be ashamed of what you had no control over. Now, let's go so we don't miss the midday meal. All this teasing has made me very hungry."

They walked out together and joined all the other cheerful pedestrians along the Promenade. Dru wanted to hold his hand and more. Her emotions were bubbling over. Not only were they finally courting, and he had given her some of his known jewelry, that everyone would be able to see thanks to social media, but he was not embarrassed of her past. Of where she was from, and she knew deep down, that this would make it easier for her to come to terms with her past as well, all of it. Even if she never told him about the guards. She didn't know if she had ever been so content as in that moment. Everything in her life seemed perfect, even though a year ago, this might have been the last thing that she would have said that she would have wanted for herself.

We must be seen in public so that people know we are courting, he said mentally. Then he added, out loud, "Drusilla."

She smiled but didn't reply. She enjoyed walking next to him. Her mind danced around her ecstatic contentment because she wasn't one to just be happy and not go over everything again and again. She had begun thinking about the weight of the known jewelry he had given her, wondering if this really was destiny or if he just shaped things to make it feel like it. The beauty of their surroundings, the purple petals loose in the wind all gave the impression of freedom, but was this freedom or destiny? Or was it destiny because it felt like she had the freedom to choose? In the end she decided that even if this had all been planned, she was happy and so she should just accept it because who's to say a destiny shaped only by her own will could be as fulfilling. But then she frowned, *But I wouldn't owe anyone for my happiness. If this is destiny, this happiness will have to be paid back in my lifetime.* She was pulled out of her thoughts when they arrived at the restaurant.

As they walked into Leld a lot of heads turned to watch them. Dru was used to this. They had a reservation for a private room which she was grateful for and she imagined he probably was as well.

"I didn't realize there would be such an audience here," he commented when they were alone.

"Humans would probably be the same if you were all of the sudden just living among us. Now, let me look at my two vegetarian options."

They had a nice lunch and the conversation never strayed into anything serious again. Ket told her about his family, his older brother Kio, who was also an Imperial Doctor aboard an Alpha Warship, but unmarried and how Dera was their spoiled baby sister that they all doted on. After the midday meal, they walked the rest of the Promenade Ring together, smiling at each other and enjoying the beauty all around them. When they had completed the ring, he flew her home in his transport.

"Where are you going now?" she asked as they stopped in front of her door. There were still some hours before the evening meal, that he undoubtedly would have with his family, but she wanted to spend time with him if he had nothing else planned.

"I'm going to go to the Grand City Temple to thank the gods you accepted my courtship and to beg forgiveness for my wandering hands today. Then I'll return home to tell my family our new status and have the evening meal with them. The gods have blessed us today."

"May the gods continue to light our way," Dru responded. He grabbed her hand and squeezed it. With that touch he transferred the sensation of him kissing her and she almost jumped at the shock of it. It actually felt like he had kissed her, but he just touched her hand.

"The mind is a powerful thing," he said with a smile and then walked away.

6

Sex in the Alliance

Dera had invited Dru to visit a women's spa with her for a couple of days before their practicals began, as kind of a reward for doing so well on their exams. Dru remembered Ket mentioning this was an important part of Alliance culture, but when she questioned Madame Bai about it and why it wasn't mentioned in her cultural handbook, she was simply told that it is something that must be experienced and never talked about and absolutely never written about. It hadn't occurred to Dru to ask Doctor Jina about it at all.

Dru was intrigued to say the least. She had contacted Jane to let her know where she was going and with whom. "Do you know anything about these spas?" she had asked as they were VMing in real time.

"No," Jane replied. "But I'm sure you will have fun with your friend," she said reassuringly. "And please no more fines."

"Ket won't even be there," she said defensively. "And he paid them all didn't he?" She suddenly wondered if Jane or Captain Kara had had to cover some. Her fine from the last time she saw Ket was over 3,000 UC and it was embarrassing that Jane knew every action the fine was for.

"Yes, he paid them all. However, it makes House Human look bad."

Dru thought Jane was being particularly grumpy today and asked, "Is everything alright?"

Jane sighed, "Fine, except Captain is due to give birth any day now and refuses to give her first command. As you can imagine this is driving Admiral Tir batty. Apparently, no Alliance woman has ever given birth off planet before and they are overly concerned as if she were going to break into a million pieces, despite John's efforts to reassure them. So, the Captain and Admiral are constantly bickering which of course leaves her in a great mood for all of us to enjoy."

Dru half smiled, she could imagine what that was like, "I'm so glad I'm not there."

Jane smiled back at her, "You should be. But this too will pass. Message me when you return from your holiday and no fines James."

Dru promised and then began to pack what she might need for a couple of nights. She looked at her pajamas and wondered if she and Dera were going to share a room and if she would be naked. And then wondered if Dera would take offense if she weren't naked. She thought about this and decided to bring her pajamas and then make a game time decision.

Just as she finished packing, a slave told her Dera had arrived. Dru grabbed her little bag, a present from Madame Bai, as she had had nothing but her day bag, and went outside to get into Dera's family transport. She couldn't help but remember fondly how she and Ket had kissed inside of this transport after the Year Assembly.

Dera greeted her and put their new destination in and

they took off.

"Tell me about this place we are going to. You were so mysterious before."

"I have to be. I'll tell you everything when we arrive. Let's talk about something else." Dera grinned and they talked about their practicals. Dera was pleased to be working so close with her mother.

The words struck Dru hard as she of course had been trained by her own mother, but their relationship had never been close even though it was not from Dru's lack of trying. She just reconciled herself that her mother didn't love anyone. That it wasn't personal to Dru.

After 20 minutes, the transport landed and the women got out and went into a stunning large stone building that was mainly lit by yellow candles. Dera and Dru approached a beautiful woman that was behind the big desk and they checked in. Then they were shown to their rooms by another attractive woman with a pleasing, melodical voice. Dru was a bit surprised that they were not sharing a room with two beds as she would have done with her human friends, but she figured that this was just another cultural difference and tried not to wonder if it was because she was human. Once they were in their rooms, Dera came through the connecting doors to her room without knocking, carrying a bottle of Alliance wine and two ceramic cups.

"Come on, let's sit on the balcony and talk. I've a lot to tell you and only an hour to do it in."

Dru followed Dera out to their adjoining balcony which had a beautiful view of a clear lake and mountains. There was snow on the mountain tops and the water was so still, the mountains were reflected in it. Dera poured the wine and made a toast, "To our futures as doctors and your becoming a real Alliance woman."

Dru drank to that toast even though it did not make sense to her completely, "Tell me now, I'm so curious. What is going on?"

"What do you know about slave artists?"

Dru shook her head, "Nothing. I know we have three surly slaves who maintain our building."

"No, those are regular slaves, slave artists are performers. They recite myths, history…" she trailed off hoping Drusilla would pick up on where she was going, but after a minute she realized that her friend really was an innocent in this regard. "Slave artists can also satisfy one's sexual pleasure. Onboard ship there are many, but men are not allowed to be with a slave artist while they are in Alliance space or on Alliance planets. As we cannot leave the planet, women have these retreats, but it is forbidden to speak about them in detail to anyone. We all have the opportunity to visit them a couple times a year for our release. And here you can do anything with anyone."

Dru was looking at Dera in complete shock, "What do you mean by 'release'?"

"Sexual release or whatever kind of release you want. Do you want to hear some myths or have a massage? Do some meditation or have sex with a beautiful slave?"

"Do you think Ket is sleeping with a slave artist onboard the *Tuir*? Do you think that is why he doesn't want me to join the fleet so he can do that?"

"I can't talk to you about Ket," she said.

"It feels wrong to have sex with someone else when I committed myself."

"Slave artists don't count as cheating on someone you are in a formal relationship with. They are part of the Contracts."

"We're here to sleep with slave artists?" Dru was still in disbelief.

"Yes," Dera said, very pleased that Drusilla finally understood.

"Your parents know we are here?"

"Yes, but it is forbidden to ever speak about what we do here out loud to anyone, especially to a man. The punishment is death Drusilla, you must remember that. Are you ready to enjoy yourself?"

Dru was horrified. A million things were running through her mind.

"I've already ordered two men, one for each of us. They'll be here soon. We'll start slow like that, okay?"

"You consider that slow?" Dru took a deep breath, "Some random men are just going to come here and ...." Dru trailed off and Dera laughed at her.

"Yes, you know when you order them you can specify everything, and I didn't think you would want to talk or hear a myth recited. I mean, we can ask for a myth to be recited instead, slave artists can do it all."

Dru made a face at her friend but didn't know how to reply. But it didn't matter because two handsome Alliance men suddenly appeared on the balcony. Dru almost dropped her wine cup at the sight of them. The men were stunning and almost naked. They wore just little green shorts. Their bodies were perfect as were their faces. They both had very symmetrical faces with green eyes. Their long black hair was pulled back in a style she had never seen before but didn't really pay attention to, as she was too focused on their other attributes.

The men didn't speak, just took each woman by the hand and led them into their respective rooms. Now Dru understood why they had separate rooms and was somewhat relieved it was not because she was a human.

The man that led Dru into her room stopped in front of her bed and immediately began stroking her hair and face with both hands. She closed her eyes and thought, *I'll just imagine it's Ket.* Then he began lightly kissing her on her face and in her hair and it felt so good, but not like Ket. Her hands drifted over his incredibly strong chest, *Strong and attractive, but not my Ket.*

Gu the artist slave with Drusilla was excited to be with a human woman. The exotic women had been the talk of the Empire since they had arrived and there were so many rumors about them, he like everyone else, was very curious and so far, he was not disappointed. Her long red hair had a floral scent and her skin was so soft. He wondered if she were fat or curvy or both underneath her dress. Her face did not look fat, so he suspected and hoped curvy. Of course, he had been with fat women before and he never had a problem performing for any of his customers, but he already had a fantasy in his mind about human women from the picture he had seen of Captain Kara's trial and her body so clearly outlined in her tight uniform. Gu began kissing Drusilla on her neck, while his hands were roaming her body over her dress.

"Stop," Dru said softly and pushed his shoulders.

Gu immediately stopped, stepped back and looked down at this lovely human woman, "Am I doing something wrong?"

"No, it's not you. It's me. Please go."

"Could I do something else to please you? A massage? A myth recited? I am here to serve."

"No. Please go."

Gu was paid regardless of what she wanted. He bowed, "Call me back if you change your mind."

Dru saw him leave and then sat on the bed and cried. Dera came in through the adjoining door just a few minutes later.

"Drusilla?" she sat next to her on the bed. "What's

going on?" Dera had no idea why the slave artist wouldn't please her friend.

"I can't do this. I know you can't talk about him and it's weird to say this to you, but I only want Ket to touch me."

Dera didn't know what to say, she couldn't talk about Ket directly, but obviously she could speak generally. "But to lead a healthy sexual life you must open yourself to others. Men are gone for long periods of time."

Dru interrupted her, "I'm not an Alliance woman. I can't do this. I'm so sorry. Just go," she finished softly.

Dera put her hand on Dru's shoulder for some seconds, the Alliance way to give comfort among friends, "We'll talk about this tomorrow. Enjoy the other activities the spa has to offer, there is no shame in sending a slave artist away. It happens. I'm sorry I pushed you without realizing you weren't ready."

Dru looked up at her friend, "It's not your fault. It's me. But I'm glad I'm learning this now and not after I married your brother."

Dera felt very sad for Ket then. This was going to be difficult for them both. She left the room with a simple goodnight and dismissed her own slave artist who had been waiting for her. Dera preferred women and was only sleeping with the man to make Drusilla feel comfortable. Being attracted to women in the Alliance used to not be a problem, you just didn't marry, and everyone looked the other way. Now it made people very uncomfortable, especially other women, as they all were supposed to be doing their part for their species and setting a good example. Especially, the Imperial Families. So, Dera's only real release came at the spas where she was free to be with other women without judgement. Dera then called in for three other women to join her for the rest of the night.

. . .

The next morning, Dru got up and dressed then knocked on the door connecting her and Dera's rooms. Dera told her to come in. When she entered, she was surprised to see Dera in bed with three other women. Dru didn't mention it, because she was sure her face said everything including, *How can you be so sexually advanced to have three women?* but instead asked, "Are you going to the restaurant for the morning meal?"

Dera looked at the women in her bed, smiled and then looked at Dru, "No, I'm not hungry this morning."

Dru nodded and then went to breakfast herself. She brought her IC with her so at least she could read her messages while she ate. As she sat down with a plate of very unappetizing food and the bland juice the staff insisted on her drinking, she opened her messages and was surprised to see one from Captain Kara.

James,

I just wanted you to know that the first hybrid baby has been born. A boy. John delivered him last night. He looks like a mix between Alliance and human and is healthy. I don't know when I will next return to planet, but when I do, I would like a medical checkup by you. There are too many men here and I feel that something is not right with me.

Kara

. . .

As Dru had little else to do over the morning meal, she replied straight away,

Captain Kara,

Congratulations on the birth of your son. The first hybrid baby. I am happy to hear he is healthy. I am always here on planet and could talk to you anytime about your health. I suspect the natural changes in your body are what is bothering you. Men wouldn't know about these things and John only in theory. As I said, I am always on the Capital Planet.

James

She wanted to ask about the slave artists on ship but then remembered she wasn't supposed to talk about it so she definitely shouldn't put it in a message. She just thought she would try to remember to ask Captain Kara the next time she saw her. She then wondered about the repercussions of Captain Kara's actions on planet. It was forbidden for men to know anything about women's reproduction and Captain Kara had given birth on a warship surrounded by men. However, maybe it was only John. She would want to ask about that too, but then she realized that's what the answer would be even if it really wasn't.

Dru finished her breakfast and went for a walk through the very symmetrically laid out garden in back of the spa. Every inch of it had been perfectly manicured and Dru couldn't help but reflect, like the entire planet and civilization, everything had been thought through and almost nothing left to chance. She wanted to be angry with Ket for not telling her about the slave artists, but she reminded herself that he couldn't have told her and that in fact, he had told her as much as he could.

She walked in the garden for some time before Dera came and found her.

"I've been looking for you," Dera said. "Let's walk to that old temple on the other side of the lake."

Dru nodded and they walked together mostly, in silence, besides some pleasantries about the landscape or the weather. When they reached the old temple, Dru followed Dera through the large, black wooden gates into the garden of the temple. The temple was made of black wood and the smell of incense and candles floated through the air. Dera walked straight into the main temple building and found the black stone statue she was looking for and stopped before it. She bowed, said some prayers and then looked at Dru.

Dru begrudgingly did the same and then whispered to Dera, even though they were the only ones in the temple, "Who is this?"

Dera didn't look at her but lit a candle and put it in Dru's hands, "The goddess of orgasm. I am praying for you and Ket."

Dru gave her a surprised look that she mentioned his name to her.

"Holy places are out of bounds," she explained. "Now tell me, do you really only want his touch or is it something else?" Zol and Dera had talked extensively about Drusilla, and what the doctors thought might have happened to her and what that meant for her sexual behavior now. But, as Zol had received copies of all of the fines she and Ket had incurred every time they met, she assumed Drusilla had conquered the

330

terrible sexual experiences she had endured as a very young woman. However now Dera was unsure. She had messaged her mother that morning but had not received a reply. All she could do was talk to her friend and try and help her.

"I really only want him," she replied quietly.

Dera considered her for a couple minutes and then tried to explain, "This is not our way anymore. I don't think Ket would accept this for you or for him. Our society is built on strictness, punishments and rewards. By taking away this aspect you are taking away a reward for both of you."

"What do you mean 'anymore'?"

"It used to be that couples who were so in love with one another," she mentioned love as if it were a shameful thing, "would take binding tattoos on their wedding night so that they could not physically be with another. They would get ill or pass out if they tried."

"How long ago was this?" Dru felt there could be some hope.

"At least four hundred years ago. Not too long, but long enough." She looked into Drusilla's green eyes and said, "We are here for one more night, could we please try again?"

Dru shook her head, "I only want Ket," then she began to cry with the absurdity of it because she knew she would lose him over this.

"But Drusilla, you just have to think of it differently. This isn't Earth. Please?" Dera had heard that some of the other humans had struggled with slave artists aboard the *Zuin*. However, she couldn't believe it because she had also heard the wild rumors about Captain Kara and the slave artist Sera.

Dru shook her head, "I can't, and I know what you are

saying, that Ket won't accept this arrangement. But I can't accept this. It's too much for me."

"Because of what happened? The rape?"

"I don't know," Dru admitted, somewhat shocked that Dera knew something about her past, but then reminded herself, *Her mother is the First Imperial Doctor, of course, she knows everything about me if her son is courting me.* "I don't think so. That was terrible but this is more than that."

"Something to do with your human culture? Your father?"

"I never really knew my father," Dru admitted and then added, "Don't say anything about it."

Dera nodded, "I wouldn't betray your secrets. We are in a holy place now. This is gods' speak."

Dru nodded.

"I think you should try again. Maybe try to focus on what specifically bothers you about it while it is going on so then you can overcome it."

"I don't want to overcome it, I don't think."

"But you cannot only be with Ket. It's not natural."

"It seems like the most natural thing in the galaxy to me."

"I don't understand." Dera sighed, "Please try again?"

Dru looked at her friend and knew that she meant well so she nodded agreement to try again.

They walked back together in silence. When they reached the spa, Dera said, "I've arranged for some women today."

"I've never been with a woman before, I ..." she trailed off.

"What is happening on Earth that you have never been with a woman before?"

"What do you mean, 'What is happening on Earth'? Honestly, Dera, you know we don't have sex spas and

332

slave artists. Well, I mean we have prostitution, but most people stay loyal to just one person in their relationships, I think."

"Until that relationship ends and then a whole family is broken apart and what pleasure did you take from having sex with the same person for so long? In the Alliance we have a bit of this excitement, it makes everyone's life more interesting and it is regulated. More importantly, it allows us to remain married to the same people and maintain social order so that we can focus on important things. I think if we could have turned off our sexual desires to only pursue academic and technological pursuits, we would have done that a long time ago as it wastes so much time, sexual desire."

"But it is a natural part of life for all species. I think, humans enjoy the constant battle for romance, to keep it alive. And we celebrate for those people who have found love. You call it a waste of time; we call it the only reason to be alive."

"Not all species reproduce according to their primal bodies' desires. Some species have managed to breed it out and reproduction only happens through science now. One of our vassal planets, JXR-25 is like that. The people there live completely asexual lives and accomplish so much. Don't you think humans could have accomplished more if you weren't wasting your time chasing after love and good sex all the time?"

"I don't know. I have never thought about it like that. We abolished marriage because it was seen as a trapping from a different era in human history that had many other detrimental elements such as slavery." Dru specifically used slavery as her example.

"Yes, slavery is bad but sometimes necessary, but you know Alliance slaves have not really been slaves for generations now, it is just a name, a class, but they choose their professions just like the rest of us."

"What is an Alliance marriage like Dera?"

Dera considered how to answer this in a way that would please Drusilla, "Being married in the Alliance is a comfort, it gives you a place, a starting point, a family. Of course, you can never walk away from it like humans can from their families, but there is some security in that too. As for your being able to find a man who would only be sexually loyal to you, I can't say."

"I don't see myself ever changing on this. I can't share."

"You never know. People do change over time. Now, it is time to think about the midday meal and your first sexual encounter with a woman."

"Dera ..."

Dera smiled, "Why are you so unwilling to try? Maybe you like women more?"

"I don't know what to do with a woman," Dru admitted. "I've never felt attracted to a woman."

"Are you not a woman yourself? Haven't you ever been curious? In the Alliance women freely enjoy all sexual pleasures with men and women. If I could never marry and always be with a woman, I would, but with the current demographics situation I know what I must do for the Empire. Fortunately, I like variety, but if you are afraid to try with a woman ..." Dera knew that Drusilla didn't like being deemed afraid to try new things.

"Dera, will you marry then?"

"If I chose not to marry it would be severely detrimental to my career and bring shame on my family. In the past, when the population was almost equal between men and women, some men and women chose to never marry and people looked the other way, now people say we must all do what's right to maintain our civilization."

"You mean pure civilization?"

"I didn't want to say it to you, but yes, that is what these people mean and there are a lot of them, as you know well. People like Rez. She thinks it's better that I would sacrifice myself than you marry an Alliance man and pollute our species."

"Do you believe that?"

"No, of course not. But I also believe that humans are the Lost People, Rez does not. Her family has never been religious, they only consult logic instead of their hearts." Dera touched her heart with one finger as she spoke of the Lost People to indicate this was something she believed to her core.

"I'm sorry that you must marry a man when you don't want to."

Dera smiled, "And this is why we are friends Drusilla. You were taken as a prisoner of war and brought here to solve our problem. Sold by your own government, but you still find it in your heart to feel sorry for me. And we will see what happens. Maybe in the end things will relax and I'll be able to do what I want."

Dru wondered then if Dera only had befriended her for Dera's own benefit to show that human women could be integrated, so that she would have a better chance at never having to marry. She knew if she asked Dera she would probably get the truth, but she did not want to hear it either way. Sometimes living in ignorance was better.

After lunch, Dera suggested they go swimming.

"I didn't bring a swimsuit."

"We swim naked. Humans have this reputation for being so wild and carefree, but I think you are all so misunderstood."

"Do you think I am so prude then?"

"Absolutely, besotted by one man, afraid to have sex with women and now you want clothing to swim in," Dera admitted with a smile. "But you are still my friend and I will just accept this as part of your humanity."

Dru didn't reply. She didn't know what to say without coming off as offensive. She just followed Dera down to a secluded part of the lake for swimming. The air was cold when Dru removed her dress. She assumed the water would be even colder. But the sun was setting over the mountains and the sky was turning red. It was breathtakingly beautiful, and she liked the experience of being so free to swim like this in nature. She followed Dera into the ice-cold water. She was trying to move at all times as to not become too cold.

"Is it too cold for you?" Dera asked.

"Possibly. Let me see if it gets better in a minute."

Dera smiled, "One minute, okay."

After one minute, two more women came into the water. One came right up behind Dru and began caressing her breasts. Dru could feel the slave's small adorned breasts pressing against her back. Dru closed her eyes and thought, *Just try to enjoy this. It is new. Be Alliance cool.*

Then the woman's hands moved in between Dru's legs caressing her lightly there and she whispered in her ear, "I heard that you were special and now I know that you are very special, human." Dru welcomed her touch and leaned back into the woman her jewelry rough on her back. She was touching her so perfectly, unlike any man, Dru thought it must be a dream.

Dera stole a look at Dru and was pleased that she had not run away yet and then went back to what she was doing with her beautiful petite slave artist.

Dru said to the woman after a couple more minutes

though, "I can't do this," and moved slightly away and then headed back to the beach. She was shaking from the cold. The slave artist followed her.

"Is there something you would like me to do differently?" she asked seductively.

"No, I just... it's not for me right now."

The slave artist nodded and walked away. Dru looked at Dera in the water being pleasured and decided to go back to the room and warm up. Once in the room, she got into the shower but at the top temperature it only got as warm as lukewarm. She washed off anyway and then looked at herself in the mirror and said quietly, "Who are you? Why can't you do this?"

Then she had the strangest sensation that she had done this before. It was her but not her. She touched her reflection in the mirror and almost passed out she felt so dizzy. *What is going on?* she thought. As soon as the moment was there it was gone and so she tried to forget about it or make excuses, blaming the cold.

She got dressed and then got into bed to try and warm up.

When Dera arrived, still wet from swimming, she told Dru she would be ready soon to go eat the evening meal, but when she saw Dru in her bed with her clothes on shivering, she came over to her, "Are you okay?"

Dru nodded, "I'm just cold. I have to warm up. Then I'll be fine."

Dera smiled, "You look ridiculous in bed with your clothes on."

"I know."

During the evening meal Dera asked Drusilla if she could pinpoint why she didn't want to be with a slave artist.

"Well, there were a couple of reasons. First, I was freezing cold. Second, I just couldn't be with another woman. I like men so much. Third, I like one man in particular so much I only want to be with him."

"But why?"

"I thought about that a lot while I warmed up in bed with my clothes on," she smiled, "and I think I just want one constant here."

"You have me."

"I know and I appreciate that, but you know what I mean?"

"I think I do, and I can't help but wonder if your opinion would change once you married and became a part of a real House."

"House Human is as real as it gets," she defended them even though she knew it wasn't.

"You know what I mean."

"I know, but I also want people to start taking us more seriously too if we are here to stay."

"I'm sorry, I didn't mean disrespect…"

"Not consciously."

"I'm sorry. I only meant that when you are married your husband and the vast number of people in a House, which House Human does not have, might make you feel more at ease and less alone."

"Oh."

"I know I say racist things sometimes, but most of us are trying to be more inclusive."

"Keep trying," Dru gave her friend a little smile. "And as far as being married and feeling more secure, I don't know if that would help. I just need to think about this whole thing for a while."

They enjoyed the rest of their evening not talking about sex or anything but their hopes and desires for their careers.

When Dera returned home, she sent a message to her

brother. "May the gods bless you; I don't know what to do. Boru Spa was a disaster. Drusilla doesn't want to have sex with anyone but you. She tried but she said it felt wrong. I tried to explain Alliance sexual culture to her, but when she tried again, she also resisted." Dera sighed, "I'm sorry Ket. I don't know what to tell you. I think she loves you and because of that doesn't want anyone else to touch her. I didn't want to speak for you, but I did tell her that I didn't think you would accept exclusivity, that no Alliance man would accept a monogamous relationship with his wife. She told me she didn't think she could have it any other way, even though she understood this may mean giving you up. May the gods guide your way."

Ket then opened the message from Drusilla. It was apparent that she had been crying as her eyes were red. He felt terrible for her.

"Ket, I am so distraught."

He noticed she didn't even greet him with a prayer and so unlike her. "My poor little tabi," he said quietly to the screen.

"I feel like I've no idea what is going on with your culture. Dera tried to explain it to me and it seems logical, but in my heart," she touched her heart with one finger to indicate her unwavering belief, "I don't want anyone to touch me but you." She began to cry again but didn't stop the VM, so he had to painfully watch her, unable to reach through the screen and offer any comfort.

Ket blamed himself, he had moved too quickly for her, even after seeing her initial Alliance medical examination and his mother's warnings. He had naively thought that once Dera introduced her to women's spas, she would naturally begin behaving like any Alliance woman. She needed to be able to have regular sex while he was away or else, she would become too strained. He couldn't have a wife who was always just waiting for him to return, she would become irritated and possibly irretrievably angry. That is why monogamy was abandoned more than a thousand years before.

"And I can't bear the thought of you touching someone else."

That stopped him. He just stared at the screen. *She can't be serious*, he thought. *She is just upset, and she doesn't understand.*

"I just can't do this. I understand if you want to end our courtship now." Then she signed off abruptly crying, again without the blessing.

He stood up confused, sat down and stood up again and went to the shrine onboard the ship. It was night and he was naked. He kneeled in front of the goddess of home and thought, *How could you send me the most wonderful woman but then have her demand this of me?* He prayed for at least an hour. He didn't feel any better. He returned to his room and tried to sleep. It was fitful. He poured himself a glass of Zota and drank it thinking about what he should do. He decided he would pray and wait for the answer to come to him before replying. If this was the will of the gods', they would guide him now.

Dru woke up and was surprised Ket had not responded to her emotional message. That was not like him at all. So, she could only assume that he wanted to break off the courtship. She couldn't' blame him, she couldn't be Alliance cool in this. She wanted someone to love, someone who was all her own and she couldn't share her body with other men, nor did she want to think about him with other women.

Days passed and she heard nothing from Ket or Dera. It was the first 4th day since she returned from the Boru Spa and she looked at her underwear as she was getting dressed. She didn't but it on, but when she went down to breakfast, one of her slaves served her Alliance bread and strawberry jam. After breakfast she went back up to her room and put her underwear on, then sat on the bed and cried. She wanted Ket so much, but she couldn't just have sex with different men to fulfill this Alliance ideal about sex and healthiness. That evening in her study rooms, she tried to open a VM to Ket. She saw that he was available and tried to talk to him, but he marked himself as unavailable after her attempt. She put her head on her desk and cried like she had never cried before. After a long time, possibly even an hour, she rallied herself. She opened her social media and began looking at what Captain Kara and the rest of the women from the *Dakota* have been doing on the *Zuin*. She was seriously considering joining them now after she finished her practicals. She wanted no reminders of the happiness here in the Capital City, if she couldn't have her Ket. He had been her one bright spot here now that everyone else had left and now he was gone too.

The next morning during her prayers, she stood before the goddess of home and asked, "Why did you do this to me? Why did you bring me here and introduce me to Ket just to take him away? You knew I couldn't sexually conform in this way after what happened to me." She actually fell to her knees crying in the shrine. Her slaves were concerned and actually picked her up and led her into the great fire room. She was wiping her tears as they looked at her. She felt like an idiot in front of them.

The three house slaves in House Human had been concerned for Drusilla for weeks now. They actually felt really sorry for her, which was uncommon for Alliance slaves to take notice of any people not from slave class. She was so lonely and had no friends. All the other humans were gone. She only had work and her Ket and now he had left her too.

"Drusilla, this is an Empire full of desperate men. There will be another. Don't cry over this one," one of the slaves said helpfully.

Dru just shook her head and cried. And the slaves just watched her, not knowing how to comfort her.

The next 4th day, Dru only hesitated for a second before putting on her underwear, but that evening in her study room she did begin a VM to Ket.

"Ket, I don't know why we can't have a discussion about this," but then she couldn't control herself, and began to cry, and so deleted the message. When she regained some control, she began looking at the adventures of the *Zuin*. She thought, *Even my slaves say there will be another, I must let him go.* Then she cried again for about an hour, it hurt so much that he had just abandoned her without a word and got very little studying done. When she left her room that night she said out loud to herself, "This was a pointless night here. I accomplished nothing except crying. No more thinking about him. He doesn't want me."

As the weeks passed and she heard nothing from Ket, Dru assumed that they were really and completely finished, so she wore no jewelry except her Human House ID necklace. She knew the other Doctors at the Capital City Hospital suspected that they were no longer courting, but she was relieved that no one asked her directly though, because she honestly, didn't know the real answer. A small part of her hoped that maybe they had not ended things and there was another reason for his silence. Dru was also happy no one asked her about him as she was afraid that if she spoke his name out loud, she might just start crying again. She had considered reaching out to Jane or Madame Bai about it but hadn't found the energy or humility yet to do it. She just threw herself into her work and tried not to think about Boru, Ket, monogamy or marriage.

Nine weeks passed with no word from Ket. Dru studied all the time now when she wasn't working at the hospital. One night she was studying late in her private room at the library when she suddenly felt very sick. Her throat contracted and she felt like she couldn't breathe. The sensation had come on quickly and completely out of the blue. She tried to stand up but fell down from dizziness. Then the alarms went off. The calming voice of the computer told her to wait there and help was on its way, that she had contracted the Uli virus from Alpha Four. Her mind was swimming. She couldn't think, so she just closed her eyes accepting the darkness almost embracing it.

Ket was working when his assistant told him he had an emergency message from the Capital Planet. He finished what he was doing and then went into his office in sickbay and closed the door. He opened the message from Dru's Alliance Cultural Guide, Madame Bai. His heart was beating faster, and he couldn't open the message fast enough, the only reason she would contact him is if something had happened to Dru on the Capital Planet.

Doctor Ket,

I am writing to let you know that Drusilla James has been infected with the Uli virus. No one knows how she became infected; the Capital City police are investigating it as a crime. She was studying in her private room at the library when the symptoms appeared a few hours ago. She is being cared for at the Capital City Hospital on floor five, room twenty. Thankfully, humans are more resilient than Alliance as the doctors say it would have killed one of us by now. They are doing all they can. Chief Engineer Jane, Head of House Human is away on the Zuin and cannot attend to her. Only members of her House or yours, with your permission. If you or your family cannot attend, I will make a formal appeal to become her guardian so that she will not be alone. However, this can take up to a week and she may be gone by then.

Madame Bai

Ket's hands were shaking as he immediately opened a new VM to the Capital City Hospital. "I want Drusilla James moved up to the Imperial Level, we are courting, this is common knowledge," he knew that someone had deliberately overlooked her new status to put her on the bottom rung of rooms. But then he also knew that she had not been wearing any of the jewelry he had given her lately, thanks to gossip columns and no doubt rumors had spread that they had split, which was not the case, not yet anyway. The truth was he didn't know what to do about her sexual expectations, it had never occurred to him that she would ask for fidelity. But now he put that all aside and was angry that the hospital would just so easily dismiss her status without asking him first. He continued the message, "I will return to the capital at once, in the meantime, keep my mother, First Imperial Doctor, updated on all progress with Drusilla and allow her visitation rights." He sent it to the Head of the hospital.

Then he left sickbay to find Admiral Ver. He found him in his ready room off the main bridge. The Admiral looked up as he came in, "How are things in sickbay?"

344

"Everything is fine. Ensign Tuz will recover with no harm done."

"Good. You haven't come down here to tell me that though."

"No, Drusilla James has contracted the Uli virus and is in the Capital City Hospital. I would like permission to go to her."

He looked at his doctor and said sympathetically, "But there is nothing you can do that they cannot do for her. I need you here."

"If she were an Alliance woman, I wouldn't ask this, but she is all alone. All the other human women are onboard the *Zuin*."

"What about her cultural teacher, Madame Bai?"

"Madame Bai has no legal status connecting her to Drusilla and to petition for one could take a week or more. Already the hospital has disregarded her new status as my intended and put her on the bottom rung of maximum. I need to be there. This was an intentional attack and the police are investigating it. I don't want whoever did it to succeed in killing her. Right now, she is alone and vulnerable"

"What about your mother or sister? Why not send them? Surely, no one would cross your mother."

"If your wife was ill in the hospital would she want to see your mother or sister?"

The Admiral laughed, "You're right, my mother is the last person my wife ever wants to see. Permission granted but Ket, remember you owe me for this. This is a personal favor."

"Admiral, I am indebted to you," Ket said and he knew that he would be called in on this debt and no doubt it would come in the form of a duel.

"Go to your human and I expect you to return as soon as she is stable."

Ket nodded, "Thank you," and left. He went to his quarters and packed a small bag and then went to the docking bay to take a shuttle craft. He would meet up with a larger ship along one of the main routes to take him the rest of the way back. It would take only a couple of days, he hoped. While in the shuttle craft he wrote to his mother.

Mother,

May the gods be good, Drusilla has been attacked and is at the Capital City Hospital. Please go and see to her. I have VMed the Head Doctor my permission. Set the guards outside her room and make sure she is moved up to the Imperial Floor. I am leaving now. May we now do the gods bidding.

Ket

Ket's mother entered Drusilla's room. She was unconscious. Zol had been monitoring her son's intended for hours, via live stream from the palace, but now was the first time she had entered her room. She went to Drusilla's side, pulled up a chair and sat down. Zol was worried, she wasn't getting any better and now this had more to do with the will to live than the initial illness. "Drusilla, I am Ket's mother, First Imperial Doctor Zol," she didn't expect a response, but continued talking anyway, "I've been worried about you ever since you returned from Boru." Zol spoke her mind now which she would have never done if Drusilla was awake, "You ask a lot of my son, our society and the Alliance. What you ask of Ket, his fidelity, will shake us to our core. Maybe we believed we were so clever in sidestepping the gods with our loopholes for our own pleasure that they are now reminding us of what happens when we are not obedient to their wills. And now you, one of the Lost People are to remind us of what is right. I'm beginning to believe you are, but to do this you must come back to us Drusilla. Ket will not give you up. You are his destiny and he is yours."

She took Drusilla's warm, pale hand in her own grey one and reached out her mind to Drusilla's. Zol could feel Dru's depression easily and it didn't take long to get to the root of it. Racism from the Alliance, alienation from all things familiar and longing for companionship, but most prominently the separation from her beloved Ket and the idea that she lost him. Drusilla was clearly choosing death if she couldn't have Ket. Zol had seen enough, she left Drusilla's mind and said out loud, to her unconscious form, "Ket is coming, Drusilla. He is coming for you, don't leave us."

Drusilla didn't stir and the computers monitoring her showed no difference, but Zol had instinctually felt she had made a small difference. She could feel it in Drusilla's presence in the room. Somewhere the young woman had heard her. She could feel it.

Zol put their House Vo guards outside Drusilla's rooms at the hospital for her protection and had spoken to Jane who was clearly distraught over the incident but didn't know what the proper protocol was so trusted Zol to take the appropriate actions. No one was allowed in or out that had not been cleared with Zol first.

Captain Kara had contacted Zol and told her that she wanted 'someone's head on a platter' for this. Zol had been shocked at the human's sentiments as she took it literally. She messaged Captain Kara back reminding her that even though she was human she was not a part of House Human and therefore everything would have to be organized through Jane. But she assured Captain Kara that justice would be done.

Dera had been sent to Drusilla's room to collect some personal things to make her feel better in case she woke up. Dera had never been to Drusilla's room before and was shocked by the sparseness of it. It felt so impersonal and empty. She opened Drusilla's closet and saw nothing personal besides her few pieces of clothing, nonetheless she took a spare dress and stockings for her. Then she saw the small things Ket had given to Drusilla on her desk in the boxes they had arrived in. She opened them up to see what was what and took the large piece of jewelry from his known collection and the location ring with her. Just in case she woke up before he arrived. When she opened some of the drawers in the desk, she found nothing but the notes that had arrived with the presents and found Ket's handwriting on three of them that had been set aside. Dera sighed, *You do really love him don't you, my poor Drusilla.* Then she looked around the room and couldn't see anything else that was personal to Drusilla or that would bring her any comfort and felt sorry for her friend then, literally having next to nothing that was hers. She knew now why her friend loved her brother so much, he had been her everything here. She said to the empty room, "You created this isolated prison for her by putting the ban on her. Ket, you better own up to it now."

Three days passed until Ket arrived.

Ket entered Dru's room silently. He went to her side

and took her hand. He did not speak out loud but mentally reached out to her with all his strength. He knew from his mother; she was willing herself to die. Over and over in his mind, he was calling out to her, *Drusilla, I'm here. I'm not going to leave you. Please come back to me.* After some hours the doctors tried to make him go, but he refused. Finally, his mother instructed the guards to not let anyone else in, so he wouldn't be interrupted as he tried to reach her.

The first night, every time he felt the tip of her consciousness, he would lose it again just as quickly as he had felt it, but it gave him hope. By the next morning, he had almost grasped it. He was speaking both mentally and out loud, which should have been unbelievably loud in her head to get her to come back to him. "Drusilla, I'm here, please come back to me. I can't let you go. I will do anything for you, just come back to me."

Finally, by the midday meal, when he didn't think he had any more energy to try, she opened her eyes. He had never been so relieved in his life.

Dru's eyelids were heavy, and everything was so blurry and dark. She saw a figure and hoped it was Ket. She hoped she had not imagined it. She thought she felt his cool hand and had heard his voice distantly calling out to her.

"Drusilla," he said emotionally.

She tried to speak but couldn't. He helped her drink some water from a ceramic cup, "Ket?"

He brushed some red hair back from her face, "Yes, I'm here."

"What's happening?" she asked confused.

"You have been very ill. Somehow you caught the Uli virus from Alpha Four. Thankfully, humans are stronger than Alliance people and your body fought it off, but then you've been unconscious for about a week."

"I had frightful dreams," she said still confused.

"I'm sure you did," he couldn't help but still be concerned. He was still holding her hand.

She looked at their hands and gave a small smile, "I like that you are near."

They were both quiet for a few minutes, holding hands.

"Are we still courting?"

"How can you ask that?"

"How can I not?"

"What you are asking is a very serious thing. We would be ostracized for pursuing monogamy and using binding tattoos." Ket could hear his guards stopping the doctors who were now outside the door wanting to come in. He also heard his mother talking to the doctors and he knew he needed to tell Drusilla his decision now because the doctors could only be stalled for minutes and then he may not be allowed to see her again for hours maybe days. "I've lived my whole adult life with slave artists. And as much as I adore you, I couldn't remain true to you without the binding tattoos."

Tears began to run down her cheeks, "So you are leaving me?" *Did he come all this way to leave me like this?* she wondered; heart broken by the thought.

"No," he stroked her hair with his other hand and made the Alliance sound to calm her a mixture of 'sh' and 'z's. "Quite the opposite. I've been praying a lot about this since I received your message and then when I thought I might lose you completely, I realized that the gods were telling me that they would take you away from me if I didn't submit to you. I'm here and I'm willing to pledge my life and body to you and only to you for the rest of our lives."

She didn't stop crying.

"Why are you still crying?"

"I don't know. Is this real? I can't believe you would do that for me. I was so sad thinking that you would leave, and I would have to join the Rez Club for pining over you."

"I don't want to lose you. We'll work this out. I'll consult some old diaries about how people managed fidelity without going insane."

"I don't think people go insane from lack of sex, Ket," she said flatly

He brushed some hair out of her face again, "We'll work it out. You should relax now." Ket mentally let his mother know she could let the doctors in now, which they all must have heard too, including Drusilla, if she had been listening, but she was tired, so he doubted it. "The doctors are coming in now. They'll make me leave, but I'll not leave the hospital. I'll be right here."

"Don't leave," she requested. She wanted to say, 'I want to make sure I didn't imagine what you said. I need to hear it again and again.' But she didn't.

"I'm not leaving you. I'm right outside." Gods, this pained him. When he had reached into her thoughts and memories, he had known that living in the Alliance had not been easy for her, but he had not realized the extent of just how depressing it was for her. That every day was a challenge. He felt like a fool that he had not considered how living alone in that big building was so detrimental. And then his silence over something that he should have told her that he was considering. He thought that would have been obvious, but instead he hurt her more.

Zol looked at her son and touched his arm using influence as if he were a boy again, "You came back, she is awake and those are the things that matter now."

"Every step of the way I have confused and hurt her," Ket countered.

"She must have liked something in the way you

behaved," Zol smiled. "I looked into her memories and I saw a lot of things you did right. I think we can only expect humans to change so much in one lifetime."

"But Captain Kara," Ket began.

"Is an outlier. There are always a few. And the other humans who are married are also having issues with the custom of slave artists, but none have been so vocal as Drusilla. Maybe it's because you were clever enough to insist Dera introduce her to the practice. Had you already been married, she would have never forgiven you, binding tattoos or not at that point."

"I can't give her up. We'll take the tattoos. I hope this will not affect our position as First Imperial House." Ket felt guilty for Dera then, her position would be put in jeopardy over this. She would have to marry now, something that they all hoped she would not have to do.

"I think if a daughter is born as soon as possible, our position will remain stable despite this archaic cultural custom being suddenly employed again. As long as it's only Drusilla demanding it people will just think it is romantic that she cannot share you. We will try to keep this a secret for as long as possible. There will be rumors of course."

Ket nodded, "One more thing, I don't want her returning to House Human. She is too lonely there. I want her to move to our home."

"No, she'll have to remain where she is, it's only for a couple more months."

"This is an unprecedented situation."

"I've seen it too, but it doesn't mean that she wants to give up when she has almost won the race. Let her decide. If she comes to me and asks for a place to live, I'll welcome her. But I'll not do it because you ask it."

Ket looked into Drusilla's room. The doctors were still with her, they were talking about a human illness he had never heard of, apparently it was similar to Uli and this is why she was able to recover. Ket could just barely hear that they were finishing up their conversation. As they left, he went in. All the doctors gave him varying looks of disapproval as they went by.

He sat down next to Drusilla's bed and they looked at each other in silence for many minutes.

Dru was so happy to see Ket, that he was really here and that this was not a dream. He looked so tired though, he had dark circles under his eyes. She reached out for his hand and he granted it. "I hope you didn't lose your position by coming back."

He smiled at her and touched her face gently, "No, but the whole Empire now can see how in love I am with you." This was something that Alliance society frowned upon this outward display of love, because it unsettled people.

She smiled.

"Drusilla, I don't like to think of you alone in the apartment building where you are now. Would you like to live elsewhere?"

"As you know I'm bound by my contract with the Empire. I must live there with the forcefield and the guards until I marry. I thought I only had a matter of months left. We are getting married after I finish my practical. We are, aren't we?"

"Of course, although I'll ask you properly."

"When?"

"When we are not in a hospital."

"Ask me now."

Ket reached out his mind to hers to just explain all of his reasons for not wanting to do it now. How it would diminish all that he had to offer her and look bad on them both.

Dru welcomed his thoughts into hers. She reflected

how comfortable it was becoming. She looked directly into his eyes and then said out loud, "I don't care about those things. You came back for me and have agreed to what I must have in a marriage. That is enough."

He looked into her green eyes and said formally, "Drusilla Anne James of House Human, my beautiful human, captured in war, traded and brought to the Alliance Empire for a new life and blessed by the gods, will you pledge your life and body to me, bound to me in wedlock?"

Dru's heart was beating so loudly she could hear it in her ears, "Ket of House Vo, Imperial Doctor and my one true love in all the galaxy, it would be my honor to be your wife and pledge my life and body to you and you to me." Dru closed her eyes then, relieved.

Ket could feel her relief wash over him.

Dru knew this pledge was binding, it could not be easily undone and would be made permanent with an intimate wedding ceremony, "You'll make the announcement?"

"Yes."

"The doctors said I could sleep," Dru murmured, "but I want to hear your voice will you read to me? My cultural handbook is on my IC. Then you will know what I know about Alliance marriages and can fill in the gaps."

Ket picked up her IC and handed it to her. She took it with shaky hands, "Unlock for Ket, House Vo, facial recognition," then she handed it to him, and he was now registered to her IC.

He easily found her cultural handbook and began reading from the chapter about courting and marriage as she drifted off to sleep. He was surprised at how much was left out and it was no wonder now how at every turn she was confused. There were too many gaps that she filled in with her own human experiences, which just didn't make sense in Alliance culture. He took a break and watched her sleep. Then he began reading again, "Now Chapter 76, Children, I'm looking forward to this chapter." She was drifting in and out of sleep so every now and then he added his own commentary and sometimes she would reply back with a witty remark, a smile or a question.

Children are sacred in the Alliance. Whether a female or male child is born to you, you have been blessed by the gods. Once your child is born you will typically pray to the gods for a name in the first two weeks of its birth. Some names are passed down through families and some names are new. Trust in the gods to help you find the right one for your child. During the first year, you should take your child to the nearest temple to be blessed. This is usually done with a sacrificial animal. This is an important step in your child's life and will help them in the future.

Dru said something then and Ket stopped reading and looked at her, "Yes?"

"We aren't blessing our child with a sacrificial animal." The idea of doing this reminded her of her childhood and she didn't want any violence near a baby of her own.

Ket smiled broadly, "No, we don't have to do that. Our daughter can be a heathen just like her mother."

"I pray every day."

"I have been inside your mind."

She sighed and smiled, "And hopefully elsewhere soon."

That night she was cleared to leave the hospital. Ket escorted her as far as the doorway to her building.

"I'll message you every day," he said. "We'll marry on

the 3rd day of the 62nd week of this year 18905, the day after you finish your practicals. It's not long." He was reluctant to leave her. "You can always move to be with my family if you need to. Don't hesitate to ask my mother."

"I'll be fine. It's not long now and I have my work," It wasn't in Dru's nature to ask for help and she definitely didn't want to do it from someone she would have to ask for help from in the future for more important things.

"Trust in the gods that they will keep you safe," he squeezed her hand and sent her the sensation of a kiss. "And may the gods continue to light your way."

"May I see their path," Dru replied and gave him a small smile and then turned to enter her almost empty building.

Ket met with his family before returning to the *Tuir*.

"She is a sensible woman not wanting to move here," Zol commented over dinner.

"Drusilla isn't like some of the other humans that I have seen," Dera made a face. "She definitely isn't like Captain Kara." The whole family made faces of disgust then.

"She won't be Empress," Zol predicted to put them at ease. "There are too many who would challenge her for it and she just isn't capable. This is why Tir keeps her off planet."

"Brother," Kio addressed Ket, "Aren't you worried of someone challenging Drusilla? Especially after what's happened now?"

It had crossed Ket's mind too many times, "Of course, but we must trust in the gods. Thankfully, it seems she has only a few true enemies."

"And they are cowards," Dera commented softly. "Rez

should have just challenged Drusilla if she wanted to kill her."

"Over what?" Zol asked. "Drusilla has done nothing, and I think most people have sympathy for her, the only human who has really embraced the Alliance. Rez would only make herself look bad by challenging such a weak opponent."

"I wish I could challenge Rez for almost ruining everything."

"Over what? There is no proof. She was very clever. We cannot prove anything and as such we cannot challenge her over it, but her time will come. This won't be forgotten."

"Ket, does Drusilla even own a proper sword? You should feel ashamed that I even have to ask," Zol berated her son.

"I know she has a sword and a teacher. It's only now that I've considered these scenarios," Ket admitted trying to defend himself.

"She has one, but I suspect it is a beginner's sword. Her guardian is more about proper manners than challenges and duels. I don't think the Empire envisioned any of these human women marrying into Imperial Families. Madame Bai was chosen to help them face more practical and cultural issues, not the power struggles of the ruling class."

"Dera," Ket said, "Buy her a proper sword and make sure her teacher is decent," it was forbidden for Ket to do these things for Drusilla.

"And the rest of us will try to watch over her as best as we can. It's only a matter of months now." Zol said and then looked at Ket, "And no more strong displays of love either, we don't need any more attention around this."

Ket said nothing. He would do it again if he had to. Drusilla would have just simply slipped away without him.

357

It was the first time in his life a woman needed him. He loved the feeling that he meant so much to her. That he provided the strength she needed to come back to them and continue this life. And he knew this was exactly what his mother feared. Human women changing their culture by putting their faith in men.

Ket was true to his word and he sent Drusilla a VM every morning before he went on duty. He also made sure she had flowers from Earth in her room every week, as Frank the Earth Store owner, had suggested. As well as a constant supply of her favorite foods and drinks from the Earth Store. Drusilla had, of course, been reluctant to name the things she wanted, so he had Frank choose different things he thought she would like and varied it weekly. He hoped that these small acts made Drusilla feel good about her future and life in the Alliance. He was constantly worried that she would suffer another attack and it might be the end of her.

He even had a necklace sent to her with their hair braided together in a tiny braid incased in a smooth circular crystal pendant. On the back was the inscription,

May our paths always meet
18905

The necklace she found out was to be worn under her clothes and would rest in between her breasts, near her heart. It also would get hot and cold depending on the nearness of Ket. Of course, it only worked if he was on the planet, but she found it very charming.

Every day she was reminded of him, the flowers, the food and the necklace with their tiny braid and she counted the days until she would be able to be with him, get married and move into her own home. She was tired of eating her meals while a slave watched and having few people to talk to. She tried to invite Dera over a few times, but their schedules never lined up. She assumed though that Dera just didn't want to come over as she kept suggesting to meet at restaurants and places Dru couldn't afford, probably not realizing that Dru had no money for such things.

As the weeks passed, she was surprised to receive a written message from Ket around midday. She was at the hospital so went into her office to see what he had to say as it was unusual for him to message her now and in a written message too,

Drusilla,

As our wedding draws closer, we must meet to discuss the small logistics of the ceremony, choose wedding bracelets and where we will spend the four weeks after. I will return to the Capital Planet next week, the 3rd day to discuss this with you. Specific details to follow.

Ket

She was excited to see him again. He always told her he wouldn't tell her when he was coming home until it was certain so she wouldn't be disappointed. She thought about the message again and wondered though if this was some formal Alliance thing and they were going to have to do more than decide which two people would be their witnesses. Before she could think about it more, she was called back into work and then forgot to reach out to Madame Bai to ask about it. Both when Rebecca and Captain Kara had married it had been quick. She hadn't witnessed either, but she wasn't under the impression that Alliance weddings required much planning, so she was confused as to why they would have to meet specially to plan everything.

Dru had taken the day off work, as she was entitled to apparently, to plan her wedding with Ket. She felt like all of her colleagues knew something she didn't know was going to happen today or that they were all just really excited about weddings. She couldn't decide. But she found their enthusiasm contagious. She put on her best day dress, the known jewelry necklace, her ID necklace and the location ring. She had not felt this happy or content with her life in years.

Dru met him outside of a park in the city she had never been to before. They smiled at each other. She wanted to run into his arms but controlled herself. He briefly took her hand and said quietly, "I missed you so much," and then let go. "There is a place in the center of the park called 'Fire'. It's a common place to discuss everything we need to talk about."

Dru nodded and let him lead the way. It wasn't a far walk.

When they reached the building, it was painted red which made Dru smile and she wondered if it was painted red to be modern and sleek or to be unstable. She wanted to ask Ket, but he was busy checking in with a computer.

Then he led her down a hallway and up an elevator into a beautiful room with floor to ceiling windows and a comfortable seating area with a computer panel on the table. It was like an Alliance hotel room but without a bed.

When the door closed behind them, Dru turned around and pushed herself into his arms. He held her very tightly and then she looked at him, her green eyes begging for a kiss and he obliged.

It wasn't long before his hands were roaming her body over her dress. He kissed her neck and said in between kisses, "You're so divine, but we really do need to decide things." But he didn't stop kissing her or groping her breasts.

"I don't care, you decide everything," she said trying to unbutton the top of his uniform.

He put both of his hands on either side of her face then kissed her and said, "Let's quickly make our decisions and then get back to this. I don't want you to be surprised on our wedding day because there is something you have completely culturally missed. And we will have four weeks to just be together after the wedding."

Dru wasn't having it, she tried to kiss him again.

He picked her up under her arms, her legs going around his waist and he kissed her again, even more passionately. His tongue exploring every inch of her mouth. After a couple minutes he carried her over to the sofa and lay her down below him. He began stroking her hair and kissing her neck while his other hand played with the nipple piercing over her loose dress. Her soft and warm hands had undone his shirt now and were caressing him. He hadn't been with a slave artist since he left her last and he was desperate for her touch. She tried to remove his shirt and he stopped her, "Not yet. Let's do the other first." Then he did reluctantly move away.

"I don't think I can concentrate on anything you say until I kiss you more," she admitted and bit her lip.

Ket looked at that and couldn't control himself either, "I'm timing this though, so we don't waste all of our time only doing this."

"We're not wasting time," Dru said as she removed his shirt and began kissing and licking his torso and then his nipples. His hands were in her hair and he was unbraiding it. Dru had never felt so sexy in her life.

Dru began undoing his trousers, she pulled them down as she got to her knees and when she saw his erect penis, she wanted to take it into her mouth. Her tongue just got to lick the top of it before he pulled her back, "No, it goes against the gods to do that."

Dru was confused and wondered if they were going to have sex then, they were almost married so maybe they were. She wanted to ask but then he was taking her dress off and kissing her torso up to her bra clad breasts, she was so pleased now she wore the long nipple rings he had given her before. It had been a last-minute decision based on the looks of her colleagues. And her mind was a blur. He expertly undid her bra for a man who had never done it before, and his thumbs and mouth were immediately on her nipples when he saw the exquisite jewelry there. She was in ecstasy under his ministrations. And after about 20 minutes she was sure he was going to make her come and she was still wearing her underwear and hadn't even touched her upper thighs let alone her vulva or clitoris.

Dru was projecting everything to Ket which made this all easy. He knew exactly what was pleasing her and what was not. He was sure that he could resist having sex with her until he saw the nipple rings and he remembered the image she had shyly sent to him, which he looked at frequently when he masturbated as he was no longer pleasing himself with slave artists, and knew that he would not be able to resist her now. Their marriage was only weeks away and if she became pregnant the dates could always be arranged through bribes as these things did happen frequently, especially at Fire, he had heard the stories. He almost laughed to himself when he thought he would be different, but his friends, who were already married had just smiled.

Dru had her hands in Ket's hair lightly, he needed no guidance, her thighs were pressed together, and she couldn't believe that he was going to make her come simply by kissing, licking and stroking her nipples. She didn't even know this was possible. The buildup had been slow, not like anything she had experienced before and now her body was so tense. She didn't know if she should say something. She momentarily lost her edge by thinking too much and then told herself, *Just enjoy it and find out the protocol later.*

Ket enjoyed listening to Dru's inner dialogue as he pleased her. He wanted to tell her that he knew she was close to orgasm because of her body's behavior, but he didn't want to interrupt her pleasure. He quickly brought her to a short orgasm, as with the breasts it was always short. Then, he abandoned her breasts and moved down her body to remove her underwear. As he did, he kissed all along the top of her vulva and thighs and murmured, "This is so unhealthy to suffocate yourself like this."

Before she could answer he was licking up and down her vulva with big strokes of his tongue. She couldn't think. She didn't know if she should put her hands on his head, but he didn't need any direction, then he took one of his hands and put her hands above her head. Then returned to licking her. He was going so slowly, just like with her breasts, and she didn't know if she could handle it. Then when she thought she couldn't take anymore; he began using his fingers instead to rub with more pressure. Then his tongue again. He kept changing right before she didn't think she could take anymore. She had never felt so much pleasure.

Ket loved how open she was. He opened himself up now too, just a little, but he didn't know if she felt it because she was so overwhelmed. He realized that this might be the first time she was having sex with a man that she liked. He wanted to make sure that it was amazing for her. He was taking as much care as he could to edge her for as long as possible. When he realized she had reached her point he used his finger on her clitoris stroking it quickly in small circles as he watched her beautiful face flushed with pink and her mouth open so attractively, he kissed all of her moans as she came for at least a minute. Then he gently continued caressing her down her orgasm, lightly stroking her saying all the while, "You're so beautiful."

Dru could feel Ket, not just physically but mentally too. She was with him; it was the only way she could articulate it to herself. She knew now what he wanted and expected. She kissed him and their minds met one another in such a way she didn't think was possible. His mental touch was almost as strong as his physical one and she knew that he wanted to have sex both ways. She was willing although completely ignorant of what he meant by mental sex. She obliged him physically though. She thoroughly kissed him, the length of his body and then rose to position herself over his large erect penis. She didn't doubt it would fit. She knew what women's bodies were capable of she just wondered briefly how long it would hurt until it didn't hurt.

Ket put his hands gently on her hips guiding his

gorgeous exotic human over him. He spoke quietly and gently to her, "Go as slow as you like." He had never been with someone so inexperienced before and had only heard stories from slave artists about how delicate you needed to be with young women. He didn't want to hurt her or rush her. He had prayed a lot over this and done extensive research about monogamy. This first times needed to be slow and exploratory more than expertly executed. He didn't want her to feel like she would never catch up to him, in terms of experience.

Dru looked into Ket's grey eyes and began to lower herself onto his ridged penis, so slowly. It was so large and thick, she experienced a mild burning sensation, as her vagina stretched to accommodate him, mixed in with extreme pleasure. She closed her eyes focusing on the pleasure. She just kept on going and then stopped when she felt she couldn't go any further. "This feels amazing," she said opening her eyes and looking down at him.

"I'm completely spellbound," he said. She was so tight around him and her innocent thoughts made him cherish her even more for this. She bent down to kiss him, and he gently urged her with his hands on her hips to slowly begin moving.

Dru loved the feel of his strong hands on her hips, guiding her. She closed her eyes and reveled in the sensations. She didn't know for how long they stayed in this position, but she loved his gentleness.

As she became more comfortable, and his need greater, he urged her onto her back. He slowly moved in and out of her caressing her hair and the side of her face. Her hands were in his hair, which she had undone, and it spilled around them now. "I'd do anything for you Drusilla," he whispered in her ear as he slowly increased his speed.

Dru felt Ket both physically and mentally again, she didn't know if she had been so overwhelmed that she had forgotten about the other half or if he had backed off, but now she felt him. He was sharing his intense mental desire for her and it was intermixing with her own emotions. It was as if their minds were running off together as well in some kind of unspoken mating. His touch became her touch and vice versa, she felt what it was like to be him inside of her and he was her. It was all ecstasy and it was overwhelming. She thought she was coming again but didn't know if it was him, but it didn't matter they were one. Then, she felt his penis convulsing and her own mental reaction riding along with his. Physically she came again too. It was the strangest most wonderful feeling she had ever felt.

Ket slowly moved out of her and lay next to her running his hands through her long red hair. He could feel her contentment and was pleased he had not made a mistake this time. He had had his doubts about his own abilities, not to rush things and to be gentle.

"Is it always like that for you?" she asked looking over at him, finding it strange to be only in her own mind again.

"What do you mean?"

"Your mind in mine and vice versa?"

"No, this was the first time. I've never had sex with another telepath before. I had glimmers of it with some other women while courting but I never had sex with them. Nothing like this. This was exhilarating. How did you find it?" He knew already because she had been projecting but he wanted to ask to be polite and see how she answered. He began casually playing with the jewelry on her right breast.

"It was magnificent. I didn't know it could be like this."

"Apparently, it will only get stronger over time when we

can really control it. And don't think I'm not nervous about that either," he said pausing to take her nipple into his mouth again, "You're the much stronger telepath."

"Am I?"

"Yes," he said confidently. "You could conjure all kinds of fantasies if you put your mind to it." He sucked on her other breast. "I've been dreaming about this for a long time Drusilla."

She closed her eyes and enjoyed his touch, the feel of his long hair over her body and the knowledge that this would be forever.

After they held each other for a while, Ket rose and said, "We do actually have to do some work, we should get dressed." He held out a hand to Drusilla and helped her up.

She wanted to use the toilet before dressing and shower if there was one.

"Don't shower, I want to smell me on you for the rest of the time we are together."

"You can smell that?"

"Yes, especially without your clothes on."

"Can other people smell that?"

"Probably, but everyone knows we are to be married and most people do this," he assured her.

"Why didn't you mention this to me before?"

"After our date around the Promenade, I didn't think you would mind?"

"Wait, what are we talking about the smell or the sex?" she asked.

"Both," he grinned. He followed her into the bathroom.

"Are you going to watch me?"

"I don't trust you not to jump into the shower."

"True. Was I projecting again?"

"No, but I do know you quite well now. Through all our conversations and in the hospital, I was deep into your thoughts, and now…" he trailed off.

She suddenly felt a moment of panic as the toilet cleaned her, "How much do you know of my life or are we talking personality?"

Ket looked offended, "Drusilla, I would never look into any of your memories without your permission. Don't ever think it."

"Sorry, I didn't know the protocol. I didn't know if someone was dying if you were allowed." She got up and then stood before him and wanted to change the subject, "Speaking of protocol, do you want me to tell you when I'm going to orgasm? Is that a thing?" She had seen some movies where that was a thing but maybe not in the Alliance. Maybe it only happened in human movies because men on Earth typically didn't know women had orgasms at all, that it was such a momentous occasion they said that.

He couldn't help but smile at her, "You are adorable. You can do what you like, but I always know from your body. Some women like to scream it out and others are quiet."

"Which do you prefer?"

"Neither, it has nothing to do with me. It's your pleasure."

"Come on, really?"

He shrugged his shoulders and used the toilet himself, while she watched him. She had a flashback then of what it was like to be him thrusting inside of her and it felt familiar and strange at the same time.

When they began collecting their clothing from the floor, Ket took her dress from her, "Let me," and he dressed her minus her underwear of course. Then he

368

braided her hair quickly and put in the hair pin, "It's not as nice as you had it before, but I know you can't braid it yourself."

"How do you know?"

"You intermittently project things all the time around me, it's sweet. But don't worry, I now always create a blocking bubble around us so no one else can hear you. Now," he said grabbing his own clothing and putting it on quickly, "we must sort out our wedding."

"What do we need to decide?"

Ket got out his IC and made it visible through the panel on the small table between them.

"I love your detailed list," she said only half joking.

1. *Location*
2. *Witnesses*
3. *Bracelets*
4. *Binding tattoos*
5. *Drusilla's requests*
6. *Destination*
7. *Drusilla's personal effects*
8. *Jewelry*

"Where should we get married? I don't want to do it from my building. I know Rebecca did but that was just strange. We were all sectioned off while her husband and his friends were there."

"No, we definitely aren't doing that," Ket agreed. "We can marry from my parents' home. It's unusual but not that unusual. Do you agree?"

"Yes."

"Good. Now witnesses, who do you want? These are usually two close friends or a sister."

"Dera is my only friend," Dru admitted. "I guess Jane as well. Who will be your witnesses?"

"My brother Kio and my friend Hez. Check the date with everyone if Jane is off planet you need someone else."

"What if I don't have anyone else?"

"Madame Bai?"

"Oh yes, of course."

"Now marriage bracelets. We will wear these for the rest of our lives, so do you have any preference of the kind we get?" He brought up different examples of bracelets with black and silver and some with different script.

"I see the differences, but I don't have a strong preference and I don't understand the cultural subtleties they carry with them. I trust you to choose."

"Are you sure?"

"Yes."

"Binding tattoos. There will be an oath to take before we give each other the tattoos and we will do that before we consummate our marriage. There are set words of course that we must recite. It will hurt. And we must decide where we want them."

"Where do people usually put them?"

"In the past, when they were commonplace, they were worn on the right forearm, so that, in women's clothing especially, they could be seen."

"Why don't we just put them there?" she asked without thinking.

Ket sighed, "Because we are being over the top by even doing this, I don't want to advertise it."

"Why not?" Dru was becoming defensive. "If I'm marrying you and wearing a bracelet that says I belong to your House, you are absolutely wearing a tattoo that signifies, 'I'll pass out if I have sex with anyone other than my wife.'"

"Fine," he said annoyed. "But you are never wearing underwear ever again," then he paused and added, "Or pajamas or any other human clothing that you know is unhealthy and ugly." He looked her directly in the eyes, more serious than she had ever seen him, "And we will have a daughter or have as many sons to prove that we tried. We are risking a lot."

She knew he wasn't really being serious now or he would have phrased it differently and made it a part of their official compromises, so she ignored his little tirade about her human comforts. "What do you mean about proving we tried?" she could tell he was exasperated by her question. "If I grew up here, I'd know, now please explain it to me so that I'll know for the next time."

"We are questioning everyone who does not live monogamous relationships now. If we have a daughter all will be forgiven. If we have many children people will just think we are really in love. If we have no children, people will think we want to revive the gods' will for monogamy and that we look down on the practice of slave artists after marriage. Everyone believes that slave artists within marriages represent the will of the gods and it's their 'right path'."

"But when did that become the 'right path' away from monogamy and why?"

"Religion is always changing to meet the needs of the civilization. I can't remember the historical influences that changed our society, but they happened thousands of years ago. By the time the law was actually changed, everyone was already doing it anyway. Right now, I just don't want to be challenged to duels because you needed a monogamous relationship."

"I hope we can have children then."

He mentally said, *We will cheat if we can't,* but out loud he said, "We will trust the gods' decisions. Now, about our home. You'll need to arrange to see it with my mother and decide what you want."

"What do you mean by 'what I want'?"

"At the moment, our house is sparsely furnished. It will be up to you to make it our home. You tell my mother what you want, and she arranges it. However, you want to change it or want it decorated."

"Ket, I have no experience with this. What would you want it to look like? I don't know anything about Alliance homes. I don't want to make a mistake."

He felt sorry for her then, most Alliance women looked forward to this most of all and she was worried about making a mistake. "There are no mistakes. What's that other human's name that was married?"

"Captain Kara?"

He gave her a look that said, 'Be serious.'

"Rebecca."

"Yes, she requested things from Earth. You can do the same. Also, I'm skipping forward here but all of your belongings from the human fleet have already been delivered to our house."

"Wow, it took them long enough."

"Well, you know. It wasn't because they didn't know where to find you."

Dru frowned, "Of course not. Can Dera help me with the house?"

"No, you must do it yourself. There are no mistakes and my mother is fond of you so I doubt there will be huge disagreements about decency as there was with Rebecca."

"What happened there? I didn't hear anything."

"Her husband told me, another time when we have

more time, I will tell you what happened. Now, we must decide where to go after our wedding. We have four weeks and there are two resorts to choose from. One is more tropical and modern and the other more mountains, ocean and rustic."

"I don't like the sun, not even the Alliance sun."

"No, me neither. That was easy. Last thing, which is good because we are almost out of time. You will receive, of course, all of my known jewelry, but I would also like to buy you some personal items which you choose. Even something from Earth? Frank has begun importing it. What do you think?"

"I don't need any more jewelry Ket," she said and then saw that she hurt his feelings. "I'm sorry. It's a cultural difference. Let me take that back and say, "I would love to have a look at what Frank has to intermix with my Alliance jewelry." He gave her a half smile then and she got up, sat on his lap and kissed him for some time. Then without getting up said, "I'm trying too."

"I know. We'll find our way." Then their time was up. They left the room and Ket had to return to the *Tuir*. He promised to be back soon.

As they said their goodbyes, she couldn't help but ask, "Is my underwear in your pocket?"

"Of course, it is."

"And you really never want me to wear it again?" she smiled.

"Well, I was just upset, we'll see."

"Can I have it back then?"

"Absolutely not." He brushed her cheek with the back of his hand, "May the gods watch over you until we are together again."

This was the traditional saying between married couples and Dru didn't think it would resonate with her the way it did now when she said the response, "And bring you back to me so we may live in their light."

It was a couple weeks before Ket returned to the Capital Planet. During that time Dru was still alone with the three slaves in the building. And life moved in a slow rhythm. Every week was identical. The only variations in Dru's days came in her messages to Ket, her requirements on 4th days and her tasks at the hospital. She also took a keen interest in the 1,000 human women still being held in orbit and had begun asking questions. In her free time, she began exploring the Capital City now that she was allowed more freedom than she was when she first arrived. Most people knew her by sight now, so she was treated with respect, which she appreciated, rather than cold and curious looks.

Tonight, after work, Dru decided to walk around the Shopping District. It was the most prestigious of places to shop and even though Dru had no intention of buying anything, she thought it was time she at least saw it. Her other motive for not going directly home was so that she wouldn't think about Ket. She knew he was on planet as her necklace between her breasts was warm and she knew by the location rings they shared that he was also in the city. But he hadn't contacted her except to say that he had some things he needed to do and then would get back in touch tomorrow. She wanted to keep herself from thinking too much about what he might be doing without her.

The perfect wide pedestrian streets of the Shopping District were full of shoppers, mostly Alliance but also other off-worlders from rich cultures. She was the only human. She casually walked along the streets and looked into some shop windows. She had been into numerous

Alliance shops with Madame Bai before, but they were all mid-range shops which anyone could enter. These shops were reserved for the highest class and even though Dru was technically considered maximum class now by her being human and even more so with Ket's rank, she still was reluctant to enter any of them.

As Dru was looking in a jeweler's window, out of the corner of her eye, she thought she saw Ket. She looked down at her location ring and it was almost clear so she knew it must be him. She continued to stare, and after a minute or two, she was sure it was him. She was going to go to him until she noticed who he was with and she stood completely still. It was Rez. They were speaking closely. She could not hear them, but she could feel them. He was angry and she was, Dru hesitated she could not identify this emotion. Then she got it, Rez was infatuated, or rather obsessed. Dru took deep breaths watching them. Suddenly, Ket said something and Rez hurried away with her head down and ran right into Dru with a force so strong Rez knocked her to the ground. Dru got up and Ket was running over to help her.

Rez spit on Dru, "You hairy human whore. I challenge you to a duel. You have used your human witchcraft to enchant one of our own. To all who hear, I am challenging this human, Drusilla James of House Human, to a duel for stealing one of our own with human witchcraft."

Dru stood in front of Rez now, defiant. She brushed the dirt from her coat, "Go home Rez, you pathetic woman. I'm not going to fight any duel."

Everyone who stopped to listen gasped at this. Ket then took Dru aside and whispered in her ear, "Say you will fight the duel now and we will sort it out later, by saying you won't, puts an impediment between our marriage."

Dru looked at Ket, "What nonsense is this?"

375

Ket said nothing more but nodded to her as a way to urge her to say she would fight the duel.

Dru looked at Rez with scorn, "Fine, I'll fight your duel only to prove that I used no witchcraft to seduce Ket. The gods' will will prove that you are just a jealous woman and nothing more."

Many of the onlookers said, "Thanks be to the gods that you seek their justice." Then the crowd dispersed, satisfied that justice would be done between the two women.

Rez looked at Drusilla, "The Alliance will rejoice when I sink my sword into your throat you barbaric human."

Dru grabbed Rez by the neck tightly. She had not been in a physical fight since she had been a young girl, but all of her instincts came back now. And all of the hatred she carried for Rez, who had made her life miserable, was concentrated in her hand holding Rez's neck.

Both Rez and Ket were shocked to see Drusilla become so violent suddenly. Neither one realized she had it in her.

"Rez, I've wanted an opportunity to kill you for some time. If I were you," she squeezed as Rez tried to reach her hand around her throat, gasping for breath and Dru could hear Ket somewhere telling her to let go, "I'd stop this nonsense now."

Then she let go and Rez grasped for breath holding her throat and she managed to cough out, "And this is what you choose Ket? This barbarian to soil our genes?"

Ket looked at Rez and just wished he had never even spoken to her, ever, "Leave Rez. You've done and said quite enough."

She gave them both nasty looks and walked away.

Dru looked at Ket, "That's it? 'You've done quite enough'? Remind me never to count on you to insult someone."

Ket ignored her and looked her in the eyes, "Are you okay?"

"Okay in that I just said I would fight a duel to the death with a woman who accused me of seducing you with witchcraft? No, of course I'm not okay. I don't want to die by a medieval sword because I was accused of witchcraft." It hit a little too close to home for Dru thinking about her life in the Exterior.

"It won't go to a duel, you just had to say it now. She is upset. She won't follow through. It would not be a fair fight."

"That's true. I picked up a sword for the first-time last year and I'm not very good." Then she looked at him, "Why were you meeting her anyway?" Dru tried to hide her jealousy, but she couldn't.

"I wasn't. We just ran into each other. She heard that we were getting married and was trying to convince me that it was the worst thing I could do, to marry a human, and you, in particular."

"How did you respond?"

"What do you think I said?" he said a bit annoyed that she would even ask that question. Then he realized he should be a bit gentler; she was his Drusilla. She was frightened by what just happened. "When she told me, I shouldn't marry a human I told her that I believed you were the Lost People and that you are my true other half. And that is when she ran off. It was unlucky you were standing right here. What are you doing here?"

"I was just looking around. My mind was restless." She looked up at him, "Do you really think I'm your true other half?" Alliance people believed that men and women used to be all one being in the beginning of time, but that they had so angered the gods that they had been split in two, men and women, as punishment and so now, men and women would spend forever searching for their true other half.

"Of course, I do," he said not even bothering to ask if she felt the same. He didn't want to hear the answer. He knew that he loved Drusilla more than she loved him, and he didn't like to think about it. "Let me walk you home now. It is getting late," he checked the time, it was a good 45-minute walk through the city to her building. "Or should we take a transport, so you don't miss the evening meal?"

"No, I want to walk. I am upset. I couldn't eat anyway," They walked in silence for a couple of minutes, "What happens with Rez now?"

"She'll go home and calm down."

"And if she doesn't?"

"She will. This is lunacy."

"Tell me what happens if she doesn't, so I don't have to waste time looking it up in my cultural handbook that will only give me a vague idea of the procedure anyway. Then I'll have to waste a couple hours shifting through the government laws about it and I don't want to have to do that."

"If she doesn't calm down, she will put in a formal request for a duel, which you don't need to answer as there were already witnesses here today that heard you say you would fight her in a duel. And then the duel will be set for seven days from today. At any time during that waiting period Rez or you can cancel it."

"What happens if I cancel it?"

"It means you are agreeing to her accusations."

"That is ridiculous. How can this be justice? Anyone can just walk around accusing someone they don't like of something?"

"Most people would never do what she has done, so

378

people take it very seriously, especially if it goes to a duel. It means that she is willing to die for her belief that you wronged her or the Alliance in some way."

"But I can't win if it goes to a duel. How is that justice? This is insane. You put a ban on me before I even met you."

"Someone from your House can fight in your stead."

She laughed because the idea was so ridiculous, "No one in House Human could win." Then almost with tears in her eyes she asked, "What am I going to do? I don't want to die like this." She remembered the scenes from the duel he had shared with her.

He put his arm around her and said, "It won't come to that. She won't make this formal."

The next morning, Dru woke up to her IC chiming on emergency alert. She picked it up and looked at it. It was Jane calling in real time, "Jane?"

"James, what the hell is going on down there?"

"What?"

"The duel. We just read about it. Captain has convinced Admiral Tir to let us return to support you. Are you really going to fight this woman Rez? How do you even know her?"

"She is a nasty piece of work who I had the pleasure of getting to know at the medical school. She hates humans and is rather obsessed with Ket. She ran into us last night and lost her mind. He said that she would probably calm down and not go through with it."

"Unfortunately, she is going through with it. Do you think you can win?"

"No."

"Okay. We will come up with some kind of plan. Captain is angry as hell that this is even allowed."

"But she's not in our house. Apparently, someone from our House can fight for me."

"Oh, but you can change Houses."

"How? Ket and I can't marry until I finish my practical at the hospital."

"I know, Captain says that she can adopt you or some such nonsense and then you will be a part of the Admiral's House and Captain will fight for you."

Dru looked at Jane with dread, "Adopted by the Captain? What would I have to do?"

"Be loyal to her forever," Jane said evenly. "Look James, it's not the best position you'd ever want to be in, I know. But it's better than death."

"And if Captain dies then what?"

"In the duel? Then I am sure the Admiral would kill you himself."

"Such a lovely culture isn't it?" she sighed. "I guess I don't have much of a choice, do I?"

"No. We'll arrive back the night before the duel. I'll file all the formal documents as you know this all has to be sanctioned, but thankfully, Admiral Tir, Captain Kara and I are all together here. When we arrive on planet though you will need to complete the change of House with a formal ceremony at Captain's home the night before the duel. I'll come and get you at our building and take you there myself."

Dru nodded. "Thank you," she said it because she had to, not because she thought this was a good idea at all, but it was her only way of possibly surviving this Alliance dueling mess.

7

A Women's Duel

Dru met Ket in a small café not far from House Human.
They found a place to sit and talked quietly. Ket specifically chose this place as it was not in the best area of town
and people would look the other way if they were too
close.

"Are you ready?"

"You know I'm not, but I've no choice," Dru said
unemotionally.

"Being connected to such a high House won't be bad.
No one will dare threaten you after this. And Captain
Kara is making quite a stand for humans. I'm surprised
that Rez hasn't called it off. If she kills Captain Kara over
this, Admiral Tir will be very angry."

"Captain may be new to the sword, but she was a born
killer."

"Good, but she needs more," he said and spoke so
quietly in her ear so it looked like they might be kissing,
"You can use your manipulative telepathy without being
detected in the arena. You'll need to do that tomorrow," he
said and then couldn't resist kissing her neck. "Rez will be

using hers, as is her right, to make your captain see things that are not there. You'll need to protect her."

"How is that fair?" Dru whispered.

Ket kissed in a long sensual kiss and answered equally softly, "It's not fair, but it's her natural skill, so she can use it."

Dru felt her stomach drop. She was very concerned she would really die now, "I want to be with you now. Let's go somewhere private."

Ket looked into her eyes, "We don't have much time."

"I don't care. I need to be so close to you right now. I might die tomorrow," Dru knew that she sounded emotional, she just couldn't help it.

He stood up, "Your room then. We'll be heavily fined and probably have to also pay penance to the Grand City Temple."

"I don't care, I may be dead tomorrow anyway."

They passed the guards on their way into her building, who said nothing to them, and Dru asked, "Why aren't' they stopping you?"

"We are engaged. I'm allowed to be here now, but the slaves will monitor us."

"Do you mean they are going to watch us?"

"Probably."

They took the glass elevator up to the living quarters and Dru decided that she didn't care if her rude slaves had to watch her have sex with Ket. It served them right for being such terrible slaves. Sure, enough, when they entered the great fire room, all three slaves were there waiting for them.

"We are going to my room to have sex," Dru announced boldly and all the slaves looked at each other, then some universal credits were exchanged, which made Ket laugh and Dru frown. Then, one of the slaves nodded and followed Dru and Ket up the stairs to her room.

Inside Dru's room, her least favorite slave took a seat in the corner and said, "Go on, I don't have all day and neither do you two."

Dru frowned.

Ket took Drusilla's face in his hands, "Focus only on me. This may be the last time. The slaves are the embodiment of the gods, no different. You and I are the only mortals in this room."

Dru nodded.

Ket began kissing her and caressing her all over. After some minutes he took off her dress and then all of her undergarments. When she was naked before him, he lifted her up and set her on the edge of the bed, positioning himself so that he could easily bring her to climax by licking her clitoris. Just before he began the slave watching asked him a question.

"You like that fiery fur then? I told her someone might like it."

Ket smiled and replied not looking at the slave, "I love it." Then reached up and tilted Drusilla's head back down to look at him, "Only me. Don't think about her."

Dru wanted to forget everything, the slave in the room, having to be adopted by Captain Kara and most of all the duel and the chance she might die tomorrow. At first her mind was swimming with all of these terrible things like a whirlpool that just gained more and more speed, but then Ket's mind was there with hers, calming her. Making her focus only on her own pleasure. Soon she could think of nothing else. She was him and he was her. It wasn't long before she was coming in his mouth, in hers. It didn't matter.

He undid his trousers, just enough to take out his erect penis, and then lifted her up, with her back against the wall. She loved the rough cool feel of the stone behind her and his strong, clothed body against the front of hers, pinning her in place as he held her up by her underarms. His ranking jewelry biting into her skin. He was plunging in and out of her so hard. It was so rough and sexy and exactly what she wanted or was it what he wanted, it didn't matter, what they both wanted. "Harder" she whispered.

"Don't break her," the slave in the corner said loudly.

"Don't listen to her," Dru replied, "harder Ket. Break me in half, it feels so good." Dru couldn't help but contradict the slave as ridiculous as it was.

Ket loved that Drusilla was beyond caring about what her slave thought now. He also loved taking her like this, roughly, while both their bodies and minds intertwined. He could feel her building orgasm again and when she came it brought on his. After the aftershocks subsided, he carried her to her bed and they lay there silently together, wet with their own intermixing fluids.

"Are you going to bath or can I leave?"

"You can leave."

"That fiery fur will hold all of that scent. Are you sure?" the slave asked them both.

Ket rubbed Drusilla's vulva and all the wetness there, "We are sure. Go, file the punishment."

The slave nodded and left.

Dru put her hands over her face, "I hate that they call it 'fiery fur'."

Ket smiled down at her, "Why? It's cute." Then he moved her hands and began kissing her again and said, "And now for one more time again without an audience." His hands were on her breasts, kneading them and playing with the nipple piercing. Then his mouth was there.

384

Dru loved it when he gave his expert attention to her breasts. The way he took his time sucking and playing with the nipple piercings. She was impressed that he could make her come just from touching her breasts and now was no exception. She was close, but then before he did that, his hand was between her legs, caressing her wet sex. Moving firmly from the top of her vulva, through her wet folds, to her anus. Then he did something he had never done before, he put a finger in her anus. She moaned then and he moved down to suck her clit again and she came hard.

Ket moved above her and gently entered her hot and wet vagina. He thrust in and out slowly, but strongly. She was looking up at him with such desire in her eyes and he shared his thought, *I love you my Drusilla.*

Dru couldn't believe what she had just heard. Alliance people never spoke or thought of love. This was unprecedented and she knew it had come from his heart. She didn't know what to do. Of course, she felt very strongly for him and possibly loved him, she hadn't really thought too much about it as it was a forbidden topic, however, now she looked at him and decided to reply back. *I love you Ket and I don't wat this to end tomorrow.*

Then he stopped moving and leaned down and kissed her. His hand wiping off a tear she didn't even know she had. "You won't die tomorrow." Then he moved back and held her legs up and over one shoulder. He began thrusting into her faster and stronger. He loved the way she looked up at him, urging him to continue. Her beautiful breasts moving back and forth as a reaction to his strokes. *You won't die,* he thought again and again as he pumped into her. Their minds were so close again, intermingling and doubling their enjoyment of the friction between them. Finally, they both came again. Ket held her for some time, his body sweaty from her warm room. "Do human women really like it this warm?"

"Yes," she said stroking his back.

"I hope you don't mind that I'll be sweaty then. It's very warm for me."

"I don't mind," she said. She would rather have that then be cold everywhere.

After a few more minutes, "I'm reluctant to go, but I must, and you must prepare for this evening."

"I'm nervous."

"Don't be. This will be purely ceremonial." Then he hesitated but thought he should tell her, "The Empress will be there. She hates your captain and will try to make things difficult. Try to remain in the shadows."

"How can I do that? This is all about me being adopted by Captain Kara."

"It's not really about that. It's about power. Captain Kara is flexing her power. Stay in the shadows my little tabi." He caressed the side of her face, worried for her.

Dru didn't like the concern she saw in Ket's eyes, "I'll do my best."

Ket stood up and readjusted his clothing. Then looked down at Drusilla on the bed. *She is so beautiful. Gods, please don't let her die*, he thought.

"You projected that," she said accusatorially.

"We are destiny. You won't die," he said confidently. "Now do you want to have a shower? I've just enough time to wash you myself."

She nodded and he picked her up and carried her into the bathroom.

"You're not going to shower?"

"No, I want to smell you for as long as possible."

"Because that is not grim considering the circumstances."

He shrugged and stood back as the water started, "I forgot it is so hot for you. I'll just have to stand here and admire you and your fiery fur."

She laughed, "Seriously, don't call it that."

Jane arrived at House Human to meet Dru a couple hours after Ket had left. She gave her a big hug in the great fire room.

"I'm so sorry this happened to you," Jane said still embracing James.

"Barbaric Alliance people," Dru said quietly.

"Don't worry though," she sat letting go of the embrace, "Captain has been practicing a lot with Admiral Tir and she's getting the hang of it. I'm sure this little doctor is no match for her."

"I know. It's just maddening this whole thing and to be bound and adopted by the Captain for it. What if she becomes Empress?" Dru asked Jane with real fear. Jane understood Dru's fear as did all who had served with Captain Kara. There were times when she was so dark there seemed to be no good in her at all. It was the fine line between genius and madness that people always talked about.

Jane took both of Dru's shoulders, looked her in the eye and spoke to her as she would her own daughter, "Captain Kara has changed for the better. She has a real direction and motivation here in the Alliance and believe it or not Admiral Tir keeps her in order. This is a good thing. She will keep you safe. We all agreed we should have done it sooner as you were all alone here. We all were foolish to think Alliance women would be so accepting of you. Thankfully, they didn't succeed in killing you."

"Yet."

"Not today, tomorrow or next year," Jane smiled at Dru then and brought out her bag. "I've something for you that will make this easier." Then she brought out a bottle of tequila.

"What?"

"Come on. I have some limes too. Let's go to the kitchen."

"I don't want to drink before I do this," Dru said while she followed Jane into the kitchen.

"But I think you should and as Head of House Human, which you are still a member, I'm insisting that you do one shot with me. Maybe two. Just to make this all a bit easier on the senses."

"One," Dru said.

They entered the kitchen and all three slaves looked at them and then went back to talking amongst themselves. Jane cut a lime, took out the salt and then poured four shots of white tequila. She handed one to Dru.

"To not dying by grey Alliance hands," Jane said and Dru repeated her toast.

Then Jane picked up another glass and handed it to Dru, "To not dying by the Captain's hands either," and they both frowned and drank.

"One more," said Dru.

Jane poured two more shots, "To making it through tonight."

When they finished, they left everything in the kitchen for the slaves to tidy up and left the building. They took Jane's transport which was from the Zuin.

"It must be nice to be on an Alpha Warship?"

"You have no idea James," she said nonchalantly. "But the crew is another matter. We've had some real issues with integration. I'll tell you about it another time," Jane didn't

crew on planet. Already she was concerned about the closeness between James and her betrothed's sister.

"Kneel."

Dru obeyed. The cold stone floor bit into her knees and her breasts were tight from the cold. She was grateful she had had three shots of tequila before coming or else she worried she might have protested more or looked less nonchalant about this change in events.

Kara nodded to a slave and he came over with a tattoo pen and began tattooing Kara's husband's family symbol onto James's back left shoulder. Then cut her own palm and dripped some blood on the tattoo. "You will be bound to me until I release you by death Drusilla James." Then hurriedly Kara added in before James could reply, "And I rename you James of House Zu."

"I, James of House Zu, will honor the blood oath to you Captain Kara."

"Mother," supplied Admiral Tir. "You must call her Mother now."

Both Dru and Kara looked at him in disbelief and he nodded, "You must. Say it again."

"Admiral Tir, if you can't get your humans to do this correctly, I'm making this whole thing null and void now," came the Empress's voice from a corner.

Dru looked up at Kara and said loudly, "I, James of House Zu, will honor the blood oath to you Mother." A shiver passed through her body when she said those last words.

Kara tapped James's shoulder, "Get up now and put your clothes on, James."

"Not yet, James, House of Zu. Remain where you are," the Empress commanded.

Dru bowed, still kneeling. Her face next to the floor. All she could remember were Ket's words, 'Try to stay in the shadows,' and think, *Snap, I've completely failed at that now, haven't I?*

"You and your captain think you are so clever, infiltrating the highest ranks of Alliance society this way. But let me make it clear to you who is still really in charge." The Empress nodded to another slave and a long black whip was brought out. "Captain Kara, you will whip your charge for planning this duel in the first place."

Kara was angry and tried to say something but Tir stopped her.

Tir whispered in her ear, "There is nothing you can do now. You'll only make it worse for the girl."

Kara didn't acknowledge Tir but then walked over and took the whip from the slave and asked sweetly, "How many lashes, Your Grace?"

Dru was still kneeling, completely stunned.

"Seven. It's just a reminder to you all."

"Your Grace," Zol, the First Imperial Doctor spoke, and everyone looked over at her for the first time.

The Empress nodded allowing her to speak.

"May I suggest another punishment for James? Something that wouldn't mar her skin. If the gods side with her she is meant to be my son's wife."

The Empress didn't want to really harm this human doctor. She knew as well as everyone else, she had done nothing wrong, but the Empress could think of nothing else to get to Captain Kara. "What do you suggest then?"

"Let me mentally shame her."

While the Empress considered this Dru looked at Captain Kara for clarification and she shrugged her shoulders.

Kara mouthed the words, "If you don't know, I surely don't know."

After some time, the Empress nodded, and the whip

was taken out of Kara's hands. Dru was told to get dressed and sit down. Next Zol pulled up a chair in front of her and said telepathically, *I'm so sorry for this, but it's the less of the two evils.* Then she put a bracelet on Drusilla's wrist that could project her memories like a movie for everyone to see. Zol then took Drusilla's hands and began searching her memories for something that would be shameful but not too shameful, she wanted to protect the girl.

Dru resisted Zol searching her memories. She didn't want anyone knowing anything about her life especially from before she joined the fleet.

Let me in, let me find something, Zol was projecting to Drusilla.

Dru was resisting with everything she had, and it was tiring her, but she wouldn't give up.

Zol finally managed to break through Drusilla's defenses and began projecting the memory of her escaping the Exterior. Zol wished she could have found another one but without Drusilla's assistance this was the easiest one to access as it was at the top of her mind and connected to a lot of her decisions.

The whole room watched as Dru walked up to the guards' house at the Exterior gates. Listened as she propositioned the guards with her body for her escape. Drusilla was crying as Zol made her relive the entire memory minute by minute in real time, just as it was happening again. The five men taking her in her mouth, her anus and her vagina. Taunting her when they discovered she was a virgin and telling her that she would be a good prostitute in the modern world, that she built for it. All the terrible things. The memory stopped when she got up and walked down the path to her freedom.

Zol didn't let go of her hands though, she healed Drusilla then. She used all of her influence to bring

Drusilla back to the stable mental place she had been at before she had brought the hurtful memory forward. And when she had succeeded, she projected, *Act sad now, really sad*, as she simultaneously took the mental bracelet off of Drusilla's wrist.

Dru did as she was bid by Zol and began to cry. She was not hurt anymore by what had happened, she was immune to it. Just like she was immune to this room seeing it, as if it happened to someone else.

Zol got up and bowed to the Empress.

The Empress wished she would have had Captain Kara whip the young doctor. This only hurt her, Captain Kara was unmoved by the terrible things that happened on their barbaric planet.

Kara, of course, knew where James had come from. It was an unspoken secret they all shared. She felt for James having to relive such a nightmare. *No wonder she didn't mind an alien's touch now. How could she ever want to be with a human man again after that?* Kara thought.

Jane had always suspected that James came from humble beginnings, but she had no idea it was the Exterior. The Exterior was full of criminals and religious fanatics. Jane didn't know what to think of James now and so she stood back in shock. She wanted to go to her but couldn't.

Kara stepped forward and took one of James's hands, "It's done now, and you did the right thing. I hope I can do the same for you tomorrow. Meet me an hour beforehand in the preparation room of the arena. Now go home and sleep. We've all done things we wish had turned out differently and we'll continue to do them."

Dru looked up, "Yes Captain."

"Mother," Admiral Tir supplied.

"Mother," Dru was quick to say not wanting another punishment from the Empress.

Kara touched the top of her head and said quietly, "You did well, James."

Dru's alarm went off the next morning, "Good morning James. Today you have a duel scheduled at ten o'clock. The time now is seven o'clock." *Apparently, it's all registered that I am officially Captain Kara's daughter now*, she thought as the computer had referred to her as 'James' the name Captain Kara had given her and not 'Drusilla' as it normally did. *The Alliance was efficient.*

Dru opened her eyes and stared up at the ceiling thinking about everything that had happened yesterday. She got up and went into the bathroom. While she was brushing her teeth something black caught her eye and she turned to look at the tattoo with the House Zu symbol on it. *Adopted by the most terrifying woman I know*, she thought, but then reminded herself, *but at least I probably won't be dead.*

Dru took a longer shower than usual. She didn't' need to hurry, she was not going to eat breakfast today. When she stood in front of her wardrobe, she remembered that she needed to wear her more formal dress, so she took it out and put it on. She thought of Ket and Dera and wondered if she would see Dera today at the duel. She wondered if the day would get any stranger, like it did yesterday. She went into the bathroom and had the mirror do her hair in an Alliance fashion with intricate braids and then she added one of the hairpins Ket had given her. Next, she put on the necklace she had worn everyday but then stopped. *No, now I have to wear this one*, she thought as she took the necklace Captain Kara, no Mother, had given her. It now showed her to be a part of House Zu. *This is so messed up*, she thought as she put it on.

Dru left the house and went to the Grand Arena just

outside the Imperial Palace. She got a little lost inside the large building trying to find the preparation room where the Captain would be waiting. When she finally found the Captain and some of the other women from her old crew, she was relieved.

James walked into the room and Kara said, "Good, you are looking the part of the Alliance fair maiden today." Kara was dressed in tight black athletic pants and a tight black sports bra. Both had 'House Zu' written in red on them. She had a small women's sword in her right hand.

"Aren't' you going to wear any armor or anything?" Dru asked and everyone laughed.

"Women don't wear armor or use shields, but we do thankfully wear clothing. I heard that the men have to fight naked," Kara explained.

Dru knew this to be true from Ket's shared memory and nodded.

Kara continued, "Don't worry James, I may not have been using these little swords long, but I'm a natural fighter and I've had much more experience killing when it really matters than your little classmate who has had her head in books for most of her life."

"Will you offer her mercy, Captain?"

Kara stopped warming up then and looked at Dru in disbelief, "No. She will not be offered any mercy. Did the Alliance offer us mercy? No. Did our own government offer us mercy when they sold us? No. We must fight for a new place in this new world. No retreat. No surrender. No mercy. Are we clear?"

"Yes," Dru looked into Captain Kara's brown eyes and was terrified. Terrified of this new world she had been thrust into and terrified of the woman she was bound to now and where and what she would lead her to if Kara became

Empress. But then she remembered her own anger from last week when Rez had originally challenged her to the duel and in that moment, she could have killed Rez. She wondered now if Captain Kara always carried that kind of anger in her.

"Don't look so scared James," Kara said starting to warm up again, "I know you're a doctor and took the Hippocratic oath to do no harm. And I won't ask you to break that oath unless I absolutely have to. Obviously, Alliance doctors take no such oath." All the other women laughed at Kara's comment except for James.

"What happens after you win then? Does anyone know? I mean what do they do with the body?" Dru asked. "I think you get to keep her sword though."

"I assume her family members will deal with it. Who knows? It's not something we need to think about. And it will be you who keeps her sword as you were the one challenged. I don't want it. I don't know this woman." Kara stopped warming up and stood in front of James, "All you need to concentrate on is not looking scared. Everyone will be watching our behavior today. They all think that human women are weak and below them. Don't let our ignorance of their traditions prove their racism to be true. We know enough about today to just pass the minimum requirement for doing this right. So, all of you, listen up. We hold our heads high and no matter what happens there will be no fear, James, look at me, no fear, no tears and to you all, everything plays out exactly as you expect it to. Understood?"

"Aye Captain," they all said and then it was silent.

"Captain, it's almost time," said Jane after many minutes.

"Captain," Dru almost forgot, "Rez will try and use her telepathy to trick you."

"Well you better block her then," Kara replied as they all left the room.

"Listen for my voice in your head," said Dru as they walked down the hallway.

Kara stopped and looked at her then, "It's really true then? You can also read minds?"

Dru nodded, "Better than most. Better than Rez."

"Good. All of you go and take your places. James, it's time, be strong."

Dru nodded and then she and Captain Kara walked through some corridors and out onto the floor of the large arena. The stands were full of Alliance women with a small section for the humans. The Empress stood in front of them on the arena floor with so much jewelry Dru wondered how she could move. She was surrounded by her female guards, all dressed in the most elaborate armor. Rez was already there standing before the Empress by herself. She wore a similar outfit to Captain Kara's but with her House name on it in white writing.

Everyone bowed to the Empress. After a few seconds the Empress addressed them all, "Today we are here to settle a matter of witchcraft. Rez of House Uz has accused James of House Zu of using witchcraft to entice Ket of House Vo to marry her. Rez is so confident in her claim that she has challenged James to a duel today. However, James has taken the right to name her own champion from her own family and has named Captain Kara of House Zu. The duel today will be to the death. James kiss your champion and then come and sit with me in the Imperial Box."

Dru bowed again and then looked at Captain Kara and kissed her on the cheek.

Kara held James's head close and tight, grabbing her

hair, "Don't let this little doctor use her mind tricks on me."

Dru replied, "Never. We are stronger."

Then Kara let go and took her position in the arena. She was just about the same height as the doctor. She motioned to get her attention, "Alliance woman, are you really sure you want to go up against me? It's not too late to say you are just a lying little loser who pines after a man who clearly doesn't want you."

Rez was so angry she replied, "I'll enjoy watching you and Drusilla die today. Humans should have never been brought here. Your barbarian genes pollute the Alliance. Today will be the first day of flushing you all out."

Kara looked at Rez across the stone floor and smiled. She was going to enjoy killing this racist woman.

Dru followed the Empress's guards through the corridors into a box just above the arena floor. She was sat behind and to the side of the Empress. On the arena floor, Kara and Rez were taunting each other. It was impossible to hear what they were saying, but Dru could feel intense anger rising from them both.

A slave then said with a loudspeaker, "It is time for the gods to show us their will. Take your places, now begin."

Rez and Kara circled each other on the floor for many minutes before either of them got close enough to strike a blow. But once they got close enough, Kara was able to cut Rez's arm above the elbow. It was a small superficial wound but psychologically set the scene.

They circled each other for about twenty minutes that way, striking small blows to each other. Kara being able to hit Rez rather than the other way around, despite it being obviously Kara was new to the sword.

After forty minutes, Rez was tired and now began using her telepathy. Rez conjured three apparitions of herself in

Captain Kara's mind, all standing in different places on the arena floor. The first time she projected this, the human just stood there in awe, trying to figure out which one was real and Rez charged her. Rez had almost managed to kill her with that blow, but at the last minute, Captain Kara struck against the her pushing her to the ground roughly.

Next Rez tried to make Captain Kara blind, but it didn't work for long.

But Rez knew the only way she would win was with mind games, so she continued to infiltrate the Captain's mind as they slowly circled one another. Sometimes the mind tricks would work, but only for a few seconds, so Rez was trying to be fast with her body and mind.

"It looks like Rez doesn't fear the wrath of House Zu. She may kill your champion, after all," said the Empress cheerfully to Dru as they watched the women below.

"The gods' are on our side. Not only are humans the saviors of the Empire, but Rez lied. I didn't use any kind of witchcraft to seduce Doctor Ket and the gods know that," Dru replied softly. She didn't take her eyes from the duel, attempted to block Rez's telepathy.

"Tsk tsk," said the Empress trying to distract Dru from helping her champion, "You can already see that your champion will lose. She's not as capable as Rez and why should she be? You humans are soft and weak. And most importantly, you are unworthy of Alliance men. It's no wonder you had to use witchcraft to secure yours."

Dru had to remember she was talking to the Empress now so she simply replied, "No doubt as Empress you have a special connection to the gods, however maybe you have been misinformed by them. Today's duel will prove, by the gods' graces,I used no such witchcraft."

"Witchcraft or possibly a setup by his lesbian sister? But I guess that is a kind of witchcraft too, isn't it?"

"I wouldn't know I'm a doctor." She wanted to ask the Empress if she were a lesbian herself as she knew about Dera, but she knew that would definitely end up with her being dead, so she held her tongue. But she suddenly saw the Empress in a new light and understood that the Empress wanted them there as much as Dera, and for the same reasons, but she didn't want Kara to be Empress and that was all.

"I thought human doctors used herbs and enchantments as well? No?"

Dru had heard this before. Alliance doctors had laughed at humans still using so much from their environment for good health. "Yes, we do. If you hadn't murdered your natural ecosystem centuries ago maybe you could have found some of the same remedies in your environment which would have been more in line with the will of the gods', no?"

The Empress didn't like Drusilla's comment so ignored it and looked down intently at the duel below.

Captain Kara, every now and then, was swinging at invisible things and Dru tried to block whatever imaginary images Rez was throwing at her. Dru was blocking Rez but some of the mind control being thrown at the Captain was coming from someone else in the arena. Dru was so concerned she actually stood up, not that she thought it would do any good, but she couldn't help herself. She scanned everyone. *Who was doing this?* she was frantic to focus on a face to block them as well. She was not going to die today. Not here and not like this.

Dru decided this was the moment to attack Rez's mind no matter what the consequence as if she didn't she and Captain Kara were both dead. She sat down again and concentrated on Rez's mind and made her see multiple images of the Captain surrounding her. She watched Rez's confusion. Backing away not knowing which one was real. Unfortunately, the Captain was also suffering from someone else impairing her vision, making her blind. Dru couldn't defend the Captain and manipulate Rez at the same time. She was trying her best to think of a way to help the Captain and incapacitate Rez at the same time but was getting nowhere.

Dera watched and knew that everyone with even a little telepathy could feel the rhythm of the soundless energy affecting the duel. She looked at Drusilla and saw her struggling with whatever she was doing and decided that she would also risk death today to save her friend and the humans. It was in her best interest as well. Not to have Captain Kara win of course, no one wanted that woman alive, but they needed the other humans and she specifically needed Drusilla to marry Ket. Dera focused her mind on protecting the human on the arena floor.

Suddenly Kara's vision cleared, and she walked decidedly towards the young doctor. They were both tired and bleeding. Kara stood in front of the young woman, kicked away her sword and then kicked her face, "Any last words, Doctor?"

Rez was too frightened to speak, she was surrounded by multiple Captain Kara's all speaking loudly at her with their swords drawn. She didn't know which one was real and she knew she was going to die now. She tried to swing her sword at all the human captains hoping one would really strike her. She silently prayed to the god of war to help her find the right one.

Kara stabbed Rez through what she hoped was her heart as she wanted to be dramatic and said, "Humans will always win." Then, she watched Rez's reactions and was assured that she had indeed hit her heart.

The arena was silent then. Obviously, none of the

Alliance women had expected Captain Kara to win. They had come here today to watch two human women be killed.

Kara stood up and wiped her bloody sword on Rez's dead body and then said to the crowd, "The gods have revealed to you all the truth of this matter. James of House Zu did not use witchcraft to seduce Ket of House Vo." The arena was still quiet. Kara was looking at the Empress, she bowed and said, "As it pleases the Empress?"

The Empress rose then and addressed the arena, "The gods have spoken, and we must obey. Captain Kara of House Zu and James of House Zu, you walk freely. May the gods shine their light on you both." Everyone bowed then and the Empress left in such a hurry she almost knocked Dru over on the way out of the box.

James looked down at Captain Kara and she mouthed the words, "Meet me in the preparation room."

Dru nodded and went back to the preparation room in the bowels of the arena. She went to the first aid kit on the wall and got it down. When Captain Kara entered with some of her crew, Dru said, "Let me treat your wounds Captain."

Kara nodded and sat down in front of her, "The first thing you should have said was, 'Thank you for winning and saving my life.'"

"Thank you for winning Captain and saving my life," Dru said and then began healing her.

The other women were rehashing the entire duel, clearly ecstatic that the Captain had won, despite the cheating and telepathic tricks. Then the Captain remarked, "This justice is just as fair and equal as any we have on Earth. I might even say better. Rez started this fight with you James because she was a bully and racist. We were able to win even though we definitely did not have the government or public's support. This is true justice."

Dru nodded to Captain Kara to let her know that she had finished healing as much as she could for now.

Kara stood up and said to the women present, the most important women to her now, "Today we showed the best of the Alliance women, the people who run this whole Empire, who they have bought and brought into their precious society. We will not be silenced or treated like slaves or second-class citizens only made for breeding. We will find our rightful place here and if we don't, we will rip it to shreds and build a new one."

Dru was alarmed by the Captain's last statement, but all the other women loved it.

"James, you find this distasteful? That's not like you." Kara looked at the rest of the women, "All of you are dismissed, except James. Go, I'll catch up with you at House Human for our celebration." Then Kara turned her attention to James.

"No, I just…Captain," she didn't know what to say.

"First, just call me 'Kara'. I don't want to be fined anymore today for you calling me 'Captain'. It has to be 'Mother' or 'Kara'. I think we both prefer 'Kara'."

Dru nodded, "Kara."

"Now, I know you are more of a sneaky person, probably very good at poisoning and torturing people if you put your mind to it."

Gods, I don't think so, Dru thought as Kara continued talking.

"But some of us have to be the front of the show and that is me. Don't take everything so literally or be so fearful. I need you to be strong and I know you are. I've seen it," she said acknowledging the shameful punishment last night. "I think being alone on this planet has scarred you more than anything that happened to you on Earth though. This ban and the isolation of being the only human." Kara looked into her green eyes and said with as much compassion as she could, "No one could foresee how dangerous or difficult it would be for you down here alone. But we all need you to stay. I need you to stay, can you do that and not go insane or become completely depressed or afraid?"

"Yes, Kara," she said obediently waiting to be dismissed and not wanting to talk about that ever again with anyone. "I'll be strong."

"Good, now there is one more thing we must discuss?"

Now what? "Yes?"

"Now, that you are a member of my family, apparently you must marry from my House. However, I don't know what you want to do? Tir said it was up to you. I assume you already had an arrangement made, or? You weren't going to marry from that dreadful building you've been living in like Rebecca did, are you?"

"No," she was relieved this was a normal question. "I was going to be married from Ket's parents' home."

"Well, that sounds incestuous," commented Kara. "Apparently, I also need to be your witness, unless you would rather have Tir or one of his family members?"

"No Capt... Kara, please be my witness," Dru said quickly. "I'd be honored," she said automatically.

"You owe me your life and even when you marry Ket and are no longer a part of my House, as far as we go," she motioned with her finger between them, "as humans. We will always share this bond; you will always be my adoptive daughter and you will always do my bidding." Kara touched the place where the tattoo was, "We are in this for the rest of our lives. There is nothing I hate more than fearful women; it's just wasted energy. You weren't scared of the Exterior and that is one of the more frightening places in the galaxy. The Alliance should have nothing on you James. And soon you will be one of the most important women in the Capital City by marrying Ket. Gods, the look in your eyes right now," she commented more to herself than to James, "How can I help you? What have they done to my bravest young doctor?"

Dru shook her head, "Nothing," but tears were escaping her eyes.

Kara did something she never thought she would do, she brought James in for a hug, "They have tried to break you and have come very close. But listen to me, they are not going to break you. Not under my watch. You are safe and I will always come for you. Do you hear me?"

"Yes," Dru said relishing in the touch of another human in this way. This comfort she had not felt in so long. The same warmness of body heat between them.

"I want you to speak to John every day as part of counseling, this extreme isolation and culture shock has done this. We must repair you. That is an order."

Dru wiped her eyes, "I think that would be good actually." It was difficult for her to admit that she needed help but when she reviewed how difficult it had become to just get through daily life she realized that she had slipped into a deep depression which was the result of her isolation from humans and most of society. She wondered then how she had not noticed it herself, but she suspected it came on so gradually and that she was so focused on fitting into Alliance society that she didn't want to admit it to herself that she was slipping.

"Good now tell me what else you can do besides read minds?"

"Nothing," she shook her head, "Just a doctor."

"Just a doctor, who can read minds and gods only

knows what else you are not telling me? And so close to the Imperial Families you can hear them breathing."

"What do you want me to do?"

"Nothing. What you are doing. Go be a successful Alliance doctor and keep me updated on your progress as if I really was your new adoptive mother."

"Yes Kara."

"Now let's go. I need a drink."

"John should see to those, you're not completely healed," Dru tried to explain.

"I'll be fine. I need to celebrate with my crew and you. However, I assume you will be late as you want to go tell your boyfriend you're alive?"

"Yes, go and then return to dreadful House Human to celebrate. Jane says there is tequila there."

"Thank you."

Kara nodded and watched James leave, thinking, *It can't be this easy.*

Dru left the arena and walked out into the city. The normal hustle and bustle around her was almost surreal after the last 24 hours. She took out her IC and messaged Ket.

I need to see you. I only have a few hours.

He replied immediately,

Meet me at the entrance to the park with Fire.

· · ·

Dru walked towards the park and saw him waiting for her at the entrance 20 minutes later. She knew it was forbidden but she ran into his arms. She didn't say anything and neither did he, he just held her. After a while he took her hand and they began walking towards Fire.

"I reserved a room for a couple hours," Ket said softly.

"Was the fine that terrible from yesterday?"

"You'll see. I don't want to talk about that now," Ket said unemotionally as they walked into Fire. He let go of her hand to register and then they went up in the elevator and into a room that was different than the one they had originally used. Ket programmed the holographic setting to a large sofa and he held her as they talked. She told him everything that had happened. Everything the Empress had said, Kara had said and how Rez died. It felt good to be in his arms.

Ket listened to everything Drusilla told him and understood that she only comprehended half of what really took place that morning. However, he was reluctant to point out what she missed in the current state she was in so he just held her and tried to calm her as much as he could.

When it was time to leave, Dru said causally, "Oh and Kara says I must speak to Doctor John every day now because she thinks I have been too lonely and it's changing me."

"Do you think that is really necessary? We will be married soon and you won't be alone anymore, you will have my family around you."

"I don't know? I've been lonely and I miss human company."

"It's up to you."

"Not really, Kara said I must."

"But still it is up to you," Ket insisted and she smiled at him as they walked out.

408

. . .

Zol contacted Dru and arranged to meet at what would be her and Ket's home located within the House Vo compound in the Imperial Ring of the city. Dru had never been to an Alliance home before, except for Kara's home, but at the time she had been too anxious to take in much, except that it was red and she knew that was considered distasteful. The only thing Ket had told her about their home was that it suited his rank. Dru was worried that it would be as large as Kara and Tir's and that she would have to furnish the whole thing alone. She had no experience with such things even on Earth and definitely not in the Alliance and not of his social rank. Her childhood home in the Exterior had been small and had only a small hodgepodge of inherited furniture. Afterwards, all of her accommodation had been provided for her either by the human fleet or the Alliance.

Dru had contacted Rebecca to ask her about her home in the Alliance with her husband Kole. She had not expected the hour-long VM she got in return or the unexpected entrance of Kole in the middle and witnessing their small argument over his mother, but it was very insightful as to what Dru could expect from Ket's family. Rebecca had married an officer in the military and his home and family were very traditional and didn't want her to have anything from Earth. Rebecca said flatly, 'They want to pretend that I'm not human at all, so it's a constant struggle.' But it didn't matter so much for Rebecca because she and her husband live on ship together and are rarely at home. For Dru it would matter because she would live the rest of her life in this house, if all went according to plan, so she wanted things from Earth. She had made a list and was planning on defending it.

Dru hired a transport to take her to Ket's family compound. She reached the gates and the guards let her in. There was no forcefield and she felt for the first time since she arrived in the Alliance the excitement of becoming a real person again, not a prisoner. *This was not a cage but a home*, she told herself, *No forcefield*.

Dru walked up to the main house, which was a massive yellow stone block with many windows. This house was far larger than Kara's house had been and Dru hoped her and Ket's house would be much smaller. She knew by tradition that Ket's older brother would inherit this house when his parents died. She was grateful the large mass of stone would never be hers to deal with. Before she got to the door, a slave in green opened it for her and told her that Zol would be out presently. Dru waited outside wondering what this would be like. She looked into the large foyer and saw a beautiful stone black floor and a glass elevator at the end of the hall. Then she saw the elevator come down and Zol walk down the hall quickly, her shoes echoing with each step towards Dru.

Dru had felt embarrassed after what had happened on the night she swore her blood oath to Kara, but Zol had assured her that she had nothing to be embarrassed about and that what everyone had seen would be kept secret for now. Then she said, 'And no one will tell Ket yet, but at some point, you must. Because there will be a time when Tir does. I reckon you have about a year before they are drunk on Zota and he says something. It's forbidden, but I know Tir and he won't be able to help himself. Or he will use this to get you to do something for him. Don't let him have either position Drusilla.' Dru thought that that was actually the best that she could have expected to come from that horrible night and resigned herself that at some point she would have to tell Ket so that it didn't catch him off guard. It made her feel a bit ill every time she thought about telling him, despite her lessened emotional connections to the event since Zol had distanced her from her own memory.

"The gods are good," Zol said as she reached Dru.

"The gods will show us the way," Dru replied automatically. As she remembered, she saw both Dera and Ket in Zol. She had Ket's grey eyes but Dera's more joyful face. She and Dru were the same height although Zol was incredibly slender like Dera.

Zol was pleased Drusilla didn't hesitate to use the common expressions. She had heard that some of the other human women refused, however she knew Drusilla was different from the few times she had met her already. "You are perfectly on time. I will invite you in here after we look at your house. Come on," she said walking along.

"Sounds good," Dru said. It was not close to a mealtime so unlike in a human meeting, there was no need to invite someone in for tea or a snack.

The women walked side-by-side silently for many minutes through a symmetrically manicured garden. Then Zol said, "I know that you aren't used to this. The Alliance or a large house or any of this. Just don't tell anyone outside the family. Inside the family we are all here to help. Ask Dera or me first about things if you are unsure."

"Thank you," Dru said quietly.

"There's no thanks Drusilla. It's just a new experience. You'll learn, there is nothing to it. It's just living but on a larger scale."

"I'm not sure what to expect as the only real Alliance house I have seen is Kara's and she painted the whole thing red."

"Yes," Zol said evenly. *Tir really went out of his way to find the only one in the galaxy just as crazy as he is,* she thought.

"I'm not planning on painting anything, but I would like some items from Earth. I have a small list."

"Of course, you would like some things from Earth. I would be suspicious if you didn't," Zol said with a smile.

Dru was relieved that so far Ket's mother seemed normal, almost friendly about incorporating some things from Earth. Soon they approached what would be her and Ket's house. It was another large stone box house with lots of windows with different beautiful geometric patterns around the building.

"This will be your home Drusilla," Zol said.

Dru didn't know how to respond. The house was not as large as Ket's parents' home, but it was very large. "How many rooms does it have?"

"There are six bedrooms and the whole house is about 20,000 square meters."

"I think I'm going to faint," Dru said and put her hand on Zol's arm to steady herself.

Zol couldn't help but smile at Drusilla and used her influence to lessen her anxiety. "You'll be fine here. It won't seem so big after a while. Let's go in so you can look around and I'll introduce you to the slaves."

"I hope the slaves are as surly as my own, so that I'll feel at home in that regard."

"I'm sure they will be." As they approached the large stone front door a slave opened it, and the rest were standing in the entryway to greet them. "These are Ket's slaves that will now be yours too. I will introduce you to everyone. The guards are not here right now but you will meet them later. After your marriage you will be much more protected than you were in House Human."

Dru wanted to say that she didn't need to be looked after but after everything that had happened lately, she knew that she was going to have to sacrifice a bit of her privacy so that she could have peace of mind and not always have to watch her back every minute. Before she could reply Zol continued speaking.

"Unfortunately, there are many who would like to sabotage this whole idea of humans replenishing Alliance women, more than I think the High Council first realized. However, you are here now, and I believe that we are making the right choice in inviting you back into our civilization."

Dru didn't have a chance to reply to Zol as she began introducing the eight slaves, four men and four women who maintained the house. Dru met them and just like the slaves in her building they were not like slaves. They questioned Dru a lot about being human and what kind of work they could expect, one even asked if she was extra dirty as she had heard humans leave hair everywhere. No one but Dru seemed to think this was a rude question, so Dru assured the woman she would try to pick up her own hair when she saw it, and this appeased the slaves.

Then Zol took her on a tour of the rest of the house. Just as Ket had said, it was sparsely furnished. It was livable but that was about it.

"Does Ket live here when he is home?"

"No, he stays in his childhood home or the barracks. He can't occupy this house until he is married."

"Who lived in it before?"

"Juh and I lived here a long time ago," she said. "Long before Kio was even born."

"Have you been married a long time?"

"Yes, almost 50 years. I married very young, like you. It's a good thing to do when you've met a suitable man."

The house had many empty rooms and Zol explained to her what their functions were, and she was overwhelmed after the tour which they ended where they began in the drawing room. "Is this your furniture?"

"No, our furniture is with us. This is your house now Drusilla. I can feel your reservations, just relax and think about one thing at a time. Now, let me see your list."

She motioned to the table between them and Dru brought out her IC and brought up the list on the 3D computer.

1. *Wallpaper*
2. *Art*
3. *Rugs*
4. *Greenhouse*
5. *Wine cellar*
6. *Heat*
7. *Viewscreen*

Zol looked over the list and then asked, "Where do you want the wallpaper? Everywhere?"

"No," Dru smiled, "I thought to put the light blue one with the flying birds in the main bedroom and the cream colored one with the menagerie of Earth animals in the nursery." She brought up the pictures of the wallpapers. "They can be bought at the Earth Store."

"You aren't worried about your future child being distracted by such busy pictures on the wall?"

Dru shook her head and tried not to laugh, "No, I'm sure it will be fine."

Zol looked through the rest of the list, "What will you do with the art?"

"It will be hung on some of the walls to be enjoyed by us and visitors. It is nice to look at beautiful pictures."

Zol didn't think so but she was slightly intrigued by the idea and decided she would read about human art later to try and understand this practice. Then she moved on, "What is a green house?"

"It's a small enclosed building to grow plants. I would like one to grow my own herbs from Earth. The owner of the Earth Store has one, but he charges a fortune for the most basic herbs."

"Give me the specifications and it will be built, but you will teach one of the slaves to do it. You know as Ket's wife you shouldn't be doing any manual labor."

"I wouldn't consider it manual labor," she protested a little but Zol gave her a look that said, 'I'm being reasonable, you be reasonable too.' So Dru nodded and waited for the next question.

"Why do you want a specific place to put wine?"

"I intend on buying wine from Earth and some of it is stored for years."

"I don't understand, but fine. Again, the specifications. What do you mean by heat?"

"I would like a fireplace put here in the drawing room, so that it makes the room a bit warmer for me. We have one in the building I am in now and it is nice. Also, in my bedroom and the nursery I want the heat to be able to be adjusted to at least 26C. I don't want any computer overrides for health. I also want the water in my ensuite to reach 45C."

"Kara and Tir's child have adapted to Alliance temperatures maybe your children will too?"

"Possibly, but if they don't, then it is already done."

"And a human viewscreen. What is that?"

"It is a place to watch fictional human dramas and

listen to music. I'll send you the specifications along with all the others."

"Fine. Now you must decide on more furniture."

"I was hoping you would help me."

"You know, I'm not allowed. You must do this yourself."

"I'm not from here. I don't even know how to begin. I wouldn't ask for help if I thought that I could do a good job myself. Please, no one needs to know." Dru was looking into Zol's grey eyes just like Ket's and then she heard Zol speak to her mentally.

I'll organize the rest with some Earth things as well from Frank's Earth store, so it looks like yours. However, when it comes to name your child, you must give your first daughter an Alliance name. I will suggest it to Ket. Have we come to a compromise?

Dru answered back, *Yes, I will give my first daughter an Alliance name of your choice in exchange for your help in furnishing this house.*

Zol nodded then and said out loud because the slaves were listening of course, "I'm sure you'll figure out something yourself. Now, there is one more thing I must show you, I almost forgot. The storage."

Zol led Drusilla to a large storage area in the back of the house. It was partially filled with long rectangular boxes and then a box that caught her eye, it was labeled,

Drusilla Anne James, care of House Vo, Imperial Ring, Capital City. Human Fleet: Personal Effects.

Dru went to the black wooden box and opened it. Inside were her few personal items that she had in life. She began going through them, a couple of obsolete human fleet uniforms, her sandalwood comb, menstrual cup in its decorated pink cotton pouch which seemed so colorful and busy after not seeing patterns in the Alliance for a year. Her small makeup bag with pineapples on it and her one nice dress that she had just bought with her first salary because she had never owned anything like it before.

She brought out the dress from the box and looked at it longingly. It was a white, silk, short-sleeved dress with bright birds embroidered down the dress as if they were swooping down to the hem of the dress which was floor-length. It had a low V-neck in both the front and back and the sides had beautiful sequin embellishments.

"Can I wear what I want to my wedding?" Dru asked not looking away from the dress. Almost thinking that it was destiny that she had bought this dress to be married in. She remembered the day she bought it. It was strange, she had had no intention on buying anything with her salary except a coffee, but when she saw the dress in the window and then tried it on, she just had to have it. The dress cost more than half of her monthly salary and it was extravagant to own a dress like this, especially since she had little else to her name, but she couldn't describe her feeling in that moment, she knew the dress had been made just for her and so she bought it. The woman selling it to her had said, 'You never know when fate strikes, and you need a formal dress.' She hadn't thought about the comment at all until now.

"Captain Kara is your guardian now. Do you think she would allow you to wear that?"

Dru looked at Zol and smiled, "Did she paint her whole house red?"

Zol smiled back, "Just don't wear it out once you belong to this House. It's not that it isn't beautiful, it's just we don't like to draw too much attention to ourselves. No one really likes telepaths, but they need us. Or that's what we tell them."

"I've brought a lot of attention lately, haven't I?"

"Yes, but this dress won't make a difference in that now. Wear it for your wedding. You're human after all and you should wear what you want, as a sign that you are coming into this marriage freely. But afterwards, at least for some time, I'd appreciate it, if you made every effort to assimilate within reason in public."

Dru nodded, "And at home?"

"Once you are married and have your first child, the cultural ban will be lifted. However, I'd hope that you would keep a nice balance between Alliance culture and your own."

"That sounds like a decent compromise that I could live with," Dru said thinking of how wonderful it will be to have more freedom to be herself in her own home.

8

An Alliance Marriage

Dru carefully applied her makeup, smoky black eyeliner, defined eyebrows and strong rouged lips, before she put on her white silk dress with the embroidered birds and sequins. She was wearing nothing underneath and she knew she would be cold, but she didn't care. For the first time, since arriving on the Alliance Capital Planet, she felt like herself, nipple jewelry, makeup and all. She left her hair down and only wore the ring that Ket had given to her the first day of medical school and her ID necklace which now had the Imperial Symbol on it, *But not the right one*, she thought, as she put it over her head.

She then put on her flat Earth shoes she had bought with the dress that matched perfectly and brought up the full-length mirror in her room. Then she said out loud, "Computer, capture image." Then she said down at her computer and sent a message to Jane who was still in orbit on duty.

Jane replied to her immediately,

. . .

James,

You look gorgeous today. I'm glad this worked out. I'll see you the next time we are on the Capital Planet. Enjoy your holiday with your husband.

J

Dru went to the great fire room then and waited by herself for Kara to arrive. Kara was going to take her to Ket's parents' home. While she was waiting a slave came out and gave her some Zota in a small glass. Dru looked at her questioningly.

The slave just shrugged, "It' makes the wedding a bit easier and we will be happy to see you go with your 4th days and other nonsense." Before Dru could reply she walked away.

She shrugged and drank the terrible alcohol.

It wasn't long before Kara arrived. She was wearing an Alliance dress with lots of jewelry and looked physically uncomfortable.

"Oh well, look at you," she said excitedly. "I love this. Where did you get this? I need one. It will make Tir explode with fury. I can see the curve of your breasts and hips and everything."

Dru looked down at her dress and had a moment's hesitation, "Do you think I should change? You are my mother after all."

"Oh, definitely not. I wasn't kidding I love it. I want one. And I love that you are part of House Zu and you are wearing it. Tir's mother is going to be so cross with me for allowing it, it's almost like me wearing it." She smiled then, "We should take a short walk around the block just to be sure this makes it into the gossip columns."

"We shouldn't," Dru protested.

"That's an order James, come on."

Dru got up and followed Kara down the elevator and outside. They walked for ten minutes outside the building. And just as Kara wanted, they got lots of stares from people walking around them.

"Pretend we are talking, and you are so happy," Kara said with a fake smile for Dru.

"I am happy, but I don't want Ket to see my dress in the gossip columns before he sees me."

"Oh, don't worry, he's with his friends doing some blood ritual. He's not looking at his IC."

"What blood ritual?"

"I've no idea. I thought you'd know. You know, these Alliance men and their punishments to prove to each other they are all alpha men. It's ridiculous. Oh well, I think that is enough now. Let's go. I've brought some champagne to drink as I'm not drinking any tasteless Alliance wine and witnessing a wedding."

Dru didn't know why she was acting like it was such a chore to witness her wedding, but she was excited by the idea of having champagne. "Thank you, it'll will make the day extra special."

Kara smiled and they got into the transport with her guards. It wasn't long before they landed and were entering Ket's parents' home. "The slaves have all been dismissed," Kara explained as to why they just walked in. Then they found Dera in the drawing room drinking wine waiting for them.

When she saw Drusilla, she stood up, "Drusilla, Gods, I have never seen you looking so human. I like it, I think.

Come and have some wine?" Mentally Dera projected, *You really look like an alien goddess.*

Kara motioned to the guards behind them carrying a case of champagne, "Hi, I'm Kara. I've brought champagne from Earth. Trust me you will like it. Put down the Alliance wine."

Dera looked from Kara to Drusilla and decided she didn't care and put down her wine. "I would call one of the slaves but unfortunately on wedding nights we have to do it all ourselves. Dismiss your guards. As hostess I will serve."

Kara dismissed the guards but helped Dera pour the champagne into the human champagne glasses that had been decorated with colorful hand painted butterflies on them.

"Interesting glasses," Dera commented. Taking in Kara's appearance for the first time. She was beautiful. Kara was wearing so much jewelry it was easy to make out her figure in the large Alliance dress and Dera reckoned her figure was somewhere between Drusilla's curvy figure and an Alliance woman's athletic one.

Kara took in Dera's long gaze and smiled at her, thinking *So there are lesbians here* and then said, "These glasses are also a gift from me to you, James. That with whatever champagne we don't drink from the case tonight."

Dru smiled. She liked this wild side of Kara and wondered why she had been so afraid of her sometimes before. Then she wondered if she was just becoming more used to life in the Alliance. More used to sex and violence, things that Kara greatly enjoyed in life. "Thank you, that is very generous of you."

"As far as I'm concerned, we need to bring as much

beauty here as possible. I'm so tired of seeing black, yellow and grey everywhere."

"Thankfully you have a red house," Dera couldn't help but point out.

"Yes, thank the gods for the color red," Kara said dramatically.

The women continued to drink, and Kara entertained them with stories from their recent missions in the galaxy. Some of which Dru already knew but others that were kept from the Alliance newsfeed. She wondered if Kara knew that but decided, Kara didn't care, so she let her talk uninterrupted. It was less than an hour before Ket, his older brother Kio and his friend Hez walked in.

Dru had never seen Ket look so gorgeous. He was wearing his formal uniform with all of his imperial jewelry for ceremonial purposes. His hair was braided in an intricate braid down his back and he carried a ceremonial sword that was much more ornate than the one he carried every day.

Ket was surprised to see Drusilla wearing a human dress. It was white with colorful embroidery and was so tight on her curvy figure he wondered if he would be able to speak to her without his hands roaming every inch of her body over that dress that hid, but didn't hide, everything. Then when she turned to him and he saw that she had painted her face in that exotic human way he knew that this really was going to be one of the best nights of his life.

He walked into the room and went straight to Drusilla and without a word took her hand for her to stand and began passionately kissing her, he had to. His hands roamed over her body, the exposed parts and over the soft silk of the dress. And he couldn't help himself, one hand caressed a nipple to see if she was wearing the jewelry he had given her, as she had none of the other jewelry on and she was. His penis became rock hard then and he projected privately for their minds only, something that Drusilla hadn't mastered fully yet, *I love that this is the only jewelry you are wearing. The one thing you never wanted from the Alliance.*

Dru heard him but couldn't respond, she was too emotional. When he began caressing her nipple to see what she had on there, she was so pleased as she had worn those just for him, as almost everything else about her appearance was totally human.

After a few minutes, Ket reluctantly pulled back and whispered in Dru's ear, "You look so exotic and gorgeous tonight." Then he pulled out the marriage bracelets from his pocket. They were black and silver and had their names on them. He took her left hand and put hers on her slender wrist and then put his own on his left wrist. "Drusilla Anne James of Imperial House Zu, originally from Earth, I pledge my life, love and honor to you in wedlock."

Dru had memorized her part over the past few days, "Ket of the Imperial House Vo of the Alliance, I accept your pledge and will bestow on you my life, love and honor in wedlock."

Then the marriage bracelets tightened, and Dru jumped at the small pinprick she got from it. She looked at her bracelet, then Ket was already answering her question, "It becomes personalized after we pledge ourselves to one another. I'll explain more later."

Kara stood then, put down her champagne glass and addressed everyone, "As is our human tradition, I need a portrait taken of the happy couple."

Ket looked at Drusilla and she was looking at Captain Kara questioningly.

"When Jane and I were researching human marriage we found all of these pictures of couples on their wedding days and we decided since it was one of the only nice things about human weddings that we should bring back the custom. I've trained a woman to do it from my House. She'll be here in a few minutes. Champagne?"

"We don't need a picture taken," said Ket. "But thank you."

"I want the picture Ket. Thank you, Kara. It's very thoughtful of you and Jane."

"We need to add our human touch," Kara said and then suddenly a woman of slave class entered with an ancient Alliance camera.

"With that?" Dru asked skeptically.

"It's vintage," Kara responded nonchalantly.

The photographer lined them up, just how she had seen in all the examples Kara had shown her and took the photos. Then she left, bowing to everyone.

"Now, you can get back to the regular ceremony," Kara smiled at them all. The Alliance people were in complete shock at their tradition being disrupted, but James smiled at her and she knew then that she had done a good thing for James today.

Ket's best friend, Hez, then came forward with an ornate black box and Ket took it from him. He opened it on a nearby table. Inside were some silver instruments and Ket took one out. It looked like a small stamp with a long pen on the end of it. He stood in front of Drusilla and asked for her right arm and she willingly gave it to him. He looked into her big green eyes and said quietly, "Drusilla James, my wife, now we will bind ourselves together not only by vows and paper but by the body as well." Then he placed the binding machine on the underside of her right forearm, below her elbow and looked into Dru's eyes expectantly.

Dru knew he was waiting for the reply. She had been so

confident before, but now she wondered if she really needed to do this. *Can I share him?* she questioned herself. She didn't care that she was making everyone wait.

Ket looked into her eyes and saw her wavering. All he could think was, *We don't have to do this Drusilla,* but he kept that thought to himself letting her make the decision without his interference. They had already decided, and it was up to her if she wanted to go through with the binding.

After a long minute she said, "Ket," and paused.

Ket was still looking at her expectantly. He thought for a minute that she would decide not to go through with it. He was hoping.

"Ket of House Vo, my husband, I accept your binding as yours will be the only body I willingly touch until the last breath I take." She looked into his eyes and nodded, allowing him to proceed.

Ket was momentarily disappointed that she had decided after all to go through with the binding tattoos, but then he reminded himself, this was the compromise he made to have her. This was the destiny of the gods.

Dru had been unprepared for how much the binding tattoos would hurt. Ket had warned her that it would be more painful than the blood oath tattoo, what he hadn't told her was that it would feel like a million cold needles punching through every nerve in her body in a steady rhythm for about two minutes. Dru tried not to cry out but she couldn't help it, half of her cry was surprise. When she recovered herself, Ket handed her the instrument to administer it to him. Her hands were still shaking from the pain when he handed her the instrument. "Ket, I asked this ancient practice of you for my own selfish desires, but as the gods have blessed us, you have agreed and for this you will always have my loyalty, my husband, I bind myself to you until the last breath I take."

"Drusilla," Kara cleared her throat to correct him and then Ket said, "James, I accept your binding as yours will be the only body I willingly touch until the last breath I take."

She put the binding tattoo to his forearm and he only closed his eyes through the pain. When he opened his eyes, she kissed him quite passionately and he responded.

All of their witnesses left the room and Dru thought it was over. Now they would be able to consummate their marriage, which was necessary for the binding tattoos to work. She had read a lot about the custom and they both needed to orgasm, at least once, best at the same time. In addition, the first time they had sex after taking the tattoos should feel like the first time they were together. She didn't feel like she had forgotten how Ket's body felt next to hers, but she was curious to see if that particular aspect was just a myth or if somehow the tattoos would really make it feel like the first time, "I'm looking forward to your hands being all over my naked body now."

"Come. We must orgasm together now for the binding tattoos to be optimized and complete."

He led her upstairs to a large bedroom, lit only by ancient candlelight with a statue of the goddess of sex above the bed. She almost died when she saw all of their witnesses there, "I can't do this with an audience."

He frowned at her, "These are our friends and family." And thought privately, *You only had a little problem with the slave in your building watching us, and even I thought, that was a little embarrassing.*

"That just makes it worse, your sister and brother?"

"This is the Alliance way. I'm proud to share my wedding night with them."

"I can't."

Kara spoke up then, "James, you can do it. I did it. Rebecca and Eve did it. They all do this. You are the only one who finds this strange." Kara was totally lying about that last part, she still found this strange and weird and especially that his sister and brother were there. But she reminded herself, this was their culture and they didn't seem to have huge issues with incest.

Ket put his hands gently on either side of Dru's face and she could feel he was using his influence to relax her. "Drusilla," he said, looking directly into her eyes, "Just focus on me, only me." Then he began kissing her. Chastely at first and then more passionately. As she began to relax his hands traveled the curve of her hips and down her back. He was purposely moving so slowly. Bringing her arousal back.

After 15 minutes of just kissing and petting Kara could not help but think, *Tir, you were right, this is going to take a long time.* She had told him she would be back early, and he had laughed at her and said that Alliance weddings usually take some time. She, of course, had not believed him, but now she was watching this thinking, *Really? You have been courting for months and you are going this slowly?* She could not help but remember her own wedding night then and think, *Yes, Maybe Tir and I are meant to be as I would never want this kind of romantic nonsense.* Kara was also pleased with herself for coming upstairs with a bottle of champagne as this was going to take some time. She poured herself another glass like she was at a sex show and refilled Dera's glass while she was at it.

Ket began caressing Dru's breasts over her dress and she was becoming so aroused that she didn't care anymore about their audience. She just told herself this was one more bizarre thing that she had now done in the Alliance.

428

Her hands were roaming over his uniform, she could feel his strong chest under it and could not wait to feel him against her, skin to skin.

Soon he was taking off her clothes so slowly and kissing her exquisitely as he went, she thought she could live in this moment forever. When her dress came off, she could tell that he was surprised she was naked. Every other time he had taken her dress off she had had undergarments on but not today.

He purposefully projected his thoughts to her, *For once I am shocked, I expected undergarments under this human dress, and you tricked me, my little tabi.*

He was on his knees before her and replied, "You look so intoxicating right now, I'm just trying to find my bearings again. Face paint and Alliance nipple jewelry, my wife," Then he ran one finger from her ankle to her inner thigh over her stocking. When his finger had reached the top of her stocking, he circled it and then began kissing her naked skin between the top of the stocking and her vulva. She almost jumped at the sensation and he then put both of his hands on her rear to hold her steady as he began kissing in earnest. After a few minutes, he rose slowly licking and kissing her body as he went. He loved her curves and the taste of her. She began to make small pleasurable sounds and he began caressing her breasts gently moving the nipple jewelry back and forth. "You are so beautiful," he whispered as he kissed her cheek.

Dru was so aroused now, not only did she not care about their audience, she wontly wanted to put on a good performance. But then she questioned whether that was her thought or Ket's as their minds were becoming intertwined just like their bodies were. She decided it didn't matter she just wanted Ket inside of her and the need was growing with every second. She began taking off his clothes, she was not nearly as slow as he was, but she gently kissed his neck and torso as she went. His body was, as always, strong and stunning. He kept himself in top physical form. As she took off his trousers, she could swear his penis looked larger than it usually did. She wondered if he was more aroused with an audience. She put her hand gently on his penis, ran her fingers along the ridges across the top and she heard him gasp. Then she began kissing all around, but he stopped her before she put his penis into her mouth.

"There will be a time and a place for that later," he whispered in her ear and then led her to the bed. He wondered privately; *Didn't I tell her she wasn't allowed to do that until she was pregnant?*

Dru assumed this meant that they were going to have sex now and that was fine with her. She wanted to feel him inside of her. She wanted to know whether it was going to feel like the first time again. She let Ket arrange her on the edge of the bed and then again, he began kissing up her legs from her ankles to her thighs and she thought, *Alliance men really do like these stockings.* And then he was licking her sex and vulva. His tongue everywhere. She couldn't think anymore. He slowly removed her stockings from her legs at the same time and returned to kiss again everywhere but her clitoris. The sensations were driving her mad. She put her hands on his head and tried to direct him to where she wanted him to be.

He stopped and said sweetly and quietly, "Don't rush me, dear Wife. We have to time this just right tonight."

Dru thought to herself and was so aroused, she projected her thought unconsciously into the room, *Just lick me already I am dying, I'm so close.*

Ket, Kio, Dera and Hez all smiled at that, as the other telepaths in the room, and Ket obeyed.

430

He began licking her clitoris with the gentlest and lightest strokes of his tongue and she leaned back and said, "Yes, oh gods yes Ket."

When she was close to climax, he put two fingers inside of her dripping vagina and began stroking her there, in and out, slowly while he worked his tongue in intervals on her clitoris. It was not long before she was coming. He removed his fingers then and kissed her so lightly on her vulva afterwards she thought she really might die of pleasure.

Their minds intermixing, she said to him telepathically, *It does feel like the first time. Is this a trick of the tattoo?*

Ket still stroked her fur and answered, *I don't think it's a trick. I'll explain the science behind it later, but technically, the binding tattoos have changed our bodies, so in a way it is the first time.*

Ket tenderly picked her up, laid her further back on the bed and laid next to her. She leaned over to him and began kissing his body everywhere beginning with his lips down to his toes, she tried to take his penis in her mouth again, but he stopped her.

Ket smiled when she tried to take his sex into her mouth again, it was somewhat adorable that she kept trying to suck his penis. He brought her up to him and kissed her passionate as he laid her under him, "My exotic human Wife, are you ready now?"

Dru was looking up into Ket's grey eyes, brimming with desire. She could see into his mind and feel his arousal. His pride at having her as his wife and consummating this marriage. The desire to plunge into her and the fear they wouldn't set the binding tattoos as he would come too soon. "Go slowly, Husband, even your fingers felt tight."

He gave her a half smile, "I know, that's why I'm worried."

"I have my own fingers," she whispered in his ear.

He began to find the entrance to her vagina with his fingers and place the top of his penis at her entrance, then he whispered back, as he began sliding into her, "Hopefully, it won't come to that, but gods, you feel so good. So warm, wet and so tight."

Dru could feel what was going on and she felt like it was the first time she was having sex too. He was so big and the ridges, they rubbed her in all the right places, but she could feel that he was closer than she was to coming after a couple slow thrusts. She then decided to take matters into her own hands. Literally. She reached a hand between them and began rubbing her clit. "Wait," she said on a loop. She didn't even care what everyone else in the room thought, they needed to do this together.

Ket continued to slowly move in and out of her as her breathing increased and she became flushed, he reached down and touched one of her pink cheeks, the same color as her nipples. He knew she was close to coming again. He increased his speed, "Wait for me, now" as he focused on them both. Their minds and bodies fully intertwining.

Dru became so lost in her own orgasm, or their orgasm, she saw black. There was nothing for her but sensation. The sensation of her sex still throbbing with the aftershocks of the most amazing orgasm and sexual experience of her life and the feeling of Ket with her. Their minds had not even fully separated. She could feel him and suspected he could feel her. They just lay together still connected for a couple minutes, mentally and physically, wonderfully spent. The room and everything faded, and it was just the two of them in bliss and it seemed to go on for several minutes. When they both came to, their witnesses were in a bit of a shock.

Kara spoke first, "If that's from the binding tattoos then we should all take them."

Dera laughed, "It's the binding tattoos and the telepathy. Telepaths have sex with their minds too."

Kara looked at Dera skeptically, then picked up the half empty champagne bottle and her glass and said, "Blessed be the gods you are married. I have witnessed it. May the gods bring you many daughters and happiness." Then she left.

The rest of the witnesses followed suit wishing them well and then leaving the room.

"Is there anything else that is going to happen, or can I relax now?"

"You can relax now. I thought someone would have told you about the consummation of the marriage with witnesses."

"No. I guess everyone thought someone else did."

"I hope it was not too traumatizing."

"The people, I know the best, watching me have sex with you? If I was still on Earth this would be very traumatizing, but in this situation, I know you all think this is normal, so I'm trying to remind myself of that."

"In the future, I'll try and warn you of things that you might find strange, but it's difficult because everything seems so natural to me. I've never lived in another culture and so it's difficult to know what others find strange about my own, but I guess, I'll know in a couple of years almost everything humans find strange about the Alliance."

"Thank you," she said a bit charmed he even acknowledged that she might find some of his culture strange now and that she just wouldn't take to it as it must be the best way to do things in the galaxy, easily throwing off her human ways. "It is both fascinating and frightening to experience a new culture. It makes me feel like I am really living all the time. As if everything is more real than it was on Earth. It's difficult to explain and I don't really want to try," she couldn't help herself then and began to kiss him. Soon they were making out and she tried again to take his penis into her mouth, and he pulled her away. "Why won't you let me pleasure you that way?"

"It goes against the gods until you are with child. I'm sure I have told you that before."

"How do you know that I'm not pregnant already?" she asked playfully and tried to move down again.

"No, Drusilla," he said firmly but gently. "You know about our beliefs and laws. Don't flaunt the gods' decrees."

"We flaunt them all the time. We had sex before we were married how many times?"

"Speaking of which, we have penance to pay for that."

"Fines?"

"Worse."

"What's worse?"

"Punishment at the Grand City Temple at the High Priestess's discretion."

"Oh," Dru said a bit terrified. "Publically?"

"Thank the gods no, but it won't be pleasant."

"When?"

"Tomorrow, but let's not think about that until the morning," he said and then took a nipple into his mouth.

They made love again and then he suggested that they walk to their home and sleep there as he didn't want to sleep under the goddess of fertility.

She enthusiastically agreed. As they made the 15-minute walk to their home, Dru felt so at home with Ket at her side and the foreign stars and two nearby planets in the sky. All felt right in the galaxy.

. . .

Dru woke up in a bed that would be hers for the rest of her life. It was large and comfortable. Next to her lay Ket who was still sleeping. Dru moved closer to him and he instinctually put his arm around her and cradled her against his large muscular body. She wasn't tired but just closed her eyes and reveled in being as free as she could be in this new second life she had in the Alliance.

It wasn't long before an alarm went off, "Praise the gods, Ket and James, the time is six o'clock you have a punishment scheduled with the High Priestess at ten o'clock, may the gods light your path."

Ket kissed the back of Drusilla's neck and said, "We have to get up."

"I don't want to."

"We have to do this so we can go on our honeymoon at the resort and then we'll have a month to just lie in bed."

When she didn't move, he got out of bed himself and picked her up and carried her to the bathroom with him.

"Don't take me in the shower with you, it'll be too cold. Put me down." She was squirming and trying to escape his arms with all her strength. The last thing she wanted was to go into the cold water.

"Next time you will get up when I say so. It's a 4th day today. Shower on."

Dru felt ice cold water pour over her and Ket and she screamed, "It's too cold! Let me out!"

He smiled and tightened his grip on her, "No little tabi. You can't be so lazy in the morning."

She tried to get away, but it was futile he was too strong. She let the cold water fall over her hoping it would end soon. When the dryer came on to dry them with luke-warm air her teeth were still chattering from the cold and then he let her go. She ran into their bedroom looking for the wardrobe. "Where are my clothes?" She had been in the house many times with Zol, as things were organized and decorated, but she couldn't remember where her wardrobe was, she knew it was one of these rooms.

Ket came into the room, took her hand and led her into an adjacent room that was filled with fine Alliance dresses, none of which she had ever seen before. "Here are your clothes."

"Did you buy these for me?" Dru was so overwhelmed by the large walk-in wardrobe which was basically another room filled with things only for her she momentarily forgot that she was freezing cold.

"Inadvertently. I wanted you to have clothes befitting your rank now. I knew you wouldn't buy any for yourself as you think all our clothing is terrible, as it's machine made, I have read your thoughts. So, Dera picked these all out. I hope you won't disappoint her?" he asked rhetorically and Dru smiled at him. He pointed out a section, "These are for work, these are for friends and family, and these are formal." Then he opened a secret closet and said, "And here is all of your human clothing. Frank suggested some things and I bought them under your account so neither of us would be punished. He said he would be happy to exchange them for other things if they weren't right."

Dru stood in front of the secret closet with the Earth clothes in it. There were sets of the silk pajamas that she had admired every time she had been in his shop. She ran her hands down one of the soft silk robes, "These are so nice Ket. Thank you." Then she went through a drawer filled with underwear and bras. Next she looked through the selection of human formal dresses and looked back at him, "Would you allow me to wear these?"

"As long as I'm with you or we agree on when. I don't

want you to give up all of your humanity Drusilla. Unlike other Alliance men, I'm not ashamed that you are human."

"Even though, we are voted the best party place every year?"

He smiled and took her in his arms, "Even with that award, because people can see, especially with you, that humans are more than just beautiful and fun. And it's good to remind people that you are human too."

She put her hands in his long loose hair, "I could be a lot of fun now though."

He kissed her and then set her down, "No, we don't have time for that. Let me show you the rest." He took her to another area of her large wardrobe and showed her all her jewelry. All of his known jewelry and many pieces he had bought from the Earth Store.

"They are all so beautiful Ket," she said admiring now what was hers. She touched one bracelet which was made of gold from Earth, "Thank you for incorporating human made jewelry too."

"I don't want you or anyone to forget where you came from. This is how it's meant to be, Wife."

Ket's words resonated with Dru. She felt a chill as she was reminded of the picture Madame Bai had taken of all of them on their first day in the Alliance and her same message. Dru looked at herself naked in the full-length mirror in the wardrobe and thought, *And I've come a long way*, taking in her naked body, save for her marriage bracelet, nipple piercings and two tattoos, one forever binding her to Ket and the other making her loyal to Kara. She had become in some ways, what she would have imagined her worst fear would have been from a year ago, bowing down to the Alliance and grateful for what they had given to her, but she thought, *If all of the world is slavery, that all of our destinies are set by the gods of some kind, then this cage is better than most and I'll be grateful for it. I'm no longer that young woman, naïve of the galaxy, naïve of the physical pleasures of life.*

Ket came up from behind her, naked and put a dress over her head. Then he put on her day stockings and took some jewelry from the wall. The first one he put on was her new ID necklace, it carried the Imperial Seal just as the House Zu one had, but this one also had the medical symbol on it and said House Vo, "I've been waiting to see you with this one for a long time. I'm only sorry it has to say 'James' instead of 'Drusilla' as Captain Kara had the audacity to change your name. But you will always be my Drusilla."

Dru looked at herself in the mirror again, watching Ket place more and more jewelry on her. She would let him have this today, because it was his day, a 4th day and that was the compromise. But she knew on all the other days she would not wear so much jewelry.

When Ket was satisfied with her appearance he kissed her chastely, "Now you look like my wife. I know you think this is a lot but on every 4th day I would like you to look like this. For me." He stepped to the side so only her refection was in the mirror, "Mirror, capture image. Send image to my IC. Now, let me get dressed quickly and then we will go downstairs together."

Ket went to his own wardrobe and put on his usual uniform as men always wore their uniforms. As they walked through the house to the dining room, where the morning meal would be waiting, Ket commented on the house, "You did a good job decorating the house."

I had some help as you know, she told him, but said out loud, "Thank you." Zol had done an excellent job blending both Alliance and human culture in their home, complete with a wine cellar and a green house. In the dining room there was a large stone Alliance table but on the walls were ancient still life paintings of Earth food intermixed with their House banners. Their drawing room also had a large modern painting of an artist's rendition of a map of the different areas of Earth featuring the Exterior. Dru had a knee jerk reaction when she saw it. First because maps usually never mentioned the Exterior, it was just an unidentified grey area and second, because she didn't know if she was ready to claim the Exterior as home, or even if she could publically be allowed to do so, without some legal repercussions. She mentioned these worries to Zol when she had first seen the painting and Zol had reassured her, 'Drusilla, you're a part of the strongest Empire in the galaxy. No human can touch you now. You should celebrate where you came from, that's what the gods intended and what led you to us. There is no shame in destiny. You must embrace it all, no matter how painful some of it might be.' And so Dru was trying to begin a relationship with her past, her childhood, but it wasn't easy. Every time she looked at the picture, she was reminded of so many things she had kept buried for so long. She wondered if she would ever be at peace with the painting and her past, but she didn't want the painting moved to an unused room or removed completely. She decided to keep it on full display in the drawing room, as a reminder to herself to continue moving forward, and a measure of how far she had come. It was not easy, but a part of her was done hiding who she was. And an even smaller part of her wondered if this were truly her destiny, to live in a religious world, be a respected Alliance citizen, and a married woman. A year ago, she would have wanted none of these things, but now she was ready to step up to these new challenges, even though she was also prepared for more suffering. All this privilege came at a cost. She knew that from the spirits on Earth and now from these Alliance gods, nothing was given freely.

After the morning meal, they went to the Grand City Temple and found the High Priestess in her personal shrine. She looked at them both and then asked them to follow her. She summoned some of her nuns to help her with the punishment.

The High Priestess took her place at the front of the small shrine and asked Dru and Ket to come and kneel before her. Then she came down and touched Dru's head, "Child, which name would you liked to be called? Drusilla or James?"

"Drusilla," Dru answered.

"Good," the High Priestess said returning to her place at the front of the shrine, Drusilla and Ket kneeling before her. "Let the gods grant mercy on these young people. Drusilla and Ket of House Vo did go against our gods and give into their physical desires as an exalted slave recorded. Now they will be brought salvation in these next hours." The High Priestess lit two candles and handed one to Ket and one to Drusilla. Then she began chanting a prayer, "Grant mercy upon these sinners, Drusilla and Ket." The nuns repeated the chant in the back, and it was repeated over and over again for about an hour.

Dru couldn't feel her knees anymore from kneeling so long on the cold stone floor but she knew they couldn't move, and her hands were burned from the candle wax that dripped on them. She kept wondering if this was the punishment or if there was going to be something more. She could see blood stains all over the floor from past punishments and she realized as well, frighteningly, there were implements of torture on the walls of the shrine. She hoped that this kneeling would be the extent of their punishment.

Ket's knees ached and his hands were burned. He hated this part, the waiting. He knew the High Priestess would have something terrible in mind for them both otherwise she would not have called in the nuns to help. He wanted to reach out to Dru mentally but there was a block inside the shrine so that telepaths could not influence the High Priestess.

When the chanting finished the High Priestess took a whip from the wall and demanded, "Sinners look at me. You defied the gods' decree and had sex with witnesses before you exchanged wedding vows. The gods now demand their due in blood and pain. Will you give it?"

"Yes, I, Ket of House Vo, give it," Ket said and then looked at Drusilla expectantly.

Dru realized they were all waiting for her after a long minute of silence, "Yes, I, Drusilla of House Vo, give it." She looked at the whip and her knees no longer hurt. She would stay on her knees all day if it meant not being whipped.

Ket looked at the whip and thought, *Well, it could be worse. Much worse.*

The High Priestess nodded to the nuns in the back who came forward and took both Ket and Drusilla by the arms, lifting them and undressing them. When they stood before the High Priestess naked, being held by the nuns she said, "Now let the punishment commence." The High Priestess handed two whips to two nuns and then the other nuns held Drusilla and Ket, side by side.

The first blow to Dru's back was so painful she cried out. Ket looked over at her and gave her a worried look, but the High Priestess slapped him across the face.

"Don't look at her, focus on your punishment."

"May the gods be great," he answered.

After the next blow, Dru felt the tears welling up in her eyes and tried not to cry out but this hurt worse than anything she had ever experienced. *There was no way this was a regular whip*, she thought.

Then, the High Priestess slapped Drusilla across the face, "You must say the words after each stroke. We have to start from the beginning again. Gods guide our hands."

Dru was struck again, it hurt so much she could not remember the words. The High Priestess had the nun whip her again and then she cried out, "I can't remember the words."

"We will whip you until you do remember them."

"I, Drusilla of House Vo, atone for my sins," Ket provided for her.

"Don't help her. Now we will have to begin this whole thing again, but I will double the number of lashes," she nodded to the nuns, "Begin."

Dru couldn't remember when a lash struck so she just repeated over and over again, "I, Drusilla of House Vo, atone for my sins." She had never been in so much pain before, she just wanted this to end. Her eyes focused on the nun's shoes on the bloody stone floor and knew now her blood and screams were being added to this shrine too.

By the time they got to ten strokes, Drusilla was in tears, the nuns had to hold her up. Her back was angry with blood and welts, as was Ket's, but when they were finished, he took hold of her and gently put her dress on even though she protested every second of it, "Not my dress, no it hurts too much, I can't."

Ket kept thinking, *We only need to make it outside the shrine, and then I can bring you comfort.*

Ket had to carry Drusilla outside the shrine as she was too hurt to walk. He did so and then immediately used influence to lessen her pain as he walked with her in his arms to the transport. He was in a lot of pain as well, but this was not the first time he had been punished in this way. Once inside the transport he took off her dress and began healing her with a med polymer. It was against the law, but he had always done it and received a fine. Then he asked her to heal him. When it was all over, they lay together in the transport, in each other's arms half naked and exhausted.

"I'm never having sex before marriage ever again," Dru said.

Ket smiled, "It was worth it."

Ket and Dru spent the next month on honeymoon in a secluded rustic home near the sea. Most days were sunny, but cold and windy. They took walks during the day and didn't sleep during the nights. They spent hours conversing in front of the fireplace with French wine and Alliance Zota. Meals were brought to them by slaves and for the first time in Dru's life she felt like she belonged with someone and that someone really understood her.

Dru watched Ket as he looked out the window and watched the rough waves crash onto the rocks. She knew he loved watching the sea. He loved every part about being there. She assumed it was because he had to be away in space so much, and because as an Alliance man, it was uncertain whether he would have ever gotten married with the demographics issue. To be here on honeymoon carried a sense of pride for him as well. She decided in this moment to project to him what she had been thinking for days now, *You are my other half, Ket.*

Ket turned and looked at Drusilla relaxing in a large chair next to the fire, *As you are mine, Wife.* Then he returned to look at the sea for one last time before going to her side and extending his hand. *Come, it is time.*

She looked at him and nodded. She realized now that he preferred not to speak but to just use his mind to communicate with her. She didn't mind at all, but she did remind him sometimes that she liked to hear the sound of his voice as well.

They went up into the bedroom and she took off her dress as he prepared the embryo from the small medical unit, they had brought with them.

She laid down on the bed with her knees up to allow him as much space as he needed. Ket activated the small robot that would guide the embryo to the best place in Drusilla's uterus and inserted it.

"Gods forgive us," he said after it was finished.

Dru didn't move or say anything. She had pushed Ket to do this. She and Zol. Zol had obtained the medical device that would go unnoticed from the Imperial Palace and Dru had convinced Ket. To promote human women within the Empire they needed to have a daughter quickly. There was already unrest with protest that the other human women, were more trouble than they were worth and only had sons anyway. It didn't help that Dru had insisted on taking binding tattoos either. It was a very unpopular move, as a lot of Alliance people felt she was questioning their whole slave artist system, and many people were upset by it.

Ket lay down next to Dru as she lay there mostly naked now. Their faces were millimeters apart. He was stroking her face. "We will be seriously punished by the High Priestess if this ever is known. I, most certainly, will be put to death."

"I know," Dru sighed putting her hand against his face, "But we can't let innocent human women's lives fall so drastically in the Empire because I have made you take the binding tattoos. We must have a daughter to show our union is in harmony with the gods' wills and I have faith that the gods will keep us safe." She put one finger over her heart, to indicate her sincerity.

"It feels as if we are pushing the gods' wills."

"No, they are pushing us to do their bidding."

Ket closed his eyes and said out loud, "I hope our daughter is better at lying than you are."

Dru smiled and closed her eyes too.

9

A True Second Life

Dru felt the strongest urge in her life to push. She almost fell over. She called the slave to get her mother in-law fast. Dru went into the largest bathroom they had, which was about 20 square meters and had floor to ceiling windows on three sides overlooking the House Vo garden below and an enormous bathtub in the middle of the room. "Fill bathtub, water temperature 40C," she commanded the bathroom and took off her clothes. In the minute that it took the bath to fill completely she got in and had the strongest urge to push. It felt like a long time before her mother in-law appeared but thankfully, she was clever enough to have brought her medical bag.

"What are you doing?"

"What does it look like? I'm having this baby. It just happened. Help me."

She put down her things and looked into Drusilla's vagina through the clear water, "Gods, I can see a head." Then she looked up at Drusilla, "I called the midwives, but I think they will be too late."

"No, really?" Dru said sarcastically. She couldn't help

it; she was somewhere else now. All she could hear suddenly were her own primal sounds and she didn't want to hear that. "Computer turn on my music. Playlist A."

"That is forbidden until you have your first child."

"She is coming, and I need it. Now," Dru was in pain now and wondered how she could have not realized their baby was coming. She closed her eyes and just focused on the music and the strongest desire she had ever felt in her life to push this baby out, no matter what. She pushed her mind away from all the births she had seen go wrong. She willed herself and this baby to make it out okay. *The midwives will be here soon. Zol is the Imperial Doctor, I am not in the Exterior and I am not going to die, and neither is this baby.* "I need you to get in the water with me, now," Dru was barely able to get out.

Zol didn't question this but just did it. She had never witnessed a natural childbirth before and nor a human's. She also knew that Drusilla had witnessed and helped in a lot before she left her hometown, so she trusted her now to know what was right. Zol removed her shoes quickly and jumped into the water. She didn't need Drusilla to tell her what to do, it was obvious. She was squatting and Zol took both of her hands to steady her. She also used her influence to dull some of the pain, however she was no midwife, so she was reluctant to get rid of the pain entirely, she assumed some of the pain was supposed to be there to make the birthing process work. There were no computers or machines to help them, this was all on their instincts. Alone. And Zol had never felt so exhilarated or alive.

Dru had never wanted something so much as she wanted the child out and healthy. She squatted and pushed when her body instructed her to do so. There was no talking now. Just the sound of her pushing, that primal sound she had heard so many women do before her, the sound of a woman birthing a child. Her mind was gone, her body completely focused on this one thing.

When the baby came out into the water, Zol picked it up as Dru fell back. It didn't take long for the little grey skinned girl to begin wailing. Zol put it to Dru's chest and helped her manage the afterbirth, not knowing what else to do and wondering where the midwives were. It felt as it had been at least an hour.

It had only taken the midwives 11 minutes to get from the hospital to the bathroom where Drusilla gave birth, but they had still missed everything. However, they were able to help get Drusilla to her bed with the baby and do all the regular checkups of baby and mother. Both were deemed healthy.

As Dru lay in her bed, with her daughter lying next to her in a protective transparent bubble, except for one button, she could feel her daughter's little mind reaching out to her and she used her own influence to comfort her. She had read a lot in her Alliance baby books about doing this for her children, if they were telepathic, which, of course, she knew their daughter would be. She had been completely engineered, telepathic, grey skin and red hair. The only thing they left up to chance was her eye color.

"I didn't know I was in labor," Dru said annoyed at Ket. The midwife said that it was supposed to hurt worse than menstrual cramps and it didn't.

"Thankfully, my mother was also at home, so you weren't alone with only the slaves," Ket said holding their daughter.

Dru laughed, "Yes, that would have been terrible. I'm sure there would have been lots of broken things from me throwing things at them to do something. I think your mother rather enjoyed it too. It was the first time she had ever seen a natural birth. By the time the midwives arrived, our daughter was already here. Now, for a name. How about an Alliance name?"

Ket knew of the compromise Drusilla had made with his mother and his mother had already told him the name she had chosen, "How about Lia?" He was pleased though that Drusilla practiced going through the charade though.

"Is that an Alliance name?"

"Yes, of course it is."

"It's also a human name."

"Is it?" Ket asked feigning ignorance. Zol had told him she had researched all the names that were both reasonable and existed for both humans and Alliance people.

Dru gave him a big smile. She looked at the baby who was sleeping in Ket's arms and said, "Lia. It's perfect." She had red hair and grey skin. Her eyes had the shade of blue that probably wouldn't remain so they would just have to wait. But Dru could feel she was content in Ket's arms. "She knows you."

"Of course, she does. I'm her father. I reached out to her every time I was home throughout the pregnancy. She recognizes my presence and my voice. It's amazing to feel her little mind reaching out to us," he said lovingly as he looked at the sleeping baby in his arms.

"I hope her hair won't be too shocking and she will not be bullied for it."

"I think it'll be quite the opposite. She's the first female born in such a long time, everyone already looks to her for hope, just like we had assumed."

"Good," Dru looked at Ket then and asked, "And I hope that you will be here for some time now? I have missed you and I want to spend this time together."

"I will. We must have her blessed as soon as possible and ..."

"I know I said I didn't want the gods' protection, but I do. We will sacrifice the animals at the temple."

Ket looked at Drusilla a bit stunned she had changed her mind, "I'll arrange it. What made you change your mind?"

"Kara messaged me and said that now that I have given birth, she needs me to do something," Dru knew that that something would not be legal, nor would it be safe.

"We must trust in the gods to guide all of our destinies now, Drusilla. I'm glad that you have finally begun to see their light. I have faith that they will protect us," Ket said and placed his finger over his heart.

Dru had the strangest feeling looking at Ket holding their daughter as if she had veered from the path set out by the gods and would be punished for it now. She closed her eyes and half thought and half prayed, *I had to have them both. Now is the time to make a deal if you want a deal. I will do your bidding.*

Unbeknownst to Dru, the goddess of home, heard her and was ecstatic at this tempting offer. She replied cheerfully from her high palace, "We shall make a deal, fiery human."

Dru didn't hear the goddess's words but knew she had been heard by a deity and that her life was truly interconnected with the gods now. That a deal had been struck in that moment. Her spirituality had been flipped like a light switch and she wasn't sure if she was ready for it to be on. But when she looked at her infant daughter and Ket, she knew she would do anything for them, anything the gods or Kara asked of her. She was ready now and knew this was who she always was supposed to be in the galaxy, the catalyst for change in the Alliance, and she would help bring the Empire to its knees for their disobedience. She also knew in this moment, without a doubt, humans were the Lost People and the Alliance had knowingly abandoned them.

Dru closed her eyes and spoke to the goddess again, *First, one more thing for me though, erase the memories of all that knew what happened when I escaped the Exterior. I don't want to carry that shame with me and longer.* Dru could feel in that instant it was done and she knew she would have to pay dearly for it, but she would never again have to confront those memories to anyone but herself. And she hoped in time that even she would forget.

Then Dru could hear the goddess in her mind and knew somehow it was the goddess of home, *Now Drusilla James of House Vo, you will do my bidding. There is a lot to be done. The Alliance people have been very disobedient. You will be my vessel for righting these wrongs.*

Thank you

Thank you for reading *Married to the Alien Doctor*. I hope that you enjoyed Dru's story in the Empire and as you can see, it's not over yet. You will see her and Ket again throughout the series. The next book is called *Married to the Alien with No House, Renascence Alliance Series Book 3*. It is Babette's story. She is a young human woman who sees Admiral Tir's advertisement for volunteers to become brides of the Empire and knows that she has to go. The next book dives more into the Alliance religion than any of the other books and if you prefer to listen to it on audio, read by the talented Janet King, please follow the link, Married to the Alien with No House

I have included an excerpt of Babette's story in the next section. I hope you will continue with me through this eight-book series. Thanks again.

Best wishes,

Alma x

Teaser

Married to the Alien with No House Excerpt:

Babette picked up her small personal bag and energetically waved 'goodbye' to her friend as she joined the line to board one of the many transports that would take them up to one of the Alliance ships. When Babette reached the front of the line, an Alliance officer with a tablet asked her, "Name?"

"Babette Thomas."

"Good," he said while marking the tablet with his finger. "You're traveling back on the *Fira* under Captain Rerg. Commander Daz will be responsible for your well-being onboard. Do you have what you need with you for the short journey?" He asked her, as if he had asked the question already a hundred times before, which he probably had as there were 1,000 women joining them.

"Yes," she said, indicating her medium size shoulder bag.

"Good," he said, looking at the bag. "You are the first

reasonable woman I've come across this morning. Everyone else seemed to think they needed a million things with them." He made another mark on the tablet and then said, "Transport number three. May the gods bless you."

Babette knew he was waiting for some set reply, but she didn't know it, so she just said, "Thank you. I'm excited." And walked away cringing thinking, *I need to learn these expressions.*

Babette viewed the line of transports and found transport number three. There was another line to board it, but thankfully it was shorter than any of the other lines for the other transports. She spotted Jade a few women in front of her in line, so she called out to her, and Jade came back to her place in the line so they could talk together while they waited.

"I'm so glad that you were selected," Jade exclaimed as she came over to Babette.

"Me too. I mean, I'm glad to see you too!" Babette noticed Jade had a lot of luggage with her. "You've got quite a bit here."

"Oh," said Jade, looking at her things, "Yes, you know there are some things I just can't be without."

"Not even for two weeks?"

"No, I mean, I probably will want to do some cooking onboard. Just to see what's going on in Alliance kitchens. To get a head start."

"Do you think they would let you do that?"

"I don't know. I'm the kind of person who usually tries things first and then finds out afterwards if I was breaking the rules or not."

Babette laughed, "I see. Well, I'm definitely looking forward to watching you break some rules and try to cook some food on an Alliance ship."

Jade gave her a smile.

The line was moving quickly.

"Why is our line so short, do you think?" Babette asked.

"As far as I could find out, there are only ten ships in the convoy brought to Earth, and for some reason they have divided us up unequally on to them. I guess we are on a ship with less humans. Although it doesn't make sense to me as the *Fira* is one of the larger ships."

"How do you know that?"

Jade shrugged, "I asked when I was asking to clear a lot of my belongings earlier. I'm a curious person."

"Maybe the other ships have more resources to accommodate more passengers?" Babette suggested.

"Or they have put all the troublemakers together to keep us under control?" Jade smiled.

"I'm not a troublemaker," Babette replied. "Speak for yourself. And besides what kind of trouble could we get into on a ship?"

"A ship full of eligible young men in top physical form looking for wives, I don't know what kind of trouble I could get into?" Jade answered in her most innocent and naïve tone.

Babette just smiled as they boarded the transport. They were surrounded by many other young women from all over Earth, and some of the women's languages didn't even register on Babette's translator. But she just sighed, and thought, *I can't wait to get an Alliance translator and then I won't have this problem.* Her translator was an older model and only translated the most common languages on Earth and not very well at that.

Once all the women were onboard and strapped in, an Alliance officer addressed them as the pilot and copilot took their places behind him, "Welcome new Alliance citizens. The gods are great and send us on our way home today. One final check, if you could please all write down the contents of your stowed luggage on these tablets as we ascend to the *Fira.*"

Then they were all given a tablet in English to write down the contents of their belongings that would be put in the hold of the starship. Babette had already seen one woman's cat being taken away from her and given to her family members who had seen her off, so she guessed they wanted to be sure there were no other animals or strange things in their luggage.

Babette dutifully filled out the form as it wasn't difficult for her to complete. She had not brought nearly as much as some of the other women for three reasons; first she didn't own very much and second what she did own, besides her clothing, was all second-hand or a hundredth-hand, as she liked to joke, and so it wasn't worth transporting across the galaxy, thirdly, something she hardly even admitted to herself, part of her wanted to start anew. To not be known as the poor girl who had worked her way up to sales assistant, who was known to be, 'not like her mother,' Of course, Babette could have always just left Natchez to do that, but it just didn't seem worth it to save the UCs to start over with complete strangers. She knew the evils of Natchez. But what the Alliance was offering her was not only a mostly clean start but also had the added bonus of extra UCs and for sure different kinds of people. More than just different people, they were aliens. And with her new life, would come new possessions, and she welcomed them, whatever they would be.

Name: Madame Babette of House Human

Declaration of Items to be brought to the Alliance Empire, 8th day of the 37th week of the year 18904

Human Clothing:
Five dresses
Three pairs of jeans
Ten shirts
Ten pairs of underwear
Seven Bras
Five pairs of stockings
Ten pairs of socks
Five pairs of shoes
One winter jacket

Human Jewelry:
One box of jewelry

Miscellaneous Human Items:
One bag of makeup
Five bars of Savon de Marseille with crushed flowers soap, rose
Three bottles of Argan Oil Shampoo
Two bottles of Shalimar-Guerlain
One bottle of aloe vera gel
A large box of À la pointe de la Fleur de Sel Noir Chocolaté
Two bottles of Heaven Hill, Green Label Bourbon

Babette was one of the first to finish her list of belongings. She held the tablet on her lap and looked around at the other women as they filled out theirs. She had a moment then when it felt like time stood still as she watched all these young women from all over Earth, busily listing their belongings, and for some reason, out of nowhere, she began to doubt her choice. She didn't know why her stomach dropped and hoped that she and the rest of them hadn't just made the biggest mistakes of their lives. *Have we all been tricked into going to the Alliance? What if they have lied to us? What if they are going to use us as sex slaves or keep us as pets?*

To buy *Married to the Alien with No House* or to read it on Kindle Unlimited, please follow the link: Married to the Alien with No House